I am

Mercy

Mandi Lynn

I AM MERCY

For Grampy,
The strongest person I know.

MARSEILLE, FRANCE—1343

"Your eyes."

The man hovers over me, gripping my shoulder. His fingers dig into my bones. I stand in the middle of the market, surrounded by people, but that doesn't change the fact that if I were to scream, no one would hear me.

"What are you?" he asks.

He pushes me away, and I stumble into a wooden cart full of barley. The merchant glares at me before turning his attention back to a customer.

"Are you a witch, girly?"

The man is large, huge compared to me. I stare at his hands; they could kill me. He wouldn't hesitate to strangle me.

"What are you?" he screams, and this time more people in the street glance over in our direction.

"I'm nothing," I sputter. "Nothing out of the ordinary." The words were meant to sound strong but come out only as a whimper.

"Silver." The man points to my eyes.

I wrap my arms around my middle. Strangers in the street stare; they want to see what this man sees.

"This girl has silver eyes! She barely has an iris!"

"No," I beg.

The man slaps me across the face and grabs my shoulder again. "Anyone who holds witness to this young girl, come

5

forward. If no one speaks to her innocence, then she must be the Devil's child."

I look across the field of strangers. Everyone in the marketplace has stopped and turned their attention to my eyes. No one rushes forward to save me or to stand witness by saying I have nothing to do with the Devil's work. Instead the faces look curious. *How will this end?* They want to know. *Will this man kill the girl he holds? Or will he beat her, rape her, and leave her in the streets, scoffing at her uselessness in the world?*

"Please," I cry. I had been saying it to the strangers in the street, but when they make contact with my eyes, they all look away. The man holding me prisoner is my only hope now. "Please ..." I look to the ground and with a shove, I'm on my knees, my skirts sprawling out around the cobblestones.

It's my eyes. The irises—they lack pigment, leaving only a small pupil in the center of my eye. It tells the public I'm unsafe, not to be trusted. Mama tells me that I've been like this from birth. I was born the day the sky grew dark. The moon and sun aligned in the sky, and all that could be seen was the circular outline of the sun's rays behind the moon. Everyone knew to look away from this turn of nature, but I was drawn to the sight. Years later, here I stand, silver-eyed and accused of being a witch.

"Will they hang her, Mama?" a little boy whispers to his mother in the crowd.

I look at him in his dirty clothes that hang from his body. He clutches his mother's skirt, as he looks back at me, hiding behind her with a muffled cry.

They all want to kill me.

A sharp pain cuts across my back. "Be there any witness to this girl's innocence?" the man shouts again, a leather whip balanced in his hands.

I haven't done anything wrong. I didn't look at anyone, like Mama told me. I kept my eyes down. I paid for my food, was careful not to disturb others, but this man looked at me. He saw my eyes, and that's all it took. Most strangers glance quickly, see my irises, and walk away, afraid to bring attention to something they can't explain. This man gripped my hand as soon as he saw me and questioned me without allowing time for answers.

The whip comes down on my back again, and I curl into a ball on the street. My body numbs the pain, and soon the tears streaming down my face are the only things I can feel.

"I've done nothing," I say in a whimper.

"She speaks lies!" a woman in the crowd shouts. "I saw her steal the kale! Look at it! She's hidden it in her satchel!"

Lies. They all lie. Why do they want me to die?

The man coils the whip around his wrist in order to bend down and take the satchel slung across my body. I release my grip on my belongings and give up fighting. Even though I know the lashings have stopped for now, it's as if the leather still drags across my skin. Hot, fresh blood warms my back, pooling on the cobblestone path. No one moves to help me.

"What's this, girly?" He holds out the kale I had purchased just seconds ago.

I shift my gaze to the merchant I had bought it from, but he cowers away. Another man from the crowd comes forward and kicks my back.

"Don't you look at him," the stranger yells.

"I purchased it." But it's just a shout among chaos. My words are nothing.

The merchant speaks up, "She bought nothing from me. The girl is a thief!"

When I look at him again, he stares at me with malice, like I really am the thief he accuses me of being.

This is where I will die. Not because of the flu or starvation, but murder. These strangers want to kill me under false charges, and no one here is willing to stop them.

"Please," I say again, turning to my would-be killer. The crowd stands over me. The man's feet are just inches from my face, and I know that, if he wanted, he could draw out my death and see just how long I would suffer before my body succumbs.

He laughs at me and uncoils the whip for the second time. The crowd gathers.

From the corner of my eye I see mothers push their children back, guarding them from the scene that is about to unfold. Men close in, make jokes, mock me, kick at my body, even though I give no fight.

My tears are cold. My hands are dirty. My body is broken, but my eyes supposedly hold an evil everyone can see. I am not this evil.

I look up at my accuser and he smiles, whips the leather

to make a loud snap. It cuts in front of my line of sight. It doesn't touch me, but a fast, cool breeze of air warns me of the danger. He takes his stance. This time, when he brings down the whip, I can tell he means to hit me.

One.

I put up my hands to block the blow.

Two.

I close my eyes, trying to forget the face of this horrible man.

Three.

"No!"

Someone screams, just as the leather cuts across my hands and face. It's not my scream.

"Aida!" she calls out again.

My hands fall away, and I catch a glimpse of my accuser winding his whip back again for another blow. He wants me to bleed. He wants the witch's blood to spill. Doesn't he understand, witches don't bleed? That's what the tales say— witches can't bleed. It's the only way to tell a Devil's advocate from a human.

"I bear witness. Aida is my friend! She's no witch! Stop yourself!" the girl screams in terror.

My head turns, and then I see her. Cyrielle.

She runs toward me, but my thoughts leave me. The last thing I hear is my own shallow breathing.

I had a dream once that I passed on and no one cared.

It was just me, lying on the dirt floor of our small cruck house. Papa decided I wasn't good enough to sleep on the thin mattress of straw. I was dying; why would it matter if I were comfortable or not? So they left me there. With no tears or goodbyes, they departed. My *family*.

A heart beats only as long as someone is there to witness its livelihood. As each second passed, the air grew colder, and the sun slipped from the window's view. Dying was strange, unlike I'd expected. I was light-headed, with a crushing pressure on my chest that kept me from moving or screaming. In my dream I cried, because I could tell nothing was happening. The glory of the Father didn't bring me salvation, like I had been told.

I was dying. I was alone.

BOOK 1

I.

Anton walks into our small home, the walls made of wattle and daub, a straw roof with a hole above the fire that Mama uses to cook our meals. He's a tall man with a strong build, perfect for working the fields. Margo married him three years ago, after Papa arranged a trade—Anton's best sheep for Margo's hand in marriage.

To Papa his daughters are nothing more than an item to sell. That's all women are worth after all, right? We're too weak, too tender, to work in the fields like men. We are to cook, to clean, to tend to our husbands. Compared to the heavy work our husbands and brothers do, we are nothing but the womb that produces the next set of workers.

Mama doesn't notice Anton at first. He's supposed to live in the next village, raising his family. He scans our home, until he notices me skinning a rabbit in the corner. When his eyes rest on mine, I drop my knife. It makes a soft thud as it comes to rest in the dirt.

"Taking your latest victim?" he asks.

I begged Margo not to marry him, but she was charmed by his very presence, with his lean muscles and dark hair that fell to his chin. He was never to be questioned. And that is why he hates me, because I've always questioned him.

"Dondre brought the coney," I say, holding up the bloodied fur. The meat of the animal rests in a skillet next to me, waiting to be cooked.

"Anton, what are you doing here?" Mama snaps at him, finally turning around. Her dark hair is gathered in braids around her head and covered by a hood, just as all married women should fashion themselves.

"I've come to deliver your daughter."

Margo walks through the threshold then, her own child in tow. Joelle is four years old, the mirror image of Margo, with light hair braided down her back, like Margo used to wear before marriage. Upon entering, Joelle lets go of Margo's hand and finds company with Mama.

"What's wrong?" Mama asks, pushing Joelle away to see Margo.

"Always welcoming, Celine."

Anton is about to pick up the knife I dropped, but Mama doesn't give him a chance to step farther into our home.

"Out with you!"

She doesn't trust him. Never has. Maybe she understands this man, like I do. Papa may have convinced Margo to love this man, but not Mama. She can see the glimmer of venom lighting his eyes.

"Fine," Anton says, taking hold of his daughter's hand.

Joelle protests, dragging her feet, dropping herself on the ground, not consenting to be moved.

"Joelle, come!"

"Papa, we just walked here!" She digs in her feet, slurring her words.

"Now." He tugs her, lifting her off the ground.

"Leave the child!" Mama yells.

Anton lets go of Joelle, and she skips away, putting the cooking fire between herself and her father. He stands there glaring at Mama, then he turns to me and spits on the ground. He walks out the door and doesn't bother to glance at his wife or daughter as he leaves them behind without the slightest regret.

Joelle finds her way to her mother. Margo sits on my bed, just barely able to hold up her head.

Now that I see her, I understand why Mama asked what was wrong. Margo's skin is pale, and long hairs hang loose from the braids piled on her head underneath her hood. All I see is skin, bone, and dark circles under her eyes.

"I'm fine," Margo whispers. Her voice is coarse. She coughs and her entire body moves as her hand clutches her throat.

"Lie down, Margo," Mama says.

Margo obeys and lies on the mattress. On the other side of the room Joelle brings her knees to her chest. She mumbles something, but I'm unable to understand her words. I wander over to Joelle's frail body, but when I do, she moves away.

"Aida, get me a wet cloth! We need to cool her. She's burning."

I follow Mama's instructions and grab a scrap of fabric as I step over the threshold. In the blinding sunlight I can still hear

Mama's voice lingering from within.

"What has he done to you?" she says. But there is no surprise in her tone—she always knew this would happen someday.

"Nothing, Mama," Margo says, but her voice is fading.

Anton. Mama didn't care when Anton grabbed me, whipped me, tried to kill me. Papa didn't care either. I was their spare child who had survived against all odds. At my birth they were prepared to let me go. One look at me and my parents knew: *this infant is only a ghost of what we wished to have.*

My eyes, my luna eyes. Once upon a time my mama loved me, because she thought I was dying. She named me Aida de Luna. *Helper of the moon.* My silver-white eyes connote purity, but also evil. They were my mark of death. Born of the sunless hour, my parents waited for my passing, but it never came.

On the side of our house a pail of water is reserved for cooking, so we don't have to walk all the way to the river's edge every time we need some. I soak my scrap of cloth in the bucket, and the droplets wet my fingers.

When I return, Margo's thick wool kirtle has been removed, so all she wears now is the thin, pale chemise that clings to her body. Her body is burning up, sweat coating her skin in a milky layer.

"Tell me where it hurts," Mama says.

"It doesn't. Anton's just being delirious, is all. I fainted in the fields, and he acts like the Devil possessed me." She laughs, but Mama's face grows serious.

"Aida," she says, her eyes never leaving Margo's.

I pass Mama the cloth, and she lays it on Margo's forehead. The water droplets slide over her skin, and Margo seems relieved by the cool touch for a moment. Mama motions me close and whispers in my ear, so Margo doesn't hear.

"Take Joelle outside. Tend to the sheep. Do something to distract her. I don't want her near Margo."

And just like that Mama prepares for Margo's decline.

No evil will infect her household. It's the reason she keeps me hidden. If I were allowed to wander the village or work the fields, people would see me, see how different I am by one look of the eye. And just like that, I would no longer be wanted. It's what happened when Anton beat me near to death. I didn't know then that, in a short few years, the man who accused me of being a witch would marry my only sister.

Cyrielle had saved me, but Papa would rather let me sleep with the sheep than in his household after word flew within the village that I was accused of witchcraft. Mama resisted his ideas of confinement at first—she might have still loved me then—but soon she stopped thinking of me as her daughter. I was the child they gave birth to, ignorant of the eyes that spoke of evil.

"Come, Joelle." I hold out my hand, but she shakes her head. I kneel down to the mattress and grab her hand before she has a chance to move farther from me.

"No!" she screeches. "Mama! Mama, stop her!"

She's not talking to me. She's not even looking at me. She looks to her sick mother. Margo doesn't glance our way as I scoop up Joelle in my arms. She screams, cries, and pushes against me until I have carried her from the room and into the daylight.

"I don't want you! I want Mama!" I put her down as fast as I can, and she stomps away. Her voice is loud enough that it stirs the sheep that graze within their fence.

"You can't see your mama right now," I say, but Joelle tries to walk back inside. I catch her arm and pull her toward me again. My grip is harder than I intended, and she stumbles, crying as if a knife had been plunged in her chest. "Shh, Joelle, your mama needs rest." I try to cradle her in my arms, but she only pushes away from me.

"No!" She hits my arm with the little strength she has, but it's done in vain. Her body goes limp; she finally surrenders, and soon her crying quiets enough so all that is left is a mumble.

"Mama will be all right." I curl her body toward me. I imagine this is what Margo looked like when she was small, but I can see Anton in this child's body. Every time Joelle looks at me, I see him in her face. The nose angled just so, the sunken eyes, but most of the similarities are in the way she holds herself. He's there when she looks at me like I'm a monster.

She must have fallen asleep because all her murmurs stop. Her body is dead weight against me. Inside I can hear Mama tending to Margo, and Margo insisting nothing is wrong. But if nothing was wrong, she'd stand up, take her daughter from my arms, and find Anton—wherever he may be. The problem is she can't. Something is very wrong.

II.

Cyrielle is a girl I've known my entire life—a neighbor's daughter who has always been a friend. She was there before people looked at me as some evil thing. To her, I was just a normal girl to play with. When I was small, Mama and Papa taught me to keep my eyes hidden, but as I grew older looking to the ground to hide my gaze became rude. The only way my parents could hide my eyes was to act as if I didn't exist. Cyrielle saw me though. Every day when she finished her chores and I finished mine, we played by the stream.

One day Cyrielle's mama found us and saw me. The woman screamed, clutched her daughter, and dragged her away. It was a long time before I saw Cyrielle again. I was only about ten at the time, and I stayed home with Mama to help care for my baby brother, Dondre. I watched Mama nurse him, and she taught me how to prepare our food, wash clothes, and clean our pots, all so she didn't have to.

Cyrielle found a way to sneak over to visit me, even after a scolding from her mama. She greatly enjoyed the art of escaping with only a whisper as her trail.

I thank the Heavens for Cyrielle. She saved me, when no one else would.

I lay Joelle across my thin mattress before leaving. Mama is gone somewhere—roaming the fields for herbs that may help heal Margo. My sister is asleep when I creep from the cruck house and leave her daughter behind. They can manage. It will only be a short time before I come back.

The village's stream is shallow, just a trickle of water compared to the ocean that hugs the borders of Marseille.

All my life I've stayed hidden. Cyrielle and I have had our fair share of sneaking away, but we always stayed inside the village when I was younger. People knew my face. We were a small community full of secrets. I was one of them. People didn't bother to look at me twice. I was just a question mark in the background. They didn't know what to make of me, but I paid them no harm.

The heart of Marseille is just outside my village, and it's a place of wonder. I've gone within its walls once, and that ended with my life almost taken after being accused of witchcraft. Since then I have hidden myself away, never setting foot onto the soil where I bled as the crowd withered away and Cyrielle took me home.

Marseille resides on the coast of France. It's our epicenter, our connection to the world. Ships come and go, and exotic foods and herbs pass through our borders. I wanted so badly to see it; I was foolish enough to wander off from Cyrielle after we had traveled there together five years ago.

The withering stream of water leads to something much grander, and I follow its path until the stream grows. Wider and wider the water expands, deepens, and brings me forward. Looking up, I see the ocean that welcomes me to the coast—the Mediterranean Basin. A chill wind blows off the sea, and the fresh air makes me want to cry with joy.

Ships dock in the port, their huge sails halting as they are pulled down and stowed away. Goods are carried off the docks, and merchants barter not far away, already making deals to sell their wares.

"What are you doing here?"

The voice freezes me, and I know it's the man who waits for me to enter Marseille again, so my life can be taken properly—just like it should have been five years ago. But he knows I will never do that again under my own will.

"Shouldn't you be tending to your sister?"

I swallow, knowing his voice from the one that haunts my dreams. "I'm getting her fresh water. Shouldn't you be tending to your wife?" My words are sharp, braver than I expect. I'm surprised because I can already feel my hands shaking. My back is to him, and I want to turn so he doesn't have an upper hand, but I'm afraid to move.

"It's the wife's job to tend to the husband, not the other way around," Anton says.

He laughs, and it makes me want to slap him, but what would that get me? A quick, painless death if I'm lucky.

"Do you even love her?" I say. Tears start to brim in my

eyes, and I wipe them away, even though this man cannot see my face.

"She is a bearer of my child, is she not?"

"You would sacrifice your daughter's life if it meant saving your own skin," I say, but a hand shoves at me and the next thing I'm on the ground. I turn to look at Anton. He looms over me, the sun at his back, making him appear as a giant dark outline.

"Care to repeat? I don't think I heard you," he says.

I bite my lip and want to pick myself up but know he will simply throw me down again.

"Now here's the funny thing. I met you before I met your sister. But your sister," he scoffs and puts a knee on the ground next to me, leaning forward. "Well, let's just say she puts on quite the show when prompted."

I don't think, and my actions are stupid. I spit in his face and he slaps me so fast I'm not even sure it has happened. But it did happen because my cheek feels as if it has been set on fire. His large hand wraps around my neck, and my head's on the ground again. I can feel water soaking my hair, and that's the funny part—I'm concerned about my hair. I spent such a long time braiding it on top of my head, and now the water will ruin it. The fact that Anton might kill me right here doesn't even occur to me.

"Maggot," he says in a whisper, like it's some secret love poem only meant for my ears. His forearm bears down on my throat, and I can't breathe. His other hand slips to his sheath, and he pulls out a dagger.

"Nothing is stopping me from killing you. No one wants you," he tells me.

"My mama would find out and take Margo from you!" I try to scream back at him, but my vision is blurring. My breaths come in quick little movements, like my chest doesn't have enough room for air. He runs the blunt side of the knife down my throat, and a small squeak that sounds like a newborn pup escapes from me.

"The same mama who lets a dying women sleep in your bed?"

"What?" The word is more of a cough, but he seems to understand me.

"A pestilence is coming, Aida. It's spreading. Kills everything it touches, and, by God, how it has touched Margo."

"What did you do to her?" I scream. I don't understand where the sudden burst of energy has come from, but it explodes from my body.

Anton doesn't seem fazed though; in fact he seems rather amused.

"Look over there, Aida. Nothing but ships, but something is on those ships."

He loosens his grip on my neck, and I dare a glance at the harbor. Just like before, ships load and unload their hauls. Nothing out of the ordinary.

"You don't see it, do you?" His hand wanders from my neck to my face. His chokehold on me is over, letting my throat gasp in air. His hand grips my jaw and forces my gaze upon one ship in particular. "Tell me what they're unloading."

My eyes try to focus, but my body is still gasping for air. It takes me too long to focus, and Anton knees me in my side. I close my eyes, and a single tear runs down my face.

"Look!"

And so I do. At bottom of the cliff, caressing the ocean, is the port. My eyes find the ships, just to the right of where the waves crash. People are gathered around like the Pope has come, but this is different. Bystanders cry out or even run from the sight. I see it then. I see what is being carried from the ship.

One by one, bodies are removed—limp, lifeless. Each man being hauled off the ship is dead. Even from this far away, I cannot pull my gaze from the scene.

"Are those ..." I lose my words.

A man crosses onto the dock and pulls a body off the ship. The dead are so mutilated by rot I can't make out any human features. A body is hauled away and thrown onto a cart with others. The dockworkers stack the dead together and on the sides of streets people cry and hide their faces. I cannot hear the screams, but I can see a woman as she rushes toward one of the deceased. Another body is tossed on top of the one she seeks, and a stranger pulls her from the cart so its contents can be hauled away.

Cold air brushes across the ocean and brings with it a deathly numb feeling. I wrap my arms around myself to shield from the wind, but I'm not sure if the chills come from the air of death or the last bit of fall saying goodbye, before the winter scatters its snow across the villages.

"You live in your own fleeting world, Aida. Out here people are dying of a pestilence. It's wiping out entire villages, and it's come all this way, right here, to ours. I did nothing to Margo. The pestilence got her. I've yet to hear a tale of someone who's hosted the disease and lived to tell of it." He backs from me and stands up.

I sit up and scoot from the man as fast as I can.

I'm nothing but an animal to him—disposable. He stands above me, as if it's five years ago again. He could kill me now if he really wanted to. No one is stopping him. He steps forward, and I think this is it. He'll finally have his way with me, but he doesn't. He leans forward and his eyes come to my level.

"I don't understand you." He grips my chin and forces me to look at him—allowing him to look at my eyes. He stares at them, memorizes them.

I can't stand to look at him. Yet I have to look at him. I can see the shift in his gaze, as he tries to process what I am— witch, monster—all the accusations play across his features. "Some say this thing that's coming is God's wrath. He's here to wipe the slate clean, and I suppose, if that is true, then you'll be one of the first to die."

He pushes me away, and I stumble back. Anton stands again and hovers over me, always looking down, like I'm something for his amusement.

"Margo is going to die," he says.

Not a question or a wandering thought—a fact. The words sting. Margo had never been the most accepting sister, but she didn't treat me like a monster, like Papa. Like Anton.

"You don't deserve Margo." I mean to shout the words, but my voice fails me, dying almost as soon as the sounds form on my lips.

My words make him smile. "Oh, I know that. I deserve much, much better. In fact that's what I plan on finding."

For the first time I look at Anton under my free will. He smiles, and it scares me. His dark hair creates shadows around his eyes, and I realize just how alone the two of us are next to this stream. My fingers dig into the dirt, and I retreat from the man I once called my accuser—the man who could still pose as my killer should he choose.

He laughs at my sudden fear.

"No one wants you," he tells me, pushing my arm with the tip of his boot. It puts me off balance, and I fall to the side. Anton watches me from where he stands, looking down at me as nothing more than a dying animal on the street. His expression blanks away to something different, followed by a change in his posture as he backs from me.

"You're leaving," I say. "What about Joelle?"

"She doesn't belong to me," he says, a simple, quick statement that doesn't make him think twice.

"She's your daughter." The words come out biting, shouting to a man who would never care for someone other than himself. "Your flesh and blood. And you're abandoning her." My words grow softer and softer, emotion erupting in my throat, threatening to close off my air. "What if this pestilence comes? Your daughter could *die*." I choke on the word. In my mind I don't see Margo getting better. I only see her dying in Mama's arms, never able to say goodbye to her daughter—her daughter who may have the same fate.

"She isn't my concern anymore," he says, never turning his back to me.

"Then what is?" I ask.

"Why, my life." He pivots now, walking away with a quick wave of the hand. In the distance I see a horse tied up to a tree—his escape was planned; he's never coming back. All this time I've wished for him to leave. But now the time has finally come, I can't stand it. My sister—his *wife*—could be dying, and he sees it as an invitation to leave.

I'm gathered by the stream, covered in mud-stained clothing, glaring at a man I hate, wishing he would come back.

III.

Papa and Dondre return from their day's work when I come home from the stream. I'm still a ways from our cruck house, but Papa's voice rings out loud and clear. He's screaming at Margo, saying she's worthless if a man no longer wants her. We're women. We are judged by the men who wish to marry us; take that away, and all that is left is a useless body that must be fed.

"Well, go track him down!" Papa shouts, continuing some fight started long ago. His voice echoes in the small space of our home. It leaves us only to mingle at the sides, in hopes he won't look at us and scream.

"I can't, Papa!" Margo is trying to scream, to get his attention, to make him listen, but it's useless. Her voice comes out muffled and broken.

All Papa sees is two extra mouths to feed if Anton no longer wants them. Little Joelle sits outside the cruck house, inside the fenced area where we keep the sheep. Dondre keeps watch over her nearby, sharpening his knife. He doesn't see me, but when Joelle recognizes me she backs up and casts away her gaze.

Dondre must hear my footsteps, because he looks up, as I close the distance between us. "You used my knife," he says.

"It was the only one I could find. Mama asked me to

skin the rabbit you killed."

His expression doesn't change; he just goes back to sharpening his knife.

"When did you get home?"

"Not long ago," he says. Papa yells again, and Dondre peeks into the cruck house for a moment before turning to me. "Margo's back."

His gaze has mild interest toward his oldest sibling, probably wondering, *why is Margo here? Is Anton coming back for them?*

If Papa found out Anton was never coming back, I don't know what he would do to Margo and Joelle.

"She's sick," I tell Dondre. "Anton didn't want to leave her alone while he worked the fields."

My little brother doesn't believe my lie. He flicks his knife to the ground, where it sticks in the gravel. "It's not fair. You know that, right?" He crosses his arms and stares me down. He looks so much like Papa when he does this that it scares me.

"It's not meant to be fair," I say.

"Don't pull that on me, Aida. Anton will come back for Margo and Joelle. I'm talking about the coney. I killed that rabbit on my own yesterday, and what did I get in reward? *You* skinned it with *my* knife."

"Is that what this is about? A filthy rabbit? I skinned it because Mama said she would cook it."

"And now it's rotting away, because Margo showed up before Mama could cook it. That's how things always go. If I'm lucky, they'll look at me for five seconds, but then you and Margo go ahead and—"

"Watch yourself, Dondre," I warn.

His face is tight, as he stares into me—never has he been afraid of my eyes.

"Do you think I want this? I'd prefer Papa ignored me, and I'm sure Margo feels the same right now."

Dondre calms slightly and the tense up-and-down movements of his chest slow to a normal pace. His hands are fisted at his sides, but suddenly it's like all energy has left him as he lets his anger melt away. We both hear Margo cough violently inside.

Something breaks in him at that moment. I see it in his eyes. His fear pulls out his true age—that of a child trying to be an adult—and I'm reminded of just how vulnerable he is. He no longer tries to mask his true emotions, and the small quiver of his lip tells me he's scared; scared for our sister's life. She can't get sick; we have no doctor.

"Is Margo dying?" he asks in a shaky voice.

I don't say anything. Beside us, Joelle's face is hidden behind a fence post, but one eye peeks out, watching. Margo's coughs become muffled and hoarse. Papa has stopped yelling, but I can hear quick, hushed whispers between him and Mama inside the cruck house.

"We all die," I say.

Dondre latches onto my gaze. He's shocked, stunned that I've just told him that our sister is going to die.

"How can you say that?"

Because it's true ... "I'm not saying she'll die now." He hears me; he doesn't want to, but my words shake both of us to the core.

"But when?" his voice snaps at me.

I catch Joelle scooting from us. I don't want to know what her face looks like as we discuss her mother's death, but I find myself looking anyway. And I regret it. Little Joelle—my small niece—looks like she's just seen a ghost. She stumbles away, tripping over mounds of dirt, and doesn't bother to hide her whimpers as she slips under the fence and goes into the cruck house to find her mother.

"Dondre ..." I try to find the words.

"No!"

I look back at my baby brother. He's so strong. Ever since he was born, I was jealous. Just the simple fact that he was a boy made my father favor him. Sometimes I wonder if he realizes how much I envy him. He is only twelve years of age, yet he's seen and experienced more than I ever will in my lifetime.

"Don't tell me that she's dying. Tell me ... tell me she'll be okay. Lie to me."

His tears stain his dirty cheeks. He uses his hand to wipe away the streaks as quickly as possible.

"Okay," I say, the breath leaving me. "She'll be okay."

Dondre runs toward me and wraps his arms around my torso. He cries into my dress and hides his face in the folds, like he did when he was a toddler. His grip tightens around me and his cries grow louder as Margo coughs again. I try to decipher which sound is worse: the suffocating coughs of my dying sister or the heart-wrenching sobs of my baby brother.

"She's going to be okay," I say again. He nods his head against me, and we're both aware we are lying to each other. In my mind all I can see are the dead bodies being unloaded from the ship at the harbor. It's the first time I had seen or heard of this pestilence that Anton spoke of, but I live in a caged world.

Joelle exits the cruck house in a silent progression. Her pace is frightful, and I see a worn, raggedy doll hanging from one of Joelle's hands. It's Margo's from when she was little—and had always refused to give it up—and now her daughter is its caretaker. Joelle comes to my feet, next to Dondre and sits. She doesn't say a word as she grips the doll and presses it to her face.

IV.

"We can't just let her die," Mama whispers.

"Well, if we try to feed two extra mouths, we'll all die. We don't have the food to feed ourselves, Celine. That rabbit is the first meat you've seen on the table in a week, and you let it rot because you couldn't stand to see your firstborn suffer. You and I both know that Aida has been looked at with fear for a reason." Mama and Papa continue their conversation outside, unaware of the growing volume my father's voice has taken.

"She's your own blood," Mama tries to reason.

"She has never been. Nothing about that child's eyes proclaim innocence."

Dondre, Joelle, and I sit, trying to eat our meal, blocking out the sounds of Mama and Papa. Joelle sits with us but doesn't eat; instead she turns every few seconds to look at her mother who has fallen asleep on the straw mattress. Dondre looks at his bowl of soup but doesn't eat it. It's made of herbs, the only thing Mama could find to feed us with the rabbit gone.

I worry Margo may hear Mama and Papa fighting, but her sleep goes undisturbed. It's the first time since her arrival that the air has stilled. The only sounds now are Mama's and Papa's voices outside. Dondre and I clean the pot used to make the soup, while the sun is still above the horizon, the two of us hovering over the basin of water. I haven't heard him speak a word since I told him that Margo would be okay.

He refuses to look at her. Or Joelle. She'll walk up to him, clutch his hand, but he'll just push her away. Dondre is everything I'm not. I've never found Joelle asking for my attention, yet here he is, pushing it away like an unwanted colt following its mother.

"Aida." Papa walks back inside and doesn't stop his stride as he talks to me. "You can't sleep here tonight."

My hands freeze around the pot I am cleaning. I lift my head to look at him, to see if he's angry or at least to get an idea of what I've done wrong. I think back, trying to remember disobeying or breaking the rules. I had left the village without his permission, but how did he know? Anton was the only one who saw me, and he's gone.

"What did I do?" I ask in a small voice.

"Margo needs somewhere to sleep, along with Joelle. We don't have enough mattresses for everyone, and you can't expect me to send your sick sister out on the street, can you?"

"You just told Mama you didn't want two extra mouths to feed." My lips stumble across the words.

"Aida!" Papa's voice is stunning in the silence of the approaching night. "You will find somewhere else to reside." He points me to the door, and I stare at him, his words final and sharp. He won't look at me.

"Mama?" I beg. My hands shake around the pot I haven't finished washing. She won't let me leave. She can't let me be removed from the family just because my bed has been taken by another.

"Listen to your father," she says. Her eyes are focused on the ground.

Why can't she look at me?

I release a breath, and I feel like screaming. I drop the pot on the ground and don't care that it may break or that it will take a week's worth of work or crops to trade for a new one in the market.

I look at Margo's sleeping figure as I step out the door. Her hair is falling from its braid and I can see almost every bone in her body. I hope the dark spots around her neck are shadows, but are probably another sign of the pestilence, and I get it— Dondre was right. This is unfair. He hunted his own meal and has yet to receive praise. Margo is dying, but Papa's only concern is that now he'll have to find more food for our family. And here I am, walking from the only home I know, because there's no longer room for me.

V.

The sky is growing dark as I make the last steps to Cyrielle's home. Jermaine, her husband, is outside tending their livestock and I'm a few steps from their fence when he looks up.

"Aida," he says. Jermaine examines me, sees my face, and leaves one of their sheep. "What's wrong?"

"Is Cyrielle here?" I ask. I mask my feelings, as he nods his head and allows me into their home.

He remains outside, feeding the sheep that wander in the fences only feet from their cruck house.

Cyrielle has her back to me, when I step through the door. With the sun setting, the inside of the house is growing dark, and I can tell Cyrielle is getting ready for bed. She wears only a thin chemise and is sitting on the mattress, resting close to the ground.

"Jermaine, I felt it kick," she says in a hushed, peaceful voice.

I can't see her face, but she cocoons her stomach in her hands.

"It's only me," I say.

At the sound of my voice Cyrielle turns and smiles in my direction.

"Oh! Aida, what are you doing out so late? Won't your

parents be upset?" Even with this she still ushers me to sit beside her.

"Did you say you felt it kick again?" I smile.

She nods, takes my hand, and places it on her stomach.

She's carried her baby for months now. Any moment she will be blessed with an infant who is already announcing its presence in the world as it kicks through Cyrielle's skin.

My hand glides over the thin fabric on her abdomen. I close my eyes and focus all my attention on the movement beneath my hand. A small, silent kick hits beneath my fingers.

"Did you feel it?" she asks, eyes aglow, as I pull away my hand.

"Yes."

She cradles her stomach again. Cyrielle's hair has been undone for the night. It cascades in long dark waves over her shoulders, all the way to her bulging stomach. It acts as a curtain around her body, and I think to myself how much of a shame it is that we have to braid our hair and hide it away when in the eyes of the public. A few moments pass in silence between us until she stops thinking of her unborn infant and looks at me.

"What happened?"

Her face is serious then, aware I wouldn't visit her at this time of night if it weren't for a good reason. Her eyes beg my soul, and I want to open up to her and scream how Papa has abandoned me, but I can't worry her. She has her own family—a growing family with a baby.

"I just wanted to see how you were."

She laughs quietly to herself. "It's almost sunset, and you don't like to walk in the dark. You're trying to tell me that you came just to check in? Besides, your father would never let you."

"I don't always need to follow Papa's rules, you know," I say.

"Until your father refuses to feed or house you," she says, laughing.

I shrink back a little. My smile disappears, and that's all she needs to know her words are true. Her face is devoid of any giddiness she may have had previously, as she registers my reaction. "Did he ... He didn't ... Aida?"

I watch as her mind turns over the possibilities, everything I would have had to do in order for my father to participate in such a harsh punishment.

"What did you do?" Her eyes are sad.

I shake my head. "That's the thing. I didn't do anything."

"But ..." She stops, thinks, and I look down, ashamed, as if I've done something horrible to deserve this. "Did your father hurt you?" she asks in a meek voice. She tries not to make it obvious, but I see her eyes scan me for injuries.

"No," I say. "No, he didn't hurt me."

Cyrielle exhales a breath. There have been multiple occasions where I've come running to her, bruised, after defying Papa's wishes.

The most prominent instance was after I met Anton in the market. Cyrielle brought me home covered in dirt, limbs shaking in shock, only to have Papa punish me for sneaking away. Mama stood inside as he hit me. Dondre was away, playing with his friends, I suppose. But I was lying on the ground after Cyrielle left, Papa kicking me, telling me that I'd lied and how I'd snuck away with boys to sell myself. I told him no, that wasn't true; but each time I spoke, he grew angrier.

The next day, when Cyrielle came to check on me, I was still in bed. She'd peeked her head through the door, seen my battered body, and begun to cry. For weeks she'd refused to forgive herself because she'd left me with Papa, but I'd told her that it didn't matter. He would have done the same, even if she had been there. It was better that she didn't have to see it.

"What happened?"

The longer I stay quiet, the more upset she grows. I don't want her upset; she should be happy. Cyrielle is having a baby, and I can't ruin that for her.

"Margo and Joelle came to visit is all," I explain. "They needed a place to sleep. Papa said they could take my bed." It's a simple lie, just a stretch of the truth, but she sees it. I look at her and try to smile, tell her not to worry.

"I don't care how despicable your father is, he wouldn't throw you on the streets for that. There's more." Her eyes are intent on me, and I can't look away.

"Margo is sick," I say. "Anton left her with us because ..." I stop myself, brush away the thoughts again. I lied to Dondre. I can't lie to Cyrielle.

"Why?" Cyrielle whispers.

"Because she's dying." I feel numb. These words aren't mine. This life isn't mine. I have no attachment to what I'm saying, yet it's still true.

Cyrielle sucks in a breath, and I can't look at her. Instead I turn my eyes toward my hands. They lie in my lap, small and feeble. I make my hand into a fist and pretend I'm strong, but it's just a façade.

"Anton doesn't want Joelle after Margo dies. He doesn't want either of them any longer."

Cyrielle gets up slowly, one hand on her stomach and the other skimming the wall to keep her balance. She doesn't look at me, just leaves. When she stands, I see just how much her baby has grown inside her. The chemise is stretched to fit around her otherwise small frame. A veil of dark hair trails behind her.

As she steps outside, I'm left alone. I can only hear hushed whispers, and I know Cyrielle is talking to Jermaine. I hug my knees to my chest and pretend everything is okay. I make up a world, a fake world, where I'm only here to visit Cyrielle, to see if her baby has arrived. I'm just waiting, waiting for the baby. I'm not waiting for their deliberation and decision.

"Is it true? About Margo?"

It's Jermaine who is at the door.

His tall shadow hangs over me in the setting sun, and I wonder if I will have to leave the safety of their house to search out another place to stay for the night. I'm surprised because he doesn't look horrified when he looks at me; he looks sad.

"Yes," I whisper.

Jermaine looks outside where his wife must be standing. I see his lips move, but I can't hear what he's saying. He sighs, puts his hand to his face, and covers his eyes for a moment. From far away I hear Cyrielle's voice. Jermaine nods and agrees to whatever she's saying.

"You can sleep here tonight. I don't know for how long you can stay, but we'll let you reside," he says.

My head snaps up in his direction. He looks tired, and I realize how much I am intruding. If I weren't here, they'd both be sound asleep by now. Cyrielle steps back into her home, her hand supporting the baby.

"You'll have to gather some hay from outside to use as a mattress, but at least you'll be inside." Cyrielle's smile is small, as she comes to me. Her steps are tiny and awkward, as she tries to balance her offset body. Carefully she lowers herself next to me.

I hug her, being careful not to hurt her, because I know how weak she must feel. Jermaine walks through the threshold as I get up. "Thank you," I whisper, giving the smallest, yet most sincere smile.

He nods, and I walk outside to find hay for my bedding. A bale is near their fence and I drag it over. In the pasture a lone cow watches me in silence, as I haul away his food.

Pushing it into the cruck house, I see Jermaine and Cyrielle have already settled in bed. In the corner, as to give them as much privacy as possible, I break apart the hay so it is long enough to sleep on. I don't have any cloth to cover my makeshift mattress, so I lie across the hay as it picks and nips at my skin. I fall asleep like that, fully clothed, and wishing I didn't have to invade Cyrielle's life.

What comforts me to sleep is the chorus of crickets, always there to lull me to a slumber. Otherwise the night is silent.

The haunting darkness leaves me to wonder how much time Margo has left and whether Joelle knows she has lost both her mother and father.

I tell myself I'm foolish. Margo is alive. I told Dondre she would be okay.

She will be okay.

VI.

"It's not safe."

The words come in the morning. The air is cool and damp. I can hear the rain making a small rhythm on the straw roof as it falls precariously to Earth.

"We can't send her away."

My eyes are sewn shut. The voices don't register with me at first, but as they continue and my mind finds its place again, I know who they are.

"What about the baby? Our son or daughter could come any day now. I can barely afford to feed just the two of us. I know Aida is your friend, but we can't give her food. I don't even know what we will do when the baby arrives." Jermaine's voice is hushed in the early morning.

I can hear other bodies stirring in the background, far away. I imagine the villagers have begun their day. With the sun in the sky, the chores begin; work awakens the peasants to their place.

"The baby feeds from my breast. You know that," Cyrielle says, pleading with her husband, but I can tell she is giving up, hearing the sense in his words.

"It's not just the baby. We can feed you, me, and our son or daughter. Not another adult." He says this fact sadly.

There's a lost hope in his voice, as if he wishes he could supply me with a home and food, but he knows the truth of our world.

The people here till the fields just to give crops to our lords. It's only in our own time that we can harvest our own fields. At home this was what I had done. During the day, when everyone else was tending to the lords' fields, I was sent to my family's pasture. The small area was planted with barley, carrots, lettuce, sometimes corn if the season was right.

Feeding ourselves became more and more of a task as each day passed. That was my only value to my family: I tilled our field. Alone. I could pretend, if not for the slightest moment, that I was working like everyone else in our lord's field—not hiding my eyes. I could offer something to my family.

"What do you want me to do?"

I open my eyes and see nothing but the wooden walls of the cruck house. I can feel myself breaking from my core outward. Everything hurts and I'm unwanted. I can feel their voices reverberating off me behind my back. I urge myself to fall sleep, to just wait and put off the inevitable. Cyrielle would never wake me to kick me to the streets.

"I'm sorry," he says.

It's true. I can hear his remorse. He doesn't want to send me away, but he has to, for his family.

"We can't help her, not this time."

"But we have to ..." The words are said to herself. She doesn't believe them and neither does Jermaine.

"I'm sorry," he says again.

Everything is still. No one moves toward where I lie on the ground. My mind spins and turns, thinking of how I can possibly get more time. My eyes are closed, but a new energy runs through my veins. Panic keeps me awake, and I know sleep is beyond my reach, but I try anyway for more time.

I don't want to listen. I scream inside myself to block out the voices. In my imagination I'm at the edge of Marseille. I can see the docks and the grand ships, but I'm not there for the sights. Instead I'm there to scream. I stand at the edge of the cliff face, the water roaring in the cascades. One deep breath and I release it. I scream to Heaven and Hell, begging someone to hear my cries.

"Look at me!" I scream, but no one is there. No one is ever there, so I stand and continue to scream until my lungs give out. Until I'm just standing there, waiting for my tears to run dry or for my muscles to release me.

But I'm here. A coward in my friend's home, hoping she will nurture me more than I deserve.

"You know we can't." Jermaine's words are final.

Cyrielle doesn't say anything afterward, but I can hear a catch in her breath. She coughs, a sound I've heard from her on many occasions. It was there every time she fell and hurt herself as a child, and it was there when her mother told us that we could no longer be friends. Cyrielle holds back her crying. Her breathing is staggered, and it's all I can do to stay in my place, to not rush to comfort her.

And I tell myself this is the closest I will ever come to being loved, and it seems right—to be loved by the one who has saved my life.

"I'll be okay," I whisper. The words are so silent I barely hear them. I wonder how many times I will lie to myself. "I'll be okay," I say again in the hushed tone, and I'm lying again.

For the first time in my life Cyrielle doesn't hear me. She's always been there to receive my thoughts and feelings, and now, when it's most important, she can't hear me. I want to say the words louder, but I can't. I don't know if they're true. Will I be okay?

Jermaine walks outside and brings Cyrielle with him, as their small house grows quiet. I'm left to brew in my own cowardice.

And somehow sleep finds me.

"Come, before it's too late," Cyrielle says. She's running to the cliff face, hopping, skipping almost. I can see the smile on her face as she talks, and I don't understand her happiness. Her dress sways behind her, and her hair is in a complicated braid around her crown. Ribbons are twined into the plait, the strips of fabric draping her shoulders.

"Before what's too late?" I rush after her. The salty air comes in from the ocean. The smell of low tide fills my senses. It's a distasteful smell, but it reminds me of home.

"Don't you see it?" She turns to me and her face

suddenly goes solemn. A corset is pulled tight around her middle, and I realize how she must have had her baby in the night. Her sleeves are tailored close but taper away at her elbow and extend to the ground in a train. The fabric is dark as night and the wind sweeps the cloth around her like magic.

"What?"

Cyrielle lifts her arm, the long fabric trailing the ground, and she's the most elegant beauty I have ever seen—she looks like the lord's lady.

Her finger points to the heart of Marseille. The white fog from the smokestacks floats up and away from the town. The church bells don't ring. All is silent.

"They are burning the dead," she says. "You can smell it."

I watch the thick smoke ascend to the sky and disappear. And yes, I smell it. What I thought had been the repugnant scent of low tide is rot. It's the odor of wasted flesh being burned. The wind off the ocean sweeps it away, but it's still there.

"What happened?" I ask.

She doesn't answer, so I turn back to Cyrielle, but she's gone. In her place a woman stands. She wears the rich clothing Cyrielle had been in seconds ago, but her face is sharper, more distinct. The women's dark hair is twisted into the same plait Cyrielle had been wearing, and I wonder how such an intricate braid can be duplicated. Her beauty is almost unfair. This lady doesn't speak a word to me. Her stare is unbroken and fierce.

"Where's Cyrielle?" the lady asks.

My voice is withheld. Papa told me never to talk to those of higher class; it could only cause me trouble.

She looks confused by my lack of words. "We have to leave," she says, frowning. She holds out her hand in an inviting gesture. I find myself stepping forward. I cover the few feet between us, and we're both at the edge of the cliff. The waves spray a mist up to us, and I can feel the cold pricks of water at my feet.

"Where are we going?" I ask, mesmerized by the water below. It sways violently, and a broken tree has fallen into its wrath. The thick wood crashes into the rock wall of the cliff and snaps in two before being washed out to sea again.

"Frioul Archipelago!" The lady lets go of my hand and holds out her arms. The wind catches her dress and whips it around her body. She's a mass of dark cloth as she sways slightly. She smiles as her lips move, though I can't hear her words. Below us waves crash, but it's like she has detached herself from this world.

"Tiboulain, Aida de Luna." And even though she whispers it, I hear her steady voice, as if her lips were at my ear.

"How do you know my name?"

"How do you know mine?" she asks. She brings her arms to her side again, and the long sleeves of her dress fall to rest at her feet. Her body faces the ocean, but her face is turned to me. She smiles.

"But I don't know your name," I say. Her smile doesn't fade.

49

"Find Tiboulain." Her feet wander to the edge of the cliff. She isn't wearing shoes. As she loses her footing, she dives into the water. She falls with unnatural grace, pulling her arms in toward her body. I don't see her face or hear a scream as she falls. I can't even decipher when she makes contact with the water—the waves are so loud.

"My lady!" I scream, kneeling at the edge of the cliff. I can't see her down below. The waves crash against the hard rock; I see no sign of the lady. A body neither comes up for air nor is thrust into the onslaught of the rocks. Everything appears as it had, just before the lady jumped. She's nowhere to be found.

I cower from the edge and push myself away. The rock I had been using to support myself falls off the edge, into the water. My limbs quiver as I lose my balance. The scream that comes from my throat pierces my ears, and it's everything I can do to call out for help in a place where I can never be heard.

VII.

I'm covered in my own form of morning dew. Sweat clings to the fabric of my thick clothing and my skin. My heart feels as if it's still leaping off the cliff edge and I have yet to catch it. I push myself from the wall and extend my body across the hay mattress. Something near my head moves and I leap away. A small mouse scurries across the ground, stopping only for a second after hearing my movement before beginning its pursuit again and escaping out the door.

"Are you all right?" Cyrielle stands at the doorway. A small frown is etched across her face as she looks down at me, frightened and awake.

"I just ..." I don't want to tell her about my dream or how she was no longer pregnant with her baby, how she turned into a stranger who jumped from the cliff. "There was a mouse."

This seems to ease any stress from Cyrielle. Her demeanor softens, and she comes to me and offers her hand. I curl my fingers around her frail bones, but I don't use her as a lever while I lift myself from the ground, knowing how much weight she already carries with the baby.

"Mice scurry through here all the time. Don't you have them back home? They don't bother much, as long as we don't leave out our food of course." She smiles at me, and I follow her outside into the day's sun. Her walk is slow as she sways with her stomach. Whenever I see her face, all I see are the tired eyes of a soon-to-be mother.

Jermaine is out in the fields not very far away. He works to unharness a plow from a cow in their field. "He wanted to talk to you," she says, not really looking at me.

"Okay," I say, but my feet don't move.

Cyrielle turns to me and smiles, skimming her hand across my arm, as she walks back into the house.

As I approach Jermaine, I can hear him cussing under his breath while he struggles to harness the animal.

"Cows are for milking, not plowing," I tell him.

He looks up at me, sweat dripping down his face. The hat he wears shades his face, so I can't see his eyes.

He laughs, taking off his hat to wipe the sheen of sweat from his forehead. "If I had a bull, I would certainly use it."

I smile, but he doesn't return the gesture.

"Cyrielle said you wanted to speak to me?"

"Yes." He looks to the sky and frowns. "Looks like it'll rain again."

I follow his eyes and see that, although it is the middle of the day, the bright sun is hiding behind the clouds. Windblown trees sway in the humid air, warning us of an approaching storm. I hadn't noticed it before, but the ground is already wet—it must have rained, while I slept.

Jermaine leads the way back to his home, leaving the cow in the field to be harnessed once I'm gone.

"Aida, can you tell me more about what's happening with your sister?"

He's far in front of me, his body strong from working, his pace much faster than mine. I try my best to walk beside him but find myself looking at the ground, so I don't lose my footing on tree roots or rocks.

"Margo?" I ask.

"Yes, she's six years older than you, right?"

Jermaine and Cyrielle's cruck house sits atop the hill that overlooks their pasture. It's larger than the home my family lives in even though we house more people, but Jermaine inherited his cruck house.

"Five years."

He stops walking and turns to look at me. "Doesn't she have a daughter that's four years old?"

I nod my head and am finally able to catch up with him. Margo married when she was young, just like any normal girl. We girls grow up, dreaming of the fine young man who will come to our doorstep with an offer to convince our father to let us marry. Margo's dream came true. Anton saw her in town one day, and soon after he found our doorstep. It wasn't long before he recognized me as the girl he had tried to have killed. This was after the wedding, however—and after Margo was pregnant. If Anton had known I was Margo's sister sooner, I'm almost sure they would not have married.

"When did she have the baby?"

I think back to the day Joelle was born. I wasn't there,

but I remember Mama rushing home to tell the news. She had been staying with Margo and Anton in their village; when the baby was born healthy, it was all Mama could do to run home and tell us.

"I think it was six months after the marriage."

Jermaine looks cross at me. "But it takes nine months ..."

"I know," I say. A drop of water lands on my hand, and I see the sky is already threatening to rain. I step toward the cruck house again. "She won't admit to anything against Anton."

Jermaine grips the top of my arm lightly, just enough to stop me. "That's a lot to accuse a man."

I look into his eyes and wonder what he sees—whether I'm the friend Cyrielle sees or if he's just pretending to like me for his wife's sake. He doesn't wander from my white-eyed gaze, and part of me is amazed by his bluntness.

"You don't know Anton like I do." I wanted to sound strong when I said the words, but instead my voice wavers over his name.

Neither of us says much of anything for a while. We just stare at each other. It's very rare that I hold my gaze with someone this long. Usually they look away, disgusted by my features, or I hide my face, so I don't get rejected in the first place.

"Why do you want to know about my sister?" I ask suddenly. And still he does not waver. His dark eyes bore into my light ones, and I wait—always wait—for the onlooker to be afraid of me.

"Some disease is spreading in the villages. No one has found a way to wane its efforts. Anyone who catches the pestilence could die as soon as the next sunrise."

I lose my breath. I knew Margo's life could have been at risk, but could she really be gone as soon as one day? "You think that's what Margo has?" And this time I'm the one who breaks the stare. I had left my sister; I could return, and she could be gone without there ever being a goodbye.

"Yes."

"They'll find something that will help." But even as I say the words, they sound unsure. I'm lying to myself. They never find a cure. The village doctors just experiment on our bodies and say it's for knowledge when they are really just killing us.

"No, Aida. You don't understand. We aren't its first victims. It's already gone through countless villages."

I nod my head and feel my eyes water. I fight back the tears.

"People have been fleeing their homes to find safety, but it follows them. Whatever it is, it's following the carriers. Rumors are that it's wiping out half the population wherever it hits."

I imagine my family in half. Margo is gone; Dondre is gone, and maybe I'm gone as well. Just like that the world decides too many of us are living and chooses the pestilence as the quickest way to dwindle our sheer mass.

I look up at Jermaine. Maybe at the end of all this he will be gone as well, and all that will be left of his small family would be Cyrielle and the baby.

I close my eyes, daring them to release the moisture that shows my weakness, when I've tried so hard to be brave. My eyes don't brim over, but I have to suppress the shudder that erupts in my lungs. I gag on my own breath, every muscle in my body tense.

"Aida," Jermaine says.

I feel his hand touch my shoulder, a kind, tentative gesture, and I'm jealous. Cyrielle is so lucky to have such a husband. I open my eyes and look at the man my best friend loves.

"I have to ask you to leave, for the baby's sake. You could already have what your sister is suffering from."

I cough out my cry and choke myself. I can't be here—I knew that. From the moment I stepped through the door of their home and saw Cyrielle carrying her unborn baby, I knew I didn't belong. I should have slept on the streets and saved myself this rejection.

A raindrop falls on my cheek and I take a deep breath. I hold back every emotion and try to look brave as I nod toward Jermaine. He looks back at me, unsure, but I find the strength to smile.

"I'll go say goodbye to Cyrielle," I say.

His eyes are pleading, and I know he wants to explain to me why I must go, but I walk away because I already know the answer—I'm unsafe.

Their house is only a few paces away. Cyrielle reaches the threshold before I do as she rushes to hug me. I try to stop her, to pull away so I don't spread whatever Margo has to Cyrielle, but her grip is final. I can feel her crying into my shoulder, and I wrap my arms around her frame, hugging her baby also. She mumbles something, but I can't make out the words. I stop trying to listen after I realize she's crying because she knows I have to leave. I comfort her, but I don't tell her everything will be okay like I had for my brother.

"I'm sorry," she says.

I try to ignore the words, but I hear them anyway. She repeats herself and acts like she's the unwanted one, when really it has always been me who no one would even look at.

I hold Cyrielle from me and smile at her. She wipes her tired eyes and wraps her arms around her abdomen again. I don't say a word to her, and I don't know if it will make our parting easier, but I do so anyway. I lay my hand on her stomach and wish the baby health. She places her hand on top of mine.

"Aida, you don't have to leave. We can figure something out," she says.

She looks so worn. I only hope that once she delivers the baby she will grow to be strong again.

I hug her one final time and it is brisk. Her fingers trail down my arm as I pull away. Just steps away Jermaine stands, staring at me like he has no idea what to do. I open my arms to him, and we hug in the way a brother and sister might.

"Thank you," I tell him. This time it's Jermaine who doesn't speak. I walk away from both him and Cyrielle. I wrap my arms around myself, as the wind grows stronger. Rain builds in the atmosphere, and I wonder how long it will be until the Heavens pour.

VIII.

The air is a mist, but it still finds a way to swallow me. Every drop of rain is just a dull ping to my senses. It coats and envelops me, making me sick with the thoughts of entrapment. Midday and the sky is dark. Clouds coat the air and trap me inside this village.

A man I don't know lies against his house on the side of the path. His tunic is covered in mud and when I walk by it's like he doesn't see me. His eyes are closed but his mouth is moving, forming words. There's no sound, not even rain. The air is still in the sleet-covered day, no wind in the sky. I count each rise and fall of the man's chest, so sure they are numbered just as Margo's. Curiosity grounds my feet close to the dying man.

His head falls back against the wood of the cruck house, and my breath leaves me. Along his neck a large tumor erupts. Its dark color looks garish, even compared to his soiled clothing. Something seeps from the wound that swells around his throat.

At the sound of my breath the man seems to hear me. He picks up his head and looks at me. I don't fear his gaze—it's too dark for him to see my irises, but his eyes seem fixated on me. He scans me, beginning at my face, lingering on my bodice, until he trails down to my feet and back again.

"What's a pretty lady like you doing out alone?" When

the man smiles, he closes his eyes again.

His voice is rough and worn, and I imagine fluids accumulating in his throat, cutting him slowly from the world until no air is left.

I step back half a foot—subtle, so he doesn't notice—and begin to plan my escape. Instead my feet catch on something and a rock stumbles under my footstep. The man opens his eyes again and stares at me. I don't know why, but I hold my breath, as if inhaling might provoke him to attack.

He sits forward and winces in pain. I expect him to lie back again, but he uses the support of the wall to force himself to his feet. He moves each of his limbs with care, but I can still hear his moans of agony as he stands.

"You here to make a shilling?" he asks. The man stumbles toward me, coughing with each breath. I wait for him to fall to the ground, to succumb to his illness, but he doesn't.

"What?"

He sighs, turns to the pouch tied around his waist, and opens the pockets, searching. "Can't you see I'm dying, girl? I can neither afford nor take part in your services."

And that's all I need to know. I've seen the young girls he speaks of, the ones who sell their virtue to gain just a bit of money. But that makes them worthless. By selling herself, a suitor will never want her, will never look at her. Papa warned me of this, told me that he'd whip me before I could think of taking part in the act.

"I'm not—" But I don't know what to call it. I've only

seen the girls on the streets, waiting for men to call upon them, until they sneak away where no one will find them.

"You don't want me anyway." He points to the dark tumor on his neck. He tries to act normal, to smile off his death, but I can see the tense muscles that lie beneath his skin, how he holds himself so that the skin around the tumor doesn't stretch or pull.

I nod to him and realize he's looking at me. I avert my eyes like I've learned to do when someone looks upon me and wait for him to sit again, for my feet to find motion.

"Well, I guess this is it, huh?" He coughs at the end of the sentence and chokes on his words.

I wait for him to quiet again before I speak.

"What do you mean?" I ask.

"The separation of the dying and living," he says in kind, simple words, like his death doesn't matter.

I look at his body, the clothes that hang over his bones, and his tunic—stained with a dark substance that looks like blood. His forehead is moist with droplets, but I'm not sure if it's the air's sleet or the man's sweat. "God's giving His mercy."

I look at him, confused. "So He's not giving mercy on your soul?"

He smiles, and he seems genuine. "That's the best part. He's giving me mercy by letting me die."

He steps close to me, and I back away, not wanting the man to get a better view of my eyes. The sky above is still darkened by clouds, and I hope the cover engulfs me in its safety.

The man doesn't step any closer, but he hunts through the pack at his waist. He coughs and instead of getting better he sounds worse as the seconds tick by. With his last cough I see a dark substance at his lips and know he is rejecting his own blood. It drips down his chin, and he wipes it away with his hand. Finally he holds out two coins.

"Take them." He opens his palm to me. "This won't be much use to me anymore."

Before I have a chance to say anything, he takes my hand and uncurls my fingers, places the two coins in my grasp, and releases me again. I stare at him for a long moment, my eyes glued to his bloodstained hands. I blink back tears, as I step from the man once again.

"Thank you," I say, and when I turn, I hear the man cough, no longer holding back his agony as he vomits.

When I see the walls of my home come into view, I can barely hear the horror that comes from within. From a distance I can only hear a whisper, a choking sound; but as I come closer, and the space between me and Margo closes, I can hear her struggling for breath in between coughing fits. Dondre sits outside, leaning against the door frame, looking inside every now and then. His face is ashen and I wish he didn't have to see this.

"How is she?" I ask, as I come closer.

Dondre's head shoots up and he stands to his feet, brushing away tears that streak his face.

"What are you doing here?" He clutches his fists at his side and stands firmly. He's copying Papa—or at least that's what I tell myself to explain his aggression.

I hesitate, the remaining distance standing between my brother and me. "Papa said I couldn't sleep here. Margo needed my bed."

"Aida," he says, and suddenly his demeanor changes. The brave exterior that he had just been trying to put forward disappears, and I see him for the twelve-year-old that he is. His face crumbles and I want to hold him like I had when he was small. "You have to leave before Papa comes back."

"Is she okay?" I ask, ignoring Dondre's warnings.

His gaze doesn't leave me, as tears drown his eyes. He doesn't lift his hand to wipe them away as they brim and cascade over his cheeks. His arms and fists are still clenched at his side, and I know he is fighting to hold in his emotions like he always had—like Papa taught him.

"No."

I walk toward my baby brother, but Dondre sidesteps me. He removes himself from the door and continues to back away.

"Dondre!" I say, but he doesn't turn or stop. "Please." My voice is a plea thrown to the air and I wonder if he can hear me or if he chooses not to listen.

I run up behind him, as he walks toward the fence that holds our sheep. I grip his shoulder and turn him, so he'll look at me. Dondre pushes me backward with more brute force than I knew he possessed. I suppose all the years working in the fields while I was hidden away, gave him the strength I only wish I had.

"Don't touch me!" he screams, and his voice breaks. The tears still flow steadily down his face, and he blinks them away.

"She's my sister too," I say. I reach out for his hand, but he cringes away.

His hand comes up and I feel a sharp sting across my face. I had barely seen his hand as it whipped to strike me, but now the pain sings out strong and true.

"Aida, I—" Dondre stutters his words.

I can't look at him. I hold my palm where Dondre slapped me. I try to ignore the pinpricks that rise in my cheek, but tears cloud my vision, reminding me of his hand across my face.

"I'm sorry, Aida," Dondre says.

My feet slink from the source of danger. The voice of my brother continues to talk in its sweet sounds, trying to coax me back toward it. My ears ring so I can't make out the voice talking to me—pleading with me. My backside hits the post of our fence and I lean against it, shifting down to the ground. My other hand covers my face, and that's when the tears come. They run down my cheeks in shameful spouts, telling the world how weak I am.

"Aida ..."

I look for the source of the voice. Blinking away tears, I clear my vision and see Dondre standing over me, his face horror-stricken.

"I'm sorry." He cries in hiccups, no longer able to contain himself and to be the man Papa wants him to be.

I lower my hands from my face and hold my arms open. Dondre enters them, like he had when he was just a toddler. I sit on the ground, and he comes to me, burying his face in my neck. His breath is hot against my skin as tears pour from him onto my clothing. I grip my baby brother and silently beg him to never leave. He's not as small as he was when I last held him, and I struggle to wrap my arms around his frame, but he comes to me for comfort regardless.

Dondre doesn't speak to me and I don't utter a word either. My tears grow quiet as the stinging in my cheek wanes, then disappears. Dondre's cries only grow louder as he stays in my arms and I welcome him. He doesn't raise another hand or force me away. Minutes pass and still his sobbing continues until I hear a soft whisper, so quiet the sound of the rain almost swallows it.

"I didn't mean it."

IX.

"Aida," Mama says, as she sees me walk through the door. She doesn't rush to greet me, the daughter who was pushed from her home. Mama sits at the far end of the cruck house in the wooden chair Papa made years ago. She can barely hold up her head and in the shadow of the dark, I can see the dark circles painted under her eyes.

"I stayed with Cyrielle last night," I tell her. I want her to be pleased that I'm safe, that I was able to take care of myself. She sighs and covers her face with her palm. I wanted so badly for Mama to hug me when I walked in, but she makes my appearance seem to be a chore, like I've created trouble for her by being here.

"Victoir won't be happy you're here."

I stiffen at Papa's name.

"I know," I say in a hushed voice. "How is Margo?"

Mama lifts her head to look at my sister, who lies on my mattress on the floor. Her hair is sprawled across the straw in waves—I imagine that Mama took out her braids so Margo would be more comfortable. She wears only a thin chemise, and even with the chill of the morning, I see the fabric is stained with sweat. Next to Margo, Joelle is curled against her mother's side. Joelle's hair is still in a braid down her back, but short wispy hairs cling to her forehead in sleep. The child has her face nuzzled against her mother, her hand resting against her mother's cheek.

"They both fell asleep a few moments ago," Mama says. "I didn't think the coughing would ever stop."

I hear Mama's tired voice. She's been up all night tending to Margo. Looking at Mama, I see her kirtle is stained across the front with what looks like dried blood. My eyes skirt back to Margo and see her dark and bloody lips. I follow her arm down to where her hand rests at the edge of the mattress, fingers wrapped around a handkerchief that is also blackened by the blood.

"You need to leave, Aida," Mama says.

I don't bother looking at her as I approach Margo, kneeling next to her on the ground. I run my hand across her cheek and feel the moist sheen of sweat that coats her skin. I pull away the blanket across her body, so she can cool off. As I do, I notice a dark-toned patch of skin on her neck, just above the strap of her chemise. I push away the cloth and stagger backward. A dark mass of skin protrudes from the crook of her shoulder and neck, just as the man on the street had.

I can feel Mama get up from her chair and look over my shoulder. Behind me she stops breathing for a moment, coming to her knees in front of Margo's sleeping form.

"No," she says to herself in a silent and hushed voice.

She mumbles words I can't make out, but when I steal a glance, I see a single tear run down her cheek.

"It's the pestilence. She has the buboes like the others."

I realize she's talking to Dondre. He stands behind us now, making a stiff nod before stepping outside again.

I continue to unwrap the blanket off Margo's body and scan every inch of her skin as I go. Looking at the bubo, I see it leaves dark trails of skin, like rivers reaching out, plaguing the rest of her body. Smaller lumps gather around her shoulder and I try my best to hold back a shudder as I continue to scan her body.

I remove the handkerchief from her hands and see the blood has stained her fingers. I don't know why, but I lean across Mama to reach for the cloth that floats in the water bucket. Ringing out the excess liquid, I wipe Margo's forehead. I take her finger in my hand and wash away the blood, holding her gently, but the blood doesn't rinse off. I release my sister's hand for a moment and dip the cloth in the bucket of water again. I ignore my mother's eyes as she stares at me, and I continue to tend to my sister's needs.

I wrap the cloth around her hand and massage the water into her fingers. After a few moments I take away the cloth, but the blood resists. I release the soaked rag and look closely at Margo's hands—blackened, stained. That's when I scream. I can hear my voice cry out in horror but don't remember opening my mouth to shriek.

"Where's Papa?" I ask, my heart hammering in my chest, begging to be released, to run away in terror. I don't know why I ask for Papa—he doesn't want me here—but the words come anyway.

"He's gone to request a priest for last rites," Mama says. She looks at me strangely and examines Margo's fingers just like I had. After a quick look, she drops Margo's hand, not bothering to be gentle. Mama stands up, her hand covering her mouth. Her eyes cloud over, as she backs from her daughter in fear. Her chest heaves with sobs that no one can hear.

So this is the end. Papa's given up on Margo. Soon a priest will be here at Margo's bed, to hear her sins and forgive her, preparing her for her trip to Heaven. I wonder if Papa had seen Margo's blackened fingers—I wonder if that told him she was near the end.

She stirs awake, her fingers nothing but stiff digits attached to her body. Her arm stays wrapped around Joelle, still sound asleep against her side.

"Mama?"

I can barely make out Margo's voice as she speaks. If I hadn't seen her mouth form the words I wouldn't have guessed it was my sister who spoke.

"I'm here," I offer. She looks up at me with bleary eyes and coughs, her entire body shaking with the movement. Her hand comes up to her face to cover her mouth as blood sprinkles her saliva.

"Handkerchief," she says, choking on her own blood.

I reach for the bloodstained rag and hand it to her. I watch as she purges the blood. Mama comes to my side and hands Margo the bowl we use to brew our soup. Margo sits up, taking the bowl, but it slips from her grasp and onto her lap. Joelle slumps against the mattress as her mother moves from her, but the child doesn't wake. I see Margo cringe as she vomits into the bowl.

She coughs a few times more, before she's silent again. "How long until it goes away, Mama?"

"Soon, my child," Mama whispers between tears. She doesn't stand near her daughter, and I realize what a good liar Mama is.

Margo lies down, curling her daughter around her body once again. She strokes Joelle's hair, and I wonder if my sister can still feel through her dying senses. Margo closes her eyes, coughing every few seconds.

"Mama?" Margo calls out in the silence. She sounds frightened, her voice touching the note of hysteria. "Mama, I don't feel right." Her bottom lip quivers and shakes in the dark and I hear her shudder as her chest rises and falls in a clumsy pattern.

"You'll be okay, Margo," Mama says, but she's doesn't step forward. She looks to her daughter across the room and glances away.

I hope she feels ashamed. I hope she and Papa realize what they have done; how they have treated us so wrongly.

"Mama, I don't think I'm going to make it." And when she says it, she begins to cry.

I hear her lungs struggle to gain breath in the musty air. She makes wheezing sounds each time she inhales; beside her

Joelle stirs.

"Oh, God ..." Margo curses under her breath. "Move Joelle. Please, Mama, move Joelle."

I look over to Mama, but she stays frozen. She just stares at her daughter in horror, having no clue what to do.

I thought the nightmare began yesterday, but I was wrong. This, right here, is where it begins. In my bed Margo's body becomes possessed by something other than herself. Her head shakes and turns, her whole body shaking. Her limbs rise and hover over her mattress, as horrific sounds release from within Margo; they are choking, drowning sounds.

I run forward and grip Joelle by the wrist, just as she opens her eyes. Her face is confused as I pull her from her mother. Finally I scoop Joelle up in my arms and put her down behind me. Joelle wraps her fingers around my arm and I usher her behind me so she doesn't see.

Margo's eyes look in no particular direction and I feel fear ripple through me as I watch her lose herself. I put my hands out to stop Margo's hands from shaking, but I can't fight her. I try to be gentle, but I find myself forcing my body over hers so she will stop moving. Joelle cries behind me, but she doesn't dare come forward.

The shudders stop at some point. Margo's body stills, and I back away. All is silent. The only sound is the absence of Margo's breathing, which—after all—isn't a sound at all.

X.

My body is being yanked away as Margo's form disappears from my vision. Arms vise around my chest and neck, pulling me, shoving me, punishing me for something I've done. I can't breathe. I'm trying to scream, but it's nothing but a muffled gag in the back of my throat. A hand comes across my mouth, and I concentrate on breathing through my nose as the room spins.

"Let go of her, Victoir!"

I think it's Mama who screams for me, but I can't see her. Looking left and right I see Margo far from me, her body still and bruised. I cry, but I'm not sure if the tears are for my sister or me.

Papa releases me and I'm thrown to the ground. Using my hands to catch myself, I lie in the dirt, trying to breathe. A pounding pressure erupts behind my ear and its pulse is the only thing I can hear. Mama screams something, my back to her, right before I feel the pain.

It feels like a fine line has been drawn down my back, and someone has anointed me with poison. My back bleeds—I can't see it, but I can feel it. The hot liquid runs down my back in streams, flowing from me. I smell the leather in the air and know someone has struck me with a whip. My arms—the only thing holding up my body—collapse, and I'm brought to the dirt floor once again. Mama's scream comes belatedly. A sharp snap sounds and I brace myself for the second lashing, but it just barely brushes the skin of my cheek—a snake slithering by with its deathly fangs.

"What are you doing, Victoir?" Mama says, in between cries of hysteria.

I can no longer smell the leather of the whip; instead it is replaced with the toxins of my own blood.

"Did you see what she did?" Papa yells in his husky voice.

I can't look at them. I don't face them. When they turn to see me, they will only see my bloodied back.

"What are you talking about?"

Mama's voice is dim. A soft whine or moan comes from the corner of the cruck house, and I know Joelle stands apart from what unfolds in front of her.

"She's carrying out the Devil's work! Look at our daughter, Celine. She was possessed," he says in a muffled voice. "Margo is dead now."

His words are light and gentle, but I can hear the accusing tone aimed at me. I hear Joelle whimper softly, hesitating to go to her mother who now lies lifeless in my bed.

I lift myself off the ground, only slightly, turning my torso toward Mama. She gazes down at me in question, as if waiting for me to admit that I'm doing Satan's work, but I don't speak.

She looks from me to Margo, back to me.

She can't believe his words, can she?

When Papa thinks of his daughters in his mind he only has one, and she lies dead on my mattress. He thinks I did that to her; he thinks I made the Devil possess her.

"Mama—" I say. I ignore the skin that pulls tight around the wound on my back as I twist more to look at Mama. Her face changes and I see the hate form in front of me.

Her brows furrow and her body becomes stiff.

"You're not my daughter?" She says it like a question.

I wait for Papa to continue to warp her mind and turn her against me as he approaches her from the side.

He doesn't speak as he places his hand on his wife's shoulder.

She releases a shudder when he touches her, and I know I've lost her.

Mama steps from him and comes toward me, leaving just a small gap between us. I crane my neck to look up, knowing it will take little energy for her to kick me in the face.

"No, Mama, I'm here. It's me," I tell her, my voice pleading. "*Aida*. I'm your daughter."

"You're not my daughter," she says. This time her voice is sure. She says it with a conviction that can't be swayed. "Get out." Her voice is a whisper.

"Please, Mama. I'm Aida. Aida de Luna. You named me the helper of the moon, remember?" My eyes cry the words that she refuses to hear. Her face is stone when I speak, and just like my entire life, it's as if I don't exist. I'm not welcome in this household.

"Get out!" Mama screams.

Her hand flies out in front of her and I flinch away. When nothing hits me, I look up and see she's pointing to the doorway. Her gaze follows her hand, but I know she is still watching me. Tears flow down her cheeks, her face rigid, trying to hold back the sobs just long enough so as not to appear weak to the Devil—to me.

I stop arguing. I gather myself and ignore the pain as my skin stretches too much and bleeds more from the lashing. When I stand I can't hear anything. My world is nothing but static, a blur of injustice.

The worst part is, when I reach the door, I want to turn around and say goodbye. I long to love this family who doesn't want me. Tonight they will cry for the daughter who has died. Maybe days from now they will find my body abandoned somewhere and celebrate their victory over my death. Or maybe my body will never be found. I'll be just like the other neglected ones on the street. When they die, no one notices. Just another person lost to the pestilence to be picked up by the cart that brings them to an unmarked grave. That's what it will be like.

I'm being left for the Angel of Death. Dark faces will chain my wrists to the stone wall, and when I move the metal links will echo in the vast expanse of my loneliness. I have no option but to run to the Angel of Death. I will not only look death in the eye but will welcome it as it comes to take me away.

I will be unloved.

XI.

The rain comes in sheets across the horizon. It flows through the wind in harmony, putting on a show, bringing on a chorus. I soak in the rain, waiting for the water to absorb me and let myself become part of this storm.

I only make it as far as the next cruck house over. When I left my home the rain had already begun, the sky thunderous as God thrust His wrath upon us. Lightning streaks across the sky and I retreat into the canopy of another's home.

I expect the owners to come for me, push me from their haven, but no one ever does. I keep my back to the inside of the home, reveling in my ignorance.

Light shoots across the sky in a brilliant flash. Seconds later a thunderous roar shakes the earth under my feet. The rain relents a little, just enough so I'm able to hear something other than the pattern of droplets.

"Miss?" a frail voice says behind me. It's a child's voice.

I turn around to see a small boy, not over the age of eight, lying in a bed. He looks like Margo had, his fingers black as he shivers under a blanket.

"Did Mama send you?" he asks, his voice growing louder, but as he gains volume he coughs. When he is finally able to stop, he looks at me with sad eyes, his lips turned downward.

"No," I say, coming farther inside. Outside the rain continues, but as I enter the sound fades into the background. Things are scattered everywhere. Broken pots lie abandoned on the floor, baskets on their side, emptied. It looks like a robber has just passed through, but the boy doesn't appear to be a victim of a burglary.

"Oh." The boy closes his eyes and sinks into his pillow He doesn't make a sound, but I see a tear run down his face.

I come forward to kneel next to the boy on the floor. "What's your name?"

His eyes pop open as he turns his head to me. He seems surprised at my proximity but answers my question with a smile. "Bernie."

Up close I see the blanket over his body is covered with sweat, but he clutches it around his frame like it's the only thing he has left. Dark circles are under his eyes and the boy is skinny enough that I can see his cheekbones.

"I'm Aida," I say, offering a smile.

"Hello."

There's a moment when neither of us speak. After a few more the boy looks away and groans, drawing the blanket closer to him.

"What's wrong?" I stretch my hand to touch his fingers that peek out beneath the cloth, but I'm shocked by what I feel. I expected thin bones, but instead it feels like my hands have come into contact with a rock. His fingers are hard and lifeless, stiff against the cloth.

"Mama left," he tells me, closing his eyes again. His voice is sleepy and grows thick as time passes.

"What about your papa? Do you have any brothers or sisters?"

He shakes his head, but as soon as he makes the movement his body stiffens. He heaves and coughs, and I wait for the blood to come, just like it had for Margo. I brace myself for the shock of the thick liquid to spew through his throat, but the boy stays strong and it never comes.

"No." He coughs. "Papa left too. They took everything with them." I look around again and realize there was no robber; it was just Bernie's parents packing their things to leave and abandon their sick child. "They left me a loaf of bread, but I ate it all." He starts to cry, fat tears rolling off his cheeks and onto his pillow. "I didn't mean to."

"Shh," I say. "It's okay. You'll be all right." And there it is again, my lie. How many times in a single lifetime can I lie before trust is eradicated?

Bernie's hair is plastered to his forehead, and I smooth it away with my fingers. Under his skin he is boiling. His sweat coats my hand, but his skin burns me like hot coals.

He turns his face to me even though the movement pains him. He looks at me closely, studying my face. All expression leaves him, as he asks his next question. "Why are your eyes white?"

I take away my hand and feel my own body cool, as I

break contact with the feverish boy. My eyes dart from his gaze, even though it's too late. I consider my options. If I lie to him about this, will he believe me? Will Bernie assume, just like everyone else, that I am someone who works with the Devil?

"I—my eyes are white because I got sick." I don't know why I say this. My story isn't believable, but Bernie looks at me with something I've never seen before—sympathy. His eyes change and he looks me up and down for the signs of my sickness. His grimace turns into a small frown.

"Are you still sick?"

I shake my head. "It happened when I was small, but it gave me white eyes." I point to them and wonder what he sees. Am I a monster?

"Did you almost die?" he asks, but I know what he's really asking. He wants to know what it feels like to defeat death; to come so close, yet live anyway.

"Well, I don't know. It was so long ago," I tell him, but he seems disappointed by my answer.

He chews on his lip and it bleeds. My hand inches out to stop him, but I know it is useless. After what I just saw at my own home, it's only a matter of time until this little boy dies like Margo did.

"Do you think it will hurt?" he cries in a sad, small way. I open my mouth to speak but his hoarse voice beats me. "Because it hurts right now."

"I know, Bernie," I say, brushing my hand against his hot skin. He looks at me like I'm his savior. His eyes gaze wide at me as he soaks in my image. Bernie smiles and, very slowly, wipes a tear from his eyes in a grimace.

"My mama told me dying doesn't hurt," he says. "She said that God will take us in His glory, and nothing will hurt."

I don't say a word, feeling like my voice would interrupt him.

He stares, unblinking, at the ceiling. A hole is in the roof, above the spot where the fire belongs, allowing smoke to escape.

"What did I do?" Bernie sobs suddenly. His chest rises and falls in a fast pace. Groans come whenever he moves and the more upset he gets, the harder his chest heaves. The little boy brings on his own pain through his emotions.

"Shh," I whisper, putting my hand over his. His skin burns against mine, and it's a while before Bernie comes to an even breath again. A long silence hangs between us in the stormy air. All that can be heard is the consistent patter of rain on the roof.

"What did I—" Bernie starts again, his voice in hiccups.

"Shh, Bernie, it's okay."

"But what—what did I do to make God hate me?"

He isn't crying, but I can tell he holds back the tears. Under my hand his body is tense. His breathing is staggered, ready to slip.

"God doesn't hate you," I tell him simply.

"Then why am I dying?" His voice is a somber whisper in the heart of the storm. I hear his words, but I don't want to.

What a cruel world it is to have a child aware that they are dying. The young are supposed to live free; not wait for death to come in its full fatigue to take them away. In this universe where death is so plain—this universe where I do not wish to live—a boy lies dying, wondering why God hates him.

"Because that's how it is," I say, feeling the flow of tears grow inside my chest, waiting to be released. I haven't grieved for my lost sister. But this boy accepts me more than my family ever has.

When I look at Bernie, I see Margo. Not when her limbs were flailing in her last moments of life, but when she walked through the threshold of our home, Joelle in tow. I see her now, as I saw her before I knew she was sick. I saw my sister at a glance and thought everything was fine and that she was just dropping by for a visit. She had hidden the buboes and blackened fingers, but my eyes had been too ignorant to notice.

"You're lucky, Bernie. God's saving you. I know you don't understand right now, but you will," I say.

"When?"

His voice is soft. Outside the sun peeks through the clouds of rain and sunlight shines on Bernie's face. He has beautiful light eyes that shine against his dark and stained skin. His eyes gleam like the facets of a gem, and I try to ignore the tears that cling to his lids.

"I don't know," I say, my voice nothing but a whisper. I want to cure this boy and make him whole again. I would rather give this boy my life so he can live. I imagine how his life could have been, had it not been interrupted by this pestilence. He'd marry someday; his round face would lose its childish looks, and it wouldn't be long until he had a lady wrapped around his finger. I mourn for the life that he will never have.

"Aida?"

It's the first time he's addressed me. This time it is his hand that touches mine, his touch a hot spark. I don't pull away from the heat—I welcome it. I feel his gaze, as he watches a tear trail down my face.

"I'm sorry," I tell him, giving his hand a light squeeze, careful not to hurt him.

He doesn't smile. His face is limp, and his hand becomes a heavy weight in my grip.

That's when I realize he hasn't been coughing. This entire time Bernie has been able to bring his rough and tired voice forward without the interruption of coughs. I don't know if this is a good thing.

His lids close. He's tired—falling asleep. I know this, but my heart still hesitates, as he stops talking to me. I sit there with Bernie, his hand in mine, watching his chest rise and fall, so I know he's alive.

"Goodnight, Bernie," I say, even though it is well into the day. I bring his small hand to me and hold his palm to my cheek. I can't stand the heat that comes from this little boy. I pull away his fingers and kiss his hand before placing it on his chest, wishing it was me with the pestilence rather than him.

I stand up but don't turn away, always watching the

small rise and fall of each of his breaths—that unsteady, staggering pattern.

XII.

The world will always continue to move. Even when there's no laughter, the tides will push and pull; insects will roam in the soil and foragers will feast over our dead bodies. Humans are too ignorant to open their eyes and see the chaos before them.

The rain is just a mist in the sky, as I walk from everything that I've ever loved. Bernie was alive when I left, but part of me knows that his moment here in this lifetime is almost up. It doesn't matter how much I hope and pray; God will take whom He chooses.

The man on the streets said God was taking mercy on our souls by taking us. At first I didn't believe him. What if nothing exists after this life? But now, after just one day, I know anything—even if it is nothing—is better than this life of watching others succumb to the pestilence before my eyes.

Marseille. The town comes into view, as I continue my pace. It's no longer in its full glory. The air is utterly still. No wind comes off the port; the church bells don't chime. In the distance are smokestacks—the only tell that people still reside in Marseille.

It's a long time before the smell comes. I'm just outside the town when I'm covered in a cloak of rotting flesh. My eyes water at the scent of burning skin. I sprint forward and cross into town. The streets are empty like I've never seen them. Any occupants are slumped at the side of the street, leaning against a building as they cough.

No one looks up when I rush through. Their eyes stay glazed over in their sickened state. I pass by one woman and I think I hear the word *help* being muttered, but the sound is lost to the rush of total fear and abandonment that I feel.

Two men pull a wooden cart down the street, already heavy with its load. One of them says something and they both stop in the middle of the street. The man lets go of the handle and bends down on the side of the road, wrapping his arms around a girl my age. I scream out to stop him, to let the defenseless girl go, but she doesn't speak. The young girl doesn't even move as he picks her up and drops her in the cart. The other man holding the cart looks up at me, but his face is as placid as ever.

The two men grip the cart firmly and continue down the street to where I stand. I shift to the side, leaning against a building wall, averting my gaze as they come closer, feeling their eyes roam over my body.

As soon as their backs are to me, I see inside the cart and the bodies that rest within. The young girl is not its first victim. There are other bodies. Young and old, male and female—all in various forms of decay. An unsavory stench carries through the air around the cart, and I wonder how I didn't realize it was full of the dead right away.

Someone grips my hand and I'm being pulled away. I'm

about to scream, but another hand comes up around my face and covers my mouth, muffling my scream. The only ones who can hear me are the sick who lie in the street. They don't bother to look my way, as I'm being dragged away.

"Hush!"

I'm being led to an alcove hidden in the darkness of an alley.

"Hush, you!"

The voice is female as one arm wraps around my torso, the other around my throat, fingers gripping my face. She isn't much bigger than me, though she feels stronger. Every time I move, her arms tighten around me.

"I'll let you go. Just don't yell out," she whispers in my ear.

She waits, just holding me in her solid grip, and I realize she wants my consent. I nod my head in a slow, rhythmic pattern.

She lets out a breath and releases me. My body surges forward and runs in the direction of the bright and open streets. A hand punches my back and I'm on the cobblestones of the alley. Scrapes embellish my skin with shallow marks.

"I'm sorry," the girl who captured me says.

Her pleading voice is far away. Part of her sounds like she might actually regret what she's done.

"I didn't mean that. But I need you."

I twist around to see my assailant. The voice sounds sweet, like a young girl, but, when I turn, I see a mature woman.

She's not much bigger than I am, but her face is aged. Not like Mama's; this woman has a divine grace about her. She's almost childlike when I glance at her, but when I look close enough, I see the frail lines in her skin. She's hooded in a dark cloak and when she approaches me, she pulls it farther over her face.

She stands above me and offers a hand. I can't see her features in the dark alley full of shadows, but I gaze at her, trying to see past her hood to the woman who hides beneath.

"Get up," she tells me.

When I don't obey she bends down and picks me up like I'm a disobedient child. Her strength is jarring as she stands me straight and proceeds to circle around my position. The woman takes note of all the flaws that are within me. Her gaze is piercing and I can feel her eyes appraising me.

"How old are you?" she asks. She stops in front of me.

I see her face hidden within the hood. She's sad. Her eyes are watering, and I wonder if she's lost a loved one to this pestilence like I have.

"Please, tell me how old you are."

"Twenty-one years, my lady."

She nods and looks to the street before she looks at me again. "You have the eyes," she tells me. Her fingers slide down my cheek and tip up my chin. She turns my face, edging my eyes to the only spot of light in the alley. "Aida de Luna, you have no idea how long I've been searching for you."

Her words stop me. Aida de Luna is a name from long ago, never fully spoken by anyone outside my family.

"Aida de Luna. Helper of the moon. Is that what your name means?" As she speaks, she circles me again. Her eyes search me, as if my body bears some treasure or spell.

I hold still, but I can feel my legs quiver under me.

"Yes," I say quietly, but my voice is powerful in its silence.

Papa laughed at Mama when she suggested that I be named after the moon. I don't understand why Mama was so adamant about having my name be a constant reminder of what's wrong with me, but I suppose that was the point. It's to tell others that I'm not the Devil's child. My eyes are shining, just like the moon, and not the Hell that my iris color screams of. No one ever saw me as the moon.

"What do you think I am, Luna?"

"Aida," I correct her. I'm Aida—helper. That's what I'm supposed to be known as, not the moon—not Luna. No one has ever called me that.

"You're Luna. Maybe not yet, but you will be."

I stare at my captor. Her face doesn't look as young and flawless now. When she stops circling me I'm able to see the age etched across her features. She seems tired. I can tell when she loses her willpower, her body swaying with fatigue. Her hand peeks out the edge of her cloak and all I see are skin and bones.

"Are you sick?" I ask. "Like the rest of them?" She doesn't seem like them. This is a different disease that eats away at her, if it's a disease at all.

She blinks. "What do you think I am?"

Her voice is harsher the second time she has to ask. The world bears down on her and she sways with the effort to stand and talk to me. I'm important to her for some reason. And even though I know I should be afraid of this stranger, I'm not. I want to help her, whatever it is she needs.

"What are you?" I ask, confusion coloring my voice.

"I'm like you. We're the same thing. I need you to tell me what that is," she says.

Her face crumbles. I don't understand what's going on. Just a minute ago this woman was holding me hostage, and now she can barely hold herself up.

"Please."

I don't know what she is.

She waits in anticipation. She leans forward, and her pupils grow large in a flash, making her entire eye black and dark.

I scream out, knowing exactly what she is.

"You're a witch!" I stagger away, but she catches my arm, her iron grip pulling me forward again. Her strength is back. I watch in wonder as her bony fingers flesh out, growing healthy and long before my eyes. My gaze follows all the way to her face; what had once been sharp and defined is now flush and youthful. The wrinkles disappear from her face, and though she had been beautiful before, she now possesses some sort of glory.

Her grip on me loosens as her pupils shrink back to a regular size.

The thin wrinkles around her eyes return, but that's all.

She still holds a strange and remarkable beauty.

"Are you a black witch?" I continue to pull away, but she doesn't let go.

Her face is somber when she looks at me.

"Black and white are one and the same, Luna."

Black. I'm sure of it. A white witch would be quick to tell of their good deeds and how many they've saved.

"My name is Mystral, and I need you."

She pulls me to her in a possessive manner.

I flinch away, but with each protest she drags me toward her in a quick motion. My feet are reluctant as I follow behind her. We continue slowly down the alley.

"What are you doing?" I'm surprised by how distressed my voice sounds when I speak. That edge of hysteria is a reminder that I can't escape.

Mystral stops in front of me, and I stumble into her. Her back faces me as she speaks, her grip never letting up. "You don't trust me."

"No."

She turns and uses her free hand to lower her dark cloak. The hood falls to her shoulders and reveals hair dark as night, braided upon her head. A plait wraps tightly around her scalp until it's tied at her nape. The rest of her hair is tucked into her hood, and she tugs it out, revealing dark tresses that cascade down to her elbow. Ribbons decorate the braids that frame her face.

I hold in my gasp.

"You raided my dream." All at once, it's like the dream is happening all over again. I see Cyrielle, no longer pregnant, running to the edge of the cliff. But then it's not Cyrielle anymore. It's a woman with ribbons in her hair and a dress that swallows her body. It's Mystral.

"You let me in," she says calmly.

Panic grows inside me. Suddenly Mystral's grip on my arm is too tight. It's like she's digging into me, but when I look down at her fingers, I see she only has a light grasp on me. If I really wanted to, I could run away, but my feet won't let me.

"Luna, what have you seen in the past few days?"

She talks to me, but I ignore her. I've heard rumors of what witches can do, how their mind games work. All my life I've been accused of being a witch myself, but others were just too foolish to realize I didn't possess the same powers Mystral does.

"What have you seen?" she asks again.

Her voice is soft and pleading and I wonder if this is still a game she's playing.

I look up at her and see the question in her eyes. Just today I've seen my sister's life taken from under my fingertips, then a boy—who I don't even know or should care about—suffering as he contemplates his death. Today alone I've been exiled by my family, whipped, left abandoned, but that's not what matters. Mystral doesn't know all this. She shouldn't know all this.

Today I saw a body being picked off the ground and

added to a pile of dead on a cart. Today I saw a piece of the world die, and I wonder why I haven't become a victim.

XIII.

Men in dark clothes stand in the street. Some don't wear a shirt, and those are the ones I fear most. Their bare backs reveal whip marks. I watch as they all take the leather and slash it against their own skin with as much force as they can muster. None scream out in pain. They make their way through the streets in a slow procession, lashing their backs, inflicting their own pain. When I smell the leather, I feel the sting of my own fresh wound.

"Why are you showing me this?" I can't help the horror that tears through my voice.

The masochistic men in the street mumble words about divine grace, salvation, and suffering in the name of Christ.

It makes me want to vomit.

"You need to see this," is all Mystral says.

We stand on the side of the street. The men come closer and closer with each passing second. When they finally walk past, I smell their blood and sweat. Some lonely women follow them and worship. They wipe the men's faces with a rag whenever they get a chance.

A man in the group whips himself, and he falls to the ground. No one stops to help him. He just kneels there, as others walk past him without noticing. And I don't feel the need to help this man. I can't find myself empathizing with him or trying to understand what drives him to such irrational action.

I hate myself for not helping him, for wanting to look away.

Eventually he gets up again and continues to follow the group. They will go village to village, attracting an audience. What do they want to get out of this? Is it really an attempt to make amends with God before their death, or is it just to have this last bit of control over their lives? If they die, then at least it will be on their own terms.

"What are they doing?" I ask. A crowd of followers gathers around the men, watching the show.

"Flagellants. They are cleansing themselves of their sins by the whip." Mystral turns away and goes into the tavern.

I rush in after her as the moans and shouts from the flagellants fade.

Inside the tavern the air is stale and smells of the different concoctions people make to see how much they can drink while still being able to stand. The streets outside are full of nothing but the sick and dying, but in here people live on, alive and well—sort of.

Mystral moves to a table with rowdy men. She throws herself over one and takes his drink in her hand. He doesn't protest but wraps his hand around her neck. She slips from his grasp in a quick motion, his drink still in her hand. She nods to me as she takes another table across the room that is empty.

"Come on. We have important business," she says,

walking past me and taking a seat.

I follow behind her and sit on an old ale barrel propped upright. Across from me Mystral puts down the drink and lays her arms across the table. "Drink it."

My eyes widen. "What?"

"Am I unclear? Drink it." She slides the drink over to me.

"How can you even think of drinking? Have you not seen what is out there? People are dying."

"You think I don't know that?" she snaps back at me, but then her body relaxes a bit. She looks around the room; the people throw themselves to and fro, asking the beer and gin to take them before the pestilence can. "Sometimes it's easier to pretend everything is okay," Mystral whispers, mesmerizing the faces in the room.

One large man has a table full of empty cups around him. He looks sick, but it's not enough to stop him from taking another sip.

The smell of barley hovers around me. I look down at the mug Mystral gave me—ale. I push it away. She looks back at me and takes the mug, wrapping her delicate fingers around the drink.

"The people in this room may survive."

I watch Mystral, but she doesn't look at me. Her gaze drifts about the tavern, never settling on one face too long. She's impassive as she continues to clutch the mug.

"Some may not ... unless there's a salvation." Her eyes

flicker over to mine, looking for understanding.

"What do you mean?"

Mystral grips the mug closer to her and sighs. She brings the drink to her lips and sips the ale. Her eyes never leave my face as she puts down the cup between us.

"A force outside of what is normal."

She's talking about black magic. I back from the table just slightly, but she doesn't miss the movement. As soon as my hands leave the table Mystral throws the mug and grips my hand. In my shock I look around the room, but no one has noticed the mug has hit the wall and shattered.

"You have the power to save lives, Luna."

Mystral tugs my arm toward her across the table, but I can't bring myself to look at her. My eyes scan the room, begging someone to glance my way, but everyone in the tavern is preoccupied with their drunken games.

"My name isn't Luna," I say. My voice is just a murmur. I wish I could sound stronger.

"Your name is Aida de Luna. Born in the day of darkness, bearer of the white eyes. With just a sliver of the sun in the sky, you looked to the moon, and you were forever cast as a witch," Mystral tells me.

The words sound strange from another's mouth. Mama only told me the story of my birth once, just so I could understand why I was cast away.

"How do you know that?" Mystral's fingers dig into my wrist even though I gave up trying to escape as soon as she threw the mug. My hands shake under her grasp, as she leans over the table in a heavy stance.

"I know you, Luna. I need you to help me."

I stare at her hand that clasps mine. Her touch lightens, and the edge of her dark cloak falls across my wrist.

"I can't help you," I say, shaking my head. My voice wavers as I feel the tears well up and my throat constricts to hold in the biting hysteria.

"Yes, you can!" She picks up my wrists only to slam them down onto the table. Her voice projects through the room, and finally someone looks over. He just watches at first, but then he motions to someone else and now I have two faces watching. One by one more people watch us as the scene unfolds. Mystral turns and sees her audience; she releases me.

"I'm sorry," she says simply.

I'm not sure if she's talking to me or to the people who sit in the tavern, waiting for a fight to break out. I take the moment to slink away. I run around the tables and out the door, knowing Mystral won't follow me with so many watching. I don't know why it matters whether or not we're a spectacle, and I don't care. I run, feeling all eyes on me, but no footsteps following.

XIV.

Bernie's dead when I find him again. I don't really know what I expected. After seeing Margo it shouldn't have been a surprise. The little boy reclines in his bed, just as I had left him, the sheet still covering his body even though he was overheated from the fever. I take the blanket and roll it off his still sweat-covered skin.

Bernie's chest is bare, revealing a large bubo that adorns his armpit. I stifle a cry when I realize the mass of infection is almost the size of my fist. The longer I look at him, the more buboes I see scattered across his skin. I take the blanket and place it over his shoulders like he had originally left it.

"I'm so sorry." I don't know why I say it. I don't even know this boy, but I feel responsible. I was the last one to talk to him; surely there was something I could have done.

I place my hand across his forehead and smooth back his hair, though the gesture is lost.

"God saved you, Bernie. I hope you understand that, because I don't." The tears overwhelm my eyes and fall down my cheeks. "I don't understand why God took you away, but I hope you understand."

His sweet eyes are closed, like he's asleep, and part of me wants to believe he will wake up in a few minutes and tell me he's okay. He looks peaceful in death, and I hope that's how it was. In my heart I wish that his passing was painless, unlike my sister's.

"May you find eternal peace."

My tears fall to his face and become his tears. Wet stains float across his face and leave behind clear trails of pale skin. I bend my head down to his and let myself leave this world for a moment. I ignore the smell of death that rots his skin and makes me want to gag. His forehead is stone against mine, and I try to forget that he is gone. I murmur prayers into his hair until I can't whisper words anymore.

I didn't know Bernie. I shouldn't be crying for him. His family left him here to die while they ran off to save themselves. They were selfish. I hope I'm never like them.

Bringing my face to Bernie's, I kiss his forehead like I'm just wishing him a good night. I blink back the tears and promise myself this is it. From this point on I won't cry, but like a lot of promises, they cannot be kept.

The cruck house burns down in flames, as Bernie receives a sad excuse for a funeral at my hands. I said all the blessings I knew, before I set fire to his home. I had no oils, but I hoped that wouldn't stop God from receiving him, forgiving any lost sins. Even as I set the first spark, I prayed for Bernie.

Bright fire burns the wooden walls of the home and sets the straw roof aflame. It doesn't take long to catch. Even with a fresh coat of rain, nothing stops the flames. The smell of burning flesh is in the air—the same scent intoxicates the air of Marseille—and now it reeks through the streets of this village too.

"What are you doing?"

I turn and see a woman slumped over. Her body is weak, the beginning symptoms of the pestilence written all over her face. When she coughs, her entire body shakes with the simple movement. Part of me wonders how long she has left to live.

"Saying goodbye," I tell her. My eyes avert, and I take a step back. She doesn't bother to look at my white irises as the flames of the cruck house consume her vision. She backs from me the slightest bit and her hands clutch at her heart.

"Is the boy ..." she says, but then I think she reads my mind.

I can see the recognition in her face, as she realizes the boy she is asking about is gone, in the flames, his body leaving this world along with his soul. "I knew him—his mother."

"Where did they go?"

She looks down at the ground, winces with the movement. "To the countryside, where it was safe. I couldn't go with them—I wouldn't have made the trip." She looks up at me quickly, then to the cruck house. The flames are dying, running out of fuel to burn. The charred and ashen wood deteriorates, the walls no longer able to support weight.

"When did he die?" the woman asks in a shy voice.

"Today, just a few hours ago, I suppose."

She nods her head, like this makes sense. It appears as if

she is speaking to herself, lips moving, but she smiles at me and says, "Thank you," before walking away. I watch her slow pace, as she distances herself from the fire with the burning boy.

The smoke drifts through the sky in dark sheets. I wait for it to engulf us and take mercy on our souls, but it floats away in the wind, dissipating until it can't be seen anymore.

Why is it me who stands here, untouched by this sickness, while every person around me seems to succumb?

When I hear steps behind me again, my head whips around to see a man dressed in dark clothing, proceeding through the village. Even with the great distance between us, I can see he's wearing a mask. He walks away from me, his back always to my face, but the longer I watch him weave through the village, the more sure I am of his destination.

Bernie's home burns to the ground while I watch as the fire licks away the remainder of the building, until it has no choice but to dwindle down. With a last glance at what is left of the little boy's life, I run home. I keep some distance from the man in the mask, but I never let him out of my sight.

The fields I had grown up on open in front of me, and I stop. The masked man continues onward, stepping through our fenced yard and through the door of our home. A few seconds later Dondre comes out, holding Joelle's hand. He doesn't see me and pulls Joelle away, outside the fence around our property.

Joelle tugs on my brother's sleeve, and finally he looks up and sees me. I'm not sure if I expected a welcome or any acknowledgment, but the greeting I get is a surprise.

"What did you do to her?" he says, his voice ragged and hoarse. He grips Joelle by the hand and pulls her from me, which she doesn't protest.

"What do you mean?"

"You killed Margo! You used some sort of magic on her!" he shouts, and I worry Mama and Papa will hear us and come outside. I imagine Papa with his whip again, slashing the thick leather strap across my back, the blood pouring out until I can't bleed any longer. I step back, not much fearing my brother, but our father.

"I didn't—"

"You did!" Dondre cuts me off. Joelle stands beside him, stone faced. "You made a pack with the Devil and killed Margo—and now Mama's sick too!"

"What?"

Dondre is trying to will himself not to cry, but he's losing the battle.

"Why do you want to take away Mama?" When he says the words, I see him as a child once again, gripping Joelle's hand for strength. She doesn't sway—even though, just hours ago, she lost her mother and her father abandoned her.

"Dondre, I didn't," I tell him. My voice is even, calm, but my brother unravels.

Beside him Joelle whispers something into his ear, and he pushes her away. She falls to the ground but doesn't pick herself up. I rush over and offer my hand, but she squirms away like looking at me would give her the plague.

Dondre shoes his hand against my shoulder and I'm on the ground. He stands above me and my kirtle gathers around my feet, tying me in place. I hear Joelle get to her feet and join his side. She's so much smaller than him, but at this moment she appears to have just as much strength as he does. Her gaze is fierce and I applaud her for it.

"Your eyes are white," Dondre says. His hands are fists at his side. Joelle looks at him and mimics his gestures.

"Dondre, you know that," I stutter the words, suddenly wary as he slips out the words everyone thinks when they see my eyes.

"Why are your eyes white?"

His words are angry, and part of me wants to believe that he still sees me as his big sister, but when I look into his eyes all I see is malice. He's just like everyone else now. Whatever has happened within the past few hours has led him to believe I'm a witch.

"Why?" he shouts and pushes my shoulders down, until I realize I'm lying in the dirt.

I stay flat on the ground.

"Dondre?" The voice is quiet from within the cruck house.

Dondre turns and leaves me on the ground. Joelle stares down at me like I'm nothing more than a dying animal, and follows my brother inside the house.

I get up quickly and rush to the threshold but don't enter. I peer through the opening, hiding my face as much as possible from anyone inside.

My mother lies on her bed, a dark man leering over her. He is masked, just as I had seen in the village, but now I can see exactly what he wears. His robes hang all the way to his feet and extend over his gloved hands. The material looks like a thick canvas, but it has a glossy coating, almost as if it had been dipped in wax. The large mask has openings for his eyes, but where his mouth slit should be is a long beak. I can't see any skin. He is a bird.

The Bird holds a wooden cane, and uses it to poke and move Mama's arms. She seems uncomfortable but listens when the man tells her to move this way or that. She doesn't look sick, but then she moves to the right like the Bird tells her and winces. He holds out his cane and uses it to move her chin up and away. In the new light I see a lump grace the crook of her neck. A tear runs down her face, as the skin around the bubo stretches. He nods and moves from Mama to a bag on the other side of the room.

Mama sits, never looking up to the worried faces around her. Papa stands stiff but doesn't comfort his wife. Dondre stands a few feet from the door with Joelle, waiting for the moment to run away.

I see a glint of metal, and the Bird comes back to Mama, a small knife in his hand. Mama sees it, but she holds out her arm, resting her hand across the Bird's wooden cane. A sweet smell fills the air of the cruck house and I think it comes from the Bird—flowers, herbs, the aroma of healing.

"We will need to rebalance the humors. Those are what keeps the body in alignment," the Bird says in a muffled voice.

Papa nods as if he understands and Dondre steps back, away from the scene that unfolds in front of him. Mama watches as the small knife comes to her skin, the Bird holding it in his gloved hand. The skin breaks and dark liquid bleeds out.

Mama doesn't even flinch. She looks up at the door for a moment, and I think she sees me—a corner of her lip lifts in a smile.

From behind me a hand covers my mouth and pulls me away. I feel the small body behind me and know it is Mystral right away. I don't fight her, for fear of alerting Papa and the Bird that I was watching. I let her lead me and when we are out of hearing distance she releases her grip.

"What were you thinking?" Mystral says, her eyes abuzz.

I brush off my kirtle and don't answer her. Instead I look back at the cruck house where Mama is taking treatment for the pestilence.

"They'll kill you," Mystral says. Her voice is steady and sure. She's not accusing Papa of whipping me or abandoning me; she just knows what he'll do to me, if he ever sees my face again. That much was clear after what Dondre said earlier.

"Who is the man?" I ask, still looking at the house. "The Bird. He wears a mask."

"A doctor. The beak of the mask is filled with herbs that filter the bad air." She shakes her head, like it is nothing but useless tidings.

"And I suppose you know how to cure the pestilence." I say the words, not expecting her to respond to them. It was meant to mock her, but instead she smiles at me.

"Yes, with your help."

"Mystral, please, I need to get back to my family." I brush past her, but she takes my arm. She doesn't turn me to face her, but her lips are at my ear when she speaks.

"They don't want you. You've seen what they've done once. What makes you think they won't hesitate to kill you if they have the chance?"

"They wouldn't," I say, looking at the home I was exiled from. All I can see is Papa's face after he brought the thick leather down to my back. Hate fueled him, but what hurt most was how easily he swayed Mama; all it took was a small sliver of doubt for her to leave my side.

"Don't lie to yourself, Luna." She lets go of my arms and takes a few steps back.

The opportunity to run appears, but she knows I won't leave. I care more for my life than my family does. I don't trust them enough to keep me safe. Yet somehow, I remain.

Mystral's hair lies across her breast and is braided in one long coil with pieces of ribbon intertwined and flowing at the ends of her hair. She doesn't fit in here. Women should have their hair hidden away; men should not see such long locks. She doesn't care though; everything about her is wrong. Her black cloak floats around her body in sheets, the hood no longer covering her face.

"You can save them, you know." Mystral's voice is quiet.

Her words curl around in the air, as they linger my way. When I don't respond, she takes it as an invitation to continue. "The pestilence will kill more than half of those you love, even if they don't love you back. All you have to do is find the cure on Tiboulain." She points in the direction of the coast off Marseille.

"Frioul Archipelago?" I ask, turning and sure enough, the four islands sit among the ocean. Not many venture out to them. For the most part they are all just large masses of rock, unable to support vegetation, so few people make the journey to explore.

"Tiboulain is the smallest of the four islands and mostly forgotten. It stays hidden, out of our sight, behind the two larger islands, Ratonneau and Pomègues. Your task is simple. Go to the island and take immortality." Mystral's voice grows in excitement, like a small child, and when I see her face I see just how badly she wants this. She clutches her braid absentmindedly and comes closer to me.

"Immortality?" I ask, growing wary the longer I talk to her.

"You and I, and whoever we choose, will live forever." Her eyes are almost kind as she looks at me, her smile softening as time passes.

"I can't take part in this ..." I think of what to call what she's doing. And of course I know what to call it. It's what I've been accused of my entire life. "Sorcery."

"Luna, no. That's not it at all. There are no herbs or

potions, like you may think. It is just simple logic."

"Then what is it?" I ask.

She looks down, suddenly unsure of what to say. "I cannot say. Only you can discover it."

"Do you even know what it is?" I watch her as my questions alter her.

Her sheer confidence in her plan diminishes, and she slouches forward.

"No, but—" she says.

I wait for her to finish, but she never finds the words. Instead I watch as she runs scenarios through her head, thinking of what she could possibly say to convince me. Finally she looks at me and her gaze pierces my eyes. "You have a bond with the moon."

"No," I say. In the past few days I've seen too many deaths, too many bodies, and she wants to lie to me and tell me something out there will make us live forever.

"Please," Mystral begs. Her voice reaches a level of hysteria and I almost feel sorry for her. Her arm comes out and she grips my hand, pleading. "Luna, I need you. Your family needs you," she tries one last time.

I push her hand from me. "You said it yourself, Mystral. My family would jump at the opportunity to kill me, so why should I gift them with immortality?"

The words sting her, of that much I am sure. She cowers away and for the first time, I see genuine fear. Her face is lined with wrinkles and I no longer see her as the young woman I first thought she was. She morphs into an aged soul before my eyes, keeping her youthful figure and looks, but her posture slumps and surrenders.

"Just ... remember what I said ... if you change your mind," she says, taking in a deep breath and holding herself upright again.

It amazes me how quickly simple features appear to change her beyond her years.

She nods at me as she walks away.

I don't bother returning the gesture, yet I watch as she leaves.

XV.

Life comes and goes. It slips so easily from our grasp and sometimes we don't bother to capture it. There are days when living becomes too hard and we push it away. We offer ourselves to death, like there is nothing to live for. *Nothing* is just ... so much.

Whenever I pass the tavern I see people living their reckless lives. They drink as much ale as they can afford, then proceed to wander in the streets. They trip and hobble and sometimes I hear their moans as they bend over, their bodies ridding themselves of the poison they've swallowed. Everyone is dying. Some run from it; others run to it.

Mama is sick for days. The sun rises and sets and I stay away for fear of my life. I know if Papa sees me he may just kill me. I wonder what is happening to us, what is causing this pestilence, but I can't find an answer. People are saying this is God's punishment for our sins, while others are convinced that it is the sign of Christ's coming. The ones who believe the latter are those who whip themselves as they cross through the towns. I choose to believe neither.

I reside in a nearby cruck house. Someone's belongings

are still strewn about. Clothes hang on the line, drying from a day's launder. Food is gathered in the corner, waiting to be prepared for the next meal. Outside a mule whinnies for attention. A life was abandoned. When I first found the cruck, I wondered what had happened to the previous inhabitants but I quickly dismissed those thoughts when I saw the men walking by with the cart of dead.

I've only been residing in this borrowed home for a few days since Margo died and already my food is running scarce. When I decided to live here I told myself I wouldn't disrupt anything, that I was just using it as a shelter in order to watch my family, but very quickly hunger called.

Dondre never sleeps inside anymore. I've been watching him through the window of the borrowed cruck, and he always stays outside. I'm not sure if Papa has asked him to leave, like he did with me, or if Dondre left by choice, but either way my brother now sleeps under the stars. It's all he does. Even in the light of day he lies on the ground and goes to sleep.

When I initially spotted him, he had looked back at me. I knew he had seen me, but his face never changed or acknowledged my existence. At first I thought I would have to run again, maybe even leave my family forever, but Dondre never told anyone that I was hiding nearby. So now I watch my little brother, as his chest rises and falls, and wonder what exactly he is thinking.

Mama's coughing never stops. Every night when I twist and turn on my straw mattress, I hear Mama having a fit, never able to sleep or regain her strength. At times I wish she would just let go, leave us, give up—let us have peace with her coming death. That's when I begin to hate myself. Awful thoughts haunt me at night. Self-preservation consumes me, and I'm willing to do anything.

Dondre coughs also, so I stop watching him through the window.

The Bird comes and goes. In my dreams he's not a surgeon but the Devil's apprentice. Instead of healing Mama and Dondre, he poisons them through their veins. His dark cloak hides his features, like the coward he is. The Bird never touches the sick, for fear of catching the pestilence, but I'm sure he doesn't know how it is spread. Maybe it is spread within the air. His herb beak can't protect him, because he is still within proximity of the sick. Nobody wants to be near me and I wonder if that's why I'm still alive. Those that are loved, those whose lives have been touched—those are the ones to succumb.

The men walk through the village today, dragging the dead in their cart. The bodies are fresh, and even though they don't carry the odor of death just yet, their skin is stained with blood and vomit. The pair are slow and quiet as they pass my doorway. My eyes are hidden in the shadows as they look to me with a questioning gaze. *Are there any dead I would like to dispose of?*

When I don't speak they continue on, looking toward Dondre who lies against a wall across from me. The old wooden walls of the cruck house are the only things supporting him and even though the two men stop and look at him, they don't place him on the cart. Not yet.

I was almost killed when I was small. I can't remember much of what happened or why it happened. I just remember chaos. Mama and I had gone to the market to trade our furs for food for that night's meal. When I was a child, I never had to be hidden. I was just like every other girl at the time. I got to help Mama with chores and I dreamed of a man courting me. It was a time before I knew I was different, when people looked at me and didn't stare. They saw my pale eyes and thought it was just a trick of the light. When I grew older, the word "witchcraft" came to mind.

Mama had let me carry the furs to the market that day; Papa had killed the rabbit the day before. We ate the meat for a meal and we were to trade the furs. It was the softest thing I had ever held and I tried to convince Mama to let me keep it, but she had assured me it would be worth much more to us if we traded it.

When we got to the market, we had searched out a merchants who was looking for furs. Their locations were unspoken, but everyone knew where to find someone for a trade.

"What do you have today?" the man had asked. He had looked in my hands, where I gripped the soft rabbit skin. He had leaned down to get a closer look and put his hand out to caress the fur. I hadn't been thinking at the time. When I could see the dirt beneath his fingernails, I hadn't wanted him to touch the soft rabbit. I pulled away, and he looked at me.

I had seen then the surprise in his eyes as he looked into mine. At first it was wonder, but then fear had been etched into the lines around his eyes and his hand had moved from the fur toward his belt.

"What is she?" He had been talking to Mama, but his gaze had never left me. I remember hearing the anger in his voice and yet not being afraid—no one would ever hurt me; I had done nothing wrong.

I was so foolish.

My gaze had followed his arm, where his hand was on his waist. With the sun in the sky a small glint of metal had shone from his belt.

"What are you talking about?" Mama's voice had been calm, so I stayed calm also, but when I looked up at her she was anything but. Mama gripped my wrist and had tried to pull me away, but the merchant was stronger.

His hand had left his belt and he had held up a knife. He dragged me to him and rested the blunt of the knife against my neck.

Mama had begun to cry and scream when he tore me from her. She had put out her hand and gripped the knife; the sharp metal had bit into her skin, and a dark liquid had leaked from her fingers. She had ripped the knife from the man's hand with a shout and had thrown it to the ground.

The merchant hadn't known what to do. He let me go easily after that.

Mama ran me home while she bled. I had tried asking her if she was okay, but she just shushed me while she cried. We had left the furs at the market and never got anything for them. Papa was mad, but his anger had diminished once he saw Mama's hand.

She had saved my life that day. It was the first of many times people had looked at me and thought I was something unnatural that should be disposed of. All my life I've wanted to return the favor to thank Mama. She's dying, but I'm helpless.

XVI.

"Aida?"

My name is whispered into the morning light. When I roll over I see a figure at the door.

"Is that you?"

The body steps through the door. *Cyrielle.*

"How did you find me?" I ask, sitting up. Out the window the sun has barely risen. The air is still cold in the morning shade and dew coats the ground.

Cyrielle comes to sit beside me. For the first time I see the bundle of blankets in her arms. She hides something there, holding it close to her body, like it may just jump away at any given moment.

"I went to your cruck, but Dondre ... he said you left. He didn't tell me where you went, but he kept looking at this cruck," she says quietly. She keeps looking down into the blankets in her arms. Her face is shallow and sunken, fresh tears stain her cheek.

"Cyrielle?"

She looks at me and I see the tears rim her eyes, threatening to flood over. The liquid slips down her cheek, but she doesn't wipe it away. Instead her arms wrap around the blankets she holds.

"Is Jermaine all right?" I ask.

She releases a smile that seems almost painful. She coughs the slightest bit when her cheeks turn up, but it's not like Mama's or Margo's. This is a tired cough, not one of a dying soul. Cyrielle shifts her arms up and brings the blanket to her face, inhaling the scent. She closes her eyes and her small smile disappears.

"What's wrong?" I put my arm on her shoulder, and she stiffens.

Cyrielle gasps for air, her hysteria rising. Her grip on the blanket never loosens and I wait to see just how long it will be until she calms down. I watch as her shoulders heave and she cries. I half expect someone to overhear and come rushing in to check on us, but it never happens.

"Aida, I don't know what happened!" She screams the words in between her cries.

I lean forward where she sits and wrap my arm around her shoulder, careful to avoid the blankets she holds so dearly.

"Shh," I tell her. "It'll all right."

I feel her head shake against my shoulder. "He's dead, Aida," she mumbles into my collar.

I lean back but don't release my hold. She stares at me, pleading, begging for help, but I can't stop my gaze from wandering to the blankets. Unknowingly my hand glides over the coarse fabric, unfolding the bundle. A small tuft of hair is hidden under the sheet. I look up at Cyrielle, but her gaze rests upon the tiny head. I move the blanket farther away and look at the newborn within. The body is so small and frail—and lifeless.

"He never cried, Aida," Cyrielle says in a whisper. Her voice breaks and I hear the tears sting her throat. She looks down at her son, gliding her fingers across his frail forehead, her movements so ginger.

"Does Jermaine know?"

She shakes her head, bending down to kiss the infant's small tuft of hair. Even now he looks so much like Cyrielle, from his face to the shade of his hair.

"I don't know what he'll do. This is our baby, and he's gone. I don't know if Jermaine will forgive me," Cyrielle cries.

"Cyrielle," I say, removing her hands from the blankets.

She protests for a moment, but when I give her a small reassuring squeeze, she releases with a small gasp. I move aside the blanket and put her infant on my mattress, turning to Cyrielle and wrapping my arms around her shaking frame. For months she had grown this baby inside her, offering herself to this new life and now—just like that—it's over; all for nothing.

She shudders against my touch, but I hug her to me, trying to reassure her. "Jermaine will love you, no matter what. How can you doubt that? He needs to know. Your son needs a proper burial."

"I can't do that," she says. Her arms embrace me, and I can feel just how scared she is. Her entire body quivers as her chest rises and falls with each breath. For a long moment we sit in our embrace, neither of us sure what we should do or how to get there. She cries for her lost son and I can't find myself to utter a tear. My eyes ache and sting, but I'm numb. I just kneel next to Cyrielle, holding her, wishing there was something more I could do.

"I—" she says. "I'll tell Jermaine," she finally says. She picks herself up, finally looking at her surroundings. The abandoned cruck stares back at her in its eerie, hopeless way.

"Would you like me to go with you?" I ask.

She bites her lip and stifles back a cry, as her arms wrap around her torso. Cyrielle shakes her head and puts on the bravest face she can muster.

I watch her as she picks herself off the ground, her hands shaking slightly as she brushes debris off her kirtle. Her eyes rest upon the pile of blankets next to where I sit. With the slowest, gentlest movement, she lifts the bundle, holding her son close.

"Aida?"

I smile at her and I see the corner of her lip rise the slightest bit. "Can you be there? When we bury him?"

I nod my head, but her eyes water when I make the gesture. Her dark hair clings to the skin around her face, as the tears overwhelm her. Cyrielle walks away before the sobs come.

She didn't tell me where to meet; she didn't even tell me when she would bury her son. Jermaine is so silent. He found me in the cruck house and, without a word, I knew I should follow him. His face was placid stone, unwavering. Even now, as we walk, the only movement in the air is our footsteps as we approach the location of the infant's burial.

Jermaine comes to a stop, and I look up to see the river that lingers outside Marseille. This was the last place I had seen Anton when he had told me that Margo would die. I can still feel the grip of his hand around my throat when he threatened my world and abandoned my sister and their child.

Cyrielle kneels at the river's edge. Her kirtle rests in the brook, where it continues to soak in water. She no longer carries a bundle of blankets, just a simple sheet of fabric that wraps around the infant's frail body. Even from a distance I can see his still face, forever at peace with the world. Cyrielle cradles him in her arms, as if he were alive. She doesn't cry.

Jermaine walks up behind her and rests his hand on her shoulder. She doesn't turn or acknowledge him. Instead he is the one who kneels beside her. She lets him take the infant from her arms.

Cyrielle looks up to where I stand a distance away. She smiles and gestures me in their direction. I join her, taking grace on her other side while Jermaine holds their child. His eyes never leave his son's face. What's amazing is how proud he looks of his son, even though he was never gifted with life.

"We named him Nouvel," Cyrielle tells me. She grips my hand and brings me closer. My knees rest in the mud that borders the stream and the water laps at my skin through the fabric of my kirtle. Cyrielle glides my hand to Nouvel, resting my fingers over his soft hair. "His name means new," she murmurs.

Cyrielle looks up at me and smiles. It's a real, genuine

smile, and my heart breaks for her. She takes Nouvel from Jermaine's arms and he doesn't protest. Instead he leans his head against her shoulder, his eyes always following his son.

"Can you reach the basket?" Cyrielle asks in a whisper. Her fingers stroke Nouvel's cheek as she speaks.

I turn and see a small basket behind Cyrielle. I take it, noting how tight the weave of the reeds are. I hold it in front of Cyrielle and she places Nouvel in it, careful to wrap the small sheet of fabric around him. She kisses his forehead for a final time before taking the last corner of the blanket and folding it over his head. I give her the basket and she grips it in her arms. Jermaine wraps his arms around her but never touches his son again.

The air is still in that moment as Cyrielle leans forward into the steam. Her knees sink farther in the mud and water laps at her arms, as she releases the basket. I fear she may fall in the stream but, at the last minute, she picks herself up again, leaving the basket behind as it floats away. It caresses itself atop the water, keeping Nouvel safe inside.

Cyrielle drags herself from the water, the sleeves of her kirtle sticking to her skin. She leans into Jermaine, and he offers his support as he wraps his arms around her torso. Silent prayers are said, as we watch the infant float away.

That's when I realize how unfair life is. A boy that never got to live, a mother that never got to love, a father that never got to be. It's all very cruel.

XVII.

The water bites at my toes. The cold ignites my senses and wakes me up to a world I never thought I knew. In front of my eyes Frioul Archipelago opens up. The moon in the sky lights their peaks, the rocky islands just an adornment to the dark ocean. Beyond the surface lies Tiboulain.

"It's not too late."

My body jerks at the voice. Behind me Mystral stands in her cloak. It drowns out her body in the night, but the hood is down. With the moon lighting the sky all I can see is her pale skin, the prominent bones of her face all the more visible. A long, simple dark braid coils down and over her shoulders.

"I know," I say.

Her eyes watch me—for what, I don't know. Everything about her is pleading. She wants something from me, but I can't give it to her.

"You could do so much," she says.

The ocean opens in front of us, beckoning us to come closer, to venture into its deep seas.

"It would be so easy for you, Luna. You could save lives ... forever." She lingers on the last word.

I imagine that we are inside a cave as the aspect of *forever* bounces back to us, pleading, telling us to come and tend to its needs. Forever.

"Mystral." When I say her name she snaps to attention again. So easily she believes I will do her biddings. "I don't want forever," I tell her.

Her face drops just as soon as it had lifted. Hope leaves her and it's like her body has caved in on itself. "But—" she begins.

"No," I say with more force in my voice. "I don't want forever—if that's even possible. You've seen this world. It's dying."

"But if you only went to Tiboulain! That is where you need to go, and the world won't die!" Mystral loses breath, and her chest rises and falls in quick staccatos.

"No," I say again, but this time my voice is gentle.

"But your family ..."

"Would rather have me dead. You know this."

She's silent after that. Her gaze never leaves my face, but, after a long moment she finally nods her head and agrees. A few seconds later she takes a deep breath and lifts her chin. The moonlight shines down on her face and she's the young woman with the aged lines again. Wrinkles crease around her eyes and her hair is limp down her side.

"You think I'm a witch," she says, looking across the ocean to the moon. "I'm here to help you, but you won't help me first." Her words are sad. With shaky hands she gathers the ends of her cloak and wraps it tighter around her frame. "I don't know what you're supposed to do at Tiboulain, but it has to do with the moon, Luna."

"My name is not Luna," I say quietly.

Mystral smiles. "Yes, it is. Your mother named you Aida de Luna, helper of the moon." She looks at me and smiles with her weathered eyes. "Take time and mend it. Stretch eternity like it may never break. Soothe infinity like it will always snap. Remember to cherish the night and seek the day. Postpone the moon and find forever, Aida de Luna."

Mystral steps into the water of the stream. Somewhere down this water path, an infant lies in a basket, his body waiting to be washed away. Mystral's dark cloak spreads out around her. To the right the city of Marseille rests, but in front of us the edge of the land appears and the ocean cascades down. Mystral never looks back as she sinks deeper and deeper into the stream. She follows it to the edge, where the world ends.

I never follow her. In fact I don't even speak up to stop her. I just watch in silence as she leaves me for one final time. Even as she trudges through the water, her pace is true. She doesn't falter or slip; she just simply is. Mystral becomes like the water of the stream, her cloak coating the surface. She bends and turns, following the edge. It only takes three more breaths and then she's gone.

No one is standing in front of me anymore. All that is left for my eyes to see is a silent river. The water cascades to the ocean below, but there isn't a whisper of a woman. I rush forward as soon as I lose sight of Mystral. At the land's edge I look down. Even in the dark I can see the sharp boulders that line the ocean's edge. Waves beat against the wall of earth, but, through it all I don't see Mystral. I listen for a scream or cry, thinking she may have fallen or jumped, but it never comes.

XVIII.

The longest day is the day without forgiveness. People don't look for the forgiveness of others, but for the forgiveness of the world. Because maybe, if everyone's lucky, the universe will have mercy on our souls and gift us with sleep. But not tonight.

Even though my eyelids are closed, I struggle with energy. My body refuses to rest. My mind won't shut down. No matter how hard I try, I cannot stop the shift and awareness of my body. Yet if I keep my eyes open, the world spins. If I turn my head this way or that, blackness tunnels my vision and I wonder how long it will be until I free-fall into my own universe.

The moon is just a crescent in the sky. I lie near the ledge, a stream coursing at my feet. The water bubbles and churns until it splashes over the ledge into the ocean. It's a long fall and the water travels the height in an almost graceful manner. Mystral disappeared into these waters and the idea haunts me. My tired mind wants to know what happened to her; my limbs even beg me to continue to look for her somewhere, but my head loses itself.

"Miss?"

The voice stirs me back into consciousness. Rocks are

nestled beneath my head and gravel clings to my cheeks. Under my nose water splashes from the drop below. All it would take is a small slip, a push forward of the muscles, and I would be gone, lost to the water forever.

"Are you all right?"

When I turn my head the muscles of my neck lock and burn, but I follow the voice regardless. Standing behind me is a young man, hair curling around his face. In the wind his dark hair sways, but only slightly. It's dawn now, and the sun illuminates his face.

"Who are you?" I ask in a hoarse voice. My fingers still cling to the ledge.

"Um—" He hesitates for only a second, seeming to fight some internal force until he finally comes forward and kneels beside me. His hand wraps around my fingers as he brings me away from the edge. "Garren," he tells me, after leading us a safe distance from the ledge.

He looks at me expectantly, his focus craning over my features as I hide my face until I realize he wants to know my name.

"Aida de Luna."

A small smile slides across his lips. "Luna? Like the moon?" he asks, as he points to the crescent in the sky. Even with the sun peeking over the horizon, the moon is a small silhouette in the dawn.

The wind blows across my face, bringing my hair forward and, all at once, I realize how vulnerable I am. The two of us sit on the ground where no one is within range of hearing if I were to need help. In a quick motion I gather my hair that tumbles over my shoulders and form a braid as fast as I can. Garren smiles at me and I feel all the more helpless.

"What were you doing? Sleeping at the edge?" he asks.

My pale hair rests atop my head in two braids that curl around my crown like Mama taught me.

"I didn't mean to fall asleep," I tell him, stepping away from this stranger who seems to take it upon himself to watch me.

My back is to Garren, but I hear him gather himself to his feet and he follows me the few steps I took to distance myself from him. My kirtle gathers in stiff sheets of cloth at my feet, and with the salty air I can only imagine how foolish I look right now.

"The question is how you fell asleep in so dangerous a location," Garren says.

His voice is just behind my back, and I have to remind myself not to look and give him the advantage in exposing my curiosity. His voice is light when he speaks, but I can't find it in myself to turn to him.

"When the mind is tired, it doesn't make sense of its surroundings," I say. That's when it hits me just how exhausted I still am. My eyes are heavy with sleep, and my body has finally seemed to find peace. My knees quake under my weight, and I feel my hand shake and struggle as it hangs limp at my side.

"Are you all right?"

And when Garren speaks I can hear his genuine concern. He positions himself so I can barely see him, but I try to ignore his presence. Instead I concentrate on the horizon. Again the islands of Frioul Archipelago beckon me.

"Are you dying too?" The words come from my mouth and I'm not sure why I ask them. I wonder if it's because Garren is the first person I have seen in days who hasn't contracted the pestilence, or maybe it's just because I wish he would leave, but either way, the words come without permission. I want to cover my mouth and take them back, but they echo inside my soul until I'm forced to hear the words over and over.

"No," he says simply.

"How?" I ask, my voice a whimper. In my mind all I can see is the sick faces of those I have loved and lost. Margo stares back at me with her tear-stained eyes and Mama looks at me for a final moment before letting me go forever. It's not fair to have life taken so easily.

"What do you mean?"

Garren comes to stand beside me and part of me wants to put distance between the two of us, but the smaller, more fragile, part of me longs for the voice—the voice of someone who isn't afraid of me.

"Everyone is sick," I tell him. "Not you."

"Or you," he says.

I refuse to look at him. I feel his eyes scan my face; looking for what, I don't know. I close my eyes to the ocean and surround myself with the sound of it all. Waves crash; wind blows; birds caw in the morning air—it's all very peaceful.

"It's not by choice."

"Are you saying you'd rather be sick or dying than alive?"

He doesn't mean to hurt me with the words, yet they sting anyway. I bite my lower lip, holding back the breath that expands in my lungs.

"I didn't say that," I say after a fleeting moment.

The silence is long. When I open my eyes again, I see Garren. His gaze has yet to leave my face and I want to push him away. I want this stranger to let me be so the pestilence can take me also. But that's not how this malady works. You wait until death honors you, and then you leave. No goodbye, no celebration, you just die.

"But ..." He stops himself before he finishes, perhaps rethinking what he was about to say.

"You don't know me," I tell him. "And I don't know you."

He doesn't say anything. Instead I see the slight nod of his head, as he agrees to my words.

"What would you like me to call you?" His question is so sudden I'm unable to understand what he is asking at first. I turn to face him and realize my mistake too late. The sun is above the horizon now, lighting up the morning and giving clarity to the world. It makes it so that, when I turn, Garren sees me for who I am. In the morning's dew I was able to hide my real self. For a small moment in time I was able to pretend I was just as any other person. A person who doesn't look like a witch. But now, my white eyes aglow, Garren sees me, and even though I don't know the man, I know I will cower at the idea of him despising me.

His face is frozen when I look at him. Garren's eyes squint as he observes my irises, and I try not to think of how long it will be until he comes to his senses and attacks me. I see time ticking away between us. Seconds pass until the minutes accumulate. I wait for him to move, to say something, but he never does.

"Your name. What name would you like me to call you?" he asks in staggered words. He continues to watch me, as he speaks.

I abandon myself at that moment. I realize that I can no longer be the person I was when I grew up. Mama and Papa will never have me again, and Dondre and Joelle will do no more than look at me. Other than Cyrielle and Jermaine—and Anton—those are the only ones left to call me Aida. So when Garren asks me my name, I tell him, "Luna."

"The moon," he says. He smiles at the words, the corner of his lips lifting to a smile.

"The moon," I agree.

XIX.

He'll ask the question eventually. I just don't understand why it hasn't come up yet. Garren sees the unique color of my eyes, but he chooses to neither run nor hurt me. In my consciousness I prepare my defense, but I find that I never have to use it.

"You have any family?" he asks.

Garren stands to my side, but I don't face him. Instead I watch the ocean and wait for it to twist and turn into a black hole—it never does.

"Yes," I say, but my throat burns on the words. Salty air consumes me, and I wonder how long it will be until my breath will come easy again.

"Are they like you?"

The words spike my senses. My family is not like me; if they were, they would not have cast me away as if I were an unwanted clothing item. What is disturbing is that he knows I'm different but doesn't choose to voice it directly. Instead he skirts around the subject, almost like he wants me to explain.

I shake my head to answer his question and I see him nod.

"My sister died of the pestilence," I say, as if this explains how my family is different from me. I've not caught the sickness, yet I live by it every moment.

"I'm sorry to hear that," he says. And after a moment, "What was her name?"

"Margo. She was older than me by a few years and was married, had a daughter—Joelle. I suppose Papa will be taking care of her now."

"What about Margo's husband? Wouldn't he be responsible for the child?"

I shake my head and only wish the words were true. "He left. One day Anton came to our doorstep, and left Margo and Joelle with us."

"But he can't do that."

"Why can't he?" I turn to look at him. Garren's eyes are bright in the morning sun that rises higher and higher in the sky. Curls of brown hair blow off his face and the ocean mist gives everything a salty spray—I can almost taste it.

"Because a man marries a lady to not only love her but to care for her."

"Until death do us part," I tell him. His eyes are unflinching on mine. "Margo was dying. The child was not part of the vows."

"But—"

"No," I say. When I look at Garren I see an upset young man. His eyes are crinkled, his forehead creased, and I can tell he wishes he could fix the mistake Anton has made, but Garren can't. "It was good he left."

"How can you say that?"

Memories of Anton flash behind my lids: the first time

he tried to kill me in public, everyone making sense of my execution because I was a witch. And more recently when he placed his hand around my throat, leaving dark blotches that outlined his long fingers. My breath falters, and Garren notices. He steps closer and when I flinch he steps away again.

"What happened?" he asks.

"Nothing," I say, but my voice isn't convincing. My words are lies, and he knows it.

"Luna." He steps closer to me in one fluid movement.

I forgot to fight back, and the next thing I know he's too close.

His fingers wrap around my chin to make me face him, but, when he sees my fear he releases me. Garren no longer touches my body, but he doesn't move away. The man comes closer, close enough that I can feel his breath on my cheek. My eyes are memorizing the ground, but his voice warms my skin.

"He hurt you."

It isn't a question, so I don't bother agreeing with him. I stare at my bare feet, and I wonder why I never put on my shoes again after saying goodbye to Nouvel along the stream. Garren has leather shoes that are worn and beaten and old.

"What did he do?" he asks.

"It doesn't matter," I say too quickly.

"Then why did he do it?"

His voice is soft and begs me to look up at him again, but I can't. This stranger makes me feel safe, and that can't be. I can't let him near me, not now. "Please."

His hand brushes against my arm and I jump back. My feet slip and under my heels, I can feel the edge of the cliff. Garren's hand comes out to catch me and before I can protest he pulls me to safety. A small yelp escapes from my throat, but then a second later I find myself far from the edge with Garren holding on tight to my hand.

"Stop!" I yell out. I pull myself from him and am careful when I leave his side, watching the edge of the cliff grow farther away as I distance myself from Garren. Shock is etched across his face, but I don't register his emotions because they shouldn't matter to me. "Look at me and tell me why Anton would never want to hurt me!" I didn't mean to yell.

He doesn't respond. Garren just continues to look at me, stare at me, never speaking as to what he sees.

I pause to breathe and regain myself. Emotions stir that have yet to be released, but I refuse to unhinge myself in front of this stranger.

"You see it, but you haven't asked why," I say in an almost whisper, but he hears me just the same. I stare at him, begging him with my eyes to accuse me, to want to execute me, like all the rest.

"What is there to ask?"

When I look at him I want to cry, and push him away.

"Ask me if I'm a witch."

He's baffled by my words, that much is obvious, so I step closer. He doesn't move away. I keep my arms at my sides and stare into his eyes, waiting for him to register my words and see me as everyone else does. My silver eyes leer into his, but he never looks away.

"You're not a witch," he says almost too quietly.

"How do you know that? I've lived my entire life hidden, so people didn't accuse me on false charges, but here I stand, waiting to be accused, and you won't say the words. I could have caused this pestilence. I could have killed your family, and it doesn't matter. You still stand close and trust me. I could kill you." I challenge him, threaten him, and push him away—I don't know why.

Garren doesn't move, back away, or cower in fear. He looks at me, his gaze steady.

"You're not a witch," he says.

I nod my head when I hear the words. I've wanted them to be true all my life, but I'm not even sure what I am myself. I grew up being called this evil thing, and I began to believe it. But now, here stands a man, and he neither fears nor harms me.

"I'm not a witch," I say, choking on my own words.

"No," Garren whispers.

A tear drifts across my cheek and I wonder if this is what happiness feels like. When the world grips me and never lets go, is this what it feels like to finally be released?

"Why are you out here?" His words are soft and it makes me realize that he must see my tears. In an instant I stand taller and appear stronger than I feel, but then I remember why it is I'm out here alone.

"My family doesn't think the same way you do," I tell

him.

He seems to understand this and nods his head.

I look onward toward the ocean and imagine myself there.

"But why here? At the ledge?" he asks.

I fight myself to find an answer, because I'm not sure why I brought myself here either. I came to say goodbye to Nouvel, but I never left. "I suppose I had nowhere else to go."

"Would you like to go to the islands?"

I turn to Garren. His face is emotionless, as if what he's said holds no significance. "Have you talked to Mystral?" I ask.

The name confuses him, and I know right away Mystral is a stranger he's never met. "Who?" he asks.

"Never mind." I brush off the subject as quickly as possible so he can't ask any more questions.

"You keep looking to them—Frioul Archipelago. Is there something there you need? I can take you on my boat." Garren points far down below us to the beach where merchant ships are docked, but between them rests a small wooden rowboat. I look off to Frioul Archipelago. In front of me are the two largest of the islands—Pomègues and Ratonneau—but behind them are two smaller pieces of land that I can't see.

"Someone I knew told me about the islands," I tell Garren.

He smiles and follows my gaze to the two large landmasses. Both are abandoned, without human contact—I suppose that's what makes them so beautiful. They rest so close, yet so gloriously undisturbed. So serene that maybe, by a miracle, it is a safe land without the pestilence.

"They are a sight, aren't they?"

"Yes," I say, a smile rippling through my core. It's possible. Maybe that's what Mystral was telling me. She wanted me to go to Tiboulain as a safe harbor. "Can you take me there?" I ask, suddenly hopeful.

"When would you like to go?"

"Sundown," I say. "I have to tell my little brother." All I have to do is convince him of Tiboulain's safety. I'll take everyone—Papa, Mama, even Joelle—as long as it means we will all be safe from the pestilence.

"Then I will meet you at the docks when the light leaves the sky," Garren says, a smile pulling at the corners of his lips.

I look back where my village resides. Pillars of smoke rise into the air, leaving me to wonder if Mama is still alive, if she'll live long enough to find safety.

"Thank you," I say, quickly grasping Garren's hands in my own and giving them a small squeeze. I look into his eyes and he doesn't look away and neither do I. I smile before releasing him from my grasp.

My gaze has always been avoided—people don't want to look at me—but Garren is different. I don't understand it, but he accepts me, witch or not.

I leave him and the ledge, fully aware that he is watching my steps as I leave. The ground is light beneath my feet, and if someone were to tell me that I was a witch, I would believe them, because the ground is no longer part of my world. Everything I see is a prop, and I'm simply an essence running through the universe.

XX.

Dondre isn't at the cruck house when I arrive. The world feels frozen, my breath making its shaky journey through my lungs. Death is high in the air, and we are under its power.

Papa's voice can still be heard. He's talking to someone, but I'm not quite sure who. He sounds angry and I'm not sure why, but fear tickles at his feet.

"What are you here for, if you can't treat her?" Papa screams out across the valley that separates me from him. In the distance I see our small cruck house and the pillar of smoke that emanates from the roof. A fire burns from within, so distinct it is ruled out by the smell of rotting flesh. I can't escape it. The only time I forget the world that now exists is when I'm at the ledge, where the wind of the ocean takes me away.

"No one knows what the cause of the pestilence is. If that is the case, how do you expect me to find a cure?" another says. A dark figure emerges from the cruck and walks away in a fast pace.

After my eyes focus on the image I see it is the Bird. His dark beak and clothing sway around him and make him a figure to fear, but people perk up at the sight of him. They think the Bird can cure the pestilence. Everyone heard rumors that there's a cure—but they don't realize that's not possible.

"All you did was come here to antagonize my wife! You experimented on her!" my father shouts as the Bird continues to leave my family behind.

"Well, what did you expect of me, sir? I do not know the cure. Experimenting is the only way." And with his final words the Bird never looks back. He continues on through our village, stopping at other homes to see the dying—to see what he can't do for them.

Papa watches as his only hope leaves. I suppose somewhere inside is Mama, just waiting for the pestilence to consume her and take her from this forsaken place. Eventually Papa leaves also, but only after the Bird is long out of sight. I make my way to the only place I've known as home and wait for someone to acknowledge my presence from within.

The cruck house is cold, even with a fire going. The smoke billows out the hole in the roof, but no one gathers around it for warmth. Instead I see Mama asleep on the other side in the same clothing she was in the last time I had seen her. Dark splotches streak across her face and neck, the skin bulging out like tumors.

"Mama?" My voice is tentative in the dark light. She doesn't look familiar. With the buboes she's just on hold until death touches her. Dark circles encompass her eyes; bruises are all over her skin. And like so many who have been taken by the pestilence, the tips of her fingers appear dark and decaying.

A hand slaps me from behind and I'm being pulled from Mama and back outside to where the morning has just barely begun.

"What are you doing here?"

The harshness of his voice catches me off guard, but I still welcome it. When I spin around to look at my attacker I see Dondre. He's no different than when I last saw him; in a dying world, he's found health.

"Dondre!" I put my arms out to embrace him, but he shuffles away. The rejection is quick and emotionless for him, but for me it is so much more. For as long as I can remember, I was always able to count on my brother to help me and to accept me for what I am. Why is it now he chooses to no longer do this?

"Don't touch me," he says in a small, yet strong voice—a voice I've heard Papa use when we've misbehaved. He pushes me away and never fully looks me in the eyes.

"Why?"

"Because you did this! You did this to Margo, Mama, and who knows what else you have planned. Am I next? Are you going to kill me too?"

Dondre spits the words at me even though I've already heard him say similar words once before. But regardless, they infect my skin and leave me feeling punched and helpless.

"Why do you think this?" My breath catches and I wait for Dondre to take back what he's said or at least show that he regrets his words, but I'm greeted with nothing but a hard face. My baby brother gazes at me with malice. His fist is clutched at his sides, eyebrows bent, face drawn, pulling him from any memories we might have shared as children. All he sees now is a witch who is killing those he loves.

"Because it's true."

Time freezes between us. Particles of debris float in the atmosphere and the air reeks of death, but neither of us dares to move. Hope dies within me in a slow and heavy flux. I thought I could save him—I thought I could save all of them.

"I love you, Dondre. I would never do this." I say the words, but I know they are useless now. I don't recognize my brother anymore. He has always seemed so young to me, but now, over the past few days, he has aged beyond compare. Ten years has been added to his brow, and I beg myself to resist the urge to embrace him and tell him everything is okay.

"But I don't believe you!" His voice drags across the words. A small cry comes at the end of his sentence, but he refuses to recognize it. Instead he chooses to stand tall and keep his chin held high as he waits for me to buckle down at his words.

"Dondre, please, listen to me."

"No!" My brother comes to me and pushes my shoulders.

Although he is younger than me, all the years spent growing up working in the fields have made him much stronger. I find myself struggling not to fall over into the dirt.

"Leave!"

He pushes me again, and this time I lose my footing and stumble into the dust. My limbs ache, but what I fear most is the young boy who hovers over me. Dondre doesn't speak to me again. Instead he glares at my helpless figure at his feet. I'm afraid to see the hate in his eyes so I pretend he's no longer standing above me.

"Leave!" he shouts again. His foot comes out and kicks me in the side. In an instant I put my hands out to protect myself, but I'm not fast enough before his foot connects with my ribs.

I see Dondre gain secure footing to kick me again, so I struggle away. I don't wait for the second blow. I just run from my horrors and my dreams. I wait for the will to live to leave me, but it never falters and I think that's an amazing thing—to survive, even when you no longer want to.

The instinct to live is stronger than I thought.

XXI.

Midnight is forgiving. It holds my secrets close and whispers words of reassurance. I only wish the daylight were so kind.

"Good morning," Garren says, waiting for me at the docks.

My kirtle hangs in a dry mess. Dirt and mud are plastered to the fabric, but I don't let myself worry about appearances. All I want is to be rid of the memories that taint this land.

"Morning?" I ask, pulling the cloak around my figure. I had found it in the streets. It was thrown across the shoulders of an older woman, long since dead. Part of me didn't want to take her possession, but everything is about survival now. I'm not a grave robber if she's not buried.

"Yes," Garren says. "Morning. Past midnight, it is morning."

"The sun has yet to even seek the horizon."

He smiles in a way that makes my thoughts seem foolish. "The sun does not need to be present for it to be morning."

I nod my head to agree with his words. My hooded cloak clouds the vision of the world around me. All I can see is what is before me and, at present, that is Garren. He doesn't look tired as my being seems to feel. The young man seems awake and alive, eager almost, for whatever it is we will uncover at the islands.

"Where is your brother?" he asks.

I avert my eyes and let the cloak's hood hide my face as I lie. "I couldn't find him," I say.

"We can wait. He'll turn up. Then we can go to the islands."

"No," I say quickly, before Garren has a chance to continue. He seems shocked by my sudden words, and I pray he doesn't hear my deceit. "My brother—Dondre—doesn't like the sea."

"Doesn't like the sea? Why?"

"Just—the water," I say, detailing false information. I don't want Garren to see my lie and then deny me passage on his boat. If I can't leave Marseille, I'm no longer sure what I'm to do. At least on the islands I can have my false hope that Mystral told the truth, when she spoke of a cure.

"We aren't waiting for anyone else?" His voice is soft in the dark air.

The pale moon in the sky lights up the morning just enough for me to decipher Garren's face. He's so sure of himself, so sure of whatever it is we are about to encounter on the islands.

Some reason compels me to look back. And for the last time, I see my old life. Over the hills and past Marseille at the foothold, the village I grew up in rots away. Life sways and washes away as God decides we don't deserve to live. It's a life

I'm leaving. I'll never return to this place I used to call home. So as I look back I remember Margo, Mama, and Papa and wish them well. I hold Dondre in my heart and tell myself it is the pestilence that makes him speak such harsh words. I pray Cyrielle and Jermaine remain healthy and produce many healthy children. Finally I thank Mystral. Even if all that she's said is a lie, at least I'll be free of this land.

"When do we leave?" I ask, my back still turned.

I hear Garren approach me from behind. He doesn't speak at first and I picture him following my gaze, trying to see what it is that holds me here.

"Now, before the sun rises."

I nod my head and say my last silent goodbye. I pray for all the dead I've seen and hope that they've found their way home, wherever that may be.

"Okay."

Garren moves away and toward the docks. The ocean waves crash in a quiet hush, a constant rhythm against the ships. Sea foam gathers at the edge where water meets land and fish swim like the world isn't fading into a hushed memory.

When I turn to Garren, he is busy untying his rowboat from the dock. The boat is small, just big enough to safely fit about six people. Only two oars will steer us across the sea. The wood is old and worn, but even so, it appears stronger than anything I've seen before. After Garren tucks the rope in the boat, he turns to me.

"Madam." He stands at the edge of the dock, half his

body poised over the boat, ready to help me step in. The man I barely know offers me a hand and I take it willingly. I cross the threshold and step away from Marseille. I leave behind all the hurt and memories.

"Merci," I say.

The sky opens for us. In the dead of night the two of us drift away to the islands. Tiboulain sits hidden and out of our sight for the moment, but we know it is there. The sea sways and makes us drift. Garren arms the oars and doesn't allow me to help. Instead he tells me to keep watch and to notify him if we come too close to land.

Part of me questions why Garren has gone through with this. But tonight—this morning—he is my captain. Once morning fully strikes and the sun rises on new land Garren will leave me on Tiboulain. I'll thank him, and he'll leave. And just as soon as I have met him, he will be gone. He'll go back to his family and I will forget mine. Maybe I'll find whatever Mystral was talking about, or maybe I'll just find my demise. Either way I have come to accept both possibilities.

When the sky turns to marble, I see Tiboulain. The two larger islands, Pomègues and Ratonneau, rest next to us and the massive rock of Tiboulain sits across the ocean like the grand structure it is. No life seems to be found. Trees, grasses, animals—they are all absent. The entire surface of the island can be scanned from our boat. It rests far from our reach, but within the hour we will dock.

"Is that it?" Garren asks. He doesn't stop paddling, but he turns to look at me. His eyes are soft in the morning light. A spark there tells me that he doesn't need me to answer.

"It isn't what I expected," I say, seeing the island for the first time in my life. It's always been hidden behind the larger of the Frioul Archipelago. A small hope inside me had told me that Tiboulain wasn't like the other rocky islands, that there might have been some life hidden there, but it's nonexistent.

Garren looks at the island and its utter emptiness. "Would you like me to take you back?"

I don't bother to look back—I know Pomègues blocks my view of Marseille. As far as I'm aware, there is nothing for me to return to, so my next words are clear.

"Please take me to Tiboulain."

XXII.

The island is a glorious piece of art. The cliffs of Tiboulain face
the sun that rises on the horizon. In front of our eyes the
morning awakens, shining into a cove of the massive rock island.
There is no beach or shore to Tiboulain. All is rock that lifts
from the water. It is a massive sandbar built by the warriors of
the sea.

"It's beautiful," I say. In front of me Garren doesn't
speak. He shifts his body as he rows us toward the island. It is
small—small enough to see across to the other side. If I wanted,
I could sprint clear across to the other end. The only thing
stopping me from this activity is the rocky surface that juts out
in random directions.

"Where would you like me to dock?" Garren asks.

"You're staying?"

"I can't leave you," he says. Garren turns to the island
that rests in its grandeur.

I follow his gaze and see it as he must: a deserted island
full of nothing but rock. Of course he wouldn't leave me here
alone.

All I can do is nod. I begin to question Mystral and her
motives for urging me here. Surely she knew what the island
looked like.

Garren brings our small rowboat to the closest edge of the island. The waves sway us toward the rock's surface, but the movement is small enough to not damage the vessel. Garren is quick as he works the rope and secures the boat to the sharp corner of a jetting stone. He's first to get off and set foot on the island.

His hand beckons me.

"Why have you come with me?" I ask.

He stands on the island, the surface about a stride's length higher than the boat. If I wanted to set foot on the land, I would need Garren's guided strength in order to do so. He stares back at me, not at all put off by my question.

"Because the only way to get you to this island was by boat. You don't have one—I do."

The ocean roars behind my ears. I want to press my hands over the sound, containing it, muffling it, and block away the world. Everything screams, and I don't know why.

"I'm just a stranger to you," I say, but the words come out as a shiver. My lips tremble and I pray Garren doesn't see.

The wind off the water brings a deep chill and makes me sway. Garren's tunic shuffles, but he stays grounded. His eyes are knowing. Everything about him speaks to me, but it's like I can't hear. Words escape; sounds reverberate, but nothing is heard over the roaring ocean.

"Come. We are here to see the island." He offers his hand again and I take it with numb fingers, I take it. He pulls me from the rowboat and onto the island without another word.

The ground is steady where we are. After such a long time at sea, with the push and pull of the waves, the stable ground seems almost unnatural to my feet as Garren leads me away. Here there is nothing to offer shelter. Anyone on the other islands could see us as soon as the sun breaks over the horizon.

The uneven ground continues on. The two of us hike, Garren always in the lead. I let him guide me, though I'm not sure what it is we are looking for. For the most part, everything about Tiboulain can be seen. The only mystery is what would be found within the crevices between massive slabs of rock.

"What were you told about this place?" Garren asks.

I hold up my cloak and kirtle to step over the rough surface. I can sense Garren's eyes on me, but I keep my eyes on my path.

"She said it could offer shelter," I say. "Somehow ..." My eyes skim the island again, having doubts about why I'm here. Garren must think I'm a fool, asking him to bring me to this deserted island that offers nothing.

"Who?"

"A woman I met not long ago," is all I say.

He doesn't say anything, just continues forward.

At some point he stops walking.

"What?" I ask.

"Who was this woman?"

"I didn't know her well," I say. I let go of my skirt and cloak and they flit through the wind, brushing against my legs. The salt in the air coats my face and hair, a layer of natural dew.

I watch Garren, but he doesn't look at me. He gazes forward at nothing in particular.

"Do you remember what she looked like?"

Mystral's face comes to mind like I had just seen her seconds ago. Dark hair and cloak, masking her for whatever she really is. The image of her body disappearing from the water replays itself in my head, begging me to solve an impossible mystery.

Garren turns to face me and I shake my head.

Something within me says Mystral is a secret best kept. It's as if saying she existed connects me to her and her ways.

When I don't speak further Garren scrutinizes me. He sees the lie but doesn't make me explain—I thank him for that.

"Come on," he says, motioning for me to walk ahead of him. I explore Tiboulain without any idea of what lies ahead. Rocks tumble and fall beneath my feet as earth is stepped over for what may be the first time.

"Do you think others have been to this island?" I ask. The Frioul Archipelago can be seen off the coast of Marseille, but very rarely are they visited. The larger ones, like Pomègues and Ratonneau, have been explored, but with Tiboulain being so small it seems like a waste of time to bother docking when its entire surface can be seen offshore.

"I don't see why not," Garren says.

In front of us is not another rock but a crater. In the center of this small island, a pool of water sits within the opening. The hole is just big enough that, if I wanted, I could slip inside. Rocks overhang the water, giving the impression that the crevice goes deep, opening wider underneath.

I bend down at the edge, my knees scraping against the rough surface. Behind me Garren doesn't say anything. I sense him coming closer, but his approach is silent. Dipping my hand in the pool, I feel the soothing sensation of warm water. When I pull out my hand again, the sharp wind greets me without mercy. I bring my hand to my mouth and taste the water—pure, without salt.

"It's freshwater," I say, putting my hand by my side, turning toward Garren.

It happens fast. When I see Garren, the first thing that strikes me is the panic in his eyes. He jumps at me, his hands gripping my arms. My feet drag against the ground as I try to right myself, but I end up slipping. Garren falls on top of my legs while my torso hovers over the water. His hands grasp my wrists as he lowers me, closer to the water below.

In the moment I forget to breathe or scream. All I can see is the fear in Garren's eyes. He looks at me, his gaze piercing, but his body is an unwilling participant. It's like he has no control over what he's doing. When I see his face, I forget the pain of his weight on top of me, but the moment I look away I see how close I am to drowning.

Garren doesn't release me, so we stay here, my body hovering over the edge of the crevice, his body pinning me to the only piece of land keeping me alive.

"Garren," I say, but it comes out as a gasp. His body

crushes mine.

"I'm sorry," he says, and his words are a cry.

At the nape of my neck, I feel the warm water embrace my hair. The braids coiled around my crown absorb the moisture and pull me deeper to the water. I feel myself slipping, my back getting soaked. The water flows past my ears to my chin. My head dips below the surface, my shoulders and torso following. The water entwines around my arms. The weight on my legs lifts suddenly and I know Garren has fully released me, no longer holding half my body in the water. My feet fall into the pool now and my wet cloak and kirtle drag me farther, deeper and away.

I can't see him anymore, and it makes me happy. I don't want to die while peering into his face, knowing he's my killer. He can't be. When he looked at me there was no malice. When he looked at me, it was like he was mourning my death.

He can't be the reason I die.

I was right; the pool of water is bigger than it seems. I'm suspended, stretching, feeling for something to grip, to fight my way out, but there are no handholds. The only thing my fingers encounter is water. The warm, delightful water.

I think I see the moon. It is only half of itself. Behind the blurry surface, Garren looks down. I see him. He doesn't see me. His eyes find mine, but when I look back at him his face shows no recognition—the only movement is his hair curling in the wind. Finally he turns away, leaving me.

I want to panic, but I can't. My body is numb to the world and I wonder the last time I felt alive.

The water loves me like no one has before. It takes away my pain and embraces me. The fear and loss leaves me until I can no longer feel anything. Happiness is beside me. I could take it and keep it, but I don't choose to. Instead I watch as happiness withers away. It shrivels into the million pieces I have always known it to be—too small to pick up. It will stay this way. Always afloat in the water, waiting for the waves to take me away.

BOOK 2

XXIII.

People don't understand what life has been withholding until they receive something beyond their wildest dreams.

The colors. The vibrant, wonderful colors that have always been in my world were mere shades of black and white, dark and dull.

Blue is the color of the water that embraces me. It is the sky and the ocean. It is so much more—and yet so little. Blue goes on forever and never stops. There are no boundaries for blue.

Red is death. Red is Bernie's cough, Margo's lips, the Bird's hands. Red is blood. The same blood that has leaked on the earth and captured us. It is what soaks our skin and makes us crawl into the corner for shelter. Blood is what threatens to leave, when our life is ending.

The sunrise is oranges, purples, pinks—all these colors have names, and no color is more wonderful than the other. They all carry on into infinity. Each color has its own tone and hue. I want to capture them with my eyes and remember them forever because I'm not sure when I'll see color again.

How did I miss this world until now? When my hair falls in front of my face, I don't see it as the dull hue it had once been. It's an astonishing golden brown. The color makes me think of wheat and barley, the tilling of fields and the harvesting of food. It is the color of baked bread, risen and fresh from the oven.

The sun rests somewhere over the horizon, not yet risen. All I know is that now, when I turn my head, I see the moon. It shines bright and radiant in the sky. A sliver of its being is still missing—a half moon in the sky. It's the first thing I see with my improved eyesight and I'm just now being introduced to this new world.

Postpone the moon and find forever ...

It's like being born again into another body, the same but different. When my eyes finally open, all I can sense at first is the brightness around me. Different shades enhance my vision, but I can't put meaning to them. The sun rises in the farthest corner to bring warmth to the new morning, but I can't feel the effects of its rays just yet. The sky appears as if it is burning away, exploding into something wondrous.

The next thing I'm aware of is the utter stillness around me. The sounds of waves echo somewhere far off in the distance, but that is all. Here, right now, I feel as if my body doesn't exist; my limbs aren't sore—in fact I don't even feel them.

My eyes peel from the scenery around me and I force myself to examine my body. And that's when I realize I am underwater. My hair floats about my cheeks, wrapping itself around my chin in golden strings. Above me the world is magnified and I am trapped below, suspended in liquid that doesn't wake all my senses.

For a moment I panic and take in the air that is in no supply, swallowing water into my lungs. My body jolts forward and my fingers find a handhold in the rocky surface that makes up the sides of the water hole I've been suffocated in. I pull myself out and on to the land above.

I feel a lack of sensation as I pull myself free from the cocoon of water. Once on land, I don't need to catch my breath. Instead I lie here, my face to the ground, attempting to take in my surroundings.

It's like a switch has been turned off. Nothing is as muted as it had been when I was underwater. I can hear the ocean, no longer far away like it had seemed moments ago. A hue of color is missing from the world when I look at the sun. It takes me a moment to think of what it is called—blue. There isn't any blue in the sunrise and I realize it is because I'm no longer seeing it from underwater.

"Luna," says someone in a quiet voice.

My head perks up at the sound of my name. I try to place where it came from, but it feels like my world is being bombarded. Colors I've never seen distort my vision and make me close my eyes to whatever trick is being played on me.

"Are you finally awake?"

The voice is familiar. It comes from behind me.

With a care I didn't know I possessed, I twist my body to see whoever is speaking. The vision that greets me is not what I expected. A woman lies on the ground withering, but her face appears to be in the utmost peace. She smiles when I see her.

"Oh, Luna, I thought you'd never wake."

Her voice is nothing more than a whisper. I find myself moving forward in order to catch her words. I kneel on the rocky land, and when I look down I see the drape of my cloak and kirtle clinging to my legs like a wet rag, but I am unable to feel a thing. I run my fingers over the fabric, but still no touch is ever felt. I take off the cloak, finding it no longer needed.

"Glorious, isn't it?" the woman whispers.

I see her face for the first time. Ripely aged, she lies across the ground in sullen movements. Her voice is a soft murmur of words that must be deciphered, but when I see the wrinkles around her eyes, I recognize the woman. Mystral stares back at me, her dark hair falling over her shoulders in waves of gorgeous clamor. She is no longer the young woman who disappeared into the water that night so long ago.

"What is glorious about this?" I say, my voice a hoarse echo into the wind.

She smiles. "We cannot feel a thing. Nothing can hurt us—nothing will ever hurt us, my dear Luna."

"What happened?"

Mystral closes her eyes for a moment, leaving me to sit within the confines of my own question. "What happened, you ask? Life. Brilliancy. Eternity!"

She opens her eyes and this time when she looks at me, it is as if I'm a dying relative who cannot be fought for. The only thing left is to pity my soul.

"Luna, you lived all your life blind to a world that did not love you. Color—there was never any color for you, was there?"

She stares back at me, waiting.

I think back to the time before I awoke in the water. The memories of my past haze together like a large mess of words that I can't make sense of. I vaguely remember my family. Mama and Papa, Margo and Dondre. Margo had married Anton—the man who had once tried to kill me—and their child was Joelle.

"You don't remember, do you?" Mystral asks.

"Remember what?"

"The pestilence."

The pestilence that killed Margo, which was the reason Anton left us with Joelle. How Dondre hated me and wanted me dead. How I left Mama on her deathbed with the Bird who put her through pain instead of easing it. Yes, I remember the pestilence.

"It is killing my family," I tell Mystral. I can feel an empty pain in my chest, a lack of emotion which threatens to engulf me. I wait in silence, expecting tears to flood my vision, but they never come.

"There's more," Mystral says. "Think back to your senses."

"I can't feel anything anymore," I tell her.

"I know. Our kind doesn't have a sense of touch. It protects us. Nothing will ever hurt us."

"That's not possible," I say.

Mystral shakes her head and closes her eyes. Her next words are more to herself than to me. "The child doesn't understand. She does not see the boldness that beholds her eyes."

Her eyes flash open and look into me. "What do you see, Luna? Think back to how the world appeared to you once. Was it filled with this brilliance? This beauty? What has changed from now and then?"

Her voice is almost frustrated, like she's explaining something I refuse to listen to.

I look around me. Tiboulain is the island Mystral told me to escape to in order to free myself of the pestilence. She said it provided safety. Nothing extraordinary is here. The island is so small I can see from one end to the other, but here in front of me, a pool rests. The freshwater travels deep into the island, but when I was drowning there was no need for air.

All I can remember is falling in the water. I thought I was going to die, but this world that I've entered doesn't seem like death at all.

"What did the rising sun look like to you before?" Mystral asks. Her voice is kind, quiet.

I look out at the water and beauty. Hues and tones I don't have a name for flash before my eyes, and finally I understand what I didn't see before.

"Those are called colors."

Mystral's voice is happy. Her words are a lullaby to my ears, and even though I'm not looking at her in this moment, I know she is smiling.

"You've never seen them before, have you?"

I shake my head, absorbing the brilliancy of color. They spray across the sky in a gradient, glowing like there will be no tomorrow and that they must celebrate their brilliancy right this moment.

"It is because you have transformed. The water of Tiboulain is magical. It took you away from the pain and gifted you this sight."

"Can everyone see color?" I ask.

"Yes," she says. "You couldn't because of your birth."

"What do you mean?" I turn back to Mystral and try to understand her words, but she shakes her head.

"You were born on a day of darkness, when the moon covered the sun—a solar eclipse. Born blind, but the moon gave you a gift—sight—but vibrancy was not part of that gift. These colors before you have names. You may not know all of them now, but they will come to you. The blue is the sky of day. The yellow is the glowing sun, and the brown is the soil of the earth."

"I don't understand," I tell her.

"That's okay. You have eternity to find the knowledge you seek."

"Eternity?"

"It's what we are given—it's what we are."

She smiles a kind grin. Her voice floats away and she is done speaking. She slides her body forward in small, slow movements making her way toward the pool of water that lies between us.

"You are my passage to eternity, Aida de Luna. The helper of the moon. You belong to the universe—*we* belong to the universe."

As she crawls forward, I see her aging. Her dark hair grows and grays as it touches the ground. Her face changes, as wrinkles mark her smile; her body thins and weakens until finally she touches the water.

Mystral skims her finger in the liquid and I see her slip away to some eternity beyond sight. Her body turns to ash in front of my eyes and with an unknown grace, the water takes her away.

Fear should not be the emotion that instills me, yet that is what overcomes my body once Mystral disappears. It's not the first time I've seen her disappear into the water, but this time it seems all too final. Nothing is left of her presence except the ashes in the air that were once her being.

I look around Tiboulain. It seems so familiar, but it is another world—another lifetime. When I look closely at the surface it appears damp, a soft gleam of moisture covering its façade. I run my fingertips over it, concentrate on the point of contact, but when I close my eyes it's as if I'm touching nothing. I wrap my fingers around a stone and squeeze, but again nothing. I open my eyes and bring the stone close. Its surface is a dull gray, darkening in spots where water has pocked its surface.

The rock is as solid as anything else in this world, but only my sight tells me it's really here. I toss the rock and it makes a thud as it hits another larger stone farther away.

The sky around me is still roaring with color, and that's what I don't understand. All my life I had never seen any of this, but now it's found me. Not only the sights, but the names just as Mystral had spoken to me. When I see the sun peeking over the horizon, I see yellow, flaming out to orange. The colors mix and diffuse into greater things—purples, pinks, blues.

And as much as this beauty astounds me, it makes me fearful, for what is unknown, for what doesn't make sense, and for what confuses me. All at once this new world has come to me when I didn't ask for it. I'm in a new life that doesn't make sense. I can't remember how I came to Tiboulain. And somewhere, without me, my family lives—or dies.

I crawl forward, and my limbs shake. It's not reasonable; I'm not cold—in fact I don't feel a thing. Warmth, cold, all sensation is lost to me; and that loss is what brings on the anxiety that rips through my core.

I near the edge of the pool. It is just big enough that someone could unknowingly fall in—breaking a bone in the process maybe. The memory of how I came to the water eludes me. I don't remember falling in the water; I don't even remember how I got here.

I lean my head over the edge, peering into something that kept me safe from the pestilence. My hand reaches forward and touches the surface, ripples of water echoing over it. When the surface stills, I see my reflection. A young woman stares back at me, her face stunned to find this new world. Her hair is golden, braided in loose waves about her head. When I look at her face I see beauty in her features, but also the utter fear that possesses her being. She is tired; she is alone, and she is me.

Dark circles encroach my eyes. I am the picture of death, but youth haunts the glow within my skin. And then I see what everyone else saw my entire life. My eyes are dominant, calling attention where it is unwanted. The irises lack color. They are silvery-white in the morning sun. They possess a metallic sheen that both amazes and horrifies any who look upon my being.

I am the witch I've been accused of.

XXIV.

The islands stare back at me. They aren't anything like I remember. Pomègues and Ratonneau, the largest islands of Frioul Archipelago, have stone buildings on their land. What was once undisturbed is now invaded. A bridge has been built between the two pieces of land, connecting them in some sick display of uniting what should be left alone.

Standing on Tiboulain, I'm left only to wonder how much time has passed. Surely a bridge like the one I see now couldn't have been built within a short span of time. The pestilence created too much chaos for this to happen overnight.

The cloth of my kirtle snaps itself in the wind. The fabric is worn and old. It has dried in the rising sun, leaving the material coarse and threadbare, ready to rip at the smallest of movements. It hangs off my body in a sad display, the color almost completely diminished. If I look close enough, it was once a brown that has faded to a lighter tan, now blending with the tone of my skin.

The waves of the island surround me. Water crashes against the rocks and splashes against its sides. Otherwise the morning is silent, yet the screams of the ocean ring out in my ears, begging me to leave. Tiboulain is small with nowhere to escape or hide.

All that can be seen is a rough, rocky surface that makes for an uneven land difficult to navigate. Crevices in the rock hide empty promises for shelter, none of which are large enough to hold a person.

It isn't until I reach the other end of the island that I see a small rowboat. The wooden hull is starting to rot as its bottom sits in a small puddle of water between jutting stones. The boat rests just feet from the crashing waves of water as if someone had carried it inland, so it wouldn't get washed away. There's a rope to tie it in place, but despite the fact that it could have been secured to many surfaces it lies untouched within the boat.

I look around, almost expecting the owner to come out of hiding and scold me for being in its proximity, but no one ever does. Instead I push the boat, steering it into the water, careful that the rotting wood doesn't brush up against the rough stones that had trapped it on the island. Despite its small size, the boat weighs just enough for me to struggle with its transport. With a final shove the hull touches the surface of the water and floats with an ease and poise that I never expected an old vessel to bear.

I'm far from the world I once belonged to. Somewhere behind Frioul Archipelago lies my home, Marseille, and for some reason, this scares me.

I've commandeered the boat which shifts and glides through the water. It lulls me into a trance that I will never understand. Tiboulain shrinks away behind me, only a diminishing memory. The images of Mystral disappearing replay themselves in my mind, speaking to me in a coded language only I can decipher. I remember trying to rid myself of her in the village. Somehow, in the end, she captured my curiosity and I was a fool who came to Tiboulain at her bidding.

Marseille rises out of the horizon, but it doesn't look the same. Just like Pomègues and Ratonneau, Marseille has also changed, grown almost. A barrier lines the ports of Marseille, a great wall rising above all else. Faraway I can see ships, appearing so small in the distance, docked in the bay.

As the hours pass, the sun travels across the sky. The rays find my skin, and as I row, all I can do is watch as my home comes into view—a home I don't recognize.

The docked ships grow as I approach. They are so much more than the meager merchant ships I grew up watching, sailing in and out of the bay. I remember memorizing the ports as I grew, always amazed by the size of the great ships that carried goods from exotic places. The largest ship had three sails that branched outward when the wind caught flight, but the vessels in front of me now make those ships of old pale in comparison.

Even from a distance the ships in the harbor appear to be two, maybe even three, times the size of the ships I had seen in my childhood—their sails more intricate, far larger. They tower

171

over the land and I watch as men unload boxes of goods from the ships' hulls.

As I draw closer in my small rowboat I feel myself growing small, almost unimportant. I can be so easily crushed. My boat is manned by nothing but a paddle. Waves crash upon the ships before me but don't sway. Out in the open I thrash around in the unruly water. The sea could so easily swallow me, and it would never be known that I was here; yet if these grand vessels were to sink, part of me feels it would be a great loss to many.

My heart beats inside me. The oar of my boat rests in my hands even though I cannot feel the weight of the wood. I float and drift in the sea. The stark colors of day eat away at me—the bright sky, the hovering ocean. It is all shouting for attention where my eyes were once blind, but it all just confuses my heightened sense of sight. The sails of ships blow in dull tones, but far behind them rests the heart of Marseille. It lies behind a stone wall that towers high above any person.

I watch as people leave their ships carrying crates and enter the town through a gate in the stone wall. Men guard the passageway, acting as a checkpoint and I realize it's useless for me to attempt to enter. With a shuddering breath I lift an oar and steer myself from Marseille.

I row myself to a beach I had known. It was a place I never had to hide from others because I was the only one who knew of the secret beach's existence.

My arms struggle against the current of the ocean, but I

push forward. As I glide over the water, I remember Mama and how sick she was with the pestilence and I wonder if she's still that way. When I left Marseille it was a dark, dying world, but when I look at the people walking across the docks, even from a distance, I see they don't bear the weight of the pestilence.

A false hope burns inside me. I see the Bird leaning over Mama, putting her through extensive procedures to rid her of the pestilence. Could it really be over, just like that? Bernie died of the pestilence; everyone was dying, and it doesn't seem possible that it could have ever ended so soon. There were buboes, blood, the smell of rotting flesh—all of it gone; it doesn't seem possible.

I allow myself a moment to believe Mama is still alive, that she was one of the many who overcame this pestilence and prospered. That somewhere hidden within Marseille, I'll find her at work in our cruck house. But the longer I scan the landscape, the more my hope is denied. Nothing is as I remember.

The world now open to me doesn't seem real. I'm not a part of it.

XXV.

The village had been burned with fire. The air was still hot with death. Everywhere I looked, there was rot and ruin. Buildings appeared as if they might have just been torn down; people sagged against their own weight on the side of the road. Even the tame animals that once trotted through the streets couldn't be found.

Once upon a time the churches here tolled their bells to signify death; now there is a frightening silence. There were too many deaths to support, too many funerals, so instead they did away with tradition. Bodies were thrown about as lives was lost, like life was a simple piece of thread that finally gave way to a great weight.

Burials became nothing more than a dumping ground for dozens of dead. Large graves were dug, big enough to fit what seemed like hundreds of bodies. The living would line up the departed, laying the deceased in rows, shoulders touching. It was a sick display and disrespectful to the dead—not giving proper funeral rites—but it was the only way to rid the air of so much death.

Priests refused the dying their final rites, fearing their own demise in the wake of the pestilence. Those once admired locked themselves away from the world, being nothing but the selfish human beings they are. Days, weeks, months passed and uncountable lives slipped from the world. Death became a common sight. It was a mere miracle if someone survived. *Why did I survive? Why them but not me?*

Life didn't make sense, because it wasn't life. It was a timeline of waiting, watching, seeing when death would come to their doorstep and take them away. The world wanted to tease them, to taunt them, to see how close death could get to them without actually killing them. Death would start with the ones they loved. A brother, a sister, a mother, a father—all dead, but not them.

Life was a cruel torture.

That's what it is—or at least what it used to be.

When I finally dock the rowboat the beach is small, the sand extending only a few feet out, but the waves come to rest at its shore in a gentle rhythm. The quiet here is a great relief. There is only the gentle patter of water against rock and the whisper of wind between trees.

Stepping onto the beach, I pull my boat from the water. The small vessel groans and creaks as I carry it to the land and I feel as if it has seen its last voyage. I release the wooden nose and let it rest against the sand, watching as the stern continues to be licked by the waves of water.

I abandon the vessel on the beach and see how, even in my secret place, my world has changed. When I came here in the past it was always so secluded, but now, off in the distance, I see what looks like a village. Footprints are scattered on the beach, impressions of a world separate from my own.

I follow the path I had always used to travel home. The ground at my feet is stamped down and worn. As I separate myself from the small beach I encounter grass, with trees not too far away. The colors glow and reverberate off themselves and I wonder if these trees had always been here or if my eyes had been blind to their beauty before.

People stare as I approach, so I make sure to hide my eyes. They go about their business, carrying baskets, talking to each other, but when they see me their eyes scan my figure. My clothing is rotten looking in comparison to theirs. One woman has what resembles my kirtle, but the skirt is too full. Her dress is a red velvet that flares out at her feet, but the bodice is tied close to her chest with strings. When she looks me over she appears repulsed and keeps her distance, as if she can catch the distaste that I carry.

I try not to notice the gazes that bore into me. These people appear as nobles in their lavish clothing, but they are doing chores. A woman walks by with a basket of bread, yet nothing about it seems to appeal to me. Another much younger girl skips by, singing to herself the list of chores she must do by day's end. Her dress is beautiful, with stitching all about the bodice, but I can't imagine a nobleman sending his child to do chores alone—that's what the servants are for.

"Miss?"

I turn at her voice, finding her finger tapping my shoulder.

"Who are you?"

A young woman, maybe just a few years older than me, stands close to my flank. As soon as she sees me, she steps back. Her eyes are scanning me, looking me over. The bottom of my skirt is ripped and so are my sleeves. I'm nothing but a beggar to her and I expect her to shun me, but instead she looks at me with fear.

"What?" she says. Her dress is a lovely pink, the color of the blossoms on a cherry tree.

When I look at her bodice, all I see is how tightly the fabric is bound to her skin and I wonder how she finds the air to breathe.

"Your eyes."

That's when I realize she's staring. I avert my gaze elsewhere, trying to find an escape.

"Was there something you needed?" I ask in the steadiest voice I can muster.

"I just ... I don't recognize you. Are you a traveler?"

When I look at her she flinches. I am still a monster to these people. While their irises glean golden brown, green, or blue, mine are a white and ghostly silver. I imagine what it is like to be a stranger looking into my eyes, seeing one's own reflection when I'm looked upon.

"I'm looking for my mother," I tell the woman.

I see her ease into our conversation, growing familiar

with the strange quality of my eyes. She doesn't study them as she had before, but I can still feel her questioning glances as she tries to make sense of my clothing.

"Maybe I know her?" the woman says, turning her chin like a tame dog does when spoken to. "What's her name?"

"Celine Leland."

Her lip puckers and for the first time I notice the small bottle she holds. A clear brown-tinted liquid rests inside the glass, but nothing marks what it is. It's small, just barely bigger than her hand, but she clutches it to herself, as if it contains the world.

"I don't believe I know anyone by that name," she mumbles the words to herself, still reviewing names and faces in her mind, trying to find a match. "Leland? I don't think there is anybody who bears the name. Did your mother live here?"

"Once upon a time, yes."

"Oh," is all she says. She smiles a little and steps back the slightest bit. Although her gaze never leaves me, I can feel her preparing to leave. "Well, I don't think I know her."

She turns her back to me, going in the direction I had just come from, but I can see her spotting the village near the beach, full of life, and I wonder if that's where she lives.

"Wait," I say.

She stops, but her body doesn't pivot to see me. "Yes?"

"What is the bottle for?"

She turns the slightest bit, only giving her profile, as she brings the small bottle toward her chest, hugging it near her heart.

"Medicine, my lady. My son ... I'm not sure if he'll make it." She tries to smile, but I can see the burn of her words as they reach across her mouth. She's frozen in some fearful memory as she speaks, and her eyes drift off to some faraway land.

"Is he sick with the pestilence?"

"The pestilence?" she asks, as if it is something unheard of. She looks at me with questions, but she never actually speaks them. "You mean the Black Death?"

My mind flashes to Bernie, how his hands and fingers swelled to a dark skin that didn't seem human. I had seen so many people succumb to it, their own flesh rotting away while their bodies still continued to live. It was all so overwhelming, the number of the sick and the dying that no one cared to ever give it a name.

I nod to the woman as she stands far from me.

"No, my lady, of course not," she says. Part of her shudders with the thought of her son rotting due to the Black Death, but another deeper part sighs with great relief that her son isn't ill with that disease.

She smiles weakly, pulling the bottle closer to her before walking away.

XXVI.

It's a long time before I reach my village. My memories tell me there should be small cruck houses surrounded by fences with sheep grazing not too far away. The land should be overwhelmed by men working farmland and crops. Yet there is none of that.

My village has been turned into a town. The roads are cobblestoned and rough. Women walk across the ground like it is nothing. They don't realize the deaths I have seen here. I question if I'm at the right location, but when I look over the horizon and see the same view I woke up to every day, I take tentative steps, seeking the perfect angle until I finally find where my home once stood.

A market takes its place, people trading food and going about their daily lives. I step to the side, leaning against a small building made of stone, watching what had once been my home. A man fights with a merchant, obviously disgusted with his offer. I see him spit on the ground and a part of me wants to hurt him.

"Care to place a wager?" a man says from behind me.

I turn, and, within the shadows of an alley, a small man sits on a wooden crate in the shadows, tossing a pair of dice in his hands. His smile is warm, inviting even, but I find myself staggering away. His hair grows down his back in an unkempt braid.

"No, sir," I say.

"Why, I'm sure you desire something."

I look down at his fingers covered in dirt, black under the nails. I see beneath his layers of clothing how tight his belt is wound, just how small and frail his frame is and I consider if this man could hurt me even if he tried.

"No, I'm just … trying to find my mother." My eyes scan the crowd within the market. People linger under tents and small children poke around the stands, sneaking small bits of food into their pockets, hoping no one is looking.

"Why, I'll help you find her! If only at a price, my dear." He offers his hand, fingers extended, expecting payment. His smile curls to the corner of his eyes and I'm both repulsed and intrigued by the stranger.

"I don't have anything to offer you."

"Of course you do! Look at yourself! You aren't from here, are you?"

I retreat at his words. He scans my figure, looking too closely at my body. Suddenly the small, feeble man I had just been talking to turns into something more dangerous. He rolls the dice around in his palm, eager with his thoughts. My feet stagger backward when I see him lift himself from his seat. As suddenly as I move, I'm stopped by another figure.

"Easy, Archie. Leave the girl alone."

I gasp at the stranger's words, surprising me. The man behind me steps around and smiles down at Archie. The stranger wears a dark cloak that extends almost to the back of his knees;

his voice gentle when he speaks.

"Take the bread and go bother someone else," he says.

The man offers a loaf pulled from his cloak. It looks stale, but Archie takes it with eager fingers. With a small grumble he shoos us away and doesn't look up again.

"Come on," the man in the cloak says, ushering me with a gentle hand from Archie. "Don't mind him. He targets those who look confused, though I don't blame him. He usually scams food from them, if he doesn't scare them first."

He turns to me so I can see his face past the shadows.

My breath stops. As soon as we're out of view of others I wind my arm back and hope—even though I won't feel the punch—that maybe Garren will.

"Luna!" He catches my fist in his hand.

I push against him, but no movement comes of it.

"You tried to kill me!" I scream, but it comes out sounding more like a cry. "You *did* kill me." And this time I speak the words sound feeble.

"Luna, hush, not here," he says.

"Where's my family?"

He pushes me from the market back to the path I came from. I put my arms against his chest, stare at the tips of my fingers, but feel nothing.

I want to hate this man. I want to drown him the same way he'd drowned me, but I find myself falling into his arms instead.

"I'll explain everything. I promise."

He looks down at me with eyes that mimic the ocean and I can't fight anymore. I pull my arms in by my side and let him lead me.

"No," I say, simply stopping. "Where's the pestilence gone? I want to see my family." Colors of violet, pink, and deep orange fill the air. The sun goes down in an ever-repeating orbit. The sky tells me to be happy.

Garren stops, also looking down, as if he doesn't know what to say. His eyes lift and I can feel him staring at me, and for a moment, I can't break his gaze.

"Luna, the pestilence has been gone for over one hundred years," he finally says.

And I feel myself fade from reality for a moment, no longer caring to hear what else this world has to say.

XXVII.

The moon glows with a beauty that must be envied. It lights the night and leads the way to a future, a passage, a place. Animals of the dark wake from within their nests and come out to creep within the pale light. They make small sounds as they scurry, but unless one looks closely, they can't be found.

Trees sway in the backdrop of the night, their leaves rustling in a gentle rhythm that I used to fall asleep to in the dark. That's how it always was growing up—the quiet stir of leaves with the ocean waves crashing against the rock face that dropped below the cliffs. Now the noise serves to keep me awake, only reminding me of what is lost.

One moment I was living my old life. Margo died of the pestilence after Anton abandoned her, leaving Joelle under the care of Mama and Papa. And Dondre, I remember the way he had last looked at me, how it appeared as if he hated me for something I didn't do. How are they gone?

In this new life, in this new world, I sit in some field Garren led me to. He told me about the pestilence that earned the name of the Black Death. More than half the world, it seemed, perished. Garren said this is one of the spots where they buried the dead. It's the same patch of land I had once stood on while watching the two men cart the dead to leave them on the ground, one after another, never caring to give a service or pray for the lost souls as they passed on. It was death, and it was brutal. And it is then I realize Mystral lied—I have no power to save lives.

The last thing I had seen in my old life was fresh soil, shoveled over the dead. People feared walking near this plot of land, as if the disease could be caught by simply breathing the same air. The massive grave was left undisturbed by all. The only footprints in the soil were the ones left by those who had covered the graves with pounds of dirt.

The site is trampled now, beaten down by careless passers-by who have no remembrance of what horror the ground holds. Everyone has forgotten how much death was seen by this soil.

I rest in the middle of it all, surrounding myself with what I can imagine are those I lived with or nearby. Their words echo through my mind: *witch, nothing but a witch*.

Even Dondre began to believe their words. He never spoke them directly to me, but in the end, when I looked into his eyes, all I saw was malice. To him, I was the one who killed Margo; I was the one who was watching Mama die, the Bird's medicine bringing nothing but torment to her already dying body.

I sit on the grave of those who hated me, of those who looked at me and only saw evil. To them I was a curse. They were the only people I had, and now they are gone.

More than one hundred years, Garren had said. One

whole century I was gone, held by the moon and now I'm here again. The world has continued on; the pestilence subsided; lives were lived, and lives were lost. The number of years doesn't seem possible—more than a lifetime.

The image of Mystral comes back to me, how she hunted me down in Marseille and told me how Tiboulain could save us all. I didn't believe her. I didn't want to believe in something like dark magic, but I was foolish and I sought out the salvation I didn't deserve when I should have searched for death.

I had always imagined myself dying of the pestilence, that at some point we all would. One by one our bodies would rot away and the world would die out. Perhaps it was God punishing us for being the awful beings we were. We cheated; we lied, and we stole; and all the while we expected this undying love from the universe. We thought of ourselves as indestructible, that we could face anything, because the world could not touch us. It was a lie. We were nothing but breakable figures. We were voodoo dolls just waiting for a misshapen savior. Sooner or later someone would set a fire that would melt the stitching of our perfect world.

But I didn't die. I'm here, and I'm alone, and I'm sitting on a massive grave site.

Margo is beneath my feet. That's why I was watching them bury the dead at the mass grave in my previous life. Mama had warned me not to follow the men as they carted away my sister's body, but I did so anyway. They dragged that cart throughout the entire village, until it was full. They disrespected the dead, throwing them one on top of the other like they were nothing more than sacks of flour.

Finally they had brought the cart to this field. Margo was somewhere in that cart. When they came to our cruck house, they had thrown her body on top of three others: a man who looked to be Papa's age, another man much older, and a little girl who was no bigger than my torso. With a heave they had piled Margo's body on the ground with all the others.

They had unloaded the dead and placed them in the grave—horizontal, side by side—and, when there wasn't any more room, a layer of dirt had been shoveled on the dead, only to bury more bodies.

I didn't see where Margo's body ended up in the grave site. I had seen a flash of her hair as they hoisted her away, but once she was placed in the massive hole I lost her. Inside the earth, the dead slept an eternal silence. Their limbs were wrought with dark sores, their extremities dying before their heart gave way. That was why they called it the Black Death.

"Luna?"

A voice stirs me awake in the forgotten morning. Light shines through the lids of my eyes, but part of me refuses to wake and face the day.

"Are you all right?"

I squint and see Garren's hand touch my shoulder blade and I don't feel the contact. I know he's here, but my sense of touch is gone. I'm numb to my surroundings, never belonging to this place I've been abandoned to.

"They're gone." I say the words clearly, even with the new shock of morning. I lie with my face buried, my body curled against the dry dirt of the mass grave. I feel the victims of the pestilence radiate their essence to my soul, begging me to join them in their death where I belong. I'm supposed to be dead. Yet I'm not dead.

"Your mother?"

I see Garren pull his hand from my shoulder, and part of me breaks because I can't feel it. He's here; I know he's here, but I'm a ghost. I curl into my body as if I'm cold, but I'm not. I can't remember the last time I felt *anything*. The sun on my face, the warmth of someone's touch—it's all just a distant memory.

"I can't feel anything," I tell him. He doesn't speak so I lift my head and look at the morning light for the first time. Off the side of the cliff the water breaks into white waves, a never-ending lull of soothing melody. The sky is pink with the new day.

Garren sits close, waiting patiently for my words. He doesn't judge or speak; he just listens.

"That's okay," he says.

I shake my head and gather myself into a seated position. I remember growing up, how Mama taught me to act as a lady and to be proper. She would have never stood for sitting on the bare ground like I am now. She would have reprimanded me for getting dirt on my kirtle, the only clothing I had that needed to be kept clean.

When I look down all I see are rips and stains—Mama would have never allowed this.

"Some people, when they lose someone, they don't feel anything—and that's okay. Just because you lost your mother and you don't cry for her doesn't make you a bad person."

Garren speaks, but his voice seems so far away. He doesn't understand.

"No," I say. "I do miss her. I miss all my family, even if they wouldn't miss me." Emotions build in the back of my mind. *Would my parents have grieved if I had died before them? If the pestilence had taken me instead of Margo, would Dondre still have despised me so?*

I watch with great fear as my hand shakes before my eyes. I can't control the trembling that overtakes my body. Emotions of grief come for my family who never loved me. I want to hate them; I want to release all thoughts of them, but I can't. Instead they rule my mind and cause me to miss them.

"It's okay." Garren speaks again, but his voice is muffled to my ears.

My breaths come in quick motions that I can't regulate and I wait for the tears to overwhelm my eyes, to blind my vision, but they never do. My cries come, my voice a whine in the clear morning, but my eyes never glaze over with wetness. I shut out the world, desperate to escape this nightmare.

When I look up, I see Garren's face just inches from my own. His fingers reach out, brushing my cheek, but I don't feel his touch. I see his fingers on my skin, but his presence is otherwise unknown.

"I can't feel anything," I tell him, desperate for help, even if he may think of me as insane.

"It's okay, Luna," he says, and I want to scream.

"No," I say. I push his hand from my face and hold his hand in my own. I look down at my skin and feel a piercing cry building in my core. "This," I say, holding up our hands, "I can't feel you. I can't feel anything."

Garren looks at me, confused. I drop our hands and shrink from him. My clothing that hangs over my body, the ground that digs into my legs, the air that whispers against my skin—it's all numb to me; it's not here somehow.

Tears never come, like the cruel curse made for those who wish to grieve. I look at Garren and wonder what he sees. A woman who is going insane? Someone who is grieving for a mother who died more than one hundred years ago?

"Why are you here?" I ask. My voice is nothing more than a whimper.

He looks at me for a long time. His eyes wander over my clothing, seeing what is there. Peasant clothing from years ago, when humanity was dying off because of a disease that came to kill anyone it touched. His gaze rests on my eyes at last and I wonder if now he will finally recoil at the sight of my silver irises.

"Because I know," he says.

I shake my head, my gaze slowly floating down.

"You don't," I say, but it is only a quiet whine, so much that I'm sure he didn't hear me.

"No," he says, lifting my chin so I'm forced to look at him. His mouth is turned down, his face serious. "I do. Because I can't feel this either."

XXVIII.

"It was black magic," Garren tells me. "We were just victims of it. Mystral was the only witch, not you. She just tricked you into doing her bidding. Tiboulain was her fountain of youth. You opened it for her. You may not be able to see her anymore, but she's still here."

The sun has been down for hours now. It must be the middle of the night, but I feel no need to sleep—neither of us do.

"Why'd she want me?" I ask.

"I'm sorry to say you were marked since birth," Garren tells me.

"I don't understand," I say, my voice a numb whisper.

"Have you seen your eyes?"

My head lifts when he says the words.

I nod, remembering each and every stare I've received. How they whipped me simply because people thought I was a witch. And it was all because of the color of my eyes. My eyes told them I was a witch and that my life needed to be extinguished, but they had no case against me. There was nothing they could do about me simply being alive.

My arms wrap around my knees and I take deep breaths, noting the rise and fall of my chest. I hold my breath and wait. Seconds turn into minutes, and I feel no need to ever seek air again. I wait for my head to spin, for my world to slip away, but it doesn't. After a few more minutes of stillness, I give in and take the air. Oxygen fills my lungs, but there is no relief or ecstasy from the sweet air.

"That's part of all this," Garren says, watching me stop breathing but doesn't do anything. "You don't need air to be alive."

In silence Garren sits next to me, but the small space feels overwhelming. It's magnified by the vast space left by the mass grave we sit atop. He doesn't dare come closer and it's all I can do to sit in one place.

"I don't feel anything," I say after a long stretch of silence. He doesn't speak so I continue. "Garren, I see the ground beneath my feet, but I don't *feel* it. Emotions overwhelm me, but a tear never comes. I'm waiting for some release, for some cry to rip its way through my core, but it never does."

I look at him and he frowns. He wants to say something. His mouth opens, as if to form words, but they never come and he chooses not to speak. I wonder how I look. My face feels rabid, distorted, and twisted enough to make me a monster in my own body. Garren doesn't look aside though; he just continues to study me, like he wishes he could take away my pain.

"I'm sorry," he says.

I shake my head. "Why?"

"Because I told Mystral about you." His eyes are sad as he speaks.

When he looks at me, I know all he can see is a broken girl.

"Mystral was looking for eternity and the moon held that power, but she needed someone to be the gateway. The moon had marked you when you were born. There are legends surrounding others like you, but none had been carried out until you."

I look away, feeling a sort of weight in his words. It makes sense, but I don't want to believe him. I don't want to be this gateway to dark magic that he speaks of.

"The moon was blocking the sun. You looked at it and were gifted. Mystral told me that, up until that moment, you had been blind, without sight. It is said that when a baby is born disabled, the moon can choose to give a gift but only during the correct time. The moon gifted you sight. There was no color, but you would never realize the difference."

"How do you know this?"

"In the streets you looked at me—but only for a moment. Once I saw your eyes, I knew there was a dark magic in you—everyone did. Even your own family was wary of you. I needed Mystral's help and she needed someone like you. I had heard she could do things, so I told her about your eyes. Mystral was on a search for eternity and you were the only one who could keep it from slipping away."

"Because of the pestilence," I say.

"She became frantic, seeking a cure or some way to ensure she would live. Tiboulain is the daughter of the moon. To be gifted with eternity you first needed to give it something in return—or, in this case, give something back."

Garren looks at me, waiting for some sign of comprehension.

"Mystral gifted me. Back to the moon," I say.

"Aida de Luna. Helper of the moon."

"*Postpone the moon and find forever*," I say, mimicking Mystral's chant.

"Postponing death is what she wanted, and that's what she received."

When I look at Garren, suddenly he isn't a stranger. He's the man who lent me his boat the night I left my family. I was so desperate for some cure or solace from the disease killing my family that I didn't bother to make sense of the events. He was the one who found me asleep on the side of the cliff; he was the one who brought me to Tiboulain, but he was also the one who drowned me in its waters.

"You tried to kill me that night," I say. The blurry image courses through me of his face as I slowly descended into the water. He looks the same—deep brown curly hair, a square jaw—but now I can see him better, bolder. I try not to remember the feel of his arms on my shoulders as he held me beneath the water.

Garren holds my gaze, but his face makes me feel as if I've just slapped him across the jaw.

"I'm sorry it appeared that way. Your body had to become the water of Tiboulain, and drowning you was the only way to do that."

"But why would you bother with all this? Did Mystral make a deal with you? All this, just so you could live forever?" My voice grows in volume as I speak.

Garren reels back from where he sits but listens to every word I say. Shame is written over his face, and he doesn't look at me when he talks.

"There was a bargain, but I wasn't the one who was supposed to live."

"What do you mean?"

He pauses, his eyes darting everywhere except my face. "Mystral was to grant my sister life. My mother and father had left us once the pestilence struck. They ran away one night, taking all the food with them, along with our horse. They followed everyone to the countryside for safety."

"There's no magic in Mystral's powers to bring them back," I tell Garren, my voice turning to a gentle lull.

He doesn't look anywhere. His eyes glaze over, but I can tell he isn't with me in the present. His mind is off somewhere, remembering what he wishes he could forget.

"I know," he says. "My sister died shortly after they left. She was one of the first in our village to pass from the pestilence, but she certainly wasn't the last. I didn't want to live forever, Luna. When I met Mystral, I was waiting to die, to join my sister, maybe even my parents, but that's not how things worked out."

"What was your sister like?"

For the first time Garren smiles. A light ignites in his eyes and I know for certain he loved the girl. "Her name was Lucie. She had just turned twelve and smiled up until that age."

"What do you mean?"

"Lucie came across a man on the street one night, when I let her walk to the market alone and he offered to pay her. She accepted." Garren stops talking, emotions brimming from within. "She came home crying—the sound was awful. I've never heard such a small being make that wail before."

Stillness grows and unfolds. The air settles around both of us, and the atmosphere grows heavy. I watch Garren as he breathes, the steady rhythm bringing me to a calm place I don't understand.

"Lucie wouldn't talk to me for a long time. She wouldn't let me touch her. Every time something, anything, brushed up against her, she would yelp. I watched her every day, struggling to get through the hours, always looking behind her, as if that man might jump out and take her again. She wouldn't tell me of that night.

"One day I cornered her and shook her. I don't know why. I was just so scared for her and I watched as she fell apart. When I touched her, she screamed and cried and when I released her, she sank to the ground. I didn't mean to scare her. I just wanted to know what had happened to my little sister."

"Then how did you find out?" I ask.

Garren's hands are fists at his sides, and part of me waits for him to lash out and punch something. But despite his eager ability to break down he doesn't do so much as move another muscle while he speaks.

"She told me. She told me as she crumbled to the ground. Lucie mumbled words of money and a man and how he touched her, even when she screamed for him to stop.

"She wasn't the same for a long time. Months passed before I saw her smile again, but then one day something changed. She was happy again and I don't know why. I couldn't understand how she could have been tormented yet still see the world like she always had.

"I loved her because of that, because—even after the world had hurt her—she had hope. Even after our parents left, she didn't question their actions. She said they were safer away from her than with her. I didn't understand her selflessness.

"But her death was slow. I watched her slip from me every day, growing sicker as the pestilence fought its battle against her beating heart. I watched her as she smiled at me, before she closed her eyes to the world and I remember thinking that I would do anything to give her life again, just so the world could remember that smile."

"So Mystral would bring Lucie back?" I ask.

Garren nods his head, looking far off to the ocean over the cliffs. "But Mystral couldn't. I helped her and when I finally gave her what she wanted, she gave me life instead of Lucie."

"I'm sorry," I say, because I don't know what else there is to say. When life has handed someone something so tragic, what else is there to do except apologize for the wrongs of the world?

"No, I'm sorry, because all this was for nothing. I've brought you into this world that you never asked to be a part of."

I look around us and see the settled ground. Time has come and passed; lives have been lived, and people have died, but the one sure thing is the corpses that lie in an eternal sleep beneath my feet.

"Nobody asked for any of this," I finally say.

XXIX.

The water is so still. My curiosity wants me to touch the surface, to see the ripples glisten across the surface as my disturbance hits it, but I'm able to refrain. I'm afraid of this pool of water. The last time I made contact with it I disappeared for one hundred years, leaving my family behind to live or die without me.

"So this is it? The place where the black magic stems?" I ask. I stand at the very edge of the pool, just a jump from the water. If I wanted, I could lean in and become consumed by the water again—I know it is deep enough. Even when I was sprawled out in the pool my feet never came into contact with the bottom, only the sides of the rocky walls.

"Yes. As I said, Tiboulain is the daughter of the moon. It is the connection the moon has to Earth. And now you are part of this connection." His voice is flat, only some background noise in the pandemonium of my mind.

"I never wanted to be a part of this," I say.

Beside me Garren shifts and comes closer. I feel his body radiate toward me, but I flinch from any contact—or lack thereof. I walk from the pool of water and navigate the rocky surface of Tiboulain to look at anything other than the monster who took away my life.

I turn toward the vast ocean instead of the islands of

Frioul Archipelago that open themselves at my back. The water is endless, nothing but a vast openness that never dares to close in. I look to the ocean and I wish I were as invincible as the waves that crash and thunder against the breaks.

"I'm sorry this has happened to you."

Garren's voice forms at my back and I want to push him away, to let me be, never to be bothered again, but he is also all I have left.

"If you were sorry, you never would have told Mystral about me."

"You have to understand. I was desperate. I didn't know what Mystral's plan was."

"Why didn't you stop her?" I ask, my voice catching.

"She promised me that she could bring back Lucie. She had me. You have to understand that. I had to do everything I could to bring back Lucie."

Garren's voice is still desperate. It's no wonder Mystral was able to convince him so easily. The boy is blinded by his emotions.

"So you traded my life for your sister."

"Never," he says, sounding genuinely hurt. "Mystral told me that you would live on as something that existed throughout eternity, just as she would. I didn't take your life—I gave you forever."

"You can't decide that for me," I shout. Eternity rests on my shoulders, and I don't want it. I want to blame the one person who gave me this curse, but when I turn to look at him he seems to be hurting more than I am. "I was waiting for the pestilence to take me, Garren. I watched as so many died, one after the other. There was no reason for their deaths. It just happened, and I didn't understand. Why would God put us on Earth just to take us away so bluntly, before we could learn to live? And I don't understand why anyone would want to live forever, because all you will ever see is death.

"You and I, Garren, from this point on, will never see life. Every moment a baby is born, we will not see the miracle of life. We will only wonder how long until they leave Earth again, because life is cruel and fragile and there is no real goal. We are just here for a moment, but now I've been cursed. I've been bedeviled, and you've created me into the witch everyone always thought of me."

Garren is silent. For a long time it is just the two of us looking at each other, neither of us knowing what words should come next. My breath comes faster even though my heart no longer beats. Emotions stir and roll inside me and I wonder what it will take for my surface to crack and finally let the tears roll. It builds inside me and it isn't until I release a shuddering breath that I feel free again. I inhale air, as if it will be stolen from me in mere seconds, only to exhale a personal poison. My chest stirs in chaotic breaths, but the tears never come—the relief is lost to me.

Arms wrap around my shoulders, and without knowing it, I had been lowered to the ground. I sit with my feet curled underneath me, my body shaking. When I look up, I see

Garren's face close to mine. His eyes are rimmed red, his face contorted into something called pain. Through it all neither of us cries.

The winds blow, but we never shiver. The water bites at our ankles, but the sensation never comes. Disconnected, we are no longer part of this world. We are rejected and left useless, only mannequins of the past.

"I'm sorry, Luna," Garren says, as his arms lock around me, but I can't feel him.

The only thing left for me is the roar of water where I had been drowned and taken from my old life and brought into a new, more unfavorable one, where all those I loved have gone and left me.

Death separates me from humanity and the boundary is impossible to pass.

Something about tears makes sadness somehow gratifying. Until I cry all I do is let the emotions build with nowhere to go; but once the crying comes and the tears run from my eyes, there is a certain relaxation in that. But when that release is denied, when it is impossible for me to cry, the pain becomes all the more unbearable.

I sit far from Garren, my back to him. I can't stand to look at him. He doesn't dare break the silence that lingers between us and I can't find it in myself to speak. There is so much to say, but I have no desire to exchange words with him.

So we sit. I face the ocean, the breeze blowing salty air through my hair. Garren looks at the islands of Frioul Archipelago that no longer appear the same as in my memories. Ships and buildings inhabit what were once peaceful islands left to nature.

With shaky hands I unwind the braid that curls around my head. My hair falls in waves and tangles around my shoulders, the golden pigment a shimmer in the sun. The strands are untidy and matted and I take three locks of hair and twist them into a single braid that falls to rest against my abdomen.

"So why are you here?" I ask suddenly. Garren stirs behind me and I can tell my voice has surprised him.

He doesn't answer right away, reawakening himself.

Rocks and pebbles move and stir behind my back and I hear him as he walks closer to me. Finally I see him standing off to the side.

With the slowest movements possible he bends down to sit next to me.

"Don't," I say.

He doesn't respond, just clears his throat as if it is a simple misunderstanding and walks off, coming to a seated position near the shoreline in front of me.

"I'm here because Lucie is not," he says when he's finally gathered himself in a comfortable position. His thick coat falls in the sand around him.

I can tell it's expensive, something that is difficult to trade, yet he treats it no differently than his other clothing.

Waves nip at his leather shoes, but he doesn't flinch away. Instead he absorbs it all, his face taking everything in, the wind brushing through his hair.

"That doesn't answer my question. Of course Lucie isn't here." Once the words are out I see him flinch and I regret my bluntness. He knows his sister is dead—of course it eats away at him. That much is clear.

His head bows to the ground.

"I'm sorry. I just—I, I'm confused. Mystral was supposed to bring your sister back."

He laughs, the sick laugh used when the world has been so cruel that one must pretend it is all some twisted joke.

"Isn't that true! I thought the same thing, my dear Luna. I gave you up, all in the hopes that Lucie would be brought back to enlighten the world again. Yet here I am, and she is not."

"So what happened?"

"I don't know," he says. His voice is quiet, somber when he says the words. "I'd like to think Mystral thought she could bring Lucie back. You don't understand how hopeful she looked when she talked about the spell that she would cast for Lucie. I prefer to think it was not all an act."

He drags his hand through the thick sand at his feet. The grit is large enough that I can see the individual pebbles that make up the sand even from the distance where I sit. He piles the sand, gathers it, and crushes it all in an endless cycle. Finally he presses a final handprint in the sand and draws his fingers to his lap again, staring off into the endless vortex of ocean that lies ahead, as open as an unbarred door.

"I suppose life is not something that can be bought or traded once it is lost. If it slips through your fingers, it's gone forever. The dilemma is we don't discover this until it is too late—until a life has been lost forever. I should have known this when Lucie died, that it was perpetual, but Mystral gave me hope ..." He pauses, his voice faltering in the wind. "I had to do all I could to get her back.

"Sometimes I think Lucie fought it. Maybe she didn't want to return to the living, because there must be something really tremendous after this life that even the thought of seeing those you love seems dull in comparison."

"When you love someone, you will do anything to get back to them—you should know that," I say suddenly. "Lucie loved you. If she could have come back to you, she would have."

Garren turns to face me, his eyes glistening with wonder. He doesn't smile when he looks at me and even though I never knew Lucie, I see his love for her in every feature of his being. He lives her; he breathes her, and he would die for her.

"I know," he says.

"We won't ever know though, will we, whether you can come back after death?" I ask.

It's an odd question. Even in my own mind I can't completely understand it, but Garren looks at me with an understanding that I've never seen from another person.

He shakes his head. "I don't think so." And his eyes are sad.

I imagine what it must be like for Garren, to love someone so much and to know in his heart that, if there is a life after death, he will never see Lucie. He will just keep existing in an ever-changing world without his sister, because he can never die.

"Mystral promised me that Lucie would have forever, that whoever experienced the waters of Tiboulain would have forever."

Forever. The word hangs like a great weight that can never be lifted. What is forever? Is it a vortex that traps me, which brings me farther, deeper, until all I am left to do is breathe? Days wavering, nature escaping. People changing, dying, living, breathing. And I'm here through it all, only existing.

"Why would someone want forever?" I say, trying to wrap my mind around the idea. How could someone want to live forever, never able to grow close to anyone, knowing that mortals will always leave this planet first?

"Because it is the only way to know life is eternal," Garren says. "We think there is a life after death, that God brings us salvation, but there is no way to know for sure."

The words are final, like a marker on a grave, settling a lifetime's worth of arguments with a few simple words.

Tiboulain is so similar to what I had only known once before. Garren brought me here when we were trying to escape the pestilence, when I was only concerned with saving myself; I had no idea of the twisted world of dark magic I was bringing upon myself. Time had passed so eagerly when I was within the folds of the water. When I awoke people had changed; the land had morphed, yet I had remained.

"Exactly how long was I gone?" I ask.

Garren takes in a heavy breath beside me. "I suppose it was at least a hundred years."

I can picture Dondre, almost happy with my disappearance because he was no longer forced to see what he had named as the source of the pestilence. With me gone, he was able to forget the pain I had caused him and grieve Margo's death without me. I was a murderer to him. I wonder if he lived long enough to see that my death didn't stop the pestilence.

"What happened?" My voice is barely a whisper and I wonder if Garren has even heard me.

"You gave yourself to the moon. It kept you for as long as it pleased," he said simply.

In my human life I would have cried. I would feel a tear dripping down my cheek, making way for emotions I couldn't handle. But here, in this eternal world, I have nothing to do but grieve in an absence of sensation.

"And all this time, for one hundred years, you've just been here?"

He doesn't speak, just nods his head as if the answer is obvious.

"Why?" I ask, and my voice is a whine. I'm a toddler being scolded, someone being punished who doesn't understand why the world wishes such poor luck upon them.

"I was waiting for you," he says, not revolted by my meager display of cowardice.

My bottom lip trembles and I can't control myself. I don't understand this world and why it wants me here, when all my life I've been castaway. Suddenly I'm regarded as this gift to the moon, the only person who can bring about forever, and I don't want it. I wanted to die one hundred years ago, when the pestilence came and took away my family, when people looked upon me as a curse.

"Why me?"

The question comes from my lips as a plea. I wait for Garren to give up on me and realize I'm not the person he's been waiting for over the past century. He needed a savior, a witch like Mystral, someone who could bring Lucie back. I'm none of that.

Garren comes to my side as if I'm a broken child. I see his arms as they wrap around my figure and cradle me to his chest. When I close my eyes, it's like he isn't here and I can't decide if it's frightening—because I can't feel his touch—or comforting—because I don't remember anyone ever touching me.

"I don't know why it had to be you," he says.

His words are muffled; maybe his lips are next to my hair.

For a moment I close my eyes and pretend none of this is real, like it is all some poor, awful dream that I just haven't woken up from yet. In my imagination it's like I'm back home with Cyrielle, when Nouvel was just an unborn baby tucked away in his mother's abdomen. When our heads were filled with dreams of seeing a child grow up to be strong and prosper. When I imagine, I see my life without death. And when I imagine, I realize that is what I have. There is no death for me. I will be like this forever. I only wished it wasn't gifted upon me.

When I open my eyes again, Garren has tucked my head against his chest, as one would console an infant. He murmurs something to me, but I can't bother to focus my mind enough to make out the words. I'm frightened by his contact and what his motives for these actions may be. He loved Lucie—would do anything for her—but I can't help her.

Whether or not he believes that I can bring her back, I ignore the pings within me that say to walk away, before I can be hurt. I take the only contact I have and embrace it, drawing closer to Garren. He doesn't flinch, but pulls me close.

I close my eyes a final time, telling myself this is okay.

XXX.

A pile of clothing falls in front of my feet. The next day's sun rests midsky, reminding me that life moves forward in an ever-so-steady motion. I sit on the rocky sands of Tiboulain, always looking to the ocean, but I haven't moved in hours.

We don't sleep. There is no fatigue that comes along after several hours that tells us when we need to rest; we just continue in our existence. Garren tried to explain it to me, how we don't need so many things anymore—food, sleep, contact. He says he still sleeps at night out of habit, the only thing tying him to the world, but last night he was here with me while I looked out into the endless expanse of ocean.

"I brought you clothing," Garren says, standing beside me, pointing to the pile of fabric extravagant enough that I feel foreign just being within its proximity.

"My peasant clothing isn't quite the standard here, is it?"

The dress is royal blue with a skirt that flares out at the waist. It's simple, but compared to my own kirtle it seems so much more. I pick up the fabric and feel the thick wool, soft as the sheep I had raised back home. When I pull the dress onto my lap I see a bright new chemise underneath, the white cotton stark compared to the chemise I wear now.

"Time has changed things," Garren says.

"Fashion of the times," I half mumble. "Well, I suppose it hasn't changed too much." I run my fingers over the cloth and realize it has never been worn before. It has no stains on the fabric. It has the rigidity of fabric not yet washed. Growing up, I had only gotten handed-down items from Margo, clothing that no longer fit her. As far as I remember, this is the first piece of clothing that I haven't had to share.

"I got it from a seamstress in the market. She saw you when you walked through the first day and thought blue would suit you well."

When I look up at Garren he seems unsure of himself, worried that for some reason I may not like his gift.

"I'll let you change," he says, stepping away.

"Thank you," I say, gripping the dress tighter.

He turns back to me smiling. "Of course, my lady," he says, bowing to me the slightest bit, his gaze never leaving mine.

He walks toward the shore, giving me a moment of privacy and I change quickly. I tear away my old kirtle from my body, the fabric falling to the sand in worn pieces. My chemise comes off next, the once-white fabric now a dull brown. I pull on the new clothing with thankfulness. The chemise covers me from the neck down, extending all the way to my wrists. When I pull on the thick wool of the kirtle, the dress envelops me, the sleeves of blue rolling to my elbow, the skirt almost touching the ground. It's like nothing I have ever worn before. All my other clothing has been frail, used, but this feels safe and sure, strong.

I look at my old wardrobe at my feet. It sits, falling apart at the seams, probably from soaking in the pool with me for so long. It's a miracle that the garment lasted as long as it did.

"Okay," I say, turning toward Garren. He hadn't gone far, just simply standing with his back to me while I changed. After hearing my voice he turns slowly, still unsure I'm giving him permission to look.

When his eyes catch me, he lights up. "Well, look at who has clothing from this century."

A smile tugs at my lips and I grasp the skirt at my sides and offer a small curtsey. "I owe you my biddings, good sir," I say, laughter rising from my vocal chords.

Garren comes closer, his hands behind his back as if taking a critical examination of my appearance.

"I suppose the woman in the market was right. Blue does seem to befit you."

I look down and see the skirt of the kirtle is draped, falling in different ruffles at my hips and cascading down. The hem at the waist hugs my body perfectly, almost as if it's a second skin.

"It's beautiful," I say, running my hand over the material. I look up to him and see his happiness in every line of his face, but suddenly I can't bring myself to feel the same way. Without realizing it my smile has deepened into a frown.

"What is it?" Garren comes closer and I see his hand reach out for mine, but at the last minute he pulls away, letting me have my distance.

"All of this is very ..." I stop, not quite sure what I think.

Everything in the past few days is too much. The dress feels like a protective layer, yet I'm leaving my old self behind. "... overwhelming," I say finally. "I don't know what to think."

Garren nods like he understands, and I think he wishes he did, but it isn't possible. I was the one gone, trapped in Tiboulain for one hundred years. Garren was always here, always existing, able to understand and change and modify himself to fit along with the world.

"Was I really gone for that long?"

I look at Garren and I see the spark that was once in his eyes has disappeared. His blue irises die down to a muted gray, lost in thought.

"Yes. I didn't leave you—I couldn't. For years I stayed by the pool of Tiboulain, watching you drift in the water, so close yet unable to touch you. It was strange. I would come close to the water, almost drop my hand in, but then something would come over me and I'd find myself repelled by the thought of being near the water—like it may take me hostage. It was years before I left Tiboulain, only because I saw the world changing. Life forming on Ratonneau and Pomègues, bridges and buildings being built on something that once used to be untouched. Eventually I realized waiting on Tiboulain made time pass slower. So I traveled back to Marseille and made my life there."

"Was the pestilence gone?" I imagine what I would have done if I were Garren. Stay on an island, hiding from death? Or risk returning home where a disease may still be eating away the human soul from the inside out?

214

"It had died out at some point, I suppose. Marseille was different when I returned. The people I talked to had this solemnity to them. There were paintings and works of art that you wouldn't believe, Luna. Death was no longer on the streets, like it once had been. Instead it was in art. Skeletons dancing their sick songs, dark figures with a beak as a face choosing those who lived or died.

"The pestilence affected life. They called it the Black Death and there were tales of how it wiped out life, as if our existence was nothing to God. Children born after the pestilence was contained knew of the Black Death and feared any man whose face was hidden, as if he may carry the Black Death itself. Life became this rare gift to everyone. They became aware of their mortality."

"Did you know of anyone who survived?"

"My parents ran off before the worst of the pestilence hit. Everyone else I knew grew victim, though I didn't know many in my village."

"Do you know if my family survived?" I'm not sure why I ask the question. I don't even know if Garren knew who my family was, but the thought became vocalized before I could make sense of it.

"I think I saw your brother when I went back—he looked a lot like you. Dondre was his name?"

I nod. "Did he seem happy?"

"If it was him I saw, then yes. He found a girl, formed a family. I'm sorry to say your parents had probably passed by

215

then, whether it be by pestilence or other courses of life—again, it was years before I came back to Marseille. But Dondre grew to be a strong man for his family."

And I suppose that's the best I could have wished for him. Part of me wonders if he had ever forgiven me for the crimes he accused me of, but I also know it is nothing worth worrying over.

"And he's gone now," I say. It isn't a question. Just a single statement that needs to be heard.

"After the pestilence passed, they gave final rites again, sending the dead away with a proper ceremony. If he died afterward, then you may find his burial spot."

"Okay," I say simply.

XXXI.

The grave is hidden within the cemetery. All the stones are the same. Just simple pieces of rock carved in a square or rounded shape, marking the burial spot of a loved one. Garren brought me to the cemetery, saying that it was the one closest to where he believed Dondre lived out his adult life. It turns out my brother didn't bother traveling very far from where we grew up. Marseille is still within visiting distance. Though to get there, it would take a day's trip by foot.

"What did you say your last name was?" Garren asks, walking ahead of me. His eyes shift side to side, checking every stone with a quick glance to see if my brother is lost somewhere within the mass of bodies.

"Leland," I say. "It would be Dondre Leland."

Garren doesn't speak again, silently checking each stone before moving to the next one. He works his way through the cemetery, leaving me behind to take a much slower pace.

There is a lack of life within the cemetery. Not just the bodies that are buried beneath its grounds, but nothing grows within. When I turn around to look past the gated entrance, I see green foliage filling the space, but once inside the confines of the cemetery a dull sort of existence begins. Grass grows but it's a muted green plastered to the ground. Some graves have flowers or other precious pieces of kindness left at the foot of the stone, but they have a filtered and foggy appearance.

I wander over to one grave, smaller than most—only about the size of my outstretched hand—but the words are clearly sketched. It's new, surrounded by trampled dirt, grass yet to be grown. The death year on the grave is 1732.

"Garren?" I call out, a sense of panic growing within me. It can't have been that long. When I left it was 1348.

Garren comes to my aid at once, looking over my shoulder. I can hear his breath at my neck, but he doesn't speak like I wish he would. Instead he just stares, unable to see what my gaze has captured.

"What is it?" he asks.

I shake my head, a rumbling choking me from the inside out. My finger quivers as I point to the four digits that tell the year this stranger died.

"That's more than one hundred years," I say, my voice weak.

Garren doesn't say anything. This information is not news to him. Of course he knew how long it has really been, but he didn't tell me.

I do the math in my head, taking my time with the numbers. Over and over I check my work, so sure that the answer I have can't be true—three hundred and eighty-four years. For three hundred and eighty-four years I was gone.

I turn from the grave to face Garren, but he doesn't see me. He looks down at the grave in shame, caught in the lie he's been feeding me. Repeatedly.

"That's almost four hundred years, Garren," I say. My hands still tremble at my sides and when he doesn't look at me, I want to hurt him like he has hurt me. He lied. "Why didn't you tell me?" And when the words come, I realize I'm screaming.

"I didn't want to hurt you. It doesn't matter how much time has passed," he says, his eyes finally leaving the grave but resting instead on the bare dirt patches of ground scattered with grass.

"Of course it matters! My brother is dead, has been dead, and you think the amount of time that has passed doesn't matter?" Breaths become heated and strong and I feel that, if I were still human, my skin would have the red undertone it always sported when I argued with Mama or Papa.

"You'll learn, Luna, that when so much time has passed, it all becomes the same. It doesn't matter if the ones you loved died yesterday or hundreds of years ago, because the pain still exists. It just fades and ebbs as you grow used to its company. You learn to hide yourself from the world to lessen the pain."

My hand crosses his face so quickly I'm not even aware of my actions. We are monsters together, unable to feel anything. A sharp slap sounds from the contact between his cheek and my hand, but the sound is the only thing that tells us that I had hit him. My palm should burn with pain, but it doesn't. His cheek should bear a red outline, but of course it doesn't.

That's when Garren looks at me. His eyes finally return to my face, and it's as if he's a lost pup, so unsure of the world around him. I wonder what he sees in my eyes. I feel wild and frantic, unable to control the urges that have come over me.

"You told me that it's been one hundred years since the pestilence struck," I say between deep breaths.

"Since the pestilence had last been in the area," he corrects me. "It came back for a time but not nearly as bad as when it struck when our families were alive."

My lip trembles and I know if I were still human, tears would be flowing with merciful grace down my cheeks. My hand comes up to cover my mouth, the shame fully spreading over me as I realize this man is about to witness me falling apart.

"Leave," I say, no longer looking at him.

"But Dondre's grave—"

"Leave!" I say, stronger this time.

I feel Garren's eyes on me, but I refuse to look at him. I wish his cheek bore the mark of my hand, just so I'm sure that this life we live is indeed real and that somehow it matters that we exist in the world.

Garren walks off, leaving me behind in the cemetery, just as I had asked. I hear his steps as he leaves, making a trail of prints in the gravel that doesn't grow green grass. The moment he steps through the gate of the cemetery, I feel alone but lifted. I come to my knees on the ground, the full passage of time falling over me in waves.

I try to fathom it. How it is possible for almost four hundred years to pass and then to simply enter life again, like the act is so simple, so easy to do? But I guess that's the point. It isn't easy to simply enter life again. The world is a body, and I am the virus; the question is whether or not I will be rejected.

Dondre's grave is hidden between rows and columns of abandoned souls. It's deep within the cemetery, so old that no one cares to visit anymore. The stone is nothing more than a thin plate of rock with words carved in its face. Names and dates label the lonely graves, but time has eaten away at the surfaces, making it hard to read the inscriptions.

I pull away dead leaves and rotted plants to reveal the small stone. It is nothing more than a foot long, the most miniscule size possible for a grave. I can barely make out the inscription of the stone: Dondre Leland, 1336-1384.

My legs collapse from underneath me. The ground seems too finite, so strong compared to how I feel. Even though I can't sense touch, I run my fingers over the rough surface of the grave, imagining how the coarse stone may feel against my frail fingers. Dondre's in there somewhere.

I'll never know his life after the pestilence. I will never see his face as more than the twelve-year-old boy I grew up with. He looked like Papa, talked like Papa, but acted like Mama. Where Papa was assertive, Mama was thoughtful. Dondre was a boy who took action with his thoughts. I imagine his life, how he may have looked. I see another version of Papa, but one wiser, sooner to stop and think before speaking or acting—that's what Mama always taught him.

My forehead comes to rest on the grave, waiting to feel something, to know my little brother is here with me.

I wonder if he had forgotten me after a time, or cared whether I lived or died, or if he was relieved by my disappearance. All these years have passed, and it makes me wonder if over the course of time feelings can change. The last thing Dondre had said to me was spoken in malice. I was his damnation. I was the reason death was upon us and even though he couldn't make sense as to why I would have caused the pestilence, he chose to believe it anyway, because that was the only answer he had.

"Baby brother," I say, my words a whisper, "can you forgive me?"

And in my heart I know there is nothing to forgive. I had done nothing, caused none of what was a part of the pestilence, but I felt responsible for something. Dondre believed I caused the death, so his words became my truth. I needed his forgiveness, even though it may be something that cannot be gifted.

"What is it like to have so many years of malice inside you?" Like a fool I wait for an answer that will never come. The cemetery is nothing but the sleeping dead.

"I wish I could give them all back to you, Dondre. All those people the pestilence took, I would give them back if I could."

The words mean nothing and everything. A wind blows from the trees that line the cemetery's perimeter, signaled by wisps of my hair moving. The breeze is at my cheeks, yet it does not affect me. My head is still bowed toward the ground, but I imagine it's like I'm able to breathe. Like there is a freshness, a release, and when I look up I see the sun for the first time and know Dondre is here in spirit.

A smile cuts the corners of my mouth, and I want to be here now, with my brother.

XXXII.

I find Garren not too far off. He sits with his back to me on some boulder outside the cemetery, shaded by scattered trees with overhanging branches. My footsteps are just a trample in a loud world as I approach.

"I found his grave," I say.

Garren massages the palm of his hand but doesn't look at me. His gaze is bowed toward the ground, listening, but not really hearing my voice.

"Garren?" I put out my hand, touching his shoulder, but then too late I realize that, unless he is looking at my hand, he will never know I've touched him.

But he looks up at me when I say his name, and his eyes linger on my hand where it rests on his shoulder. He doesn't shrug me away; he just looks at my hand like my touch is a gift. He places his own fingers over mine.

"I'm sorry I didn't tell you," he says in a tired voice.

That's when I see just how exhausted he is. Time doesn't take a toll on us, but here he sits, looking as if he hasn't slept in days.

I don't say anything. Am I supposed to forgive him? Hundreds of years have passed and he didn't tell me. He lied to me, letting me believe the world wasn't able to pass so freely without me.

"I didn't know how to tell you," he says, still looking at our hands. "I didn't want to hurt you."

He looks at me, his eyes pleading, but I can't find my voice. My lips waver, so eager to make the somber tone of his eyes disappear. We look at each other for a long time, each of us waiting for the other to speak first. Finally I look away, settling next to him on the boulder. Off in the distance an evening bird chirps its song, but here under the trees, the most definite sound is the rustle of leaves in the wind and the soft muffle of our breathing.

"I just ..." I say, but words fail me. A space sits between the two of us and I urge it to disappear. "I don't understand what happened," I say.

I turn to face him, and when I do, I see he is already staring at me.

"You don't have to understand it. You just have to face it," he says.

My breath comes in unsteady rhythms, and I realize this is as close as I will ever come to crying again. There will never be that release I crave from my emotions, just the tease of pain. I close my eyes, wishing I were stronger.

"Luna."

Garren's voice is a soft murmur next to me. When I open my eyes, he smiles at me in a sad way. He looks down, and I follow his gaze. He has cupped my hand in both of his. "It'll be okay," he says.

I stare at our contact and wonder if this is what it means to have someone care for you. His fingers wrap around mine, and even though I can't feel it, I imagine what his warm skin might feel like against my own.

"It will be," I say, looking up at Garren.

He smiles at me again, the light returning to his eyes, making them glow the translucent blue color of the ocean.

I believe my words when I speak them.

"So what do we do now?" I ask. The two of us walk through Marseille, the market in front of us. Stands are set up to the sides, merchants eager to trade their goods for money. Garren takes the lead, smiling and greeting faces I've never seen before. His ease with the world is astounding.

"We live," he says.

My pace is slightly slower than his and I find myself struggling to keep up. Bodies move and stir around us, a constant hustle of people. Voices mingle, and people speak of the latest gossip and complaints about the merchants charging too much.

"Forever?" I ask, dodging bodies and weaving in the market. Garren looks back at me and slows down for me to catch up. He offers his hand to me, smiling. I stare at his palm and long fingers, but I shake my head. If he's bothered by my rejection, he doesn't show it, just gestures for me to walk in front of him.

"The thing about forever is it doesn't last," he says, pushing me forward into the crowd.

"What do you mean?"

He doesn't say anything to me. People I don't know walk by and make a small inclination of respect as they see Garren. Their eyes wander over to me, wondering what lady Garren has found to occupy his time. Suddenly I'm pulled to the side, away from the crowds, stumbling over my own feet. When I look down, I see Garren's hand wrapped around my elbow.

"It means I thought you were gone forever," he says, taking me from the market. Strangers pass and smile, saying a quick hello to Garren before making their own greeting to me, even though they don't know my name.

"I still don't understand what happened to me," I say, my thoughts lingering on the idea of centuries passing without my knowing.

We meet at the edge of a tavern. Shouts can be heard from inside the stone walls, reduced to a muffled murmur of voices, people drunk over ale. When I look at Garren, all expression is gone. His lips lie flat, his hands fall to his side and the glow of his eyes is gone—an iris of nothing but pale gray, a ghost of blue.

"I suppose I don't need to understand it," I say.

Garren nods his head, leaning against the stone wall.

Around us people still pass, but they don't look our way anymore. We are cast to the side, nothing but a familiar shadow.

"You haven't accepted it yet," Garren says abruptly.

His gaze finds me and I feel as if I'm being accused of a crime.

My mind chews on the words. I have to accept what has happened because I'm sure there's no way to change it. Sometimes I wonder if it would have been better to have died along with my family. Succumbing to the Black Death seems so simple now, so final. It seems wrong to have my own death taken from me.

"No," I say, wrapping my arms around my elbows. I fight for some security, but in a world of so little sensation, comfort is lost within the shadows.

"Luna …" he says, his voice choking on a lost emotion. "I'm so sorry." His gaze lifts and bores into me and I want to make it stop.

I want him to stop looking at me like I'm hurt, a lost girl who can't find her way home.

I shake my head, trying to ignore his words. "You had to save your sister," I say. "You loved her."

"But that does not excuse the crimes I've committed against your soul."

I shrink from him. Why does he stay around me if all I cause for him is guilt from his own actions? Both of us have the ability to walk away and start new lives, lives without memories of the horrible things we have seen. I could step away now and pretend to be someone who lives and dies. I could make friends, fall in love, fall into life. But I will always continue on, and any bonds I form will be torn away because forever doesn't extend to mortals. My life would be a life spent alone, and I wonder if that's why Garren clings to me.

But then I think of Lucie and how I was once his only hope of bringing her back. Mystral was using me for her own purposes. And when she couldn't convince me to go to Tiboulain, she let Garren do it, claiming she could make Lucie live again. I was nothing but a pawn. Mystral lied to both of us.

"Why don't you leave?" I ask.

His eyebrows furrow, confusion etched into his forehead. "What do you mean?"

"All these years you have stayed in Marseille, when all that lies here are memories of the past, of what will never be. Why stay?"

His expression softens but never truly disappears.

I watch his thoughts dance over his mind, confusion and questions being put before him.

"I didn't want to leave," he finally says.

"But why?" I say, the tone of my voice on the edge of annoyance—and confusion.

"Because, even though I thought you were lost forever to the moon, part of me always wished you would come back. And I felt responsible for what I had done. I wanted to be there, to help you, when you finally awoke to the world again."

When he speaks it is like he is speaking of Lucie—the way his eyes glow—but it is me. It is my name that crosses his lips.

"Would you like me to leave?" His voice is small when

he says the words.

This time when I look at him, he appears broken, the years alone finally weighing him down. I see the fear of me leaving reflected in his eyes.

"I don't want you to leave," I say, and as the words come I'm astonished by how true they are.

XXXIII.

"Garren!" someone shouts from behind us.

We stop our course through the market to wait for whoever called out his name to catch up with us. Garren turns to look and I follow suit as he guides me.

"Camila," he says, recognizing the woman who finds her way over to us.

I'm surprised by how fast she is able to catch up to us, a large basket in tow.

"I've been looking all over for you!" Camila comes to a stop when she's within arm's length, taking a moment to gain her breath again as graying hair falls in curls around her face. She smiles when she looks at Garren, wrinkles forming around her eyes.

"It's good to see you again," he says, a light laughter filling the air. "This is my friend, Luna. I was just showing her around Marseille."

Camila tucks hair behind her ear, noticing me for the first time. She adjusts the basket in her hands, nodding to me with a slight bow of respect. "Very well, Luna," she says with a smile. Her gaze lingers on my eyes, but she doesn't let her demeanor change.

I mirror the gesture and notice how age has taken its toll

on Camila. Her body is twisted and bent forward, her eyes a dim shade of green in the sun. Skin sags around her figure, but despite all this her spirit shines brightly from within.

"I wanted to bring you bread, Garren—as a token of my appreciation." She fumbles with the basket in her hands, uncovering it to reveal a large loaf of risen bread. My mouth waters at the sight, noting the value—what my family would have done for risen bread.

"I told you it was not necessary," Garren says quickly, holding up his palms in defense.

Camila frowns for a moment, but she picks up the bread anyway. "Give an old woman peace of mind knowing you are well fed."

He surrenders, a small smile rippling across his cheeks. She wraps a cloth around the bread before handing it over, leaving the basket empty.

"Thank you," he says.

"No, thank you for working my fields. I don't know what I would have done without you. I can't tend to my fields like I used to. I'll have to sell it soon." She says the words, saddened by the betrayal age has given her body. But then she comes forward suddenly, placing a hand on my shoulder. "He's a good man, Luna. He'll teach you this city well."

My head snaps up when she speaks to me. Her words are almost foreign, hard to comprehend. When she finishes talking, my eyes linger on her hand on my shoulder and the unfeeling contact frustrates me. I see her fingers skimming my clothing, but the moment is lost to me—no matter how hard I try, there is no sensation.

Camila lets her hand fall away, self-conscious of something. When I look at her again, her lips are in a fine line, her arms limp at her sides. "I'm sorry," she says quietly, taking a backward step from the two of us. "Thank you again, Garren." And she turns to leave.

Next to me all I hear is the faint rustle of fabric as Garren opens his coat to place the bread into one of the hidden pockets within. The next thing I'm aware of is being pulled away again, and when I look Garren's hand is clasped firmly around mine.

"Why do you help her?" I ask, trailing behind but keeping up a steady pace.

"There's no sin for acting with kindness—especially if you are given forever."

His words are simple, yet hurried, like this subject isn't what he wishes to speak about. I hush up and follow him like an obedient child who's trying with all her might to not cause trouble.

We don't rush through the market; we just pass through, like any other person, except we don't gawk at the displays. The farther we go, the more secluded we become, until the market ends. All that is left is a sporadic group of commoners. In the distance is the beach, our small wooden boat pulled up on the sand.

"Garren?" I say, pulling back on his hand to show him I

want to slow our pace.

He follows my lead but doesn't turn to look at me. Beats pass and our silence continues. We stumble forward, walking slowly, our footsteps a dying rhythm until I stop altogether. Garren drops my hand.

"Do you ever get used to it? Never being able to feel anything?" I wrap my arms around myself, cupping my elbows, like I would if I were cold—but of course I'm not. The wind blows but I never shiver.

Garren turns. He runs his hand over his face, like he could wipe away his exhaustion. He comes closer to me, releasing a deep breath.

I look away, breathing in my own universe, trying to understand it all. I understand I wouldn't feel his touch, but it still hits me like it's something new I've discovered.

"I don't like it, Garren," I say, closing my eyes. I imagine how my life had been once before—how I could feel the hurt of a leather whip against my skin. Painful as it was, it was real. But this, whatever *this* is, is not real. Nothing tells me that I'm standing here. I don't know if I'm living anymore.

"I know," he says.

I lift my chin and open my eyes to Garren's hands cradling my face. His fingers stroke the skin I can't feel, easing me into something I don't believe in—life. His eyes are so kind, so full. I want to fall into them and hope he can take this all away.

He leans forward and a fear awakens within me. I don't

want this. I don't want him to touch me and have it mean nothing. But he does it anyway. His lips come to my forehead, and I pretend I can feel it—so I can have this moment, a moment I never had as a human.

"I know," he says again, a murmur against my skin.

I close my eyes, trying to remember the touch of skin between two persons. At the time it seemed so unimportant. A shake of a hand, a brush against the shoulder, but now it means so much more than that.

His lips linger on my forehead, and I imagine what it would be like to feel the warmth of someone else's skin against my own. How radiant it must be. The fantasy grows and takes shape, until I convince myself of its truth.

I live a beautiful lie—pretending the moment is real.

Garren pushes the rowboat through the grains of sand. I stand at the edge of the beach, where the sand meets the rocky gravel and becomes nothing more than the usual piece of land.

"Why are we leaving?" I ask, the wind blowing between my breaths.

The small wooden boat touches water; it floats and sways with the rhythm of the ocean waves. I watch as it radiates with the life of the ocean.

He lets it drift an arm's length away before tugging the rope attached to the bow.

"Isn't that what you wanted?"

I don't speak as I feel the weight of Marseille gain on me. Even with the city to my back I feel it overwhelming me, seeking attention I refuse to give.

"We can stay," he says, pulling the rope taut. The small vessel floats toward the beach again until it meets with the sandy bottom of the shore, unable to come any farther until Garren tugs with more strength.

"No," I say quickly.

His hands stop, loosening his hold on the rope. Waves break and the boat floats on the ocean again where it sways with a cadence only nature possesses.

"Then we'll be leaving now?" he asks.

I nod and join him. He doesn't say anything else or question why I must leave; he just lets me be. A thankfulness lies within our silence, and neither of us dares to disrupt it. He tugs the rope and brings it to a steady hold where the water breaks, gesturing for me to step in. I pull up the hem of my skirts, stepping over the water and into the rounded bottom of the boat. I settle on one of the two benches and wait for the shift and sway that happens when another person steps in, but it never comes.

"What are you doing?" I ask.

Garren opens the lapel of his coat and fishes something out—the bread wrapped in cloth that Camila gave him.

"I almost forgot that we don't need this," he says, unwrapping the bread from its fine cloth. The bread is still fresh looking, and I imagine the days I walked to the market alone, savoring how magnificent fresh bread like that would smell, yet too poor to afford leavened bread. And that's when it hits me—there is no scent.

"May I?" I ask, turning up my palms toward him. His gaze locks on mine for a long moment, questioning, but finally he places the bread in my care.

The cloth is nothing to me. There is no soft contact, but I have begun to grow used to the lack of feeling. What disturbs me now is yet another of my senses is disconnected. I hold the bread in my hands and bring it close to my face, begging my nose to pick up some indication of smell.

"Nothing," I say. Hope leaves me as I drop my hand and lower the bread.

Garren reaches to take it from my hands, wrapping it in the cloth once again.

"I'll be right back," he says quietly before taking brisk strides along the beach.

It seems like a long time before he returns, but when he does, he steps silently into the boat. The motion wakes me from my own private world of thought. Garren makes soft muffled sounds in the bench across from me, working the oars as we glide through the water.

"We can't feel or smell anything, can we?" My question must feel like a blunt jab to Garren. When I look at him, his face is laden and worn. His eyes close as he takes a deep breath, and when he exhales I watch as tension radiates off his skin.

"No," he says.

"Touch, smell, it's all lost to us," I say, running the

information in my mind. "But we're here. We're like ghosts—immortal in the most common sense—but people can touch us. They can hear us and see us, but we can't feel them. We are part of their world, but they aren't a part of ours."

Garren doesn't speak. His arms run in circles, bringing the oars down over the surface of the water as we skim across the ocean waves.

"Why tease with a world we cannot be a part of?" I ask. My voice is lost over the roar of waves and ocean wind, but I know Garren has heard me. I know it because as soon as the words release, I see a sadness form that most people would crumble under.

"I don't know, Luna. That's just the way it is," he says.

I watch his movements—the firm push and pull he makes as he forces the oars to break the water's surface. We stream over the ocean in slow motion, the island of Tiboulain seeming frighteningly far away.

"What did you do with the bread?"

Garren raises his head when he looks at me, a befuddled look coming over his eyes.

"What?"

"The bread. You said we wouldn't need it."

A small recognition occurs and he returns his focus to the task of dragging the boat over the ocean. "We don't need to eat, so I gave it to the first beggar I could find."

The information isn't news. It makes sense in a cruel way. Why bother eating something if you don't need its nourishment? We are eternal beings. Food and sustenance are nothing but a memory.

"Okay," is the only word I can mutter.

XXXIV.

I stand at the edge of Tiboulain's pool, the water reflecting my image, a perfect mirror. Everything seems so still, so pure, but when I lift my head to look elsewhere, I'm reminded how the world has changed without me.

"Luna?"

Garren's voice breaks the silence. Around us the sun sets—another end to another day. Colors light the sky, the horizon on fire with brilliancy. Every cloud and stream of air declares its unique beauty, but despite this I can't find it in myself to look at Garren.

"What happened?"

His voice invades me. I wrap frail arms around my body, wanting to shrink away so he may forget I'm here. But I feel his gaze on my back as he stands watching.

"How can you be a part of a world that so readily rejects you?" I ask. I want to be angry. I want my voice to carry the cadence that comes with sharp emotions, but when I speak I'm nothing but a small element in the backdrop.

"Because I have no other choice. It's just how it is."

"But what if it doesn't have to be that way!" I shout, my words more certain than ever. I turn to face him, spinning until I see his face. His body is only an arm's length away, but I still find myself shouting, as if the roar of waves might overpower my voice. "Wouldn't you change it, if you could?" I feel as if I'm begging, like my knees might give out due to weariness, and I wonder if that's possible for someone like me.

Whatever we are—the eternal beings who don't have all five senses—can we be exhausted? We don't need to sleep, eat, or breathe. Everything we operate from comes from habits of our old and familiar human life. There is no requirement for sleep now, but as I stand in front of Garren I feel as if my head will spin until my mind finds rest in the night.

"We don't have a choice, Luna," Garren says simply.

His face is placid when he talks. It makes me want to stride the small distance between us and shake him until he understands my words.

"How can you know that?" I ask, but my voice becomes desperate. Any energy of hope dies off in a quick fury. I look at him with pitiful eyes and wonder why he doesn't understand.

"I'm sorry, Luna," he says.

"My name is Aida," I tell him.

Garren steps forward, arms reaching out to console me, but I step away, my feet slipping against the rocky surface of the island.

I stagger backward and lose my balance the instant my right foot doesn't find flat ground. A yelp escapes my airways, and Garren jumps forward to catch me. His arm is coiled around me, both hovering over the edge of the pool of water. When I look down my heel is soaked in the water. I push Garren away, stepping out of the water and away from the edge.

"Luna—"

"Don't call me that," I say, cutting him off before he can say anything else. "I'm not the moon." I hold my hand between us and lower myself to the ground. Everything inside me screams for rest. My head spins with more thoughts to put into action, and when I do lift my head, images blur together until it's all just one large abstract painting.

"Are you okay?"

I bring my knees to my chest, wrapping my arms around myself. Tiboulain sways around me and I want to lie down until it all just falls away. Terror and panic rise in me, but I force myself to breathe, to stop thinking, but to still breathe.

"Leave," I say, my voice a thin sound.

"But—"

I hear his footsteps as he walks toward me, but I shake my head in protest. He stops and an exhale comes from within me. He doesn't leave, but he also doesn't come closer. Around me the world hovers on the border of calm until I'm able to make out the lines and images again. I close my eyes and rest my head against my knees, feeling a small comfort grow from the containment I've been able to create.

"Please," I whisper.

There's no reply. I wait for the sound of footsteps, for some remark, but neither ever comes. I lift my head slowly, but when I look up Garren isn't here and a frown forms on my lips. I'm left wondering just how long ago he had abandoned me.

The moon reflects its beauty on the water in the night. The sky is bright in the full moon's glow, making everything a magical hue. The world seems so still and silent. A hush of water slaps against the shore, the wind off the ocean has disappeared to nothing more than a whisper of hair against my cheek.

I dip my finger in the smooth pool of water and watch as the ripples cascade across the surface, echoing to the other side. I sink my hand lower, watching as it disappears beneath the surface, my skin taking on a white tone under the moon's shadow.

With one fluid movement I bring my hand to my face, cupping water within my palm. I sip at the liquid, shocked by the sheer nothingness that accompanies it. There's no sensation as the water slides across my lips and down my throat; the lack of touch makes me mourn something I thought impossible to lose.

"Why tease us?" I look up to the moon that floats in the sky and wonder what it is it wants from me.

"The world isn't trying to torment us."

My head whips around to the familiar voice and I see Garren just behind me. He doesn't move to come closer as he stares at me, and even though I feel as if I've been invaded, I don't want him to leave me again.

"I thought you had gone," I tell him. I pick myself off the ground and brush away dirt from my skirt, patting away at my sleeves, suddenly aware of the fact that the new clothing I had been gifted with has already become worn.

"No," he says in a low voice. "I would return to Marseille, where I've found a residence for the time being, but I didn't want to leave you on your own and—and it appeared you didn't want to stay within the city."

"Because I'm a ghost, Garren. They may see me, touch me, but to me, I'm nothing more than a ghost."

He nods, accepting my words as they are. I watch him and I think he may agree. Surely he must agree. We live the same life, such as it is. All that time I had been trapped by the moon within the pool, Garren had been forced to live his eternal life alone—I find myself lucky to have him.

"How would you prefer to live an eternal life?" he asks, still standing so far away.

His brows furrow in some thought he isn't inviting me to experience, leaving me only to wonder what he may be considering.

"You know I wouldn't want this," I say quickly, and he laughs—just a small chuckle of amusement.

"But, if you had to live it, if you could choose, how would you live it?"

And this time when he speaks, there is a smile in his eyes. Some of the seriousness has melted away into the lines of his face.

I let the words sink in, imagining how I might fashion it, were I able to choose. "If I had to live forever, I would want to experience it all. The touches, the smells, the tastes of what could be an eternal bliss. I would want to hold a baby and feel the softest skin that only comes with an infant, and I'd want to feel them kick when they're upset. I'd want to live fully to know that something matters."

Garren looks at me with wonder, his gaze never leaving me as he walks close to my side. The space between us seems so precious and intimate, but I don't mind as he closes the gap.

"What are we?" I ask. His blue eyes seem to glow in the night and I feel so vulnerable in the darkness, but when Garren takes my hand in his my fears melt away. I want to fight, to run away, and to never let this man touch me again, but I also know he's all I have left in this world, and, as much I don't want to be around him, I feel as if I can't be without him.

"Luna, what we are does not matter."

"But I'm not human—not anymore at least."

"And neither am I," he says, his face so serious in the night. "But you, Luna—you're just a beautiful essence of everything that is good in my life."

He says the words so boldly, as if nothing in the world scares him, and I'm jealous. It only makes me wish that I may someday possess the bravery he holds in his heart.

"I'm not," I say, shaking my head, turning from him.

"You are."

His fingers grip my chin, forcing me to look at him. His gaze is gentle, as he coaxes me toward him and I give in. I allow myself this one moment of rest, to stop fighting and to let matters be, if only for a moment.

"Before you woke up, I was alone, Luna. I talked to strangers every day, and I suppose I even made friends, but they die. A few years is all I'm given until they realize I don't age and I have to move to another place to live until they too see my eternal grace. But you, Luna, I've been waiting for you to wake up every day. I've been waiting for you to come to me, and when I saw you, I wasn't sure it was you. You seemed so different, so sure of yourself, yet so lost within the world. You were Aida de Luna, the one who gifts eternity when death was a normality."

His fingers drop from my chin and I can't help but look down. When he speaks of me, it is as if he worships my being and I don't understand why.

"Luna," he says firmly.

I look at him again and realize his hands are wrapped around the tops of my arms. His gaze is so eager, but I can't find it within myself to look at him. Instead my eyes drift to his hands. I watch his touch, but I can't feel it, and it eats away at me like maggots in rotting flesh.

"I can't feel you," I say, my voice lingering within a cry that will never produce tears.

Something changes in Garren and he drops his arms to his sides, and although I can't feel his touch, there is a sting in his rejection.

"You can change it." And when he says the words, they are so different—so unemotional—that I want to run away.

"How?" I ask.

"You'll never regain the lost senses, but you can fully become the ghost you speak of, if you so desire. No human will see you, hear you, touch you, but it may make living this life easier—you would be separate from the world."

I imagine a life in the shadows, no one ever seeing my face again. No one will ever remember me, but I also won't be able to influence the lives of those around me.

So I'll be a ghost, the beautiful essence Garren sees. I'm not meant to be seen.

"Embrace the moon," he says, gesturing to the pool of water at my back.

I turn and watch the white glow from the reflection of the moon.

"Will you still see me?" I ask.

"I'm not human."

I face him again and try to read what his voice doesn't convey, but his expression is so neutral, so plain. Part of me feels that if I do this I am somehow hurting him, but I don't understand how.

"Do what will make you happy," Garren says.

With strong legs I walk away and find the edge of the pool. At my feet the rocks along the edge drop into the water that lingers so deep in this island. I turn to face Garren to see if he approves, and when I do I see a small smile cross his lips, but it seems forced. A final deep breath builds within me, and I take off the leather shoes Garren had given me, exposing my bare feet. I feel foolish when I look up to the moon as if it were a god, and even more foolish as I dive into the water.

I drift through seamlessly and when I open my eyes the world around me is magnified by the dark liquid. The stone-lined pool cocoons me in a final embrace, a wall around me. The moon looks down and I ask for it to take away the pain. I ask the moon to hide me from the world. To give me a gift within a curse, a gift that will allow me to only exist spiritually.

I want to become an essence. A beautiful, exquisite essence.

XXXV.

I feel as if I'm falling out of the water. Gravity no longer obeys; the world spins and I'm being thrown against the ground like an old rag. My body slumps into the strange contours of the sand and stone on this island, my arms held over my head like in worship, legs twisted around each other, feet still kissing the edge of the water. As a human I'd be suffering, but here I am— everything that's nothing.

My wet clothing clings to my body, capturing me in a way that restricts my movement. Exhaustion engulfs me, haunts me, eats away at me from the inside out until I surrender and let the lids of my eyes seek darkness.

"Luna."

Garren.

I don't look for him; I don't even lift my head or move my body in response as my soaked clothing creates a personal vise. But he comes to me still. My body moves; legs turn, arms wrap around themselves and I know he's holding me. I've been cocooned within myself like an infant and I imagine Garren holding me close, like I am something more precious than what I believe.

Light comes with the morning. It ignites, sets fire, and reminds the world that today is another day. A new start. Another beginning.

I find it odd that we don't need sleep, yet we can still do so, if we choose. When my eyes finally open, I crawl away. I'm shocked by the simple idea that even ghosts can achieve such human habits. Beside me Garren lies with arms folded inward, asleep on the ground. He rests so innocently, trapped inside a perfect dream, only because it is not the reality that we have to face.

I seat myself farther away and let the sun shine at my back. My clothing flutters in the wind, beating against my legs, reminding me that I am here. I watch Garren and am jealous of his rest. He looks different in his sleep. His dark curls are matted to his head in short tendrils, and even in the dull morning light his skin seems to glow with a freshness. I watch as his chest continues in its steady rise and fall and wonder why it is we still breathe in the oxygen of the world when we no longer need it.

"Habit," I answer, inhaling deep as if I could taste the air.

Garren stirs, perhaps awoken by my voice, but doesn't open his eyes. His body shifts and he turns to face me.

"Garren?" I say quietly.

For a moment I get no response, but then a moment later he opens his eyes to me.

"Luna," he says, sleep still deep in his voice. He comes to the present and lifts himself off the ground and into a sitting position that mirrors my own.

"We sleep," I say.

He looks at me and sees the questions in my eyes.

Why do we sleep? Why do we sleep when we do not need it? Why do we breathe when we do not need to?

"Yes," he says. "It is all part of our human memory working for us, I suppose."

"After all these years?"

He shrugs. "After all these years."

I watch him. I'm not sure if I understand why exactly, but I do. I stare as his eyes fully awaken and his face opens into a smile as the sunrise's array of colors shine over his skin. He's in front of me, and I watch when he opens his mouth as if he might speak, but no sounds come at first.

"Luna."

I give him my undivided attention, and when I do he freezes as if my gaze pierces him. For the first time in a long time I remember the power my gaze holds. I remember how my silver-white irises had marked me as some sort of evil, which I never asked to be, and I realize that I'm still a monster. I look down, shame taking over me, and concentrate on the contour of my fingers. How my palms are printed and drawn with thin lines, sketches within my hands, small and nimble.

"I want you to be happy."

I lift my face and I see Garren's fingers wrapping lightly against my chin once more, cradling me.

"I'm sorry I brought this upon you, but I'm willing to do

anything to make this eternity something good for you."

"Am I a monster?"

He seems shocked by my question. His fingers almost drop from my chin, and even though I can't feel his skin against mine, the thought of losing contact with him frightens me.

"Why are you a monster?"

"All my life my eyes have been a sign to everyone that I was something to be feared, to be extinguished. I was less than human." And I can't help but remember how Dondre couldn't even bring himself to forgive me. How Mama might have died with Papa telling her how I was somehow to blame for the pestilence. How I loved so many without ever being loved back, because I was perceived as a witch.

"You are no monster," Garren tells me.

"I don't want them to see me," I say, but the words are nothing more than a whisper. Yet he hears me and nods to accept my thoughts as they are; he doesn't try to change them. "I don't want them to look at me anymore."

"I know," he says. "I don't think they'll see you now."

"What do you mean?"

He smiles, drops his hand from my chin to brush his fingers against my cheek. Instead of feeling the tingle of his touch, I watch the gesture from the corners of my eyes, skimming my gaze back to his face to see the look of nurture and care etched into his features.

"Remember the moon? And how it can give you gifts?" he says, and I smile.

There's a beautiful thing in having the ability to walk through a crowd and not be interrupted. At first I don't even believe it's really happening, but the farther I walk the surer I am of the simple fact that even if I step in front of someone, they are oblivious to my existence.

The streets of Marseille open and flood in front of me, but for once I'm disconnected. Faces pass and conversations make waste in the air, all while I stand, watching.

"Garren, they can't see me," I say, a thrill forming inside me. I turn to find Garren, but he stands off to the side like he is hiding. His face reveals surprise, like maybe he himself didn't believe the change would actually occur, that the moon would gift me something when it had taken so much.

"I see," he says, a smile reaching his lips, but his voice holds another emotion entirely. A man walks by, just inches from Garren, and I watch as Garren steps back so the man doesn't stumble into him.

"Garren?"

He looks up at me and I see he is hiding something, but he smiles anyway. In a single breath of air I swear my eyes trick me. A young girl comes running down the street, but when she reaches Garren, she doesn't see him. Instead she runs straight through him as if he didn't exist. I stare at Garren, waiting to see if he will blow away like dust, but his image never wavers.

And it's like a mask has just left his face. The smile he

once held disappears as he realizes what has happened—every fiber of his face reads certain and utter shock.

"Garren?" I say again, this time with a small shrill hinting at the edges of my voice. And I realize that the moon has given Garren the same gift given to me and I'm not sure if this is a good thing.

XXXVI.

Garren brings me to his home. It's nothing like the cruck houses I had known growing up, made only of simple things like clay and straw. What stands before me is something I'd imagine nobles possessing—a miniature castle. Four stone walls with a thatched roof that looks like it could stand for years to come. This is where he has lived while waiting for me to awaken.

We walk in silence over the threshold and inside I'm greeted with a small touch of home. Wooden furniture is scattered across the room but the most surprising thing is the stone walls within the building that divide the space. In my human memory this is nothing we ever had. Cooking and sleeping had always been within the one room; privacy was a dream, not a reality.

"So it worked," Garren says, sitting down on a chair that is upholstered with a thick and worn fabric.

His words remind me. How a girl walked through Garren's body like he was nothing. How I was the one who took away his physical being because I was both selfish and fearful.

"I ..." I start, but I don't know what to say. Instead I just stand within this room, so unsure of everything around me.

"Sit," Garren says, holding out his hand to the chair across from him.

It is like his, covered in cloth, but wider, like it could seat two.

"Please, sit."

And I don't understand why his voice is so kind to me when all I've done is take away his presence in the world.

I gather myself and find peace in the seat. "How long have you lived here?" I ask.

"Only a few years," he says. "I move once people notice the lack of years on my face, but I never travel too far."

I look around the room and see that, although the house is furnished, nothing says he has really lived in the home: no trinkets possessing memories, no stains on the floor, no marks on the wall when he moved things because he grew bored of the view. This is a place to wake up, to sleep, to reside, and nothing more.

"I'm sorry," I say.

His brow furrows. "Why is that?"

"I took you from this. From your life." I point to the inside of his home, but he doesn't follow my gaze. Instead I hear him move, and when I look he has come to sit beside me. Our knees touch and his body is angled toward mine—I let the moment last.

"Luna, I would have had to leave soon anyway," he says, his voice gentle. I'm afraid to see his kind eyes.

"I didn't want people to see me, Garren. I didn't know, by offering myself to the moon again that I would take your physical body from you also. You had friends, people you knew.

Now you will be gone to them."

He doesn't say anything for a long time and I wonder if he's finally hearing me; if he's listening to my words and realizing that I'm right and how he should leave. And I'm happy for him because I feel as if I'll never deserve him. But the thought—the simple thought of him leaving—it bites at me and begs to disappear so it can't haunt my mind any further.

"Luna," he says, but he isn't angry.

I dare a look and his face is so close. My gaze drifts and I see he is holding my hand in a gentle cradle.

"I'm the one who took you away. And for that I'm sorry."

He looks at me, and I don't understand what he sees because I've never had someone look at me like this before. His eyes don't flicker away or waver. He just stares into me and I can't find myself looking away.

His hand comes to my face and I'm aware of his touch as his lips meet mine. I close my eyes and I swear that I feel his skin against mine even though neither of us are human. Warmth builds between us, and for a second I believe we are something again, something alive and bursting, just waiting to be awakened.

The sensation leaves and when I open my eyes, I see Garren's face still just a breath away. His forehead rests against my own and I hear his small breaths, so close to me. His eyes remain closed. We are spirits floating away into something beautiful. We are creating our own world of sense and allure because we are no longer human.

"I know what we are," I say in a breath.

Garren opens his eyes, his expression tentative as to what I have to say. His eyes are so full of life that I wonder how I had ever thought we were anything less than alive.

"We are spirits. Not ghosts, but something else," I say, but my words are fumbling.

He smiles in the smallest, most innocent way, and it's like our minds are connected.

"Something that exists spiritually but not physically? Wouldn't that be a ghost?" he says, a hint of laughter in his voice.

"No," I say, dismissing the ghosts, dismissing a subject that everyone only believes has the power to haunt. "An *Essence*."

This time when he smiles, it isn't something timid. It is full and lively, and I want to remember this moment forever because I know it will never last an eternity like our lives might.

"A beautiful essence of everything that is beautiful in my life?" he asks, mimicking the words he had said to me once before.

"An Essence," I say. "Yes, that's what I'd call it."

XXXVII.

I stand in the middle of the market and wait. Voices sing, and gossip travels, but I'm always here. A little girl clings to a young woman's skirt, and when I look closer I see small tears dripping down her cheek—oh, how such a simple act is taken for granted by humans.

People rush by without any awareness of my presence. I stand in front of a merchant, and it doesn't matter if I glare at him; he will never see me. My silver eyes will never threaten another person again—including me. I'm no longer a monster to the world. I am something different. An Essence, we call it.

The world is dancing around me and all I'm left to do is observe. A husky man plows through my body and I'm amazed by the simple fact that I don't feel a thing. I don't lose my footing or even feel a tickle of pressure. For a split moment this man and I were one. It's an amazing feat—it's quite frightening to think about really.

Far off in the corner somewhere I see Garren come into view. I find my way over to him, and when I do his face is detached and oddly neutral. He smiles at me when I come closer, but it looks like a mask, out of place.

"Okay," he says. He comes to grip my hand and walk me from the marketplace. He swerves and dodges crowds of people even though their bodies don't affect us.

"What did you write?"

Though Garren had to move and restart his life every few years to keep up the act of being human, he had made friends each time—people who cared just enough to wonder what had happened to Garren when he disappeared physically from their lives. His plan had been to write a note to explain his absence.

"I said that I was leaving," he says simply.

We continue to walk at a brisk pace, never slowing, but never seeming to come closer to the beach that will bring us to the open waters.

"What about your home?" I had only been in Garren's house once, but it had been so much more than I had known growing up in my family's cruck house. Garren's was large enough for a family, maybe even two. It seemed like a waste to leave such lavishness behind, but I knew that if Garren left his human life behind, his home would have to be left behind also.

"I mailed a note to a good friend. I told him that he could have my home, as long as he made good use of it."

"Do you think he will?"

"Yes," Garren says.

Our pace finally slows as the sandy beach finds the bottoms of our feet. I watch the grains push away under my soles, and for a moment I'm tempted to take off my leather shoes to feel the sand between my toes, until I remember what it means to be an Essence and push away the thoughts with a new eagerness that I hadn't known before.

He drops my hand to fetch the boat. It seems every time I look at it, the old wood is more worn. The bottom is rotting, becoming soft and pliable. Garren pushes the boat into the water and I watch as it floats calmly on the surface, swaying in small motions against the waves. I stand by it, the wind blowing hair into my face, detangling it from the braid that rests over my chest.

"My friend," Garren says, "he was homeless most of the time. Just begging on the streets or at the market. I used to give him jobs so I could pay him somehow. Recently he took residence as a worker for some nobleman, but the work was unkind. I'm hoping now he won't have to live there."

"That's very kind of you," I say.

He turns to me. One of his feet sinks into the salty water while the other rests on the dry sand of the beach. He offers his hand to me while holding the boat steady.

With a sure grip he takes my hand and pulls me toward him. Once I'm closer he lets go of my hand, only to wrap his arm around my torso and lift me off the ground. For a moment my feet don't touch the sand, and I'm being held close to Garren. Then the next second his grip is gone and I'm standing in the boat.

All this happens, every touch with him happens, and even though I can't feel him or know he's really there, it's like I don't need anything physical anymore—because he holds my hand and I know he's here. I look at his skin and I can't feel the heat of it, but at the same time I feel his Essence here with me.

Garren joins me in the rowboat and grips the oars to take us from the beach. We float away slowly, every now and then the waves urging us to the shore again, but then Garren steers us from the land.

"Are we coming back?" I ask. We hadn't made a plan. We have the rest of eternity and we don't know what to do with ourselves. The only thing we know is that Garren has to disappear from the human life he had created. We are just spirits in this world, and we cannot bother the physical life that inhibits this place. Marseille is grand in its appeal even as we float away. Life radiates off the shore and leaves memories that are a permanent part of life.

Garren doesn't pause in his attempts to carry us away. His arms continue in their circling motions, dragging the oars through the ocean waters. "We'll be back," he tells me. But that's all he says. Neither of us speaks of what eternity will be like.

The waves push and pull us into motion and Garren turns as if he hears something. He stops suddenly, holding up the oars in the air mid-row.

"Luna."

"What?" I ask, but he doesn't look at me.

His eyes are watching something behind him and I try to see what he's looking at. Tiboulain rests easy like it always has, but now a large ship has made port on one of its rocky shores. The vessel has sails that reach high into the sky, and when I look close enough there are dozens of crates stacked atop each other on the deck. There is movement on the ship as Garren and I watch figures unload a ramp, extending from the ship to the island.

"Luna." Garren says my name again, this time more urgently. Something has snapped into place and suddenly he comes to life, rowing us to Tiboulain as fast as he can.

"What will we do?" I ask.

"We have to cover the pool in the center of Tiboulain."

"But why?" I ask.

"Because it is the reason you and I are alive today, and will be alive every day after."

"But ..." I say, his words confusing me. I thought Garren and I were the only ones, *could* be the only ones. "Others can become an Essence?"

Garren continues to row and I see frustration grow within him. He doesn't ignore me; he looks and pleads with me with his eyes, but he never slows his pace to reach Tiboulain.

"Yes," he says. His eyes dart around, exchanging glances between the ship docked on Tiboulain and me. "Anyone who touches the water can be trapped in eternity."

XXXVIII.

We steer our way around the island, doing our best to keep our vessel out of sight. Although Garren and I are invisible, our small vessel is not. As we near I realize that the large ship belongs to some merchants, the bow full of goods. The only people on it are its crew to guide the vessel from one location to the next. It ships goods, nothing more, so why is it here on this uninhabited island?

Garren jumps from our small rowboat that docks on the opposite side of the island from the merchant's ship. Ocean water splashes around me, and I watch as Garren makes frantic motions to pull the wooden rowboat to the rocky beach. The water comes to his waist, and, even though I know he can't feel the cold, part of me has to bite my tongue as I watch him drag us through the bitter ocean water. Finally the bottom of the boat glides against land and I jump out, the water making my thick skirts cling to my legs, only working to slow me down.

"What will we do?" I ask. I struggle to follow Garren even though he has to tow a boat by a rope. Once the boat is upon land he releases the rope tied to the boat and lets it drop to the ground as if it's nothing.

"We hide the pool. Cover it, bury it, whatever it takes to keep it hidden from others."

"Why are they here? They're merchants. They should be bringing their goods to Marseille, not stopping at an island so small you can view its entire perimeter in one glance."

I try my best to keep up with Garren, but I'm always a few steps behind, trying to navigate the rough terrain of Tiboulain. I'm watching the ground to find my footing rather than watching what Garren is doing. Every time I glance at him, he is farther away.

"They won't be here long," Garren shouts from ahead. "They sometimes explore the islands for anything they deem useful. They've done it in the past when you were still in the water. I would cover the pool with a boulder so they wouldn't find you, but as soon as they left I would uncover the pool in case you woke up."

His voice grows farther away and I have to strain to hear him. When I look up I only see an outline of Garren's body. I slow my pace, growing aggravated with myself. My breaths come quickly, like they had at times when I was human, but I don't feel a heartbeat in my chest. I hold my fingers to my neck and there's no pulse, yet I fatigue as if human. And even though my limbs don't ache, I can't find it in myself to push farther.

Too much time has passed when I come across the pool of water. Garren is already working and straining to push a large boulder—almost twice the diameter of the pool—over the opening before the men of the ship notice anything here on the island.

"Garren," I say, but he doesn't hear me. His focus is

solely on the task at hand. I watch as he pushes, strains, and tries so hard to do something that seems impossible. But the boulder moves across the ground and rolls over the lip of the pool.

"You need to leave, Luna," he says. A hint of urgency is in his voice. He abandons the boulder and comes to me. "I don't want you here, in case something happens."

"Garren ..." I look at his eyes and they stare into me and plead with my soul to understand whatever danger he speaks of. I watch as his hand cups my cheek and I close my eyes, begging myself to feel this moment, to feel the touch of his skin.

"I need you to be safe," he tells me.

I open my eyes again and look at him. His eyes are glassy even though we can't cry; we are so close our breaths mingle.

"Please leave," he says.

The words echo—the same words I have spoken to him—and they sting. I feel myself pull away, though he is the only person I have ever grown close to. I know he is protecting me, but I feel a small burn of rejection all the same.

I push his hand from my cheek and drop my gaze, no longer wanting to see him but also not wanting him to realize how much his simple words have hurt me. When I try to leave he doesn't let me. His hand grips my own, and I tug away with a gentle and tired motion, only to give up a few seconds later. I'm a child in his arms, waiting for something.

"Luna," he says.

I can feel myself being pulled closer to him and I hate it.

I hate that he has control over me and that I'm weak enough to concede to him.

"Look at me."

His hand clutches my arm close to him, but his other hand comes to guide my face, tilting my chin, so I have no choice but to look him in the eye.

"What?" I say, but my voice is so defeated. There is a definite broken note in my word and I know he has heard it. As soon as I speak he changes, becomes softer as all tension in his body leaves.

"I have to stay here and make sure they don't uncover the boulder."

For the first time I realize how vulnerable we are out here. Garren glances behind me, where the merchant's ship is docked.

"But you need to run. They can't see you or me, remember? We're just ghosts to them—an Essence. But even those who exist only spiritually can be hurt."

"What do you mean?"

But he doesn't let me speak. Instead he tugs my arm once more to close the small space between us. His lips caress mine in a kiss as I close my eyes, and there it is again—a small tingle of heat, a sense that tells me I'm here in this world even when my form is not. I'm swallowed by the realization and even though I don't understand it, I let it consume me.

Garren pulls back too soon, looking at me with an ever-building urgency as the large ship sends crewmembers to our side of the island. "Please, do this for me," he says.

He drops his fingers from my cheek and pulls my hand to his mouth to kiss the top of my palm, curling my fingers in as he releases me.

I shrink away, blinded by confusion and the need to be near him. I'm disoriented as I retreat from Garren, my gaze never wanting to leave his, but agreeing to his words and desires anyway.

"I will," I tell him, whimpering away.

XXXIX.

I watch from a short distance as men explore Tiboulain. Their voices are rough against the otherwise soft hum of the ocean. The men interrupt the calm island as they intrude on the land and leave prints behind that don't belong. Their words mingle and carry offenses that should never be heard in nature.

In the center of the island Garren guards the pool of water, and I watch as the men wander and push themselves like playful pups. Some of them walk with stumbling gestures, and I realize that the majority are drunk. When one man comes close enough I see a bottle of ale clutched in his hand, already half empty.

And that's when I hear a scream from somewhere within the ship. The men don't seem to notice. The shrill sound echoes over the air and only one sailor who looks particularly drunk cocks his head at the noise—but that is the only awareness he offers.

I watch as they slink away to explore the island in small groups. Someone on the ship shouts a command to the men ordering them to stay near, that if they aren't back soon the ship will leave, with or without their bodies.

Another scream comes from the ship again and I follow the sound. I balance myself on the thin wooden ramp set out on the shore and walk along it to the ship, not an eye noticing my ghostly figure.

The crew still aboard are checking bindings and examining the sails. The wind blows steady on the mast, shifting the ship back and forth on the water.

I jump and almost scream when a body emerges before me and I realize that a man has just walked through me. He walks away, leaving me with the view of his back as a reminder he was ever near me. With tentative movements I continue forward, spotting an opening in the floor that leads below to the hull.

I lower myself into the opening, dropping my feet down and finding a ladder secured to the side. It is too dark below to see everything. There are large dark rectangles that could be more boxes of goods from merchants, but in the corner a small glowing light appears. Above me the boards groan under the weight of the men, but even as the nearby voice whimpers and wavers the men don't notice anything.

The cries come from the direction of the light, but it seems muffled. It's female—that much I am sure. She seems to almost hum to herself, but a hint of hysteria can be heard in her song.

"Hush, by the moon. Hush."

The voice is so quiet, so small, I'm almost unsure someone is really here. But then I step closer, following the light to see the body that accompanies the voice. In the farthest corner of the cabin a candle is lit, and a woman not much older than me lies across the floor in a gown so glorious that its layers blossom around her. The dress is dark blue and makes her pale skin glow in the dull light.

As I look closer she isn't alone. Her attention is preoccupied enough that she doesn't move or shudder as the men above make a loud commotion, the ship groaning and creaking. In her arms she cradles a baby so small and frail that I wonder how it's alive.

And for a heartbreaking moment I question if it is. I watch the woman closely as she nestles the baby. She's so weak that she can barely keep her head up, but a mother always finds a way to tend to her baby despite her own needs. The infant coughs and the sign of sickness is a glorious reminder that the small human is still alive.

"Sabine!"

A man's voice comes from the ladder I had just climbed. He doesn't make a move toward us, but his voice is impatient and when I look at the woman—Sabine—I know that she is expected to come to him.

Her attention drops from the child in her hands, and I watch as she gathers herself and pulls her body up enough to stand. She carries her baby in one arm while she works to straighten the folds of her gown. Once she stands I see another gown on the floor that she had been using as a cushion.

"Shh," she whispers into the baby's ear. "I'll be back, Clara."

And just like that she bends down to place her child on

the other gown. Clara, only an infant, sinks into the clothing and I watch as she disappears into the folds, not making so much as a whimper. Sabine straightens herself again, gazing down at her child and there's a fear that rots away her features.

"Sabine!" the man shouts again, this time louder.

Her head snaps up and she rushes past me, completely unaware of my presence as she goes to the man. Her figure disappears up the ladder, but I don't miss the small quivers that course through her arms as she pulls herself up the rungs and into the daylight where many more men await her.

There are shouts and I think it must be Sabine who screams up above. In the hull the air is still, but above my head the wood of the floorboards shift, and men shout. I go to the corner, stopping at the edge of the gown stretched out across the floor. It is orange silk, and even though I can see it is worn, there is still delicate stitching in the skirt.

"Clara?" I whisper to the baby like she may respond to her name. Soon after I bite my tongue, feeling foolish—she can't hear me.

The gown doesn't move. I hold my breath, waiting for any sign of life, but it doesn't come. I kneel down to the wooden floor and search the fabric. The silk flows against my touch and I realize how soft it must feel to the infant's skin.

Finally I find Clara in the center of the gown. Her skin is pale—paler than a child's should ever be. Her eyes don't open to me, even though I've removed the cloth from her face. Small tufts of light hair cling to her scalp, but it is nothing more than a small gathering of curls. I remove the gown to reveal the rest of her body and see that her limbs are smaller than any infant's I've ever seen. When I hold my hand out in contrast her arm is barely longer than one of my fingers. It's as if she is only a few days old.

Clara is curled within herself, her hand bundled to her chest like the small point of contact might give her more warmth. I lower the gown over her small form, watching as the infant shivers. She doesn't wear any clothing. A hushed cooing noise comes from her, but the sound is muffled. When I bend closer I hear her breathing—slow and labored. It sounds suffocating, but when I step back I see she somehow has a steady rise and fall to her chest.

My head snakes up when I hear a scream overhead. There's more shouting from the men, and a few seconds later a weight drops against the upper deck. I can hear some men laughing. They speak in a harsh tongue, and even though I can't make out their words, there is a mocking tone to their speech.

A moment later comes a small, frail cry; I'm not even sure if I heard it. But what scares me most is that, even though the sound was so quiet, I know who made the cry. I look at Clara, knowing it couldn't have been her and fear the worst for her mother.

All is quiet in the hull. Clara rests in her nest within the gown, unaware that her mother may be in danger. At the ladder, light pools in from the deck above. It's blinding for a moment until my eyes adjust and I can make out the forms of the men moving about the ship. More people are aboard now and everyone moves with quick and rehearsed movements. They tend to the sails and pull at ropes that steer the vessel with the wind and rudder.

"We leave with or without!" shouts one man. He walks about the deck, making orders but never actually doing anything except barking commands. I climb the ladder but don't step onto the deck. I search for any sign of Sabine, but there is none. Everyone moves so fast, and it's like the screams and whimpers I heard moments ago had never existed.

On the deck I see something. At the farthest edge is a small pool of blood, bright red against the dull brown of timber. I fear the worst; that it may belong to Sabine, but she's out of sight and I hope that maybe one of the men took mercy on her and brought her to get aid or at least some shelter.

"Go clean up after the woman." The voice comes from somewhere else. When I turn I see the shouting man push a bucket and brush into the arms of a boy roaming the deck. He doesn't say anything but takes the items and brings them to the stained red floorboards. The boy is small and thin and I watch as his frail muscles work to scrub away the blood—he looks no older than Dondre and I wonder what it is he had done to get himself on this ship.

"Go below deck, in the hull." The other man kicks the boy in the back.

The boy doesn't say anything; he just takes the blow, showing nothing but the small wince that accompanies his pain.

"Yes, sir," he says, taking the bucket and brush in his arms to go below.

I rush down the ladder and into the darkness where Clara rests undisturbed. It's as if the rest of the world and its noises disappear when I listen only to the boy crossing the floorboards and down the ladder. Each groan of the rungs sings out his arrival and I crouch next to the newborn.

Everything in my body begs me to push away the thoughts of how Sabine became victim to this, but as I remember the look in the men's eyes, how they were so willing to escape this reality by drinking their ale, it becomes evident these men are fully capable of inflicting their awful drunken deeds upon this woman.

In the dim light of the hull a candle burns, giving off small flickers. The boy's face comes into view and all is still—and I swear I can hear Clara's labored breathing close to my ear. I sit atop the gown next to her, not daring to move as the boy comes closer. His face is covered with dirt, eyes dark and tired. Bones protrude from the thin clothing he wears, just a scrap of fabric against his skin. His body is host to scrapes and bruises all over, and I know this boy is just another victim like Sabine.

Beside me Clara lets out a wheezing cough. The sound makes me flinch, fear of her tiny lungs failing, but then I see the boy's face change. He seems intrigued by the sound, confused by its presence.

He comes closer, but I reach for the gown, pushing it from me without disturbing Clara. The boy freezes as if he's seen a ghost, and I realize he has.

I shift forward to pick up Clara, intent to save her from the cruel men on this ship, but when I do her body slips through my arms. It was foolish of me to forget I'm an Essence. I watch her body, helpless as she rests on the gown.

All at once I slip my arms under the folds of the gown, scooping up Clara, still cradled in the silk. I watch in amazement as her body rises with the gown and she rests in my hands—for a moment I'm left in awe as I'm able to hold her, though only through inanimate objects. As I lift her, she seems to stir and a small sound emanates from her. It's only a quiet whine, but as I jostle the gown and get a better grip on her Clara wakes up and breaks into a shrill cry. And it leaves me to wonder if the men have always heard her cries and have chosen to ignore them.

When I glance at the boy he doesn't see me. All that he can make out is the floating gown that wraps around a crying baby who he wasn't even aware was on the ship. I wait for the boy to scream, to do something, but he stays rooted in place.

For a long moment he just watches, frozen in fear.

I try to calm Clara as her bright green eyes stare up at me. I rock her back and forth like I had seen Margo do so many times with Joelle when she was just an infant.

"Please leave," I whisper, fully aware no human can hear me. I don't watch the boy. I just continue to soothe Clara and wait for her cries to soften.

A still silence fills the air, and when I look at the boy he isn't afraid anymore. His face is helpless and I watch as he inches closer, peering into the folds of the gown to look at Clara. She quiets, her cries turning into a mumble that fades into the background. But the boy doesn't step away. He becomes daring, no longer a coward.

"Don't touch her," I say, directing my gaze toward him. I put all my concentration into the sound of my voice like it might matter, but he doesn't hear me so he doesn't let up. He doesn't see me, unaware of the protective stance I have taken, wrapping myself around Clara.

"Leave!" I shout. And this time it's like he has heard a whisper. A small flicker of recognition appears as his gaze on Clara falters. He stills, listening as if thinking someone on deck has called to him.

I grip Clara firmly in one arm and use my other hand to check the edge of gown that hangs over my arms. I pull the fabric up and over Clara to block the boy's view. And finally I see fear in him again. He backs away, suddenly frightened by my quick movement.

"Leave," I say again, my voice firm and directed to the boy. This time I'm not sure if he has heard me or not. There is no sure sign of recognition like last time, but he cowers away to the ladder. I watch him climb the rungs, stopping to look back, but I don't give him the chance to see Clara again.

XL.

The sky is dark by the time I have wandered above deck again. The push and pull of the ocean makes the boat tip side to side ever so slightly, as if to only lull one to sleep. When I stand at the edge of the deck, all I see is water.

No waves appear in the sea. No white water crashes against the shore with the tide because there is no shore, no land for the water to break upon. The boat has left Tiboulain. I've left Garren, not by choice, but by accident. When I heard Sabine crying from the boat, I didn't even think of my own safety. Panic rises within me, but I hush it away, urging myself to do whatever is needed so Clara can be alive and well.

The crew is quiet in the night. Most have gone to sleep, but others are awake and tending to the affairs of the vessel. If I try, I can make out individual conversations, but they are all in the backdrop of my mind. The night is clear enough to see the stars and constellations—not a cloud in the night sky—and I can see far into the horizon, far enough that I know I am a long way from home.

The crates on the boat remind me this is no place for passengers. But Sabine and Clara had become part of this unwillingly—and now so have I.

I look around the ship, searching for her captors, hoping

they look and talk differently, but all the men seem the same: vulgar, uneasy, and short-tempered.

I walk across the deck to the spot the boy that had been scrubbing earlier. The blood has faded with his cleansing, but there is still no sign of Sabine; no female on this boat screams for help. My stomach drops as I look around the ship now, not searching for kidnappers but maybe murderers. They had been laughing, laughing out of their mind as an infant struggled for life.

A lifetime's worth of guilt presses down on me. Could I have saved Sabine?

I watch Clara as she breathes. The small wheezing continues in her lungs, reminding me that she is one loose thread away from death. But the world is taking mercy on her when it did not on her mother. The boy, the only boy who is even aware that Clara exists, ran away and has not spoken of the infant nor of the ghost within the hold. He keeps silent for reasons I don't quite understand.

Up above, the world continues without note of what's lurking below. The men within the crew shout orders to each other and speak of awful events. Though their words are muffled, from where I rest with Clara I can make out their conversations just enough to know that, yes, they had kidnapped Sabine.

They had found her roaming near one of the ports where they had docked. A man they call Dimitri had taken her. As the men talk about it, they laugh, mocking how she had screamed and kicked all throughout her capture. Dimitri had kept her on the ship, storing her in the hull where she had stayed. His voice is louder than the rest when he speaks, talking of how he invaded her, stripped her of the only thing she had left—herself. He scoffs to his crew, telling them how he had done this almost every night and how now he'll need a new princess since Sabine is gone.

But he didn't even know her name. Whenever I hear him speak of her, he calls her Princess. At some point she must have become pregnant. For nine months Sabine had lived with these men, mothering a child that she loved despite the fact she was only given the baby because of dreadful circumstances.

I sit with Clara curled in my arms. The gown drapes over my legs, and I hold Clara close to my heart, my ears always piqued to hear her breathing. The infant amazes me. Just her existence in this world is a miracle. Sabine somehow cared for both herself and her child in this hellhole.

Wooden crates are scattered about the room. Most are bolted shut, but those closest to me have been tampered with. One lies on its side, canvas bags pouring out. I lift myself, placing Clara on the floor once again. The candle in the corner of the room brings a dull light to her face, so pale.

The canvas bag is about as big as my torso, and when I come closer, I see it has been torn open, grain spilling out. I finger the frayed edges of the canvas, realizing Sabine had been brave enough to seek out food for herself.

I take a handful and turn to Clara, and just as quickly, I let the grain fall between my fingers. It rains down to the wooden floor like a tropical storm, a constant rhythm until nothing is left. I look at Clara—an infant of only days—and realize I am useless to her. Her only source of nutrition—her mother's milk—is gone.

It all passes too quickly. The men must have been kind enough to bring Sabine fresh water when she was their captive, but now they leave the hull alone. To them, there is nothing more down here than crates of goods to be sold.

I sit with Clara in my arms, watching her fade away. I know I can't feed her, but I'm helpless as her thirst goes unanswered. She's too silent in my arms; I'm not even sure if she's sleeping. She moves and stretches in my arms, clearly uncomfortable. The infant opens her mouth, seeking her mother's milk, but always coming up short.

At one point she begins to cry. The sound is piercing, a constant ringing, and I fear the men will come down to quiet the child. But they never do.

I watch Clara cry. For the first time she opens her eyes to reveal mossy-green irises. But she doesn't see me. And just as soon as her eyes had opened, they close again.

I imagine Garren is here to save me, to save this small child. That by some miracle, he might just appear and breathe life into her pale skin. Instead there is just the creaking of the ship as the waves push it side to side.

I watch Clara as her life slips away in my arms, and all I want to do is run my finger over her skin to let her know I'm with her. I can't help her, but I'm here. Any attempt at touching her skin results in my finger passing through her. I hold her in the gown, the fabric acting as one of the few solids in my world as an Essence.

And then she grows silent, and I wish she would cry. Cries mean she's alive, alive enough to scream to the world for help. But now she's giving up. Every few moments she coughs, just so silently. Her skin grows pasty before my eyes. Whenever she opens her mouth I see her small tongue and how dry it has grown.

Through it all I can do nothing. I hold her tight, willing myself to be here with her while she leaves me.

With her silence, stillness grows. At first she would just stop moving, making me think she's finally given in, but then she would bless me with a cough—a reminder she is still here. It all lasts so long, yet passes so fast. I keep wishing she would move on, wanting her torment to be over, but then I grow selfish, willing the infant to keep fighting like it may make a difference. But eventually it all gives way.

I don't know how, but I know she's gone. It's like a whisper has passed through the room, the ghosts I can't see welcoming the newest member to their family. And I am here, an Essence. Not human, not ghost. So unwelcome in this world.

And it's all so unfair. Those men on board this ship rape,

kill, and yet they live. They live and prosper, like they deserve riches even though breath shouldn't be passing through their lungs. A mother is tortured and killed, and for what? For their mere sport?

A baby who has only seen the world as a dark place within a ship is dead. Infants are the epitome of innocence and those who are innocent should not be hurt. But I look at this child in my arms and realize it doesn't matter. Life comes and goes. We are nothing but pieces of a game, betting wages on our lives, seeing how long we will last until our luck runs out.

And I'm afraid Clara had little luck to start with.

XLI.

I don't know how long the voyage lasts. Time seems endless as the sun sets and rises on the deck above. The only way I'm able to keep track of days is by the light that filters in from the opening at the ladder. The lit candle in the corner eventually darkens, using up the last of the wick and sputtering away.

In the darkness I think of how I've failed Garren, of how he may never forgive me for leaving him—all for a child and her mother, both of whom could not be saved.

I hold Clara in my arms for a long time, like she might just be asleep. The ocean rocks the boat and it acts like a lullaby. Every now and then I find myself humming, finding rhythm in the ocean waves.

I don't look at Clara after she has passed. Instead I hold her in the gown, always looking forward, mesmerized by the changing light near the ladder from the deck above. If anyone from the crew walked by the opening, their figure would cause a shadow to dance across the floor.

I can feel Clara's body stiffen in my arms. When I adjust my hold, she won't give. It's like she's a rigid doll. As long as I sit here with her, I'm telling myself that she is okay.

When I finally look down at her again, I see her face, and it's nothing like the child I had first seen. Her skin is ashen and almost bruised looking. She looks so cold, so frozen with her lips still hung open. Clara's eyes are closed, and for that I am thankful. But through it all she finally seems at peace. Her brows aren't hunched like they had been—always in discomfort. Through her death I suppose she found a place where there was no such thing as thirst or hunger or pain.

I pick myself off the floor and walk toward the candle that has gone out. It's just a pile of wax fused to the floorboards of the cabin, but I settle Clara's body next to it. It all seems so futile. I look at the child and see nothing. The body in front of me is but a carcass of the past. I back away from Clara, leaving her wrapped in the gown. The orange silk of the fabric makes Clara appear all the more pale and lifeless. I lean forward to drape a corner of the gown over her face and retreat once more.

I hope and pray for the small child, wishing for her soul to find her mother's. Through all of this, at least they can be together again.

The ship shudders and for a moment everything has stopped moving. The constant sway of the ocean that I had grown used to, over what must have been days, finally stills. Above me the crew is loud with activity, but it isn't one of chaos like it had been when I had last heard Sabine's cry for help. The sounds from above are shouts of men at work—a controlled action.

Daylight filters in from the ladder. Shadows pass by and

footsteps ring out across the boards of the ship. All the voices and shouts of the men mingle together into a black noise that fades away into my subconscious.

The ship sways again and I feel the steady rhythm of waves pushing and pulling against it. The shouts from above grow louder and movement comes more often.

It continues like this for several minutes and I sit in the hull, waiting for all to quiet. But then the light filtering into the dark cabin is blocked by the figure coming down the ladder, and while the darkness lasts for only a moment, I find myself cowering beside the crate I had been resting against.

The man turns to one of the closest crates and drags it to the rungs of the ladder. I watch as a rope is dropped down into the hull and the man ties it around the frame. Just like that the crate is being pulled upward to the deck. The wood whines and creaks as it ascends, but it never gives. The man continues until few crates are left. I watch as he works his way across the room, and as he grows closer fear instills me.

I turn to the gown piled in the corner. The remains of Clara's body still rest within the fabric, undisturbed. What would they do with her?

After all the crimes they had committed, it is the blatant disrespect for an infant's passing that angers me most. After a soul has passed the body deserves to be put to rest. Yet as I watch this man grow closer, I fear he may take Clara and throw her away like they had done with her mother.

When the man's back is turned I scoop the gown in my

286

arms. I run across the hull toward the ladder. He faces me then, still blocking the only exit. And just like the boy, he doesn't see me. To him, the only thing that exists is the gown that floats in the air. He isn't aware of me or of Clara's small body held within.

He freezes once he sees the gown. I can't be sure whether it is shock or amazement on his face as he gawks at the gown. His jaw hangs slack before he tries to compose himself. His eyebrows furrow and his face turns to stone as he observes the scene.

"Dimitri," he says in a low voice.

The name shocks me, causes me to stumble backward before regaining my footing. At my reverse movement the man tilts his head like a docile dog may after hearing something.

"Is that the last of the crates?" another shouts down from the deck.

I freeze and hold Clara closer to me. The gown cradles her figure, blurring the outlines of her limbs. To the man watching the gown, there is only fabric.

"There's still more to be brought up, but I think you'll want to see this," the man says. He seems intrigued, as he watches the gown. Feet come down the rungs of the ladder as the man Dimitri comes into full view.

I'm face to face with Sabine's killer. He's nothing. Just a man in need of a bath and a good shave. His body reeks and holds weeks' worth of filth. His hair has grown long and greasy with the salt from the ocean air glossing and knotting it. And then as I see him, I see Clara's eyes. His eyes, so much like hers, are a bright green. They scream of life—something I had not seen when Clara had opened her eyes for me.

"What is that?" says Dimitri. He stands next to the other man. His face is all harsh lines and seriousness as he stares at the gown.

I look at Dimitri—Clara's father, her mother's murderer—but I don't find myself afraid. I want him to realize what he has done. I want him to see his dead child that I hold in my arms, but I'm selfish. As much as I wish for the man to know the distress he has caused, I don't want to gift him with the ability to see his daughter.

"You killed her," I say, knowing he cannot hear my voice. My speech is hoarse, going so long without any words, but as I continue, I find myself gaining strength. "You raped Sabine. She bore your child and loved your child, and you *killed* her."

My arms tighten around Clara, and I feel her alive with me. Her soul, though gone, whispers through the hull. And I swear Dimitri feels it also. For just a flash his face goes wan, the slightest of frowns crossing his lips, and it's all I can do to relish the moment. His hand, which has been a fist at his side, goes slack as his fingers hang down.

I want to push him away, to escape this awful place and to bring Clara someplace where her body can finally be at peace, but I know whatever attack I make on Dimitri will go unnoticed when my hands slip through his body.

Dimitri returns to his old self, tensing up, like he wants

to jump across the small space between us and rip the gown from my arms. When I look at his green eyes now, all I see is hate, like he knows what is in the gown and wants to destroy any evidence of the crimes he committed against Sabine.

"Dimitri?" the other man asks. He stands to the side, firm but wavering. The man maintains a strong front, but I can see it in his eyes as he watches the gown float in the air, how he wishes to run from the scene. He can't explain what he sees and wants to escape before the memory becomes a permanent fixture in his mind.

"Coward," I say. I face the man when I say the words and he flinches away. He doesn't hear me when I speak, that much I am sure, but he turns to look at Dimitri.

"What?" Dimitri faces the other man, slightly annoyed.

The man waits before he speaks, as if he's waiting for some movement in the air. "Nothing," he finally says.

Dimitri turns his attention back to the gown. I make no movement to shift. With all my will, I tell myself to stay completely still, waiting for the men to lose interest and walk away. But I know that no matter how long I wait, they will not leave. I've found their attention, and now all that is left is to satisfy them.

I glare at Dimitri, begging for him to see me, the ghost. But he focuses on the gown. His eyes roll over the silk and he gropes at it like a woman still wore it. And I think how sick it is for him to look at his dead daughter and to bear no grief for her.

I try so hard to stay still, but something builds in me that

I cannot control. Energy radiates around my body, twisting and winding over my limbs, hugging me to this spot in the universe. I feel my arms shake, but I don't look down to see if it makes the gown move.

It must because, at that moment, as my arms lift and lower the gown, Dimitri looks at me. His eyes shift and our gazes lock. When he sees me, he doesn't cower away like I wished he would. Instead he smiles, like my appearance is a sign of weakness. And I want to rip the smirk from his lips.

"You killed her," I say, and I'm surprised by the measure of control in my voice.

And just like that, I feel my energy flicker. Dimitri looks away, avoiding my eyes, and I fade from the human world once again. His eyes drift to the gown that floats in my hands, but I see his disappointment. It's like seeing a ghost satisfies him— another prize to the game he plays.

And I hate him because he looked me in the eye and didn't back away. He is the one person I had hoped would look into my silver eyes and see a monster. But he didn't. He smiled, thinking I was something else to mock, another show.

I don't know if he's heard any of my words or why he was able to see me, even if it was only for a handful of seconds. But I push away those thoughts as I rush past him, cradling Clara and the gown in one arm, then pulling my way up the ladder.

The man whose name I don't know jumps in my direction, but he holds himself back, both afraid and waiting for direction from Dimitri.

Dimitri stands back, watching as the gown floats away, never giving the other man permission to stop me. Dimitri does not flinch as I take his daughter from him forever.

We escape without looking back.

XLII.

The inhuman ability of an Essence to run forever is never stopped. My limbs never tire. My body has no need for food or water or energy or sleep. Fatigue is just a word, a concept, but it doesn't actually exist. So I run. I run until time passes too fast to be sure what is presently in this world. I run toward Garren, hoping to find him but knowing I won't.

The ship is docked at an unknown port. People were there as I ran across the deck, over the wooden ramp, and down the dock, never seeing me, only what I carried in my arms.

Voices mingle and languages I have never heard fill my ears. Foreign words are all around me, but only a murmur of a lullaby is in the back of my mind. The voices of strangers are the sounds that keep me grounded, that tell me I am here in the universe.

Most people don't notice as I run by. To them I am only a gown. Some eyes linger and watch as the silk floats by in a quick dash, but they never follow my path. If people see it they look away, thinking it may have only been a trick of the eye.

I jog around others, avoiding bodies, knowing that although I can pass through them like a ghost, the gown cannot. People push themselves out of the way for me. If they see the gown they stare and step back, but never gaze too long. The humans don't want to know what they can't explain, so they look away.

Buildings with brick walls taller and more immaculate than I ever remembered pass by. Faces flash across my vision that don't look like the people I had known at home. They seem to vary in color, shape, and size, and all of it seems so unknown. There are trees of numerous kinds that I don't have names for. The land is flatter than the rolling hills of Marseille, but the trees stretch so much higher. Even the air feels different, less dense, like I'm more able to breathe.

But I run, and I'm not sure how far it is I have traveled before I stop.

The sun sets and rises in the sky. The air grows moist and thick and freezes at night. Gravel exchanges itself for soil; soil exchanges itself for stone; stone exchanges itself for gravel. The land just keeps going. No matter how far I travel, it stretches on. Lakes and rivers flow in quiet rustles; wind whispers between tree branches; and animals roam among the bushes.

After a long time mountains roll up in front of my eyes. I don't know how long I have run with Clara in my arms. I keep her wrapped tightly in the gown, like she may leave me if I don't hold her near.

The world disappears behind my back. I have run through villages, some bigger than others. They seem so different from the ones in Marseille, but there were women and children peeking through the windows all the same. The mothers kept to their chores, and the children played idly until they felt the gust of wind as I rushed past. Most didn't bother to look up, but some of the small faces followed my trail. One girl stood and pointed at the gown, and I remember her saying something to me, but I continued without stopping.

But now silence is in the air. Hills and valleys appear before me, the land untouched. There is no path for me to walk, so I slow down my pace. And when I do, I don't rush to breathe or feel the fatigue in my limbs; instead I just want to run farther. I reach a forest next, dense and lush, preventing me from picking up my speed. So I make my way through the brush, hugging Clara close to me.

Trees are in front of me. The ground drops away as I near a cliff. There's a lagoon below and I carry Clara into the valley. The water licks the rocky edge at my feet, and the cliff of stone we were just on raises high above my head and cocoons the rest of the water. Rich green moss climbs the surface of the stones and envelops it. The water of the lagoon is clear enough to see the pebbles and stones at the bottom. I wander closer, curious as to how deep it may be. But even then, the crystal quality of the water makes it hard to judge.

Everything glows with light and I think this is the first time I notice the darkness. Everything is muted in the dull evening, but the moon shines high in the sky. It appears full and gives the nighttime forest an eerie feel in its silver light.

A type of peace is here. I can't put it into words, but for

the first time, I feel myself settle. A boulder sits at the water's edge and I lean against it. I let the gown fall limp in my arms. It's like I've run dry of all need and desire to go on. My eyelids don't droop, but I want to lie down.

With careful hands I unwrap the gown in my lap. A part of me feels broken as I look at Clara. She isn't the infant who I had seen on the boat. Her body has mutilated itself, turning a deadly purple color. It's as if her entire body has been bruised and her skin swells over her small bones. As I strip away the silk further I find myself barely able to look at her.

So I don't. Her body sits exposed in my arms. I study the reflection of the moon in the water. It's just like the one I had seen back on Tiboulain. And for a moment I'm amazed that, although I have no idea where I am, the moon is still the same. It will always be here with me.

The water is so still, the surface undisturbed and serene, that I feel my presence is unwanted in the lagoon.

My arms tremble. I think of burial and what it means: a final resting place, a goodbye, giving back to the earth what it owns. I cradle Clara in my arms as I stand. The soil at my feet seems so rich and fertile and I know I should bury Clara—finally let her be at peace—but I can't do it. I can't dig a grave, no matter how small, and watch the soil pour over her skin and suffocate her.

I walk to the edge of the water. My leather shoes meet the rocky shore and absorb the liquid, but I don't notice the cool tendrils as they soak between my toes. I imagine what it might be like to stand in cold water—how it would be like needles biting into my skin.

The water comes up to my knees before I stop. My skirt floats out around my legs in the water. Ripples cascade over the surface, echoing rings over the water. I lower the gown into the water, watching as the orange silk grows dark in the water. The fabric floats until Clara's small body touches the surface. She weighs down the gown, but I hold her up. Her bruised skin grows darker still as the water laps at her skin. And it's like I'm watching her decay in front of my eyes.

I pull away the gown from her small body and clutch the soaked fabric to my chest. My right hand goes to Clara, offering to hold up the infant, but again my hand passes through her body. And she sinks.

"I couldn't save you," I hear myself whisper. "I'm so sorry." My voice chokes on the words, never wanting to say goodbye.

I back away, dragging the orange gown with me. I can't see Clara in the water anymore. All that is left is the bright reflection of the moon over the surface. My movements create more ripples over the water, only distorting the image of the moon.

I try to justify her death, but I can't. She is like me—a sacrifice to the moon.

All seems luminous in the full moon tonight, but I can't stop looking in the water, searching. Searching for the body of an infant who had been here for a short time, only to be taken away so cruelly.

BOOK 3

XLIII.

Through it all I find myself shaking and I'm not sure why.

It's the first time I'm alone. Trees stretch out around me, their green foliage coloring the forest. Mountains rise up high above me like I've never seen before. Their peaks are hidden in the clouds. They're nothing like the hills of Marseille—things here are so much larger. Even the trees seem to find a way to reach higher in the sky—and I realize I have no idea where I am.

There's no way to find Garren. He and I, we are two things separated, living out our eternities alone. I tell myself to search, to keep running, but we are worlds away. I had never known anyplace besides Marseille, besides my home.

I bring my gaze downward. Even though the lagoon water is clear, I see no sign of Clara's small body. It's like the water has taken her away—truly finding peace in her resting place—but her missing body just makes me feel as if it were all a dream. That nothing had happened. There was no ship, no man named Dimitri, no running away. But most of all I remember Garren and wonder if he too is just a part of my imagination.

He had touched me as an Essence, and somehow, against everything we had learned about our existence, I had felt something when he kissed me. The prickle of heat, the whisper of something that the mind can't comprehend. A reminder that I was more than just a ghost.

The sun rises across the horizon, finally letting me see the world around me. It all glows with colors of pink, orange, and purple as the clouds shade the morning. The lagoon casts a shimmer in the dawn that captivates the eye and draws me closer. I feel it in me, a need to stay near this place. Clara is here—she is within these waters somewhere—and even though I feel as if I'll never forget her, I can't bring myself to leave this place.

Birds echo their songs through the air, speaking to each other. Happiness fills their hearts as they bring the forest to life with the new day. I sit on the boulder by the edge of the water, still clutching the gown that had held Clara. In my arms it feels like nothing, but I find myself drinking in the fabric. Pretending I can smell her baby skin, feel the soft silk against my fingers. Remembering her small wheezing.

Through the branches of the trees the stars call out. Small points of light radiate in the sky, dotting the night with reason and hope. The moon rests within the center of it all, opening my eyes to something beautiful. It isn't as full as it had been the night before. A small sliver of the circle is missing, but it is graceful in the same manner it has always been.

The water is so still. The surface appears like ice, untouched and perfect in its own sense. A part of me wants to reach out and graze the surface, just to see the ripples, but I stay rooted.

Wind blows around me, brushing my hair into my face.

The golden strands escape from the braid that hangs over my shoulder, and I remind myself that it's been days, weeks, maybe even months since I had last run my fingers through my hair. The world spins and continues in its rhythm around me, like it has no idea of the evil I have seen.

I miss my family. Mama and Papa, no matter what they may have thought of me in the end, had loved me at one point in time. They cared for me enough to raise me, even when I held the eyes of a monster. I miss Dondre and how he used to act like Papa, trying to be the man of the household, because he knew it was a role he would have to grow into one day. And Margo, how she cared for Joelle like it was her dying wish to see her daughter grow strong. But I miss Cyrielle. She was someone I could turn to always. And I'd like to hope I had been there for her in the way she needed when Nouvel passed away.

There is so much I have lost, but the feelings toward my human life seem so distant. They're like a dream—some pleasant, others nightmares. The memories don't always seem to be my own. It's like someone has told me a story they wish to pass on, and I'm nothing but a solemn listener.

The memories within my new existence haunt me with clarity. My life as an Essence seeks my attention. I see the bold colors the world has offered me, but I also see Garren. His face seems embedded in my mind, like it is a part of me somehow. I want to make all these memories of him go away, but they never do. Even as I watch a bird fly from tree to tree, I see Garren and think of how he would view this lagoon. It's similar to Tiboulain in its own way—secluded, hidden by its own nature.

With an aching chest I feel a part of me is missing, and I wonder what this awful sensation is. It is that feeling in my stomach which occurs only when I've been hurt and worn thin in an unforgiving world. It's a feeling Mama told Margo about, when she married Anton. Mama spoke of men and how love gave them the power to truly hurt women, crushing us, or building us up, but only if they choose to treasure us.

Mama wasn't aware I was listening. It was a conversation meant for Margo and her ears alone. Maybe it's because Mama never thought a man would love me, but I heard her words just the same. She spoke of this frightful thing called heartbreak, how it trapped people in its tendrils initially with beauty and life, only to choke them in the end. Margo had laughed away Mama's warning, but it wasn't a long time later that Margo came to us in tears. Anton had hit her. She said she still loved him, but she also feared him.

I shiver despite the growing sun in the sky. I shudder even though I shouldn't feel cold. And the truth is I feel nothing. There is a missing piece of me, and I'm afraid I've given myself away in the same way Margo had given herself to Anton.

I fear that these emotions, this desire that will never be satisfied until I see Garren, might just mean I feel more than just gentle care for this man.

The possibility of love haunts me. It makes me fear that I've lost something I never should have traded. But the memory of being loved ignites me. It gives me hope that I've seen something, experienced something that cannot simply be put into vain words.

I think of how he had kissed me and how it had never occurred to me that I may have loved him. It makes my head spin and my stomach clench like I may be sick in a broken, dreadful way.

None of that matters now. He's gone. We're separate beings. Maybe he's searching for me, or maybe he's waiting for me to return to him. But I've failed him.

The next morning the sun shines, high and beautiful. The sky is warm with blue radiance, not a cloud to be seen. Just above the tips of the trees, mountains reach into the Heavens, their peaks the highest and grandest sight of all. And despite all this, I sit and wonder how I had fallen in love without knowing how to be loved.

XLIV.

The rock wall of the lagoon is beautiful in the sunlight. The individual rays shine upon the moss that covers the wall and makes the green of the forest vibrate with life. The leaves, the moss, the grass all seem to reflect on the water, giving it a cast of color. I search the pool, thinking maybe just algae gives the water its earthy color, but it is still clear and pure. Clara's body, however, is out of sight. There is no sign that these waters are her resting place, leaving me only to wonder what the moon has done with its sacrifice.

The stone at the opposite end of the lagoon stretches high above my head. Trees take root at the top, an extension of the forest. The stone wraps around the lagoon, almost hugging the water. The only exposed portion is the rocky shore. The water licks at pebbles as they slope down into the water, descending into the lagoon.

I hug myself to the stone I've found so familiar. It rests just before the shore of the water. It keeps me close, yet I feel protected by the unknown waters. My eyes wander, always looking and searching, like someone will come from the trees and save me—take me home.

A small hole is in the rock wall. The cave's opening appears just tall enough to pass through without having to bend for clearance. I find my way over, peering into the opening, only to realize how dark it is inside. Despite its large opening, no light seems to find its way inside.

My hands skim the cave walls. When I look, I see the ragged surface of stone, but pressing my palms into it, I'm greeted with numbness. The walls of the cave open up once I pass through the entrance. Darkness continues around me. Nothing tells me whether the wall ends or continues down a path. All I see is black.

As my eyes focus, things become clearer. The stone walls come into view, and the cave continues onward. It is narrow but long enough that I can't see where it ends. There is only a slight angle in its turns, but still I find no end point in the path.

The walls come into greater focus with added clarity. The cave becomes lighter, and I realize that the sun has found its way in. The rays rest on focal points in the stone; embedded in the walls, shards of crystal mirror the light. They are small—only about the size of the tip of my finger—but the crystal seems to line every facet of the walls. There is no dark corner or lost piece of the cave. In the light, there are no secrets.

I follow the path of the cave a little way, gazing at the crystal that seems to go on forever. It dots the surface, a personal guide, and it doesn't seem like there's an end.

I round the first corner and see that the crystal goes on farther—diluted now because less light is reaching the rounded corner. But then my eyes find her. Clara, so peaceful and human-looking. Her small infant body lies against the side of the wall. Her legs are sprawled out like the sleeping baby she is, arms folded inward, close to her face for protection. Even in the dull light I see how healthy her skin looks. It is still pale, but a small blush of color glosses her cheeks. The bruises and decay that I had seen such a short time ago are gone. The death of her body has reversed itself, leaving behind a healthy baby.

I crawl to her side. My breath seems too loud as I kneel down next to her, but as I approach, my heart loses hope. No matter how beautiful she appears, I see past the façade. Clara doesn't move. There is no rise and fall to her chest.

And once again I find myself mourning for a child I had only seen alive for mere minutes. Her light-colored hair falls in thin waves, just barely able to cover her head. Clara's eyes—her beautiful green eyes that she shares with her father—are closed. When I see her face, I can't remember how she may have looked when she cried. Instead I see how she is now: at rest, an eternal and peaceful everlasting rest.

It's all I can do not to scoop her in my arms. Instead I curl up next to her on the ground, afraid to even touch her and disrupt the haven she has finally found. She's so small, so vulnerable, but when I look at her now, she is stronger than any other infant I have ever seen.

The crystals of the walls shine over her skin, making it glow. The moon has taken her. She is here—always. I don't understand why or how, but I find myself accepting the fact.

So little space is between us, yet I've never felt so distant in my life. I reach out to her, my hand seeking some contact. My fingertips skim against her temple halfheartedly. I trace patterns across her skin in delicate circles until I realize what I'm doing. My skin finds hers and there is no moment where I pass through her. Instead we are the same. An Essence maybe—like Garren and me. But I'm thankful to finally touch her.

I cower away, aware that Clara is no longer human—or at least not part of the living world. She is beautiful and lost and small. I wanted to protect her, but the cave carries out my wish now. Despite my best efforts a part of me feels I could have prevented both Sabine's and Clara's deaths.

The light in the cave wanes. The crystals dull as the sun disappears, setting in the horizon, ending another day. I pick myself off the ground, watching as everything around me darkens, telling me my visit with Clara is over.

I exit, never looking back at her where she rests. I fear seeing her, that if I saw her again, I would fall into the façade and question whether she is really gone. So I don't look at her. Instead I find steady footing and go to the lagoon again. The sun sets and the moon rises.

XLV.

I find myself compelled to do this. I strip one of the trees of its branches. My first efforts don't do much of anything. I bend the wood, but it is too healthy and alive to break. I twist and tear at the branch and tug at the leaves until I feel the branch start to give. With a subtle ripping sound, the branch breaks away and falls to the ground with my hand still wrapped around the thickest part.

The opening of the cave stares at me in the evening sky. Dusk approaches, leaving only a muted color to the world, but it is enough to see the cave. Within its walls are crystals which I know will shine if light touches them, but farther within Clara lies forever. Somehow her body has found its resting place, but I find myself cowering away.

I take all the branches I can gather and lean them against the opening. I tell myself that if I can't see it, then it does not exist. If the cave isn't here to remind me of Clara's death, I can pretend it never happened.

The leaves and branches pile up. They turn the opening in the rock wall into something else. The healthy greens vibrate with life against the gray stone, and I find myself looking forward to the passing days as the leaves wilt and die, just a fixture against the backdrop.

I stumble away. It's a mess. All of it. But I don't care. Instead I find myself on that familiar rock by the lagoon, curling into myself. My knees come to my chest, and my arms lock around my legs. The sun runs away like it's being chased by an unnamed god, and before I know it the night is black. The only things left are the stars and moon. And I remember the moon, because it's the same no matter where I am. Garren and I share the same moon—that much I am sure of.

It comes that night. Sleep finds me and I wish I could say it was a relief, but it wasn't. Because an Essence only sleeps out of boredom. The act isn't from exhaustion or for rejuvenation; sleep comes because it is night and there is nothing else left to do. In a way I am just resorting back to human habits. The sun sets; my mind quiets and I drift off. No dreams or images speak to my soul; there is just nothing. It's a way to pass time; that is all.

In the morning birds chirp. The air breathes the fresh breeze of another day, but even with the new start I find myself haunted by the pile of leaves in the corner of my sight. I turn away, leaving my back to the cave, begging myself to forget.

Instead I focus on the sounds around me. The morning is quiet, leaving only the birdsong and the brush of leaves, as a small wind curves and twists through tree branches. In the distance is a stomping sound, an animal running through the forest. It grows closer, and as it does, I'm able to better focus on the rhythm. It's not a trot like I've known to accompany a four-legged animal. There are two sure footfalls as the steps grow louder and louder, thumping against the soil of the forest, kicking fallen leaves out of the way in intervals.

I turn to look behind me, the sounds growing frighteningly close. That's when I hear the rushed and unsteady breaths. Behind the heavy exertion is effort and pain—so entirely human. Whoever is running is losing energy. I can hear them as they slow, yet their breath is labored and strained.

A girl emerges from the trees. She stumbles through, pushing her way forward. Her hair is tied back and a dress of silk is wrapped around her bodice, yet the thick skirts don't seem to slow her down. Her clothing is from a different time entirely. It seems similar to what Sabine had been wearing on the ship, but it's simpler, less artistic.

I can see the rise and fall of her chest as she struggles to find the air needed to run. Her pace slows and I can see her better. The girl is young, no older than sixteen, but her dress is an attempt to make her appear much more mature, with its plunging neckline and intricate stitching. Her face is delicate, and small tears stumble down her cheeks as she tries to navigate through the forest.

She doesn't see me—of course she doesn't see me—but it still comes as a surprise when she rushes toward me. As she draws close, she slows, and I can see a calm melt into her exterior. Her muscles relax and she attempts to breathe steady once again as she comes to a stop.

Her eyes seem glossed over as she walks blindly to the lagoon. The girl is watching her surroundings, but all she can concentrate on is the lagoon. Her eyes gaze into the water and the beauty of the lagoon casts a spell over her. Her feet shuffle forward until she's only an arm's reach from me. Her face is void of all expression as her feet touch the water.

Panic shocks me. I watch as she moves forward, letting the water soak her gown. It folds out around her. It's an emerald color—beautiful in every way—but she doesn't notice anything except the water. She stops, looking down. The air is so still in this moment, so quiet that I swear I can hear her hushed breath.

With slow movements she bends into the water, plunging her arm to the bottom. She straightens a second later, holding something. She cups it in both hands, uncovering a silver stone. It shines in her palm, and there is a moment of relief as she stands with the stone like this is exactly what she ran all this way for.

I feel my body relax. Air releases from my lungs that I hadn't realized I had been holding as I give a sigh of relief. But then the girl's face goes blank, and I watch as her body drops into the water like a limp rag doll, like the one Margo had when she was small.

This girl doesn't move. Her body floats on the surface, legs hanging underwater. Her mouth is closed, her face cupped by the surrounding liquid. Hair streams out around her as the intricately brushed and combed style falls apart in the water.

Everything is still for a moment. No sound comes from

the forest. The birds seem to have been scared away by the splash of water she had created. Ripples cascade through the lagoon, creating circles around the girl's body. The only sound is the soft whistle of wind that rustles the leaves against their branches.

There's no rise and fall to her chest. I slide off the rock I have been sitting on, taking careful steps like my movement may stir her awake. When I reach the water's edge, her body settles and sinks. Without thinking, I step into the lagoon and grasp her shoulders. I pull her out, wrapping my arms around her chest. Once I'm on shore again, it becomes harder to pick up her weight, and I find all I can do is drag her torso against the soil, leaving her bottom half in the lagoon.

Her face is serene despite the fact that she may have been running for her life. At her side her hand is clenched into a fist. I make my way to kneel beside her and grip my fingers around hers, working open her palm.

My hands drop away the instant I realize what I'm doing. Despite the fact she's human I touched her and was able to drag her from the water. I look at the girl and wonder if somehow she is an Essence like me, but then I remember the tears so willingly shed down her cheeks. I watch my hand stretch out next to her. My fingers wrap around hers but don't slip through her skin. Instead I'm able to grip her delicate hand and open up her fist. A small rock drops from her palm and onto the pebbles of the shore. It's the stone she had picked up from the lagoon, but it's no longer the silver it had been seconds ago. Its smooth surface shines with a slight green cast.

I remember how this girl had fallen at the touch of the stone, unable to control her body. I stand up and leave the girl at the shore, her lower body still emerged in the water. The girl looks like she's asleep, but she doesn't breathe—the lagoon has taken her life. I back away, wondering how long it will be until her body decays, like those I had seen when I was human, watching the world rot away before my eyes. Even as I retreat from the green-cast stone it grows brighter, and I can't help but see it as poison.

XLVI.

I didn't want to leave her. But I did. I left the lagoon and all that it is, because I couldn't face seeing another dead body. Every time I see a human so still, so silent, all I can remember is that it is something I will never have. And it seems so selfish, so cynical, to want death, but it's what I want. I waited for it when the pestilence haunted me, and I still desire it when eternity breathes down my neck.

I'm jealous of the girl in the sick way that I want her death. I want the peace she and every other human being find one day. But then I also mourn her passing into oblivion. I don't know her or what kind of life she lived, but I know in the pit of my stomach that she has lost something great, something magical, which she will never get back. I want her to know that if we could have traded places, I would have taken her death so she could have lived—but that's not how death proceeds.

Instead I wander away, plagued and haunted by this curse of eternity. I picture myself in this world, always lost, looking for Garren, hoping that he may miss me the way I miss him.

The forest grows dark again—another day ending—so I settle in the grass. The trees are dense, making it difficult to see the moon in the sky, but I know it's there.

I find myself mystified by human habits and how they stick. I sit on the ground, completely aware of the fact I'm not tired or in need of rest, yet I still want that slumber. The night's solace tells me to be quiet and lulls me to sleep.

I lie on my back, looking up at the sky. In between tree branches I can make out small stars. I close my eyes, aware of the animals that rustle in the bushes and the crickets that chirp their lullaby. But I also notice the silence—the dead silence of it all because I'm alone.

I'm a wanderer in the morning. There was no rest in my sleep and I find myself pacing and hovering, looking around like maybe an answer to all my questions resides within the trees. But the truth is I can't find reasons for my restlessness—I just am. My feet scuttle about, my mind muddled with thoughts.

I want to go back to the lagoon. I don't know why, but it keeps calling to me. I see the water and the stone wall and see a solace that I can't find anywhere else. But I can't return. The girl is there, still motionless without life. She'll have begun to decay by now, like Clara had as I held her in my arms. I can see the young girl in my mind, how her flesh may discolor and contort against her bones, and I know I won't be able to look at her.

And Clara—she's still in the cave with the crystals that will never shimmer in the sun again, because I had closed it off from the world to be soon forgotten and never to be discovered—the way Garren had covered the pool of water on

Tiboulain.

I wander, walking in circles, occupying myself in hopes of freeing my mind of this torment of the lagoon which I had begun to call home without consciousness. The trees all look the same as I walk. There's no sure path where I step, but I make my way through the branches and bark.

I'm leaning against a tree for support when I see her. The girl steps around the trees in a haze. She stumbles as if she's just woken from a deep sleep. My gaze cruises down her body, watching the hand she clutches at her side—her fingers form a fist.

Why isn't she dead?

"Miss?" the girl speaks up. There's relief in her breathy words as she speaks as if she can't believe someone is here in the forest with her. "Can you help me?"

She looks at me with scared eyes, observing my old ratted clothing. Her gaze pierces me like she will hypnotize me into doing whatever she wishes, yet her stare makes me look to the trees for cover. I take a small step away, feeling a growing sense of danger rising in me.

"You can see me?" I ask.

"Yes." But her eyes squint with the words, like she isn't sure of herself. "Miss, I don't know what has happened, but ..." She bites on her own words. "I woke up in the water."

"You were supposed to be dead," I say.

She rebukes my words, but at the same time there's an understanding as she hears my words. "Did I drown?"

I walk toward her, seeing the emerald color of her gown—just like it had been the day before—except now the color is muted and dirty. Her hair is a matted mess at her scalp, falling over her shoulders in dark knots. She looks like she had drowned, yet here she stands.

"No," I tell her. "There was a stone. It poisoned you."

Her face drops, and I see fear overcome her again. It's like I may have killed a hope inside her as she brings her hand to her chest. Her fingers are still wrapped in a fist and it looks like she may cry. With an unsteady arm she opens her hand to me, revealing a bright green stone in her palm.

"I can't let it go," she says.

I look into her eyes and see the utter fear. With wide eyes she looks to me as some sort of savior, offering the stone she can't let go. It shines bright against her light skin. The surface of the stone is grainy, distorting the green pigment.

"Why can't I let it go?" she asks me.

I look up at her and see a bright young face. There are no signs of lost sleep or fatigue, but I see her hand quiver. I push down her hand gently, allowing her to wrap the stone in her fingers once again. She succumbs to my actions, defeated, and lets her arms hang at her side.

"What's your name?" I ask.

She smiles at my words. "Hadley," she says.

Her voice perks up at the familiar inquiry, and I know this one ordinary question is what she needed.

"Why were you running?"

Hadley's smile wipes away quickly. She doesn't speak at first, only loses her gaze as she opens her hand to look at the stone once more. It isn't until she closes her fist again that she speaks.

"Valen … he was supposed to meet me in the forest for a picnic," she tells me. Her lips form a smile when she speaks his name, but she also seems to mourn at the memory. "Mama didn't like him very much, so we had to sneak out together. I went into the woods like we always had, and he would bring the basket of food. He didn't come so I was alone. There was a rustling in the leaves and I thought it was him, but it was some animal. I don't know what—maybe a bear, because I've never seen a bear before—and it saw me, so I ran."

"You ran all this way, from a bear?"

Hadley purses her lips and I can practically see her working through the memory, trying to decode something she doesn't understand. "I don't know. I thought that's what I was running from, but after some time, I knew the bear wasn't chasing me, but I couldn't stop running. It was like I had to be somewhere—I'm just not sure where."

And she looks around as if for the first time in that moment. With the stone still clutched in her hand she scans the forest, trying to look at it in a way that makes sense of where she is and how she got to be here.

"What's the last thing you remember?" I ask.

She smiles and it makes no sense to me because I saw her last moment—or what I thought was her last moment. She stepped into the lagoon like I had, except she was sacrificing her own life, so unlike the sacrifice I had made of Clara's body.

"Peace," she says. "The peace of mind and body that I had never known before. It was as if I were dying. And I remember not being afraid." As soon as her words end, Hadley's face drops. "What happened?" Horror fills her voice that I don't wish to remember.

I offer my arm to her, resting my fingers over her shoulder, like my touch may somehow relieve the tension I see radiate off her body. My ability to touch her makes me realize— she is no longer human.

My hand drops back to my side again. Hadley lifts her eyes to me, pleading. She is just a child, a child who ran when she shouldn't have. I see it in the light of her eyes, in the fresh glow of her skin, but also in the ignorance of her words. She has yet to see the world and it's already been taken from her.

I guide her back to the lagoon silently, knowing we both have questions that neither of us wishes to answer. She doesn't speak as we walk toward where she had come from. Instead she curls her fingers around the stone in her hand, making circular rotations over the rough surface.

Clara's body comes to mind as we walk. I know it's hidden behind the leaves and brush at the cave's opening, but as I walk with Hadley, I know that barrier must come down.

XLVII.

It's painful to watch. Hadley stands above her own body, a sick and disjointed mirror that doesn't make sense. A limp girl lies on the floor of a cave. Her dark hair is still a beautiful masterpiece of locks. Her face, her eyes, her lips, all are so relaxed and serene that I'd guess she was only taking a nap. But Hadley hovers over the girl—this body that is no longer hers to possess—and weeps. She shakes and slowly lowers herself to the ground, crying without tears running down her face, but she doesn't notice the lack of tears. She only has eyes for her body, and it has betrayed her.

Hadley does not look like this girl. Hadley's hair is knotted to her scalp, and her dress is no longer emerald green. Instead the skirt is a dusty brown at the hem, weighed and wilted by dirt and debris. She curls her arms around her torso, looking at herself, and I watch as she cowers from the form, like she's afraid to touch her own body.

At first she couldn't stop looking at her body, but now I watch as she struggles to even be near it. She looks at the stone walls of the cave, the crystals that line the corners and light up when the sun hits it—but she doesn't look at herself, and I see her expression crumble as she attempts to wrap her mind around the idea of seeing her dead body before her.

"Hadley?" I stand apart from her. She doesn't lift her head or heed my voice. Instead she cries. I try to bring her back to reality, away from the nightmare that unfolds in her mind where she can't explain the phenomenon in front of her eyes.

"I want to go home," she says. "I want Valen to take me home."

I walk toward her with slow steps. She lifts her head when I approach, but she is careful to be sure that her body is outside her range of vision. Her face is dry.

"I know," I tell her. "I want to go home too."

I offer my hand to her. She looks at it, almost as if it's another piece of poison, but then she grips my palm. I pull her away, and she sways for a moment before regaining herself.

"Where's your body?" she asks.

It's a simple question, but it's also one that never occurred to me. If I were like her, there would be a body. But I'm not like Hadley. She is like me, this spirit that has been caught between deaths, but I'm not like Hadley. I don't know where my body is, whether it be back at Tiboulain or if it never left me in the first place. But Hadley isn't like Clara, who died, yet her body sits in the same cave as Hadley's. The only reason I can find as to why both of their bodies are found here is the shared element of water: because Hadley's soul left her body in the water of the lagoon and Clara was scarified in the water.

"I don't know," I tell her. She seems disappointed by my answer.

"I'm dead." She says the words so plainly. They seem to

make no difference to her, but I see the wilt of her figure as she speaks. She's dead. She's dead, and she doesn't understand how that has happened.

"Hadley," I say, so she'll look at me. She's given up, that much I can see when she stares at me.

A dead and tired expression comes over her features, and she makes no attempt to hide her sadness.

"*Essence*. That's the word for what we are. Not dead."

"Essence," she says, nodding her head.

She repeats the word silently to herself, convincing herself that she never died, but I can see it is a lost attempt. The more she runs over the word, the more I see her sink within herself.

"What does that even mean?" she asks quietly.

And the truth is I can't answer her question, because I don't know. There is so much to this life that I have yet to discover. Garren and I together were supposed to uncover its secrets and decode this concept of eternity, but I don't even know where he is. Instead I'm lost with this girl who has somehow found herself trapped within this same eternity I am in.

So I let Hadley know the truth. "That's what I'm trying to discover."

Hadley spends each night with her back to the lagoon. Instead of looking at the water as it reflects the moon, she watches the path she had traveled to get here. With a stillness I will never possess, she maintains a constant watch over the trees of the forest. She doesn't mutter a word. I watch her, waiting for some change, but it never comes.

"Hadley?"

She turns to me quickly, responding to her name, and smiles before returning her attention to the trees again. Her arms are wrapped around her legs as they have been every night since she has arrived here.

I can't say exactly how much time has passed, because it all blends so effortlessly.

"Have you ever loved someone?" she asks suddenly. Her voice is soft, like she's afraid of the words she speaks.

I come beside her to sit on the ground. Our skirts pool around us in a dirty heap. If we were human, we would never let such clothing touch the ground, but as an Essence the fabric's beauty doesn't matter anymore.

"I didn't know it at the time," I tell her.

She turns to look at me. "What do you mean?" Her face is so young, so innocent, and it is amazing that she finds the ability to speak of love.

"There was a man. I think he taught me what love was. And I didn't realize this until he was gone."

"What happened?" Hadley's face softens. Her eyes shine a bit at the promise of a story—a love story.

I smile despite myself. It creeps over my lips, and the memories are pleasant rather than hurtful reminders that love is something so hard to obtain and grasp. "I don't know what happened. I discovered there is more than what we can see in the world. Magic and stories and travel—it's all very beautiful and dangerous. There was a man named Garren. We discovered an island called Tiboulain. In many ways it destroyed me, but it also saved me."

Hadley turns her torso to look at the water behind us. As she comes to face me again, I watch her hand uncurl the stone in her palm—still green. "Was it the moon?"

She's caught on fast. As the days have passed with her here, I've tried to explain this new world to her, expecting her to believe none of it, yet she has come so far with accepting the unimaginable. I watch the moon shining over us. The sun has just gone down, leaving a violet glow to the sky. The moon is nothing but a faint outline, but it is there.

"I believe it was the moon."

"But you loved him? Garren?"

I smile. It's the first time I've heard his name spoken by someone else. It shouldn't make a difference, but it does. "I still do."

"So what happened?" Her brow furrows.

All her attention is turned to me and I realize that, although she is a small adult in stature, she is still just a child. Her body is that of an adolescent with a tiny frame and bright eyes. She leans forward at my words as if this is all nothing but a fairy tale.

"We were something when we were together. Then we

became separated, and it wasn't until I no longer had Garren that I realized how much I needed him."

"Did he love you?"

Her words hurt, and they shouldn't. But the simple fact that Garren may not love me haunts me to the core.

Hadley sees this.

As I cower into myself, she too shrinks away for a moment, as if by providing me this space I may heal in a special way. But did he love me? I remember our time together. We cared for each other, but could he have loved me? He kissed me. On my forehead for comfort, but also his lips were against my own and for the first time since my human life, I had felt warmth and life—if only for a moment. Was that love?

"I'm sorry," she says.

I shake my head, dispelling the thoughts. I try to smile at Hadley in order to let her know I hadn't been hurt by the words.

"No, it was a good question. But I don't know the answer."

She stares at me with open eyes. An understanding is there. She holds my gaze for a long time before dropping her eyes to look at the stone in her hands. She hasn't let it go—I don't think she can. Whenever I see her remove it from her hands or let it rest on the ground, she is quick to pick it up again.

"I don't know what love is, Luna," she says. Her voice hints at sadness. There is a tug and pull in her emotions, the only way to read the confusion in her thoughts. "Valen—the boy who was supposed to meet me in the forest—he was supposed to be there that day, but he wasn't. And I kept waiting. I waited for him to come through the trees and save me, but he never did. We always snuck away to see each other—we never got caught. I taught him how to dance, even though he dragged his feet too much. And sometimes I would sing to him, and he would just watch me—he'd never look away."

I rest my hand on her shoulder and she looks up at me. She's so young, but the hurt she feels now is the same I face every day when the sun rises without Garren or when the moon peeks through the clouds at night, yet I'm still alone.

"I still wait for Garren too," I tell her. It doesn't help Hadley to know that we all hurt the same or how that feeling never goes away—it just becomes bearable—but she seems to release some long-held tension in her body as she breathes now.

"Do you believe Garren will come for you?" she asks.

"Do you believe Valen will come for you?" I ask in return. It's not a fair question. I know nothing of Hadley and Valen's love story. For all I know, the love story was in Hadley's imagination, but when I look at her I know that's not true. Her stare carries a loss that only comes when love has been taken away. It leaves the face slack and lackluster; it disregards us, leaves us scarred and beautiful at the same time, because we've experienced something glorious.

"I want to believe he'll come," she says, "but I also fear it may be impossible." Hadley stares at the greenery of the trees again, searching, always seeking the one thing she wishes for most, but it never comes.

"Then we'll believe," I say, but I don't stay with her. In slow movements I pick myself off the ground and cross back to the lagoon. In the time that has passed, the sky has grown just dark enough for the moon to shine in the night. It reflects off the water, like it has every night, and I'm reminded that Garren is out there without me.

XLVIII.

Hadley leaves in the night. She fights the human habit that tells her to rest in the darkness. Instead I find her creeping away each nightfall. When the darkness comes, we always find our separate spaces. I reside near the lagoon, always looking to the sky at night, and Hadley finds herself drawn to the forest. We're both able to disconnect ourselves from the reality around us, but whenever I glance at Hadley, I see the aching in her as she leans forward from where she sits.

When the moon is highest in the sky, she always chooses to leave. Her parting is quiet and small—nothing more than a rustle of leaves as fall approaches. For a long time I didn't notice her absence because I find sleep on peaceful nights, but I've found myself keeping watch now. She always comes back by the morning after I've already woken, speechless as to where she has been.

But tonight I stay awake, refusing to let the moon lull me into a sleep like it seems to do every sundown. Instead I watch Hadley from a distance as she sits on the grass near the trees far from the lagoon. Her face studies the woods as her fingers trail through the grass, picking away at the green growth.

Her body is still, the only movement coming from her fingers that constantly massage the grass. Hadley's head lifts suddenly, looking up in the sky to where the moon shines in a small crescent. She picks herself up, brushing away any debris her skirt may have collected—and, just like that, she walks away without a glance over her shoulder.

I don't stop her. I don't feel as if I can. Instead I watch as she makes her quiet exit. Even in the dark I can see the stone she clutches in her hands. Her knuckles are tight in their grip, like she's afraid she may drop it. It only takes a few more steps before the darkness encloses her and she is out of my sight.

I wake in the morning, and Hadley is already back at the lagoon. I don't know when I had fallen asleep, but I find myself curled against the rocky shore of the lagoon. Hadley sits at the edge of water, running her fingers through the liquid. She watches the ripples that jump around her touch as she speaks.

"I'm going back to him," she says.

I sit up and gather my skirt around me, wondering how she knew I had woken without looking.

"That's where you go every night, isn't it? You visit Valen."

She simply nods her head. "I still love him, Luna," she says. Her words are happy, and she speaks as if she wishes she could stop loving him to alleviate her heartbreak. "I watch him as he sleeps, and I find myself wanting to reach out and touch him, but I can't." Her small voice breaks as she says the words. Hadley doesn't choose to look at me.

Her gaze bores into the water, concentrating on something other than the thoughts that plague her mind. "I've tried, but I pass through him. I'm nothing. I'm nothing to him." Anguish reverberates off her. Hadley takes her hand from the water and wraps it around the green stone she can't seem to let go of. Her body shakes in the small way it does when someone cries and can't control their sobs.

"I know," I say, but my words anger her.

"No, you don't." Her voice is angry, but also tired and worn—frustrated. "You don't know love. I love Valen, and he loves me. If he can't come for me, I'll come to him." Finally she turns to me. Her eyes open wide and clear, so sure of herself, so full of emotion she doesn't know how to control.

I flinch and turn, unable to return her stare.

"I know what love is," I say. I'm surprised by the strength in my voice. The words become clear and I walk away, leaving Hadley to stare at my back. But all too soon I feel my face drop like a mask, and the full effect of her words stings me.

"Hadley, you can't return to that life," I say, my back still facing her.

"Why?" she asks. Her voice is softer now, defeated. The anger has diminished, and it's like she knows what I'm saying is true but isn't willing to admit it yet.

I turn around when I speak to her. I see the hurt in Hadley's eyes, how she is still crouched on the ground next to the lagoon. A corner of her dress has slipped into the water, but she doesn't pay it any attention. Instead she looks in my eyes, like I can fix the world and make this nightmare end.

"You and I, Hadley, we're not a part of this world anymore."

Her face is broken. Small pieces of innocence and hope are torn away as she comes to terms with my words. Her eyes dim; her lips frown, but most of all, she detaches herself. I look at her and she looks at me, but I know if I speak to her again, she won't hear me.

"But I love him," Hadley says. Her face drops from my gaze.

Her hands wrap tighter around the stone in her palm, and I'm shocked by the white glow her knuckles take from the tension.

"This wasn't supposed to happen," she tells me.

"I know," I whisper. I step forward and bring her to me. She doesn't protest as I take her in my arms, but I feel the wall she has built up against me. I no longer feel like the broken child. Instead I see this quality in Hadley. The young girl shakes in my arms, breaths coming quick as she cries without tears. Through her cries I feel a strength in myself, as if I may take away some of her burden.

It's unfair. All of it is unfair. But she thaws in my arms. The rigidity of her limbs melts away, and she leans into me for support. The two of us lower to the ground. The pebbles of the lagoon surround us, and the world moves on without us. For this moment, we are here. Just the two of us as we sink into our sorrow, and I support Hadley and breathe for her, wishing only to make this life easier for her.

For what seemed like eternity, she sat in silence in my arms, just breathing and listening to the world unfurl around us. The sky grew dark, and once the moon shone bright in the sky, she left without permission or a parting word. Hadley just broke from my grip and walked away. She pushed from my arms and left. I couldn't find it in myself to stop her—I knew what drove her motions. I also knew that if Garren were out there I would do the same.

The moon is still a crescent in the sky. Its glow is small, but it sparks the clouds to life. I can hear Hadley walking through the forest behind me. With every step leaves crunch or tree branches are disturbed.

The still water of the lagoon is in front of me. I bend forward and slip my leather shoes off my feet. They give and bend against my fingers. I wonder how long it will be until I'll be forced to find new clothing, replacing the tattered dress Garren had given me when I first woke from the water of Tiboulain.

With sure steps I dip my feet in the water. I pick up the skirt of my dress so it doesn't get wet, but as I go deeper and farther, I feel the tail of my skirt catch the water and drag behind me.

The pool glows with the moon, just enough to reflect on my skin, creating an eerie white glow of a ghost.

I ask the moon for solace and protection. For how much

it has taken, I ask for something back. I stand in the waters of the lagoon and wish for peace within this world. I don't ask for eternity to be taken away, because I know it is a wish that can never be fulfilled. Instead I ask for some way to make this easier. To make moving on somehow possible, to separate our world from theirs.

I know this is selfish. I know I'm taking yet another thing from Hadley, but I also know this will be what she needs, even if it's not what she wants. Yet at the same time, I know this will not only keep Hadley in the lagoon, but me as well. Doing this takes away my ability to search for Garren, but I will not let Hadley suffer or leave her to the lagoon alone.

The water opens around me; the moon shines above me, and I ask that somehow Hadley will never escape into the night again.

But maybe, just maybe, none of this will work.

XLIX.

Hadley returns. She sits silently at the edge of the lagoon, content in her loneliness. I watch as she toys with the stone in her hand, passing it back in forth through her fingers, holding it over the water like she is tempted to throw it from her grasp forever—but she never does.

"You loved Garren?" she asks quietly. I don't answer so she turns to look at me. "Did you?"

Her eyes are wide, and I see now how much of a child she is, how little she has seen, but when she speaks she tells a different tale. Her words bring years of not wisdom, but knowledge—knowledge that no child should have to face.

"Of course," I say.

She smiles. "So this is hurting you as much as it's hurting me?" She pulls her fingers around the stone and brings her hand to her chest, exactly where her heart is.

Her lips waver and I know if she were human, tears would be streaking down her cheeks in a cascade of emotions.

I come to her, sitting along the pebbled beach. "I look at the moon each night, thinking that Garren may be seeing the same thing I do. That, somehow, our sharing the same sights will bring us back together. I'm always hoping he may come, but I'm not so sure that will happen."

Hadley watches me. My words make her lips turn down, but I see something change in her eyes. She's no longer saddened by her own loss, but mine.

"But if he loves you, he'll find a way to come."

I want to believe her, but then I think of all that I have done to Garren and how it is possible he may have forgotten me—I don't even know how long ago it was when I first got onto that merchants' boat. Garren took away my human life for his own gain—to hopefully save his sister. And I don't know if all that time we had grown close to each other was simply because we were the only two Essences left in the world.

"Does love die?" Hadley asks suddenly.

She seems frustrated with her own words. In a way it seems she wants them to be true so she can let go of Valen and move on, but it's the clutch of her fingers that tells me she hopes love never dies—that's not how it's supposed to work.

"I suppose time will be the one to tell us."

She brushes away my words like I had never even spoken.

"I don't want to love him anymore, Luna. It hurts too much." The syllables come out rushed and slurred together. She stumbles upon her words, and a constant tremble moves through her limbs.

All I can do is nod my head, because I understand all too well how she feels. Some nights I look at the moon and know Garren is the cause for the ache in my heart, the ache that can only be mended if he were here. The pain is physical in a way emotions never should be. It makes me weak; it makes me useless. My heartbreak is a hindrance, an ache and pull on a life that must continue, even if I'm unwilling.

"It will go away," I tell her, but it feels like a lie. The words come but mean nothing. I don't know if Hadley believes them, but she hears me as she nods her head, dizzy with lost tears.

"Okay," she says.

The moon is high in the sky and Hadley still sits within proximity of the lagoon. I can see her face contort through the night, under a constant debate as to stay or to go. Stay and be brave and settle into this new life. Leave and remember what love is, only to be tormented by the impossible notion of the concept.

I don't speak to her. Instead I let her decide what to do. Hadley is the only one who can make this decision to move on. Even if I forced her to stay she would wander, always wondering about the possibility of seeing Valen again.

She gets up slowly. Hadley finds my face in the darkness. Her eyes are lost and she looks to me for permission to leave. She stands but doesn't move. I keep my face neutral, but the longer her gaze holds mine, the more I feel my features slip into a frown. Finally she steps away and finds the familiar path she takes every night through the forest.

She doesn't go far. I can just make out the silhouette of her figure when she stops. Hadley drops to the ground on her knees and makes a quick shrill cry. It isn't for Valen—this is much more physical. As fast as she can, Hadley pushes herself through the trees of the forest and comes to cower near the water. Her hand clutches at her chest.

"Hadley?" I go to her aid, kneeling next to her on the ground.

She breathes fast labored breaths. Her eyes are frantic as she looks at me. Words linger on her lips, but she can't seem to find the breath to speak her words. Instead she opens up her hand to me, uncurling her fingers to reveal the stone she must always clutch. The surface is rough, as I had last remembered it, but the color is off. Instead of the vibrant green I had known, it has faded to almost white. It takes on a transparent quality, as if I can see straight through it to Hadley's palm beneath.

"It hurts," she says.

Her eyes dart across the lagoon in frantic, scared little motions. She's like a small pup that has just been scolded for acting disorderly, whimpering, looking for the source of her mistake.

"What happened?" I ask.

She doesn't speak for a long time. She doesn't hear my words at all. Her eyes dart and survey, looking—for what, I can't imagine. Her fingers tread across the surface of her stone, a constant motion that does little to soothe her mind. Dark hair falls over her eyes as she shifts, shading her face so I can't make out her features.

"Hadley?" I offer my hand, brushing my skin against her

shoulder. She jumps when she sees my hand, and when I see her face again I realize just how scared she is.

"I—" she starts.

Hadley's fingers shake around her stone and I watch as she takes the time to breathe deeply, closing her eyes in the simplest of ways.

"Hadley," I say again.

"I just wanted to see him one last time," she says. "I promise. Last night was going to be my final visit to Valen."

Her eyes open bright and glossy. Anguish radiates off her like an aura that announces its presence to all within the perimeter.

"It's okay," I tell her.

She shakes her head, looking past me to the trees at my back. Her eyes glaze over without focus, staring at the forest as a whole instead of one focal point. As the time passes and her gaze continues, I see her lose herself to the vast landscape of the trees.

"Hadley," I say again.

She jumps at the sound of her name and brings herself back to where she stays rooted at the lagoon's edge.

"What happened?"

"The forest," she says. "It hurts to go there." She watches the stone in her hands, running her fingers over the surface like it may disappear.

It has returned to normal again—the bright green I had always known it to be. Hadley seems more relaxed now, running the stone over her hands, sure that it is there.

"When I went between the trees, I felt myself shift. I couldn't breathe—and that shouldn't matter, because I'm an Essence like you told me, Luna—but it mattered this time. I needed air. It felt as if I was dying, and I don't understand how that's possible. But there was a ripping, like someone took hold of my heart and was tearing it from my chest—so familiar to how heartbreak can be but much more physical. And I looked at my stone and it was gone."

She stops to bring the stone to her chest again, the sight of the stone no longer enough to assure her it is here. She needed to feel it against her skin, but even that is impossible.

"You dropped it?"

"No," Hadley says, quick to disregard me. "It was in my hand—it's always in my hand!" Her words echo across our small expanse.

I see emotions build in her that she is trying so hard to mask and forget.

"I felt it slip away. No matter how tight I clutched it, I felt it disappear." Her voice is quiet and reverent. "I can't be with Valen," she says.

Her voice is so strong in this single moment that I'm sure she's only lying to herself, but when I look at her I see a strength I'd never seen before. She holds herself with determination, and even if she is trying to convince herself to believe her own words, I feel she may be able to live them.

"He's human," I say. "You're not."

"Yes," Hadley says. She nods her head like my words are

the simplest, truest form words can take, but she acts as if it doesn't bother her. "I'm not human. I can't leave this lagoon in the night to escape to him anymore."

"What did you see when you're with him?"

She smiles in a tired way. "He was always asleep. I never woke him because I was afraid that if I did, he wouldn't see me and that ..." She stops to take a deep breath. "... that would hurt so much more than never knowing I was there."

We kneel on the stony beach of the lagoon, the night already passing in a fast motion that we can't control. Only subtle movements stir in the forest as animals scurry across the earth and through the trees. Crickets murmur their songs, singing a lullaby of sleep.

"He thinks I'm dead," Hadley says suddenly. "They searched for me, but when my body was never recovered they pronounced me dead. I don't know how Valen mourned for me. I thought that if something ever happened to me, he would stop at nothing to save me. But every night I visit him, he seems so content. I thought he would be up until the morning's daybreak, thinking of where I may be."

I don't say anything. Her words flow, and a struggle comes with what they could mean—that maybe Valen didn't love her as much as she had thought.

"But I suppose it doesn't matter because in the end, I'm dead, and he's not."

I want to refute her words, but I don't.

Hadley runs the stone in her hand, a constant motion

she doesn't seem aware of. And the night goes on, like nothing has changed.

L.

"Luna?"

Hadley's voice comes from behind me. The daylight sky is bright as birds chirp their familiar songs. The atmosphere speaks of nothing but peace, but when I hear Hadley's voice, a hint of attentiveness is in her words.

I turn to face her and see her holding the orange gown that I had used to transport Clara's body. The fabric has faded and some of the stitching has been pulled, but otherwise it is unharmed. "What is this from?" she asks.

I walk forward and take the gown from her arms. The simple piece of silk seems so empty because Clara is no longer within its folds.

"There was a baby—her name was Clara—who was long dead by the time I came here. But I think this was her mother's," I say.

Hadley doesn't ask any questions as to who Clara was or how I knew the dress belonged to her mother. In fact Hadley never asked many questions. She's always taken my words for what they are. Even when I tried to explain the concept of being an Essence, she didn't deny my words or prove me wrong; she just took it as fact. And now she holds this stone that shines green, acting as if it is a mirror to her soul, unable to let it go.

It's been weeks since I'd seen her fall to the ground, screaming in pain as the moon shone bright in the evening sky. She hasn't attempted to leave in the night since then.

"Clara. Is she the one in the cave?"

My head shoots up at her words. I hadn't realized Hadley had seen Clara. The only time I took Hadley in the cave was to locate her own body.

"You saw her?" I ask. My grip lessens on the gown and for the first time I see the cave behind Hadley, open and unmasked. The sun's rays travel through the darkness and catch the edges of the crystals embedded in the walls. A small spark of light peeks through the darkness.

When Hadley nods her head, she does so slowly, like she's afraid she may have broken an important rule. "I wanted to see if I could find your body, but I just found Clara—and the gown was near her." She points to the fabric wrapped around my hands. I look down at the silk, and when I do I can almost picture Clara's small form when it had peeked through the folds.

"My body isn't in there," I say.

Hadley nods her head, like this is what she expected. I wonder at all the thoughts that must run through her head, how there must be so many questions, but none of which she ever chooses to ask. She possesses a certain wisdom and bliss that I only wish to master.

"Have you worn it?" she asks.

"What?"

Hadley takes the gown from my hands and holds it by

the shoulder seams so we can see the skirts fall toward the ground. The bodice is a lighter shade with darker orange stitching, while the skirts fade away to the same shade of orange. The sleeves stretch all the way down to arm's length, bearing tight until the wrist, where they flare out. It's like nothing I've ever seen.

"Have you worn the dress?" Hadley asks, clarifying this time.

She holds out the dress and examines it, looking for any tears that may qualify it as unusable. But the fabric is untorn as she holds it out for me, seeing if it may fit.

"Why would I wear a dress like that?"

Hadley smiles, folding the gown in layers over her arms. She makes sure to not let it touch the ground. "Don't you want to be beautiful when Garren comes?"

It almost hurts to hear his name said from another's mouth. I don't speak up and tell her how Garren's coming for me seems impossible. How I left him, and he doesn't even know where I am.

"Come," she says. With one arm she holds the gown, but she uses her free hand to offer her grip. We go to the cave, and she doesn't slow as the crystals glow faintly and come into focus as we near. "Put it on."

"Hadley," I say, trying not to take the dress, but she drops it in my arms anyway.

"Please," she says in a clear voice. "If not for me, for Garren."

346

And again his name stops me. Small memories form, and a scared voice in my head tells me not to let the images surface because it hurts to remember him, to remember he isn't here; that maybe he doesn't want to be here. But I ignore the voice and let myself imagine Garren coming for me and seeing me in this dress as something beautiful—it seems so dangerous to have such a hope.

"He's not coming back, Hadley," I tell her.

Her face drops as her smile fades away. And I think for a moment that she must understand how I feel—what it is like to hope the one that I love will find me, even when it seems impossible. As she backs from me the smallest bit, Valen's name whispers off her lips, almost unperceptive.

"Can you put it on anyway?" she asks.

Her voice is less sure now, like my answer doesn't matter. In spite of it all I grip the dress in my arms and turn my back to her to change. Hadley's smile returns in a meek way, as she leaves me to put on the dress.

My worn skirts fall from my body, like an old skin. Garren had been the one to find me this clothing. He had gotten it from a woman in the market—I can't even remember her name anymore. Taking off the kirtle and chemise seems like an act of betrayal, but I push away the old clothing and step into the gown Hadley insists I wear.

The delicate fabric glides across my body like silk, and once again I stand as an Essence, wishing only to feel the touch of the fabric against my skin, the soft caress of the fibers gliding across a landmine of senses.

"Hadley?" I speak softly.

She comes almost immediately and doesn't need me to instruct her any further as she steps behind me and ties the corset around my bodice.

"It fits like a wonder," Hadley says.

She finishes with the back and I turn to face her. The dress bows out at my hips, the skirts flowing over one another. The two shades of orange seem so vibrant in the forest scenery. The sleeves are tight around the bend of my arms until they reach my wrist, the silk flowing out and away.

"Here," Hadley says.

She takes my braid in her hands, working to unwind my hair. As she does so, I see the long golden tendrils flow over my shoulders as they never have before. Mama wouldn't let me wear my hair down—it wasn't proper.

Hadley twists the hair around the back of my head, letting some of the strands frame my face.

"What are you doing?"

"Making you beautiful," Hadley says. "You may not see your hair, but it's a mess." She tugs and pulls until the strands run through her fingers without trouble. "There."

I step away. Hair no longer falls over my shoulder in a braid. Instead all I see are a few strands hanging around my eyes.

"I pulled up all your hair, like the way I wear mine," Hadley says.

I imagine we both look like we are ready to attend a ball

348

where we are meant to meet our suitors, when in reality it is just the two of us in the forest making quiet wishes in our hearts.

"Why?" I ask.

Hadley wavers at my words, but I don't see the light ever leave her eyes. "Because you and I, even if the world never sees us again, we deserve to be beautiful."

There's sadness in her voice which she wishes to conceal. Her face displays a smile, but a hitch in her words tells me that, even though she may believe the words she speaks, she doesn't want it to be this way. She wants to be alive and human, and to fall in love and live a life that can be seen and heard. And touched and smelled.

Hadley comes forward and hugs me. I'm not sure if she does it because she believes I need it, but when her arms wrap around me I realize she is the one who needs the comfort. Her small frame falls against me like she's given up. Her shoulders shake in my arms, as if a child crying.

I wish I could take away the hurt.

LI.

Hadley and I watch as it happens. A man wanders through the forest. It's midday, a bright afternoon, and he's alone. His clothing suggests he might be a peasant where I come from, but the pack of food in his hand speaks another story. He seems lost in the forest as he wanders along the path without any real direction, but at the same time he seems completely at ease with the idea of never finding society again.

Hadley was the first one to spot him. She came running to me, trying so hard to keep her voice down, like he might hear and come to investigate.

"There's a man. I don't know who he is, but I think he's come from town." Her eyes are frantic with the words, like she may have seen a ghost approach from behind.

"Where?"

She turns to point me in the direction she had come from and I see the outline of his figure between the trees. He's tall as he careens through the branches, but his build is small enough that, even if I were human, I wouldn't fear him as much as most men I've seen in my life. He could hurt me if he wanted to, but only if he put all his energy and effort into the act.

"Quiet down," I whisper to Hadley.

She seems to stop breathing at my words.

I look at her, trying to alert her about how important it is that he doesn't discover where we are. We are an Essence—he shouldn't be able to see us, but the idea that we may be discovered still worries my heart.

The man stumbles. He holds something in his hands, and as he comes closer, I see it is a glass bottle. It's empty, but even then, he holds it with a fierce grip. As he tries so hard to keep his balance, I recognize him as the same type of man I would see in the tavern.

"What's he doing?" Hadley asks, next to me.

I push her behind me slightly, in a way to quiet her.

We watch him together. He doesn't seem to grow farther away like I wish. Instead, with each stumble and step, he comes closer, crossing the distance between us. He doesn't see us even as his head lifts and looks in our general direction. He seems so drunk that, even if I were human, he wouldn't see me.

"What do we do?" Hadley says in a quiet voice.

He continues toward us, clutching the bottle.

So many paths are in this forest, and this is the one he chooses to follow. It's one that will lead him directly to the lagoon. His steps are flawed and he sways from side to side within the path, but sure enough, he makes his way closer to where Hadley and I stand.

"Luna?" Hadley speaks up again.

Worry radiates off her as she tugs at my arms for attention, but I don't let my gaze leave the man. He could end up just like Hadley, going to the lagoon and becoming its next victim. It's a simple process—all he would have to do is step in the water and his human life would be over.

"We can't do anything," I whisper back to her. The air is so still and quiet in this moment that I fear my voice will upset the balance in nature.

The birds have quieted; the wind has died down—the only sound is the man's feet kicking aside debris from the path.

Hadley becomes silent next to me. I wonder if she remembers the last moments of her human life, how she had so readily taken hold of one of the stones that called her to the lagoon in the first place—the same stone she can't live without now. And it makes me wonder if this man feels the same thing—like he *must* go to the lagoon. It's not a choice for him; he must simply go.

So he does. He walks within feet of where Hadley and I stand. We are quiet as he makes his journey to the lagoon. His steps seem more certain the closer he gets. Behind me I hear Hadley stir, like she is putting all her effort into not running up to the man and stopping him from what he is about to do.

His feet touch the water. His leather shoes become soaked, but he doesn't flinch or slow down. The water is almost up to his knees before he stops.

"Please," Hadley says, her small voice breaking against the words.

The man's head snaps up at her words, looking in her general direction but unable to find her.

She freezes, so surprised by the possibility that he may

have heard her.

The man turns in our direction, searching for the sound, but just as soon as we had his attention, it is gone again. He bends down into the water, letting the water lap beyond his fingers, reaching his elbows. When he straightens again, he holds a silvery stone. And just like Hadley, the action is so simple. He looks at it and faints.

Hadley jumps up from behind me and goes to his aid. She must think he's human. She must assume he is in danger of drowning.

"Hadley," I say, catching her arm before she can touch him.

She pulls and pushes against me, so ignorant to what is happening even though her own human body has faced the same thing.

"Don't."

"Luna, he'll die if we let him drown!"

"Hadley," I say in soft voice.

Her tugging weakens as she hears my voice and turns to look at me.

"He's already dead."

"No. Luna, he's human. He's from my town. I grew up seeing him every day in the square. He's not an Essence like we are—he must have just been wandering around drunk and got lost. He does that, Luna, but if we don't help him, he'll drown."

Her eyes are pleading with me. Her expression softens as she begs me to loosen my grip and allow her to help. Her strength wanes until she watches my eyes, waiting for me to change my mind.

"He's not human anymore. That stone he picked up, it is the same type you chose when you first found the lagoon."

She must hear my words, but she doesn't respond. All Hadley does is turn from me and look to the man in the lagoon. His body occupies the middle of the water, floating like driftwood in the ocean. He doesn't look dead—he looks radiant. The sun reflects off the water and makes his skin glow, like he is a lost angel who was never meant to fall to Earth.

"His name is Edwin." She walks up to the very edge of the water, just close enough so the hem of her skirt skims the shore.

"Did you know him very well?" I ask.

She shakes her head. "My mother always told me to stay away, but I never feared him like the monster everyone thought him to be. Of course I never spoke to him, but he seemed nice enough. Just a little ... lost."

She watches him like this is the last connection she has to her previous life, and I suppose in a way it is. There is no way for her to see her mother or father or Valen. But here is Edwin, a person seen but never spoken to, and he has just landed himself in this life. Neither Hadley nor I asked for him to be here.

"Why can't I touch him?" Hadley finally asks.

I have no answer. For some reason the thought of anyone moving him from the lagoon makes it feel as if we are disturbing him. But who am I to say whether he should be moved or not? When it had been Hadley, I had dragged her body from the water the first chance I got before leaving her by the shore.

When I don't answer, she steps into the water. It hugs around her legs like a second skin as she goes closer to Edwin, wrapping her arms around his torso. She drags him out, never so much as asking for help when she reaches the shore.

His clothing clings to his skin; water droplets roll over his forehead. He doesn't gasp for air as he is pulled from the water—his human life is over. So fast, so unnoticed he is gone. And it's like he never made a whisper.

LII.

"He heard me," Hadley says.

It's night. The moon is high above us now, full in its shape. Days before Hadley would have left me to visit Valen, but here she is next to Edwin, the only part of her human life she has left. She never leaves his side, because she is afraid for him— for this life he has to wake up to.

"How could he hear me?"

It bothers her; that much I can tell. It bothers her that he may be some monster who can hear an Essence. Hadley looks at Edwin, a man who was lost within himself, and she combs over him with her piercing gaze like he may have a secret.

"He heard me when he was still human. Is that possible?" she asks. Finally she looks at me.

"It's not supposed to be," I tell her. Garren had made sure of this for me. He said an Essence can go on unseen, unheard. It used to be we could roam the earth like any other human, but then Garren changed that. Humanity forgot our kind. They walked through our bodies, ignored our voices, and forgot our images. Yet Edwin could hear Hadley, and Dimitri heard me before I ran away with Clara. It shouldn't be possible, but it is.

"Why?" Hadley looks at Edwin.

I'm not sure what it is she sees when she looks at him, but I think it may be sorrow. She lost her human life when she came here, and no matter how simple Edwin's life may have been—wandering through town without a family or home—it is still a loss.

"It's emotion," I say.

Hadley seems to be considering this.

"Why did you say please?"

Hadley sits up to face me. "Because I didn't want him to pick up the stone." She opens her hand once again, looking at the green gem there. It's a burden to her; it took her life away. Somehow by looking into it, she left her human life behind forever. "I didn't want him to do the same thing I had done."

She cared. Just like I had cared about Clara when Dimitri had heard me. I wanted to yell and scream, make him aware of everything he had done to murder a mother and consequently her child, but I couldn't. Yet somehow, after all Garren had done to make it impossible, the man had heard my voice.

"What happened? When you picked up the stone?" I ask.

"I saw myself. I don't know why I picked up the stone or why I even bothered looking at it, but I didn't see a silver stone in my hand. When I looked down I saw myself. I saw my eyes, and how alive and frightened they were. But I felt so lifted, so alive—and peering into my own eyes, I couldn't have looked away even if I wanted to. I don't remember anything after that."

Hadley turns her head to look at Edwin. He is at rest, his clothing now dry. I don't know how long it has been since he fell into the water, but he shows no sign of stirring awake. His hair is trimmed almost to his ears, and his clothing reveals he knew the streets well. If I hadn't seen him fall into the water, I would have thought he was just asleep now. His hand is tight around what must be the stone he had picked from the lagoon.

"Was I this peaceful?" Hadley asks.

I didn't stay with you, I want to tell her. I dragged her from the water and left her half on the shore, half in the lagoon. I wasn't watchful and nurturing like Hadley is now, but I remember the relief on her face right before she dropped into the water. So I tell her, "Yes."

She nods her head and there is silence between us for the rest of the night. We don't discuss how Edwin's human life is over or how, when he wakes, we will have to explain to him what it means to be an Essence. How we exist without the world. How every night, when the sun sets and the moon rises, we must be within the confines of the lagoon area within the forest.

He lies on the shore in a sort of bliss that is only temporary.

It's morning with the light first shining when Edwin finally moves. He turns over to his side, and as he does his spirit separates from itself. He moves and crouches on the ground, yet his body remains in its fixed position. I turn to Hadley to see if she has seen the same thing, but when I do I see she had fallen asleep at some point during the night, her mind quieting enough to fall into human habits. When I look at Edwin again, his body fades away until it is gone completely. But I still see him, strong as day, in the form of an Essence.

I lean forward and stir Hadley awake.

"What?" she asks in a dazed voice.

"He's awake," I tell her quickly.

At the sound of us speaking, he turns in the direction of our voices. As he does so, his face lights up and he smiles. "Hadley!" he says, coming to his feet to join us.

"Daddy?" she says. She stands also, picking up the hem of her skirt so she can go to Edwin.

"Hadley?" That's her father?

In that moment I'm lost outside their world. Edwin doesn't hesitate as Hadley steps forward and hugs the man who is no longer human. When she wraps her arms around him, her head rests against his chest like the embrace is something so familiar to them both, though neither can feel each other's touch.

"I thought I lost you," Edwin says. He holds her at arm's length, looking her up and down. His eyes are full of wonder as he looks at Hadley, and all she can do is smile in return.

"I've been here," she says.

"Hadley?" I ask again. This time she seems to hear me, turning from Edwin but not stepping away. "I thought you said he was someone who wandered your town. You didn't say he was your father."

Her face lowers with my words, like I've interrupted a fairy tale. She opens her mouth to speak but then thinks better of it and remains quiet. Behind her, her father looks at me for the first time. I can't tell if his gaze is critical or accepting, but when he sees my silvery irises, he takes Hadley by the shoulder and pulls her away slightly.

"Who is this?" he asks Hadley, a protective grip on her arm.

Hadley tries to step away, but he doesn't let her. Instead she just speaks with his back to her. "Daddy, this is Luna. She told me what we are, and she'll teach you also."

His eyes are sharp on me now. "*What we are*?" he asks. "What are we exactly?"

Edwin pushes Hadley behind him, so she can't look at me—this stranger who has his daughter. She doesn't protest, but her head peeks around his frame to watch. She smiles at me, but it is forced, almost scared as her father acts like Hadley might just be a piece of property.

"Sir, your daughter and I aren't something you've ever heard of. We're something that exists only in the spiritual sense. And now that you've come here and picked up that stone you hold in your hand, you've become one also. We're an Essence."

His face contorts with brewing anger, but he lifts his hand and opens his palm to the stone I had seen him pick from the lagoon. Surprise crosses his features as he toys with the stone he hadn't even realized he had been clutching.

"Did you kidnap my daughter and tell her these lies so she'd never come home?" he says with such sudden fervor that I'm taken aback by his tone.

"No, not at all," I say, trying to sway him to listen.

"Daddy, she's telling the truth," Hadley says.

"Quiet! Don't you listen to her!" Edwin shouts.

Hadley whimpers at his words, like he had just hit her.

I can tell by the broken features of her face that no matter how much she may agree with my words, she won't speak out against her father again.

"You need to understand, this isn't something I can control," I say. "You picked up that stone and it took away your human life."

He listens to my words, but his face doesn't soften. Instead he glares into his hand that holds the stone. It's dark blue, intense with a frigid sense of energy that I can't place.

"What makes you think we only exist in spirit?"

I can hear the skepticism in his voice, but I take a moment to convince him of the life he now has to live.

"Humans can't see us. We can't touch them, and they can't touch us. And they can only hear us if the proper emotion calls for it. Being heard isn't something we can always control."

He doesn't look at me and I can feel his distrust. He just rolls the stone across his fingers. Hadley watches him but doesn't speak up or move. Instead she stays in the spot her father had pushed her to, like she was a small child in need of punishment.

"And that stone," I say, "It has your soul, and that's why you're unable to put it down."

His hand stills. Edwin looks at me and there is something more than challenge in his eyes as he bends down, placing the deep blue stone on the forest floor. Without breaking eye contact, he stands again, this time with empty hands.

I can see his desire to give me a smug smile, but it is overpowered by his driving need to touch the stone. He tries to hold my gaze, but after a few moments his eyes flit down to the stone. He bends to pick it up again.

I don't say anything, and neither does he. Edwin doesn't tell me that I'm right or how, without the touch of the stone, he felt an anxious need to see it or touch it—to just have it in his possession. He doesn't confirm the suspicions I've formed after watching Hadley fidget when the stone was out of her touch.

"*Essence*?" he asks.

"Yes, sir," I say.

He nods his head, finally believing my words. Edwin looks to Hadley. She stands with her hands in fists at her sides, as if she might be tempted to run to my aid if needed but knew better than to step forward. When her father looks at her, she relaxes.

"What happened?" he asks her.

Hadley bites the bottom of her lip, facing something that she thought she had left behind forever—her human life, her father.

"Daddy, I didn't mean it. I was supposed to meet Valen, but he never came." Edwin stiffens at the boy's name, and Hadley instantly backs away.

"I told you—"

"No, Daddy, you didn't tell me. You demanded!" Her

words come out fast.

Hadley says them before her father is able to finish his own sentence, and I think I see regret in her eyes as the words come. "I love him," she says in a defeated voice.

Edwin doesn't scold Hadley. He stands there and takes her words, but I have a feeling these are words and phrases he's heard before.

"Valen looked for you every day for weeks, until he finally gave up," Edwin says.

Hadley's eyes light up. "Really?" Then they are heavy and weighted, like she's so tired of wanting something that she can't have.

Valen loved her enough to search for her. That's all she had ever wished, for him to find her, but sadness shows in her stance. If Valen came to her, he would also become a part of this curse; if he didn't come, she would be without him forever.

"Yes," Edwin says.

Hadley's eyes look everywhere except at her father and me.

I can see her mind working as she ignores our presence and puts together thoughts I don't trust her to form. All at once she gathers herself and walks into the forest, following the path she used to every night when she would visit Valen. This is the first time I've seen her step out of the vicinity of the lagoon since that night.

"Hadley?" I call out her name, a few steps behind her, but she doesn't stop to acknowledge me. "Where are you going?"

"Does it matter?"

"You can't leave," I say, watching as she slowly grows farther and farther away.

Behind us is the lagoon; Edwin stands alone, waiting for some answers to his new life. But Hadley moves forward, never taking a moment to gain her bearings as she pushes away branches and leaves to maneuver the path she's created for herself.

"I'll be back before nightfall. I promise you."

"You can't visit Valen," I say.

She stops and turns to me.

I expect to look at her face and see nothing but disgust for my words, but instead I see love and longing.

"I have to," she tells me. "What if he can hear my voice?"

Her words hang over us. The silence that follows is long and pleading as I remember all the times humans have heard us speak. It could be possible for us to communicate with the human world, and it's a hard offer to let pass.

"Luna, I have to say goodbye. I have to tell him that I love him."

She doesn't walk away yet.

I think of what I would do if I were Hadley, if I had the chance to tell Garren that I loved him and to say goodbye. And the answer is simple.

"Hurry back," I say.

I'm just barely able to see her smile form before she slips into the trees, heading forward with a renewed purpose and motivation. She's a girl in love, and I'm jealous of her ability to love and be loved so fearlessly.

LIII.

Edwin is sitting near the shore of the lagoon when I step from the trees. He hears my approach and in an instant his back straightens, like he's afraid of being seen as anything less than weak.

"She's gone off to see him again," he says, never bothering to turn to look at me.

"Yes."

His hands cover his face as I step alongside him. I sit a distance away, my gown spilling out around me in piles of silk. He sees this and laughs in the light way that only happens when dealing with simple emotions scattered between tragedies.

"Why the old gown? Dressing for your suitor, so he can take you to the costume gala?"

I watch his face as he speaks, but he never bothers to look at me. "I don't know where I am, let alone where the man I love is. Hadley suggested I wear the dress, if he were to ever find me."

Edwin releases a heavy breath. "Sorry," is all he says.

"She's your daughter?" I ask.

"We have the same smile," he says, but he doesn't smile, so I can't say if he's right or not.

Instead he seems intent on staring forward into nothing,

like the world will give answers or gifts.

"She didn't tell me that you were her father," I say. He never so much as responds, so I try again. "Hadley referred to you as the man who wanders around drunk, the man her mother told her to avoid."

His shoulders hunch forward at the words, like I've taken a whip to his back for a lashing. His eyes wander to the ground.

"Her mother passed away a few years ago." For a long moment that's all he says. I don't push him for more, but with patience he speaks again. "I drink a little too much, so her mother would probably say that."

"You don't approve of Valen?"

"No," he says in a hard voice.

"But why? If he loves her, that's all that should matter."

Edwin turns to me and finally looks me in the eye. He sees me as something smaller and weaker than himself as he speaks.

"You don't know anything. Love is a fairy tale. My own wife doesn't love me today, didn't love me yesterday, and probably won't love me tomorrow. Life is about getting by, not finding your *soul mate*." He scoffs at the words. "Hadley wasted her time falling for Valen and look where it has taken her."

"That's not true," I say.

"Isn't it?" he says, getting to his feet. He stands over me and sways the slightest bit.

In that moment I can see him as the drunken man Hadley had described.

"You must have seen reason enough though. You loved a man, but here you are—getting by, just as you should. Not writing some love story."

"There's nothing wrong with a love story," I say.

Hadley comes back before dusk like she had promised. The sky is just starting to glow with a purple and orange hue as she walks through the trees, gliding her fingertips over the edges of the bark. Her step has no rush or energy as she approaches. Defeat fills her stance but also contentment. Her body screams surrender, but her face seems more placid and calm.

"Did you find him?" I ask. She seems to be in her own trance, but she lifts her head to my voice.

"Yes," she says. Her voice reveals nothing.

I find no hint of emotion in her. Instead Hadley just looks around, turning her body so she can see behind me. "Is my father here?"

I turn to look. He had been by the lagoon the last time I had checked, but now there is no sign of him. I had warned Edwin of the dangers of straying from the lagoon after dark, but he seems to have run off, if only for a little while. But the sky is still bright; he has time to come back if he wishes.

"He'll come," I tell her.

Hadley nods her head as if the information means nothing to her, but then she lets out a deep sigh and seems to surrender to herself. "I told him goodbye," she says, brushing past me to sit on a large rock that juts out from the ground. She smiles in a happy way as she lets her shield fall away.

Neither one of us needs to say who *he* is—it's the boy she loves. His name is Valen, even if we don't speak it.

"He heard you?" I sit next to her on the stone. Hadley seems so exhausted as she speaks, but I see the happiness radiate off her skin and into the air.

"I found him in town. I followed him for a long time until he was alone, and then I told him goodbye."

A smile creeps across her lips, even though I know she never wanted to tell Valen goodbye—not forever.

"How?" I ask.

"He was carrying something to another town close by—a basket of some sorts—but I stepped up to walk with him. And, Luna, he stopped walking when I was close to him. He looked around like he knew I was there but wasn't quite sure of my location. So I gave him space, and after another moment he walked again.

"I whispered to him that I was okay, and you know what he did, Luna?"

Hadley looks at me, like she can't believe her own words. In her mind the memory is something just short of a miracle—something she wanted and asked for but never thought she would receive—a final goodbye.

"He whispered my name." Her words are so final. "And I stood off to the side and he found me. He couldn't look at me, but in that moment he knew exactly where I was. I told him that

I loved him and that I was okay. He heard me, Luna, because he whispered back, 'I love you too'."

Hadley's lips quiver, but what I see is so different than the sadness I had seen earlier. This isn't heartbreak; this is love.

"And I told him goodbye, Luna. I said goodbye, and he didn't say anything back, but I know he heard me because he dropped the basket he was carrying and came to me. He stood right in front of me and couldn't see me, but it didn't matter because he knew I was there. I told him I had to go and that I would always love him, and he shook his head and cried. I had never seen him cry, and it hurt so much."

Her words slow down, like the memory is becoming too much for her. But soon her body relaxes again, and I can tell she is ready to finish her story.

"He fell to his knees, and I knew there was nothing in this world I could have done to take away his pain. He begged me to come back somehow, to take him with me, to do something so we could be together again, but I can't do that to him. So as he knelt, I bent forward and kissed his forehead."

Hadley locks her gaze on mine. "We can't touch humans?" she asks, her voice quivering and scratching over the syllables.

"No," I say, my words so light against hers.

Hadley bites the bottom of her lips, like she is holding in tears, but then she takes a breath and continues. "I left after I passed through his body. I didn't want to be his ghost."

Every emotion seems so potent. Next to me Hadley tries

to compose herself. I watch her as her quivers subside and she takes control of herself once again.

"Luna?"

When I turn to look at her, she doesn't look broken anymore. Hadley looks tired, like it's been days since she has been able to sleep, but at the same time she seems so alive, so ready to fight if it were called for.

"I think there's more to this than we can understand. I know you said being an Essence means you can't exist physically, but is speaking physical or spiritual?"

Her question rolls over in my mind, and once again I can't find an answer for her. Speaking doesn't seem either physical or spiritual. So what does that make it? And what does it mean that humans can hear us?

"I don't think we are as cut off from the human world as much as we may think," Hadley says.

LIV.

There's something about eternity that suddenly makes time pass in a different way. When I was human it had a certain hum, a certain pace that says things can only happen during a specific time. Nothing can happen too soon or too fast. But eternity awakens a quickened tone.

Years lapse without much certainty. A day seems to possess only glimmers of reality. The sun rises and sets in a faster course. Weeks for a human seem only to be a day to an Essence. It all fuses together, because there is no distinction. We have nowhere to go, no places to see, no escape. Each day at sunset we must be here, in the forest, around the lagoon.

I've made note to watch the seasons. Green leaves turn to bright red, orange, and yellow, until finally a burnt brown allows the trees to shed their leaves. The trees make their own coating on the forest floor until the sky releases the white snow of winter. When the snow melts, the trees bloom and the cycle starts again. I count each cycle, and I'm amazed when the years pass. The three of us live together in the lagoon, wandering during the days when the sun is high, and coming back at night before the sun whispers its last goodbye of the evening.

Hadley speaks to her father but only in clipped words.

Neither mentions their past or even their future. Edwin talks to me, but only if I say something first. They put up with each other. That is all. Edwin is Hadley's father, but no one would know it by just watching them. Hadley never speaks ill of him, and the only time she has touched him was to hug him when he first came to the lagoon. Edwin has a hold on her though. She acts differently when he is around, like she feels she must behave or get reprimanded. And when I watch Edwin, I see why. He looks at her like she is property—not in a protective fatherly way, but in ownership, like no one can touch Hadley without his permission.

Hadley watches the town. She watches for Valen. He grows up without her and falls in love again. Hadley never learns the name of the girl, but she isn't much younger than Valen himself. Many nights the two of us stay up speaking to each other. Hadley knows never to ask of Garren. She had once, but she knows it only hurts me. Instead Hadley tells me of Valen and the new love he has found. I expect her to mourn her loss of Valen, but she never does. Instead she seems happy for him. And only a few years later they marry. Hadley is a ghost at their wedding, standing in the corner of the church without anyone knowing she is really there.

One night I asked her why she watches him after she had said goodbye. Hadley told me it was because, even though he can't love her anymore, she still loves him and she can't change that. She had said goodbye because she believed in love. And, to her, love was making sure he was happy, even if it was with someone else.

The sun had just begun to set. The orange sky is a warning sign that screams out retreat. Hadley is already sitting at the edge of the lagoon when I break through the trees, but Edwin isn't in sight yet.

"Have you seen your father?" I ask.

Hadley stands as I approach and wipes at the skirts of her gown. The bright green, once the same color as her stone, is now muted and dull. A vine necklace hangs across her collarbone, the thick natural cords wrapping around the stone that conceals a piece of Hadley's soul. Her arms hang loose at her sides, no longer wrapped tightly into a fist like they had been for months until Hadley made her distinctive piece of jewelry.

"I saw him in town today."

"He doesn't go into town," I say.

Edwin leaves the lagoon every day, but never once has he set foot in town. I had asked him why, and he said that seeing faces he knew go on without him wasn't worth his time. He said he'd rather walk through the same forest every day than see people he knew make something out of their lives, all when he had lost his.

"He said it's been long enough."

I run through the amount of time in my head. It's been years; that much I'm sure of. Seasons have come and gone. Snow has coated the forest and frozen the lagoon, except for the steady rhythm of water that never stills. Ice crystals have formed transparent stalagmites, only to melt away within a few months, weeks, or days. But I'm not sure if enough years have passed to allow Edwin's generation to disappear.

The sky is purple now. Hadley watches the sun hover over the horizon and realizes her father only has a handful of time left before the sun goes down. Neither one of us knows what happens if we don't come back to the lagoon. Hadley had been caught between the trees once after sundown, and I can tell by the way her fingers dig into her palm that she doesn't wish that pain upon her father.

A look of worry coats Hadley's face as she glances through the trees near the perimeter of the lagoon. She turns her gaze back to the sky to see how much time is left.

"Should I look for him?" she asks.

I shake my head. "He knows better than to stay out."

"But what if he got lost? It's been years since he's gone into town."

I give Hadley a stern look. She and I both understand that her father, no matter how long it has been, would know his way around town enough to get back.

Hadley continues to look between the trees and the sky.

She's almost calm in a way, but at the same time I can see her cool exterior slip as the seconds go by. It amazes me how this man has never acted as a father toward Hadley, yet she still loves him.

"He'll get here," I say.

Hadley nods her head but doesn't reply. Her attention turns when a low scream bursts from the forest. The sky is darker now, much darker than it normally is when we come back to the lagoon at night.

"Daddy?" Hadley runs off. She stops just shy of where the border of the lagoon ends. The pebbles of the beach stop, and the ground where she stands turns to a soil with small bits of green in it. It's almost as if a rope were tied around her waist, stopping her from going any farther as her fingers reach out to the forest. There's an invisible barrier in front of her, a warning that she should go no farther.

As I come up behind her, I feel a presence growing upon me, making it harder to walk forward. Once I am next to Hadley my chest and neck constrict, making it difficult to breathe. In my mind I keep reminding myself how I'm not human--how air shouldn't matter—but panic swells within me regardless.

Edwin is lost within the trees. He stumbles over rocks and branches that reach out across from him. He trips more often than not, but that doesn't seem to be what is slowing him down. He looks like he's in pain. As he comes closer, his eyes are barely open.

"What's wrong with him?" Hadley asks, next to me.

Her voice is tight, and I realize she must feel the same constriction as I do here at the edge of the lagoon.

I turn to her and she looks back at me. She must know; she must remember the pain she had felt when it had been her outside the lagoon after the sun had said goodnight once again.

Except this time it is her father. Hadley doesn't say another word to me as she turns to watch her father fight this battle against the night.

Edwin is within arm's reach. We could put out our arms and touch him, but the only movement we are allowed is backward. Edwin doesn't look at us as he covers the final distance to get within the lagoon, and when he does, he falls to the ground with a muted thud. Hadley goes to work as soon as he crosses the invisible barrier created by the lagoon and pulls her father in deeper. I join her, scooping my hands under his armpits and dragging him away. As we edge from the forest, the crushing and suffocating force that made it difficult to breathe lessens until it is gone completely.

We let go of him and back away. Hadley cowers at the edge of the water and dips her finger in, disrupting the smooth surface. As the ripples echo across the water she seems to calm. One hand dips into the water while the other clutches the stone at her neck.

I watch Edwin as he shakes on the ground. He's frantic, searching his pockets for something, rolling over on the ground to get a better angle without actually getting up. Finally he seems satisfied when he pulls an object from his trouser pocket and brings it to where his heart would be. Both his hands are wrapped tightly around the object, but after shifting and moments of panic, his fingers move enough to see his stone clutched there. It glows a dull red against his skin.

Free of the forest, I feel a release within me. It was as if someone had been crushing me with their weight, forcing me to lie on the ground as a heavy stone was placed on my chest until I couldn't breathe any longer.

"Edwin?"

Hadley and I both hear the unfamiliar voice. We lock gazes, and even though we stand opposite each other with Edwin between us, it is like we are connected. Neither of us know the voice, but the voice knows Edwin—her father. He lies on the ground, still winded. He doesn't speak, but he's heard the voice. His own eyes are turned toward the trees where the voice had come from. He knows who this is. And it scares him.

LV.

"Who is that?" Hadley is the first to speak. Her breaths are staggered and hard, but anger withers at the edge of her voice.

"Just someone I used to know," Edwin says. He tries to get up, but his strength fails him as he stumbles and falls to the ground again.

In the trees I hear whoever it is come closer. He continues to call out for Edwin, but a response never comes from him. Hadley remains silent as the stranger comes closer. All three of us are able to hear his footsteps crunch across the forest floor. Hadley has slowed her breathing enough to become quiet, but Edwin still makes haggard attempts to gain oxygen he doesn't need to survive.

"Who is that?" I ask. When I speak I'm surprised by the exhaustion in my voice. Any energy I exert is greeted by the same weight that had accompanied me at the edge of the forest.

Edwin turns to look at me with a small sadness, like maybe he is sorry for what he is about to say. "I knew him when he was only a boy. I trained him to dock the boats."

He doesn't say anything else. A commotion comes from the trees, but none of us turn to look.

"Edwin!" someone says.

It's a man, that much I can tell from his tone. Edwin

turns to his call and looks at whoever has just walked in. I shift my gaze to see a man standing at the edge of the lagoon where the forest begins.

He freezes and looks at Edwin.

I watch back and forth between the two of them. The man's gaze locks on Edwin as he remains on the ground. The man sees Edwin. That shouldn't be possible.

"What happened to you?" the man asks. He's no longer the boy Edwin had known when he was still human. He has grown to be a man, almost as old as Edwin when he became an Essence.

Edwin doesn't respond to him. He just closes his eyes and pretends like the man isn't even here.

I step forward. The leaves crunch under my feet, but the man doesn't turn to look at me. I continue until I'm standing in his direct sight, but still he sees through me to Edwin.

The man's eyes waver the longer he remains still. After a few moments I can see his attention wane, but he doesn't leave. Instead he steps forward, walking toward me without realizing it.

I put out a hand to stop him, but my palm passes through his chest. I move out of the way before he is able to completely walk through my figure.

"Edwin, why can he see you?" I ask.

"I don't know," he whimpers, still on the ground.

The man walks forward. I wait for him to stop to speak to Edwin, but he doesn't. Instead he continues on, stepping around Edwin where he lies. The lagoon's clear water calls to the man until he steps to the edge of the shore. I look up at Hadley where she stands far off from the scene. Neither of us says a thing, but we both know what the other is thinking—this is it; his human life will be gone soon.

The man steps into the water. Nothing stops him. I stand close by, still stunned by the fact that the man can see Edwin—and only Edwin. The man had seen him, but now Edwin lies in the dirt, offering nothing. Someone Edwin had known as a child is about to lose his human life, give up his soul—Edwin must know this—but he never steps forward.

"Do something," I whisper in a harsh voice.

Edwin responds by shaking his head no. He doesn't bother to watch as the man wades through the water, looks at the sandy soil beneath his feet, and bends down to retrieve a stone.

"Don't do it," Hadley says. She closes her eyes and doesn't see how he freezes at the sound of her voice. The moment is only frozen for a short time before he's trapped again in the trance the lagoon holds over him. Then he looks into the palm of his hand.

I don't watch after that. I know what will happen. Even with my eyes pulled away, I know his body falls into the water and makes small waves in the pool. I hear the splash but don't bother to run to his aid or try to save someone who is beyond my care.

No one speaks. I can hear Hadley whimper as she stumbles away. She isn't able to travel far though. The darkness of the coming night closes around us as the sun finally says goodbye for another evening.

I walk up to Edwin and bend down to look at him. His eyes carry exhaustion where there shouldn't be any, and fear where I had never seen it before.

"I don't know why he could see you or why he can hear Hadley, but you could have saved him," I say.

He looks back at me with an open vulnerability I know he will wipe away as soon as this is all over.

"I was trying to run from him. I didn't know he could see me," he says, his voice full of suffering.

"Next time," I say, "if another human comes within the confines of this lagoon, you do all in your power to stop him or her. If they can see you, you may be able to touch them and stop them from ending their human life. Their soul is at stake, so do something about it."

He doesn't say anything in return. I rise slowly to a standing posture, waiting for some rebuttal or defense, but it never comes. Maybe he agrees with me. Maybe he will regret allowing this man he had known to take away his life, or maybe he just doesn't care about my words. Either way I turn my back on him.

The lagoon traps us here for another night. There is no escape for us within the forest. Our souls are lost, captured within these stones that control our existence. I had once thought there were rules, regulations of being an Essence. No one can hear us, yet Hadley has a voice which humans hear. No one can see us, yet Edwin has an image visible to the living. None of it makes sense. All I know is these people who had once been human are victim to the lagoon. And I will do all I can to save any others from its pull.

LVI.

Edwin and Hadley are asleep when the sun comes up the next morning. Like most nights they've fallen into their human habits, but I couldn't. Through the darkness of night I just looked at this man and wondered how it was he became a part of all this.

It had started with Mystral. She was one person who had a plan, a mission, and that was to have eternal life. She didn't care what happened to others, so long as she got what she wanted. And here it is, hundreds of years later, and so many human souls taken and traded for this thing we call an Essence.

Through the night I mourned for the man I didn't know. Although I was now accompanied by three others, I had never felt so alone. Edwin curled against a rock near the lagoon in his slumber and Hadley didn't say much all night. She was doing the same thing I was—examining this new person who just became a part of our world for no particular reason.

When she finally fell asleep I was left to think of Garren. I want him and need him, but he isn't here. He isn't anywhere that I know of. I wonder if Garren is in Tiboulain, guarding his own waters, preventing it from taking human lives, if either of us will ever be able to leave to search out the other.

The next morning comes slowly. It inches its way across the horizon like a tease, never fully allowing me to escape and to push away the thoughts. I love him—I know I love him—and I need him. Not in the way I need support or kindness, but in a way I used to need oxygen to breathe. I keep waiting for him to find me and save me from whatever this nightmare is of waking up every day, never able to stray too far.

I see Edwin stir in his sleep, propped up against a rock. At his feet is the man he had known when he was human and who now lies sprawled against the stony beach. Edwin had eventually pulled that man from the water, long after he had picked up the stone. I had accused him of refusing to save the man, and in truth, I still believe he could have saved him if he had only wanted to.

The man spent a long time with his body floating in the water, no one bothering to give him a second look, never mind bringing his human body to peace outside the hold of the lagoon. Eventually Edwin pulled him out. Hadley and I didn't say anything. We watched him, but he refused to look up after I had spoken to him.

"What will we do?" Hadley's voice is hushed beside me.

When I turn to look at her, I see she has yet to uncurl herself from the tight ball she makes every night. Her gown makes its own form of mattress, providing just as much shelter as a thick blanket would.

She looks at me when she speaks, but her attention is behind us, where the forest begins.

"Are the humans just going to keep coming?" she asks.

It pains me to hear her speak of humans in that way, like

she was never one of them herself and can never connect with them again.

I turn around and see the forest that Hadley sees. It is open and beautiful. Trees scatter the floor to disguise anything that may hide within the forest, but it is also open enough to easily make one's way through the woods without struggling to find a path. With the sun rising, birds that can't be seen make their morning calls out in the wild and small animals scour the ground looking for food. It's a beautiful world, and it's a world we must say goodbye to.

"Come," I say, getting up from the position I had found myself in all night. Hadley gets to her feet, but I can see the questions in her eyes as she watches my every movement for some sign.

"What are we doing?" She looks to where her father rests on the ground with the other man. Edwin is fast asleep, and the man looks as still and silent as he had all night, while I waited for him to wake into this new life.

"Preventing others from coming," I say. I wrap my hand around Hadley's wrist and pull her away with me.

She doesn't protest, but still turns to look back at the lagoon.

I expect her to be watching her father, but when I follow her gaze, I see she is looking at the man who appears to be nothing more than a lifeless body.

"You knew him," I say. I can tell in the way she looks at him that this is a face she's seen before.

A small recollection appears in her eyes but also confusion, as she sees the changes the years have brought to someone she had known.

"That's Giles. He was younger than me when I was human. My father taught him how to dock the boats."

Her mind fades away as her words blend together. I tug her into the forest, but I can tell she is elsewhere as her body pulls to go where Giles is.

"He looks so different," she says.

Hadley walks with me then, finding some satisfaction in recalling his name.

"Has it really been that many years?"

I keep my grip on Hadley's wrist as we walk, sure that if I release her, she will drift away and I'll lose her. "How old was he when you knew him?"

"He was thirteen. My father was unkind to him most of the time, but when he taught him the docks, he had nothing but kind intentions."

Giles is no longer thirteen years old, that much is obvious. The man back at the lagoon must be near forty years old.

More time has passed than either of us were aware.

"What are we doing?" Hadley asks.

We haven't gotten far. I can still see the lagoon and Edwin, but we are just outside the invisible line created every night that we are not allowed to cross.

"Hadley, we are protecting others. I can't let anyone else

get trapped in here with us, so I need your help. We will plant trees. They'll grow around the lagoon, shutting us in. We can still leave during the day, but it will deter any curious eyes. To the humans it will just be a thick settlement of trees. They won't bother coming closer."

"Where will we get the trees?"

"We're not," I say. Her brows furrow together in confusion until I bend down and find an acorn on the ground. "Today we'll be planting." I hold out the acorn to her and she takes it, rolling the seed around in her hand.

"It will be years before it grows into anything that will resemble a tree."

"I know. And others will find this lagoon, and they'll pick up the stone and they'll become an Essence. But we can do nothing more."

I bend down again and kneel on the soil of the forest. Patches of grass are everywhere, along with small rocks and broken branches, but hidden beneath the rubble are acorns. I gather them in my palm and soon Hadley does the same.

"Where are we planting these?" Hadley asks, standing up.

I hold onto the acorns that will be trees in the years to follow and come next to Hadley. "You remember the line that is created every night?"

"Of course." She takes a deep breath. We had both seen and experienced that line only a handful of hours ago.

"Dig a hole and place an acorn along the line. Give them

about five feet of separation—enough room to grow strong but not so much as to let curious hikers pass."

She nods her head, and soon we are both at work creating a border along the lagoon. Working in opposite directions, we move away from each other. It's simple work—digging a small hole, placing the acorn inside, then covering it again—before moving on to the next spot. We continue this until we've covered the entire circumference and meet again. Hadley's dress is covered in dirt, and for the first time, I realize how ridiculous the both of us must look in such extravagant gowns.

She turns her head in surprise, realizing we've covered the circumference of the area. She laughs a little before standing up.

"This place is bigger than I thought," she says, brushing the dirt from her hands.

"Look at our dresses." We both look at each other and then at our gowns. I join in Hadley's laughter as she tries to brush away the dirt to little avail.

"Well, I think the look is just darling, don't you, Luna?" She smiles at me. "We must look proper in our gowns for the men in our lives."

I feel my face fall. Any laughter that had just been here floats away to a whisper as Hadley comes to terms with what she had said.

"I'm sorry," she says. "Sometimes I forget." She stares at me, and I realize how broken I must look to her. I'm the one who, after all these years, cannot forget or let go of someone I'm not even sure loved me. "You never got to say goodbye?"

"No," I say. "I never knew I was leaving."

Hadley watches me, so I try to smile. It's foolish of me to wait for someone I know will never come back, but it doesn't stop my heart from hoping.

I wipe the stains of dirt that scatter across the hem of my dress. The gown is no longer beautiful. I imagine Garren coming back and seeing me and being repulsed.

"I can't wear this," I say.

Hadley catches my hand so I can no longer fidget with the fabric. "I'll clean it off for you so you can wear it." She looks at me in a way that says I have no option.

"He's not coming back," I tell her.

"So what if he never comes back? Luna, that doesn't mean he doesn't love you. It means he can't find you. Wear the dress because it makes you beautiful. It's not for him anymore. It's for you."

Hadley smiles at me. It's a wonder how she looks no older than sixteen but has wisdom beyond her years. Part of me reminds myself that she must be nearing fifty or sixty in a human's time, but then I remember this is the same wisdom I had seen when I first met her.

"Okay," I say.

We both end the subject and make our way back to the lagoon. The sun settles in the middle of the sky; only a few clouds are to be seen. Voices can be heard as we come closer, and

I'm able to see Edwin's back as he sits facing the water. Someone else is beside him.

"Is that Giles?" I ask Hadley.

She squints forward. "He woke up already."

"Edwin," I shout. He turns and when he sees us he stands, but doesn't move any closer.

"Luna, this is Giles. I knew him when he was just a boy," Edwin says.

"So I've heard."

Giles turns to get up also. When he stands he comes to meet me and offers his hand. He's handsome—someone all the girls would have noticed in the village—with dark hair at his temples, but his handshake is weak and unsure. He holds himself like a man, but at the slight touch of his palm, I'm able to see just how afraid he is.

"I'm Luna," I say in a level tone.

He notices my eyes and balks for a moment, but accepts me and attempts a smile. "You discovered this place?"

I look around and see it as he does. The lagoon is the heart of the land, with its bright beautiful waters and the rock wall that cradles it all. But then the stone beach and small outcroppings of greenery and trees appear. It's a sight to remember—unless trapped here every day.

"Stumbled upon," I say.

He smiles and looks beside me where Hadley stands. A frown is locked on her face for a moment, until recognition takes over. He doesn't speak to her or offer any sign that he remembers her, except for raising his eyebrows the smallest bit.

"I suppose we all seem to stumble into things," he finally says. Giles looks around again, taking in the forest. "What do you call it?"

I don't speak at first. I've been here longer than I can keep track, but I've only ever called it the lagoon. It seems so improper now to not have something more to identify this spot. It's a place, a location, but it has no name. It's an illusion of beauty but also a home.

"Phantom Lagoon," I say. Hadley turns to look at me, but I don't look for her approval.

Edwin stands at his position on the beach, but he crosses his arms over his chest—there's a pride in his stance.

"Phantom Lagoon," Giles says. "Fitting."

"What happened?" I ask him, then turn to look at Edwin when I speak.

Giles joins me and turns to look at him also.

"I went into town and Giles saw me," he says, never moving to uncross his arms.

"You saw him? When you were human?" I ask Giles.

Giles nods his head slightly but drifts from the subject. "While you were away, Edwin was telling me about this. ... We're an Essence?"

"Yes. We exist only spiritually," I tell him.

Hadley speaks up from behind me. "But we think there might be more than that to it."

Giles looks at her now, examining her more than he had

before. Hadley shrinks away from his gaze and comes closer to me, blocking his view slightly.

"Edwin," I say, "what did you tell Giles?"

He comes to join the rest of us now, retreating from his lone stance on the beach. As he does, he seems to grow softer, more human than we've seen him over the years.

"We live forever. We can't be seen, heard, or touched. Every night we must be here in the lagoon or we feel pain—simple as that. I don't know what happens, but it hurts like hell to be outside the border when the sun is down. We have no sense of touch and our physical bodies are in the cave. And these stones," he says, pulling out a cord with his ruby stone tied to the end, "are somehow our souls now, and we have to keep them safe."

I look at Giles to see if this information has been heard before. He looks down at the stone in his hand that is an earthy brown with a violet hue in the sunlight. He holds it with great care, and the look in his eyes makes the moment so private that I wish to look away.

"Giles," I say quietly.

He looks up at me and covers the stone with his fingers.

"You saw Edwin while you were human?"

All eyes are on Giles now. He passes the stone from one hand to the other, turning his gaze over the three sets of eyes that watch him. He looks first to Edwin, flits his gaze to Hadley as she hides herself behind me, until he finally looks at me.

"He apprenticed me when I was just a boy. When I saw

him walk through town, I thought maybe it was just someone who looked like him, but then he looked back at me and smiled. I didn't understand how it was him, but I just knew. I tried to speak to Edwin, but when I did he ran away. So I followed."

We're all silent for a moment.

Giles isn't sure who to look at, shifting his gaze between me and Edwin, but I look at Edwin, waiting for some response.

"You said humans can't see us," is all he has to say.

"I think we have powers," Hadley quietly whimpers, so unsure of her words being spoken.

We all turn to look at Hadley. She seems paralyzed with fear for a moment. No one speaks up to disagree with what she's said, but she acts as if we've shunned her for her ignorance.

"What do you mean?" I ask.

She seems encouraged by my question and holds herself taller before she speaks.

"Humans can hear me. Valen heard me, Luna, and I know you said it has to do with emotion, but others have heard me also. I don't have to try in order for a human to hear me. When I go to town, sometimes I whisper in strangers' ears just to see if they notice me, and they do."

I let her words hang in the air. Once she's done three gazes turn to me. They wait for a reply I don't have.

"Okay," I say.

LVII.

The moon is cut in half tonight, the sky dark with speckles of small lights from points of stars. It makes Phantom Lagoon a beautiful mystery. Crickets call out their soothing sound that can never be replicated as they click their heels in the trees. The wind is only a soft hush against my cheeks, my only awareness of the sensation being the strands of hair that move across my fingers.

"Why isn't your body in the cave?"

A voice comes from behind me. I don't know the voice well, but it belongs to Giles. He's soft in his approach, joining me. I've found a solace from the lagoon itself while still being within the boulders. There's an unclear path to the top of the cave in Phantom Lagoon. Its backside acts as the rock wall of the lagoon itself, but the mouth of the cave is still blocked off to avoid the sight of the bodies of those victims to the stones. I sit on what is the roof of the cave. If I walk forward, I would meet with the edge of the cliff face and look over everything that is Phantom Lagoon.

Giles sits next to me on the ground. Solid rock pours out in all directions around us, but neither of us can feel the rough surface beneath our feet.

"You went into the cave?" I don't look at him at first, embarrassed to have my private spot discovered. Hadley and

Edwin never let the lagoon leave their sight anymore. Their lack of curiosity allows me to be left alone, if only at night.

"Edwin told me about it. I wanted to see if it was true."

I let out a sigh when I look at him. I can't imagine what it would be like to see my dead body. It's an experience that isn't natural—that shouldn't occur—but it does for an Essence.

"I guess I just wanted to know why your body wasn't in the cave," Giles says.

I gather my gown in my fists, holding the fabric closer to me. The hem is still brown from kneeling in the soil to plant the trees. It makes me feel exposed and vulnerable even though the clothing covers almost every inch of skin.

"I'm not like the rest of you," I say.

"What do you mean?"

I don't want to tell him my story. It all seems too much for a stranger to know, even if we will be spending eternity together. No matter how many others come here, I don't want everyone to know I was the cause of this—that I carried the moon's curse and brought it here when it could have stayed on Tiboulain, where fewer lives would have been taken.

So I lie. "I burned my body."

Giles seems put off by my words or at least unable to respond. The silence between us is comfortable. I don't push him, and he doesn't push me. For a long time I think he'll leave it at that and won't ask any further questions, but it's too soon when I hear his voice again.

"Why?"

I brush away a fern embedded in my skirt. This gown no longer makes me look beautiful like Hadley intended me to be.

"To forget. To let go. To remember I'm not human."

Giles just nods his head next to me like he understands. "Did it hurt?" he asks.

I'm confused by his question. "We don't feel anything. It may have been my body, but Edwin already told you that we don't have any sense of touch."

"That's not what I mean." He repositions himself to look at me.

I imagine how Hadley and Edwin are so close to us, yet they have no idea this piece of Phantom Lagoon exists. Below us they sleep on the beach, growing bored and falling into human traits each night, but this newest Essence doesn't. The one who is most likely to remember what it's like to be human sits in front of me, just as awake as I am.

"Luna, you burned your body. You stood there and said goodbye to your physical self forever. You saw it go up in flames in front of you. You saw your own death, and you tell me it didn't hurt?"

I stare into his eyes and realize how easy it would be to tell him the truth. How I can tell him of Marseille and the Black Death that killed everyone I knew. How no one was able to love me because I appeared to be a witch. How Mystral saw that and took death from me when I didn't want her to. How I fell in love with someone, who I'm not sure ever felt the same. How all I wish is to rest in peace but can't, when I've made others fall victim to Phantom Lagoon and taken away their human life. I've trapped their souls along with mine.

But I can't tell him that. I look at him and see his brown eyes that only display kindness and don't flinch as I say nothing of the truth.

"Of course it hurt, but it hurt more knowing that it existed. I let go of my hopes, of the slightest possibility that I could be human again."

Giles wrestles with the idea. He opens his mouth to speak but then shuts it again. He turns away only to look at me again, wishing to challenge my idea. But then he doesn't. Giles studies me one last time before standing up and walking away. I hear his footsteps as he leaves me at the top of Phantom Lagoon.

He believes me.

LVIII.

The trees planted around the lagoon grow slowly. There are gaps in our system. Some of the acorns sprout with small green plants that grow from the ground—others don't grow at all. Hadley and I make our rounds, checking to see which ones have grown weak after planting and replant in the areas that don't sprout anything.

The green saplings look like unfed infants compared to the large oaks that stand mighty and strong just feet away. The small sprouts of trees could be pulled out by the root, if I so wished. The stems aren't any bigger than my finger, and the youngest trees only stand a foot or so tall. The other trees that Hadley and I had to replant after the first round of seeds didn't grow, are just a tiny sprout in the ground; only to be seen if someone looks for them.

As more seasons come and go, I'm reminded that it will be a long time until these trees are able to act as a safeguard for the humans.

A woman enters Phantom Lagoon in the middle of the night. She's wearing a torn nightgown, and from my view atop the cave I can see her tears. I watch her as she navigates through the dark and finds her way to the lagoon. She's aware of everything around her as she walks. Her head turns from side to side. The woman has more control than Edwin, Giles, or Hadley did when they stumbled upon the lagoon.

Edwin sleeps on the beach in a corner where I can't see him. Giles is close by—within sight of this woman, had his body been visible to humans—but of course, the woman stumbles past him.

I have yet to understand how humans are able to see Edwin and hear Hadley.

The woman is quiet as she walks through the lagoon. It's clear she has no real destination while she zigzags over the stony ground, never showing any sign of slowing down.

Hadley is at the edge of the beach, sitting awake in the night. When she hears the woman approach, she looks up to where I stand atop Phantom Lagoon's rock wall and cave. Her eyes plead with me as she waits for another person to lose their human soul.

The woman is younger than Edwin, but some unknown grief weighs down her heart. Hadley watches her as she walks closer and closer to the water.

"Please go home," Hadley says. She stands at the side of the woman, allowing her the choice of stepping into the water or not.

"I can't," the woman replies. She doesn't seem shocked or frightened by Hadley's voice. In fact the woman smiles like some great mystery has been confirmed for her.

She takes tentative strides across the beach, bits of gravel pushing against her feet. She steps into the water, and for the first time, I notice she isn't wearing any shoes. Her bare feet go farther into the lagoon as her nightgown floats over the surface of the water. In the night sky the moon shines above the three of us. Hadley is on the beach with nothing more to say. The woman is up to her knees in water and I'm left to stand on the rock wall, watching it all.

The woman has silent tears running down her cheeks as she kneels in the water, the liquid soaking her chest. Her hand skims the bottom of the lagoon as she picks up a silver stone and looks into it. She sees herself within the surface, observes her soul, and then she's gone. Her body falls into the water, and Hadley turns her gaze on me.

We both look at each other, wondering if we'll ever save someone, or if there's no turning back once you've passed the border.

"Brielle."

The woman tells us her name. I've spoken with her since she woke. In the morning Edwin and Giles are surprised to see another body pulled up on the shore, but they don't ask any more about it. Instead the two just leave once the sun rises and aren't likely to be back until the sun sets. Brielle already knows what being an Essence means. She's taken the information flawlessly, in a way I'd never predict from a human who's had their life stolen.

"Forever?" she asks.

I sit with her at the edge of the water. She hasn't touched it since she woke, her wet nightgown still clinging to her. But she's not chilled, as no Essence can sense cold or anything of the like.

"Brielle?"

She runs her fingers through her long brown hair when I speak her name.

"What were you doing wandering in the forest last night?"

I've told her everything about staying safe in Phantom Lagoon, and she acted as if it were just a simple set of rules for a game. She had no emotions or reactions, and all the while I wonder how she ended up here.

Brielle's demeanor cracks then. Her placid face turns into a frown, and I watch her features change as she runs human memories over and over within her mind.

"My child died," she says.

I hear footsteps walk through the forest, and I turn to see Hadley stepping back into the perimeter of the lagoon. I motion her to leave again, and she stops, seeming a bit confused, but obeys me and turns around. She had gone into town to let me speak privately with Brielle, but Hadley's back too soon. I turn around with the sound of Hadley's departure and wait for Brielle to continue.

"I don't know the name of the man, but he was a soldier. He came into my family's home and ordered us to allow him to sleep there. Housing a soldier is part of the law, and my parents couldn't turn him away, so a group of soldiers took refuge in our home. They weren't kind all the time, but they were kind enough. The soldier, he found me alone, and I had to obey orders."

Brielle looks at me and I see the ghost tears that want to pour down her cheeks.

"They left the next morning. I knew I was pregnant a few weeks later and I wanted to curse the man, but I couldn't be happier with my gift."

Brielle makes a motion to wipe tears from her eyes but seems almost disappointed when she pulls away her dry hand. "I had a baby to take care of, and it was all I could ask for because I thought my life was over. I never married, and I knew as I grew older, any hopes of having a family were diminishing. The truth is I should have been ashamed to have a child without a husband, but I couldn't bring myself to not love her."

She smiles. "I was happy to have the baby. My father was ashamed and tried to remove me from the household, but my mother wouldn't let him. Instead she helped me grow strong for the baby."

"What was the baby's name?" I ask.

Brielle weakens at the question. She lets out a breath that almost sounds like weak laughter—the type that occurs when our emotions are so worn they don't make sense anymore.

"I never had a chance to name her," she says. "She was stillborn. My mother helped with the labor, but when she came into the world, there was no cry. My mother let me bury her in private, but I had no name to put on a grave, because I never took the time to think of one. I was going to name her once I saw her eyes, but they were never opened."

"I'm sorry," I say. But my words don't help her anguish. Every soul in the world could apologize for the death of her daughter, but that changes nothing. A life was lost and forgotten before an infant's eyes could open and see her mother for the first time.

"Her body was blue when my mother handed her to me wrapped in a blanket. I told her that I was taking her away to be buried. And I did—out in the forest where no one would ever disturb her. But I couldn't bring it upon myself to go home. Instead I just kept going farther and farther in the trees, though I knew my mother was expecting me."

I look at Brielle again as she clutches her nightgown to her body. She wears her sorrow and grief that speaks more than words ever could.

"At some point when I was walking through the forest, I didn't have to think about where I was going. Instead it seemed like something else was guiding me. I know I should have been scared so far from home, but I wasn't."

"Did you hear a girl's voice when you stepped into the lagoon?" I ask.

Brielle's next words are a whisper. "I heard her, but there was nothing left to hang on to. And there was something—I don't know what to call it—but there was a sense that if I just went into the water, it could somehow bring me peace."

She opens her palm to me to reveal her stone. The surface has scrapes and chips, but it glows amber pink. She smiles when she shows me her soul, seeming so proud of something that most would want to push away. I don't understand how, but she's already accepted this life. Part of me feels it's because she had nothing left, but then I realize Brielle made a choice. Hadley spoke to Brielle, told her to go home, but she refused. Now her soul quivers with a fierce radiance that no human is aware of.

The trees that wrap around the lagoon aren't enough. Their trunks grow in diameter and height, but never enough to stop wandering humans. Some are just hunters, like Theo and Jackson. The two men had guns in hand when they stumbled across the border. It was during the day, when Hadley and I had traveled to town, but Brielle had stayed behind and watched them as they entered Phantom Lagoon and stepped into the water. When Hadley and I came back, there was nothing left for us to do but help Brielle drag the men from the water, hiding their guns in the woods where no one would find them.

Theo was the first to wake up. I spoke to him in private as we left Hadley and Brielle watching Jackson. Theo didn't want to speak to me, so instead I spoke as we walked through the forest. I told him how he was an Essence and how he had to return to the lagoon each night. I told him that he may have powers to communicate with humans, but there was no way of knowing unless he tested it. He didn't object to anything I said, but he also didn't ask questions.

Jackson took longer to wake up. Theo was at his side the entire time, always rolling his stone around in his hand. Its surface was smooth, except for a chip deep enough to trap dirt and debris. Theo's soul was blue, not like the sky, but much richer in tone.

Jackson woke up three days later, but Theo wouldn't let me speak to him. Instead Theo told Jackson everything he needed to know. It was a long time until I was able to speak to Jackson myself, but he seemed calm. When I asked to see his stone, he held it out to me, its face covered in bumps and ridges of vibrant purple.

The two newcomers adjusted privately. In the light of day they visited their families, offering a silent protection, but always coming back long before the sun went down—just like so many of us.

LIX.

Days will always come to a close, no matter how long the hours may seem. Tonight the moon hides behind clouds, but its glow still peeks out over the sky. I stand at the edge of the lagoon and I can feel an anxiety grow somewhere within my core that warns me. I back from the dividing line, feeling peace come over me as I go home to Phantom Lagoon.

The safeguard of trees are close to being fully grown now. Their trunks are thick enough that, if I wrap my arms around them, my fingertips would just barely touch. There is room to pass between the trees, but people would have to walk sideways to fit.

Over the decades the trees have grown and protected Phantom Lagoon, but some humans still find their way. Along with Brielle, Theo, and Jackson, others have come to the lagoon. Emily and Melissa are sisters, only a handful of years older than Hadley, who came to the lagoon in the early morning before anyone was awake to see it happen. Instead those who have already resided within the lagoon greeted the morning with two new bodies floating in the water. When the sisters woke they both held lilac stones, though Emily's stone was a darker shade.

Conor came to Phantom Lagoon in the night. I watched him as he snuck through the trees, some unknown force driving him forward. I ran to wake up Hadley to see if she could say something to stop him, but by the time I found her asleep underneath a tree, Conor had already picked up a stone. I didn't bother disturbing Hadley after I heard the splash as he fell into the water.

When he woke a few hours later I wanted to ask what he had been doing in the woods in the middle of the night, but he attacked me with so many questions about this new life that I could do nothing other than fulfill his curiosity.

Gravis is an older man, a gentle soul who simply stumbled upon the wrong place at the wrong time. Brielle was the one who saw him the day he came to Phantom Lagoon. He walked in dazed, and like the others, it was as if something had control over his body that made him walk into the pool, not his mind telling him to do so.

"I touched him," Brielle would later tell me. "His feet stood in the water of the lagoon, and it scared me so I grabbed on to him. I didn't pass through him like I should have, Luna. I touched his skin, and he turned around. His eyes were facing me, but he couldn't see where I was."

Her words did nothing but add more confusion as to what it means to be an Essence.

But tonight—tonight the trees do what they were designed for. They stand tall and protect the land of Phantom Lagoon. And for that I'm thankful.

"Luna?"

I turn to the voice and see Giles standing in the

darkness. Behind him the others of the lagoon scatter about, distracting themselves with simple things to make the hours and days pass. Hadley is sitting with Emily and Melissa, playing at the edge of the water, splashing each other even though they squeal when the water touches their gowns.

Brielle sits farther away, watching them like a mother might keep an eye over her child in a busy market. Edwin also watches the girls but rolls his eyes at their games. Conor, Jackson, and Theo stand on the other end of the lagoon, passing jokes between them.

"I've been speaking with Hadley. She's told me as much as she knows about the lagoon, but when I ask her about you, she gives me no answer. She says it's not her story to tell," Giles tells me.

I look at Hadley again and see that innocent smile I've known day after day for years—the one that doesn't age. She plays like a child and looks like a child, yet when she speaks, she's so much more than that.

"My story isn't one of great joy," I say to Giles.

"Are any of ours?"

I don't retort. We've all had our lives stolen from us. Some more than others. I've learned it's better to live in a happy ignorance than to ask the others about their human lives. I stopped asking after Brielle. Her story haunted me, not in a way to cause me anguish, but in a way that I can't look at her without seeing the pain she still faces. Some days I study Brielle and see her happiness, but then it is as if she removes a mask and the world has slammed a door on her soul.

"Do you believe we have powers?" I ask Giles.

He seems put off by my question. It takes him many attempts at forming words before he is able to put his thoughts together. "All these years I've thought of it over and over. I've watched Hadley speak to the humans in town and watched their confusion when they couldn't see the source of the voice. But I've also watched Edwin walk through town as the humans clear a path for him to pass by, as if he's one of their own. They don't walk through his body like they may for you and me. And Brielle—well, she still hasn't discovered the full potential of her touch. She refuses to leave Phantom Lagoon, but I believe that she has the ability to touch, if only she tried again."

I nod my head. These are the same things I've observed, but part of me didn't think or want it to be possible. The ability to connect with humans makes all this—being an Essence—so much harder. How are we expected to leave our human lives behind if we retain contact with them, even if only in a small way?

"I believe it has something to do with love," Giles says.

"What?"

He takes a breath like he wants to pitch an idea to me. "*Love*. Hadley was in love with Valen. Brielle loved her daughter. And Edwin, he may not speak it, but he loved his wife—Lilly. She died from the flu when Hadley was eleven. She was his everything, even after she passed away—though he didn't handle her death well. To Lilly though, he was just her daughter's father, but Edwin was willing to give her the world."

"But don't we all love someone?" I ask, challenging his idea.

"Some more than others." He doesn't back down or shy away when he speaks.

My question seems to empower him more.

"Hadley said you've spoken to a human before—once—but you thought it had to do with emotion. Love is an emotion."

I look at his eyes, see the small purple hue of his stone that hangs across his chest in leather, and wonder what it is he is trying to get at.

"Who did you leave behind?" he asks. His voice is gentle now, so much softer than it had been seconds ago.

He knows the subject is a bruised and still healing place in my heart. And I feel my body weigh itself down as soon as the words hang in the air.

"He isn't a concern," I say.

"Yes he is. Because I see it in your eyes. You're broken in the only way a heart can be when it's left to heal with jagged edges."

All this time I thought I had pushed Garren away. I told myself that he was gone forever and how it didn't matter whether or not he loved me once or loves me now, because I'm here and he isn't. I was supposed to make Phantom Lagoon safe from humans, and that is all. I'm not supposed to be heartbroken. But Garren's name hasn't been spoken aloud in decades, and with the name haunting my mind, the wound is as fresh as ever.

"What happened?"

Giles speaks kindly and it makes me want to run away all the more. How dare he do this to me? When I was moving on and forgetting, he breaks open the wound again.

"It was before Phantom Lagoon. I fell in love with a man, and now he's gone," I say. My voice is hard, and the words don't feel real. I had gone years, decades, without speaking of Garren, and now I'm being forced to do it again.

"Was he human or an Essence?"

I think back to when I had met Garren. He was most definitely human, but I don't know when I first began to love him. In truth I didn't fully realize my feelings until we were separated, but that seems like such a small fact.

"He was human," I say, but it's a lie. He's an Essence, and he's here somewhere, but I don't want to pretend like he's coming back. So I lie and I pretend like the person I love has died some time ago.

Giles nods his head like this makes sense.

"Did he love you also?" he asks.

I try to keep my face calm with this question, because it is the same one I used to ask myself every night until I was able to push Garren from my thoughts.

"We became separated," I say, ignoring his question, pretending like separation is the only natural thing to occur when an Essence is in love with a human.

"But it's love, that binding love that lasts forever—that's

the love that gives an Essence the ability to connect with humans," Giles says.

"So you're saying I don't love Garren anymore, because I was only able to speak to a human once and never again?" My words come out quick. I didn't mean to say Garren's name for him to hear and it sounds so foreign in the air.

Giles opens his mouth to say something but thinks better of it.

I turn to leave, humiliated by my own openness to speak about the one thing I wanted to keep to myself, but Giles takes hold of my arm.

"Maybe humans can't hear you, but that doesn't mean you can't connect with them another way."

My back is turned to him. His grip on my arm isn't strong, but I don't feel the need to pull away just yet. I want to walk off and leave the subject behind, but curiosity creeps in the night as he speaks.

"The only way to know for sure is to test it."

"Giles," I say, turning to look at him. "I've gone into town time and time again to no avail. They can't hear me, touch me, or see me. I understand your theory of love and connection, and it may be true, but I'm not part of it."

He watches me with sad eyes. He's lost his fight, but it's a fight I wanted him to win. In my heart I feel he must be right about love and how it gifts us the ability to communicate with humans, but it's a gift I'm not a part of.

Giles releases me, dropping his arm to his side. I watch

him for a while, feeling as if I've somehow broken him in a way.

"I believe you though. I see it in Hadley, Edwin, and Brielle. I see the love there," I tell him, joining the others in the heart of Phantom Lagoon.

The night is still cloudy as everyone settles into what we consider sleep. It's not when our bodies rest and rejuvenate, but when we surrender to another day.

LX.

Hadley and I walk through town like we do most every day. We watch faces as they pass by, observing what we can. Hadley and I, we notice different things. To Hadley these buildings she's grown up with are home; they are what she had seen during her childhood.

Time has passed, but the dress Hadley wears now isn't all that different from what the other women wear. Their dresses are full in skirt and cinched at the waist, but the colors are duller than what I'm used to; their hair pulled back in knots rather than braids. In a way I miss my peasant clothing from my time. Compared to the lavish clothing I wear now, it was just a rag.

But that was my human life, and some moments I feel as if that life were just a dream. Yet I wear the gown that had once wrapped around Clara as she died in my arms.

"Is that Brielle?" Hadley asks.

We both stop walking and the humans around us continue, passing through our bodies without knowledge of our presence. Hadley's voice can be heard, but with all the lost chatter in the streets, no one stops to listen.

"Where?" I ask.

Hadley lifts her arm, pointing to a small building opposite where we stand. Brielle hovers at a doorway, her hands resting at the frame as she hides herself, only her head peeking in. With her back to us, I'm unsure if it's actually her, but when she turns, I'm certain it is Brielle. Her face is worn, making her age seem more so. Her hair falls across her shoulders in abandonment, the lines of her face drawn across her mouth and eyes. She lets go of the door frame and leans against the outside of the building for support, clutching the stone that rests against her collarbone on a leather cord.

"I've never seen her in town before," I say.

"Should we make sure she's okay?" Hadley asks.

Even from the distance I can see Brielle struggling to maintain whatever small composure she has found. After clutching her stone for a handful of breaths, she turns again to look into the building, completely unaware of the rest of the world around her.

"I'll speak to her," I tell Hadley. She moves to protest, but I don't let her. "You can't speak very much with humans around. Let me talk to Brielle alone."

I can tell Hadley wants to stay, but she nods her head in agreement and walks away without looking back. When I see Brielle again, she is still peering into the building.

"Brielle?" I say in a soft voice.

She's startled by the sound of her name and turns quick, hiding from whomever she is watching inside and bumping into me.

"Luna," she says, still trying to gain some sort of calm.

"What are you doing?"

She rubs her dry eyes like there might be tears. "My baby sister is in there." She tries to smile at the mention of her family, but by the end of the sentence her face has fallen.

I twist around her to peer inside. The building is even smaller than it appears from the outside. It reminds me a lot of the cruck house I grew up in. There are no rooms like many of the new houses being built over the years. This one only has a singular room with a bed, table, chairs, and what looks like a small wood oven with pans and skillets strewn about.

A woman rests in the bed with a man aiding her. His hair and beard are speckled with gray. One hand curls around the woman's face, stroking her cheeks, while the other is wrapped around the woman's fingers. She doesn't open her eyes, but even then I can see Brielle in her sister. She looks older than Brielle, with a long mane of gray that floats over her pillow. Her face is sunken and shallow, and even though she's pale, I can see how overheated her body is as she sweats.

I turn away, facing Brielle where she leans against the outside wall of the building.

"She's dying," Brielle says. Her voice contains little hurt. As she speaks, it is more fact than emotion. It's as if she's spent all morning facing this one known concept—her sister dying— and somehow she's become okay with the idea of her family passing on without her. "That's her husband in there. She's had a fever for a while now, and they don't have the money to see a doctor, so he's just trying to make sure she is comfortable."

"Brielle." I move to put my hand on her shoulder, but

she shakes her head.

"I'm okay. She's lived a long life—sometimes I think it was to make up for the loss of my life. That is why she's lived so long. I've been watching her. She was only nine when I came to the lagoon."

"How long has she been like this?" I ask.

"She was sick yesterday but not nearly as bad. I came as soon as the sun rose. I just didn't feel right. I needed to make sure she was okay. She was like this when I came. I haven't heard her speak—she's just been trying to sleep, shifting and turning. The fever's getting to her."

Brielle turns to look in again, her eyes always tentative for something, a sign that maybe her sister is leaving. A fear is in the air, a fear that maybe her sister will pass in the night when Brielle is unable to say her goodbye. It makes me worry that Brielle will become so wrapped around her sister's passing that she'll lose track of time and forget to return to Phantom Lagoon before sundown.

"How long are you staying here?" I ask.

She looks up to the sky and I can see the hurt there as she measures her time. The sun hasn't begun to set yet, but it rolls across the sky in threatening power. When Brielle turns to watch her sister again the conflict is painted across her features.

"As long as possible."

"Okay, just ... don't forget," I say.

She nods her head, grief striking her like venom. No matter how true or important my words are, Brielle doesn't want to face that part of reality just yet. In this moment she is here for her sister, and that is all.

When I leave, Brielle is watching her sister, never making a move to step away or leave.

I'm unable to find Hadley in town. I wanted to ask her about love and whether those were the feelings she still harbored toward Valen. Though I search for her, I come up alone.

The question seems so irrelevant now. Of course she still loves Valen. Love isn't something that simply dies or flickers away. It's always burning, even if the tone of the flame changes. One can love another as family or as a lover, but it's still love. So, even if Hadley only loved Valen as family or a friend, that was still a love which allowed an Essence to connect with humans.

In truth I want to ignore Giles's theory of love and connection. It makes our life and rules appear as a fairy tale, but deep in my heart, I do want love to be what drives our ability to interact with humans. But it worries me also. Because if I can't be seen, heard, or touched by humans, does that means I'm incapable of love?

I wander the paths of the cobblestone streets, escaping the town that is so full of life. Instead I find a cemetery. The fence is wrought iron, coiling into a point. There's no gate, just an opening in the fence that I step through. The grass inside is unkempt and abandoned, leaving weeds as the only greenery.

The graves of the dead litter the ground and what I had found as a human site of mourning is something that is only a dream to an Essence. To be human is a blessing, because then at least I could be granted mercy in death.

A man is at one grave. He is young and leans forward, using the hard stone for support. He cries silently to himself, never truly revealing his pain. As I step forward, I see a flash of red in his hand. After a few moments he uncurls his fingers and crushed rose petals fall to the ground.

"Sir," I say, but he doesn't hear me.

Giles told me to test my abilities, but there might not be any to discover.

"Can you hear me?" I say louder now, yet still he doesn't turn. All I can think of is how, if Hadley were here, she'd speak to this broken man and provide some comfort. Maybe she would act as an angel, telling him that his loved one is somewhere in Heaven, finally at peace.

"It's okay," I say, but I know he can't hear me. And that's all right. I lift my hand, watching this man, seeing every bit of pain he feels. I don't know who he's lost, but all I've ever seen in my human life was death, and it is so familiar.

I kneel down beside him, reaching out my hand. I have a small hope in my heart that maybe, just maybe, I'll be able to touch him and make a difference. My movements seem so awkward in the air until I'm close enough to touch him. But just the same, I pass through his skin.

There's a warmth though. It's foreign in a way that

scares me, but instead of pulling away, I find myself going toward the man. I concentrate on the position of his body, the way he breathes and somehow, in one last fluid movement, my body becomes one with his. Life and feeling erupt from my core in a beautiful show of senses. I am within this man, feeling the ground he kneels on, the cuts from the rose's thorns which have torn into his flesh, the gravestone he rests his forehead against.

Anna, I can't. Not without you. Don't make me do this without you.

His emotions seem too much. They cloud my own thoughts and scream out. I hear a distinct pulse of blood that I don't remember as a human beat. But when I was human I also didn't take time to feel the ground beneath my feet—it was all too familiar then, so many things I had taken for granted. Now all these senses seem so rich, so full that it's just too much. His heart beats as if it's my own.

The man I don't know buries himself in grief. Tears run down his cheeks. I'm on fire with how feverish his emotions have grown. Sweat covers his hands and mine. The tears that come cool us and mark trails of relief down our face. As he leans against the grave I realize it's not only from grief, but from sheer exhaustion.

"Please," I say in the back of his mind.

Something changes then. The man is able to focus on something other than his grief when he hears my voice.

Anna? he says, but there isn't any hope in his thoughts.

I want to tell the man yes, but it seems too cruel to lie.

No, I say. But the words are only in his mind, the mind that I also occupy.

Memories flash through his consciousness. They come in erratic moments, the beat of each memory changing and progressing. A young woman smiling, laughing, crying. She has a small face, golden hair falling down her shoulders. Tears of happiness flow as she holds a bouquet of flowers on her wedding day. The same woman—Anna—older, holding a small infant in her arms. Anna in the grass, playing with a toddler just learning how to walk. Anna lying in bed, so sick, too young to be sick.

Where is she?

I don't answer. We just both stare at the grave that reads her name.

Is she okay?

I can feel his loud heartbeat—too loud. With each passing moment her face flashes through our minds. Smiling, laughter, crying, pain—Anna was in pain.

"Anna is okay," I tell him, though I know nothing of the fact.

The man seems to find comfort in my voice, and I let him embrace that. His thoughts continue to stream, but they are whispers now, a constant background to his reality. His heart rate calms until it comes to a steady beat again.

I love you, Anna.

Memories flash through his mind again, this time slower. I see her, much younger. Her hands interlocked with this man whose name I don't even know. I share the memory of their first kiss, how nervous and thrilling it all felt. But the last, most distinct memory is Anna in bed, barely able to lift her hand. The man wraps her in his arms and carries her outside. A young man works in the field—their son. They watch him. The man holds her, kisses her forehead, and Anna cries, but it is unknown if the tears are of happiness or sadness.

He continues to remember, happier somehow, just knowing her. The moment seems so private that I want to pull away. As beautiful as it feels to experience life again, I also feel a need to leave. The wind pushes against his skin, carrying a chill as I leave his body.

And just like that, there is no such thing as cold or warmth or touch.

LXI.

The forest is a flood of color and shapes as I pass. Beneath my feet gravel and soil give way to my steps, but some moments I feel as if I'm trapped in quicksand that threatens to take me under. Branches of leaves overhang my head, but the world glows in colors of orange and pink. I can't see the sun, but I know it's passing. It's the last moments of day, when the world is more alive than anything.

I push and shove away branches as the sun shrinks, telling me my free time is almost up. I can feel an urgency in my spine that travels to my chest. Breathing is hard. My lungs gasp for air, but no relief comes of it—there is never enough air. I have no stone to clutch like the others. I'm bound to Phantom Lagoon just like all them, even if no stone possesses my soul.

My pace slows the farther I go, and the lagoon is so close. I can see the trees that have created a solid fence, but I'm dragging myself. I can feel a scream about to erupt in my core, begging to be released, to be heard, but I don't allow it.

I try too hard to look toward the lagoon, but I want to curl in on myself and forget. The lagoon calls to me in a possessive way, and no matter how badly I want to follow that call, I can't do it.

The trees are only a few strides away when I stop

completely, feeling crushed. I gasp for breath, but it only results in wheezing. Pressure pushes into me from every direction as it chokes my lungs.

"Luna!" someone screams out, so close.

I turn my head and see Hadley. Her face peeks out between the branches, but she keeps her distance. The sky is growing dark, pushing in on me, and I think this might be it. After all these years, I've faced the end of my life. My story ends here. It only seems fair after living for so long.

I don't believe I'll go to Heaven, Hell, or any place like that. I can feel it as if I'm being pulled from the world, that I'll simply cease to exist. Maybe that's what happens when an Essence lives so long on Earth. I've already had my afterlife.

I want to tell Hadley to leave, to let me pass, but she doesn't. Behind the confines of our barrier she tries to find some way to help me, but it's hopeless. I'm here. She's there.

All at once Hadley stands her ground. "What about Garren?" she shouts to me. "What if he comes to find you and you're gone? What am I supposed to tell him?"

Through all the pain I'm able to hear her, but I don't want to listen to the words. My Essence is leaving me. Why can't she understand this?

"You're not a coward, Luna," Hadley says, but her voice is off—if she were human, she would be crying. "Please, fight. We need you."

I'm an Essence. There is no sense of touch in my world, yet at this moment, I feel what humans must feel before death.

It's not the light at the end of the tunnel that glorifies and lifts; it's the robber that slams you in the back and corners you into a tunnel. I have given up, but I look at Hadley and I feel the fight come.

"Garren loves you. You know he does," she tells me.

I want to speak, to tell Hadley that she is wrong, that Garren couldn't have possibly loved me, but hope lives within me. What if he does love me?

I fall against one of the trees, my body nothing but an Essence without purpose. Hadley watches me as I fall to the ground. She smiles once I start walking toward her, but as soon as I trip, her face falls.

The world is taking my soul back. The weight becomes so much, and then, all at once, it is gone. My soul is floating from the forest with the pain—the memories. Nothing becomes everything. Black becomes color. Death becomes life. Dust turns to solid ground.

And there is Garren, waiting for me. Hidden in the trees, he was always here. His face is as kind and genuine as I had remembered, and I hear a whisper.

"I love you, Aida. I'm searching for you."

I no longer have my human body or form, but there are tears. I don't know how they're here, but I am crying. I am an Essence and I'm crying.

I don't want to leave.

BOOK 4

LXII.

It was all yellow. It was soft and kind and I didn't ever want to leave, but I was gone all the same. There were moments in time where nothing existed, and times nothing was everything. It didn't make sense, because it didn't need to.

But it was yellow, and I saw my soul, and it was beautiful.

She's dancing. I don't recognize her at first, but then the face reveals her to be Brielle. She looks younger, closer to my age—something closer to twenty years old. She's alone in her dance, but it makes her happy. Everything is so bright that it takes longer for me to see the other woman with her. She's also happy, but she doesn't dance. Instead she laughs. It's her sister; her hair is lighter. It isn't gray like it had been the last time I had seen her, but her winkles and sunken skin have also disappeared.

Without thinking too much about it I know they are dead, passed on. Even Brielle, without coming back to the lagoon, has moved on with her sister. And moving on is something that is so beautifully okay.

I'm anchored in place. Not in a suffocating way, but in the way that, no matter how hard I may try to tug or pull, there's no real use in the effort. So I don't struggle. I let myself sink and propel in something deeper that I don't completely understand. Colors and shapes shift over my vision in a display of sight and movement. I feel tempted to reach out and touch the array, but I have no desire to lift my limbs. So I float on.

I'm not in Heaven. There are peeks and small sights, but it's nothing more than a preview. I see my mother and father. I see Margo with Joelle, and they're happy. I don't know where Anton is, but they don't look for him. Dondre is there, older than I had ever remembered him, and he's with a woman he holds close. She loves him—that much is clear.

There are no clear images. Faces blur together and morph into memories and moments in time that I wasn't there to witness. In the reflection of Dondre's eyes I see the day he married, though I don't know the name of his bride. My mother and father are younger, happier, blissfully unaware I'm missing from their Heaven. But in a way they each hold their own Heaven. They exist together, yet separate. Mama kisses Papa and he smiles back at her. In their eyes I see my face, when I was just an infant. I see the fear Papa felt toward me when he looked into my silver-white eyes and didn't know what to do. But the fear is just a vague memory now and nothing more.

I see Garren, but he's not as clear as my family. He seems so dull in comparison, but something so very alive, so very different from my family. I see his soul glowing a deep red, almost as if he had his own stone from the lagoon, and I know he is not here with my family. He is elsewhere, without me, still wandering, searching. And there is love in his heart.

Joelle sings without words. She runs and jumps, and Margo watches her, as vibrant colors of life and ease radiate off her soul.

It seems like such a tease to see them in Heaven without me, but I don't feel jealousy. I've achieved bliss in my own way, my own Heaven, though I am so completely separate. And I know I'm nothing. Not alive or dead, not a human or an Essence. I'm floating and yet I'm anchored. I'm something and yet I'm nothing. My soul left the world in a whisper, and it's being pulled down to Earth again, screaming.

There's no light when I awake. I lie across the ground with a rock wall that towers over my head, cocooning around me. The closer I see, the more clarity I am granted. The walls are embedded with stones of crystal. Around me familiar bodies come into form—I'm inside the cave, the one by the lagoon.

Emily and Melissa are seated next to each other, leaning against the wall. Brielle lies across the floor, her long legs curled in. Conor sits with his head resting against the wall. Jackson is slumped over to the side with Theo lying nearby. Giles is curled in on himself, propped against a rock. Hadley has her hands folded in, her gown pooling out around her like a blanket. Clara is separate from the others, only an infant. She's in a small ball, hidden away in a corner. They all sleep in peace, bodies without an Essence.

Light enters the cave as ray upon ray of sunshine echoes off each of the crystal-embedded walls. It gives the cave light but also puts emphasis upon the stillness of so many familiar faces.

"Luna?" someone says, a few seconds later. "Oh, my God, you're awake."

I lift my head to see Hadley. She's exactly as I had remembered. Her hair still sits in beautiful curls atop her head, dressed beautifully for Valen. She's the same. I'm not gone. I'm here and Hadley's not in Heaven. I'm not in Heaven.

Hadley rushes toward me, putting out her hand as I kneel to the ground. She comes beside me and wraps her arms around my shoulders.

"You're back," she says, and her voice breaks in uneven breaths that tell me she wants to cry the dry tears of an Essence.

"I was gone," I say. My breath shudders like I had just been resuscitated. All at once the world is being handed back to me.

She pulls away to look at me, and the smile across her face is larger than any I have ever seen. "The sun went down, and you weren't here. You were gone, but I gave you a stone once you finally made it back. You never woke, but the stone changed color, like it has for every human who enters the lagoon. Giles carried you to the cave."

For the first time I see the stone wrapped in my fingers. The color is a deep pink, richer than that of a sunset, and it looks almost like the color of Garren's soul. The surface is smooth like glass except for a side that is scarred and jagged.

"It split in half when I gave it to you. The other half crumbled once it fell from your hand," she tells me. Her voice pauses as she looks at the stone in my hand. "It used to be yellow."

My soul isn't the glowing yellow I had seen outside Heaven. Without knowing how, I'm an Essence once again.

"Where were you?" Hadley asks me. Her voice is sad and I want to tell her what I've seen, but I don't feel I can. The things I have seen aren't meant for those on Earth; and I don't know why I'm here any longer, but I can't tell her all the truth.

"Elsewhere," I say instead.

She looks at me, waiting for more, but I don't offer it. After a few more breaths she's able to nod her head and let it go. "Okay," she says.

"Where's Brielle?" I ask.

Hadley looks at me, unable to speak. I wait for her to answer, but she never does. Finally she just closes her eyes, as she shakes her head.

She's gone. I saw Brielle—she had moved on. Heaven welcomed her soul with open arms and embraced her while it left me on the outside, watching, but unable to take part.

"She never came back after dark," I say.

Hadley nods her head.

I want to tell her that I saw Brielle, that she's safe and at peace, but there are so many things I can't explain, so many

433

things I feel I shouldn't explain.

"Have any other humans found Phantom Lagoon?" I ask.

This time Hadley smiles with innocent eyes. "Yes, but it's beautiful, Luna. We're something more than just lost souls—we're family. Some of us have powers, like my father and me. We can be seen, heard, or touched—some can even have more than one power. I don't understand why, but it's possible to hold on to something of the human world. And it's beautiful to witness."

"Are there others who fail to come back after dark?"

Hadley's smile is short-lived. It dies off once the question comes from my lips. "Sometimes, yes. I've tried very hard to explain to them why they can't do that, but something always calls them back to their human life."

There's hope in her words that she isn't aware of. The human life and that calling might be what brought Brielle to Heaven, and I can only hope the other Essences—the ones I haven't met—that they might have found Heaven also.

I can see Hadley is confused as to why I don't mourn the loss of an Essence and their spirit, but that is something she will never see. They've moved on. And I want to tell each and every Essence how to move on to Heaven, but telling such a thing isn't possible. It's like an Essence must be drawn by his or her own love to their human life, like Brielle had—anything other than love will end in the withdrawal from Heaven—able to observe but nothing more.

I look at Hadley, wondering how it is she brought me

back to this world.

LXIII.

I step through the cave until I meet the foliage that covers the entrance. The leaves as vines give way, and the world is open to me once again. No light shines into the cave. The sky is dark except for the moon that hovers over us in a sharp crescent. Hadley lets me step out first, following close behind. She doesn't introduce me to the new faces, as we step out.

Many are asleep in the night. People gather into groups of friends, crowding around each other as they fall into the human habit we called sleep. A group of women is near the lagoon—Melissa and Emily are with them—and another smaller group of men, still awake, sit scattered around the large rocks on the ground. They stop speaking when the vines fall back into place behind Hadley. Theo, Jackson, and Conor are in one of the groups. At the sight of me they raise their eyebrows—surprised, but not entirely taken off guard. Conor seems confused as he looks me over, but once he is able to determine that it is really me, he gives a small wave.

Farther off I see Gravis asleep against a large stone. Giles is sitting at the edge of the water with a woman. Both their backs are to me, but like the men Conor is with, he hears my approach and turns. The woman Giles sits next to looks at me, but her face is unfamiliar. Giles smiles when he sees me and turns back to the woman, whispering something. At his words she smiles before turning to face the water again. Giles nods his head in what seems like approval as I exit the cave and enter this lagoon I have found.

The night is alive. More unknown people have come to this place, but peace is in the air. Some sleep and some whisper in small conversations. There's harmony to it all.

"Look," Hadley whispers.

I follow her gaze and see the trees we have planted. They have grown wider in the time I've been away, creating a barrier for any humans who may wander in. But most prominent are the branches that reach above our heads. Leaves cloak the edges of the lagoon and overcast the water. An eerie, almost magical aura fills the air.

"It's magnificent," I say.

Hadley smiles next to me and takes me by the arm. She leads me to the highest point in the lagoon—the path that winds to meet the top of the cave. She doesn't follow me; instead she pushes me forward and walks away. I gaze over the sleeping and quiet bodies below, most of whom I don't recognize.

I see the faces of people I thought had disappeared long ago—personal ghosts of my world. I see Cyrielle and Jermaine cradling little baby Nouvel. I see Mama and Papa, Dondre—the spitting image of Papa. Margo plays with Joelle, and, by the movement of her lips, I know she's singing to her daughter—and if I listen close enough, I can hear the whispered song through the trees. Sabine holds Clara in her arms, smiling and rocking her child in a slow, continuous rhythm. Clara sleeps soundly, peacefully in the way only an infant can find repose.

Heaven dances in front of my eyes in a disarray between life and death. Mama and Papa smile up at me, but they don't speak. They are whispers, ghosts, reminders of what is beyond my reach. As much as I want to be with them, I don't feel bound to them. I feel myself in this earth. I'm the soil beneath my feet and the leaves in the trees. I'm within each Essence that rests in the night below. And I see that this—life, death, and spirit—this is what love looks like.

My family fades before my eyes, leaving me with a blissful goodbye to the night of reality. Once again I'm left with those I've never met and those that I wish to know. Hadley has found her place with the group of women, finding a spot to sleep. It only takes her body a few moments to find peace and lull away.

She is the only one who knows my story. She's the only one who's heard of my waiting soul. She knows I wasn't in love with a human, but an Essence who is still out there somewhere. Garren is a secret I don't want to share. And I look at Hadley and hope she can somehow understand why it is I've lied to her in this night. Why I haven't told her what is outside Phantom Lagoon in hopes she will find it herself.

LXIV.

Another day closes, but not all faces are present. The familiar and unknown souls of the lagoon swarm within the confines of the trees. Someone is missing. I scan within the groups—Conor, Emily, Melissa, Gravis, Jackson, Theo, Giles. They're all here, including those I only know by their faces, yet to determine their names. I try to place Hadley, but she isn't anywhere in sight—neither is her father.

"Giles," I shout above the group.

The groups chatter along, and even though my voice is loud, they aren't alarmed. Giles comes forward at the sound of his name.

"Have you seen Hadley and Edwin?"

Giles walks toward me as I speak, but once he hears my question he stops to scan the faces within the lagoon. I can see his confusion mount as he isn't able to find their faces within the crowd and turns back to me.

"Edwin hasn't been out past dark since the first time. He's careful enough to come back at least an hour before sundown," Giles says.

I look past the trees, trying to make out any movement that might mean they are both on their way. The sun floats across the sky, kissing its last goodbye. Only a handful of minutes remain before the sky turns dark and takes away any Essence that isn't within the lagoon.

I know where they're going after dark—to hover outside Heaven—and I don't know if that's what's right for their souls. Being kept from Heaven is torment, but it's also beauty. I saw the bliss before me, but I can never be a part of it.

"Luna?" Melissa comes up behind me, her eyes sad and distressed. "Hadley is on the border of the trees. We can't get her to come in. She's asking for you."

All at once I abandon Giles and follow Melissa. She guides me past the cave within the lagoon and to the border of its edges where the trees are thick and dark in the approaching night. When we reach Hadley, Emily is sitting next to her on the ground speaking to her, but Hadley never makes a whisper.

"Hadley?" I ask once I'm an arm's length away. She turns to look at me, and I see her eyes are streaked red as if she were a human crying.

"Luna," she says in a faint voice.

Emily moves so I can take her seat beside Hadley. The sisters stand behind us and Hadley never bothers to look at either of them. I turn to Melissa and mouth the word *go*. Their procession is quiet as they fade away.

"My father isn't coming back," Hadley says, once we're alone. Her words are slurred and torn.

"What do you mean?"

"He said he's done. He doesn't want to be here anymore." She hiccups the words. I think of how much she must love her father, when all her human life he had done nothing for her. The only time I was ever sure Edwin loved Hadley was when she went missing, and he searched for her only to become an Essence himself. "He said he couldn't stop thinking of Lilly—my mom. And he said he didn't care about the pain outside Phantom Lagoon as long as it put his misery to an end. Luna, he wants to die." Her words choke. "Can we even do that?"

She looks at me in broken pieces, begging for an answer I have but can't give. So much is outside Phantom Lagoon, but I'm terrified that by speaking of it, it may ruin Hadley's chances of ever finding it herself.

"I can't let him do this," she says, letting her face fall into her hands. I wrap my arms around her shoulders, feeling her chest rise and fall as she cries into herself.

"You have to let him go," I say.

My words only open up her wound.

"But he's my father."

"I know."

She continues crying but grows quieter as each second passes. The sun sinks and the trees in front of our faces seem to act more and more like a fence as the night approaches and closes us in. Edwin will find Heaven tonight. Not the Heaven any human receives, but the Heaven that a lost soul accepts. It's the one that holds us at a joyous distance but also grants mercy.

Hadley lifts her head and lowers her arms. "I want to go also." Her words are strong.

I'm not able to respond at first, unsure if I heard her

right.

"Please, Luna."

My breath catches. I can't stop her, but I can't go with her. I want to. I want so badly to go where she is going and to see Heaven where my family is, even if I can't be with them, but Garren isn't there. He's somewhere else. Somewhere so far away, yet so incredibly close.

"Are you sure?" I ask, but it is my voice that wavers. I want Hadley to find peace. I have doubts that maybe I'm wrong about finding Heaven. But Hadley doesn't expect to find anything. She wishes to leave, to simply stop, just as her father wishes. And I have to let her discover whatever it is that lies ahead for her.

"I'm sorry," she says.

She looks at me with tired eyes as if she can't do this anymore. This is the girl who knows all my secrets. This is the girl who knows what it means to love someone enough to want to give up everything for them. This is also the girl who loves a father who I'm not sure reflects the same amplitude of emotion. And she's giving up everything for him.

"It's okay," I say, trying to smile for her. I stand and offer my hand to help her up. She hugs me, and in that moment, I know she'll really leave. This isn't just some idea anymore. The sun is setting and she'll leave with it. "Be brave."

She pulls away and looks at me as if she might know what happens when her soul leaves Earth. Hadley nods her head and wipes away the tears that aren't there—so human.

She steps away and walks to the border of trees. Her hand rests against the bark of the oak we had planted so long ago as she looks back at me. "You've done great things with the souls within the lagoon. Keep them safe," she says.

"I will."

She smiles in the small way that she does when she tries so hard not to cry. The evening is turning colors of orange and purple; Hadley only has so much time left. Her hand quivers, but her voice is strong.

"And don't forget Garren—don't doubt love," she says.

Just like that, she says the last words I will ever hear from her. Hadley takes the steps between the trunks of the trees and beyond the border of the lagoon. Her breath catches, taking in every inch of pain that comes with being beyond the lagoon at nightfall. The sun is setting and crushes her soul, threatening to take it away. She never wavers. She treks on, ignoring the instinct to turn back to safety.

The night grows dark and she goes farther. Hadley never screams out in pain. Her soul fades away. As she goes farther her figure shrinks, but I see the emerald glow of her soul as it makes its last shout into the night. Then, all at once, she's gone.

Her retreat into bliss is a quiet one.

LXV.

Melissa and Emily are standing apart from the rest of the group. Both women look to me for answers, but I can't find any words.

"Where's Hadley?" Emily asks.

I suck in a breath, feeling as if I've lost the one person who truly knew me in this world. When I don't answer Melissa comes and wraps her arms around me in an embrace. I welcome the hug even though I can't feel it. When I close my eyes it's like she isn't even here, so I look to the group, remembering that this person is willing to be here with me.

Emily looks past me, out to the trees in shock. She covers her mouth with her hands as if she's just spoken some fatal words that have wounded me. Melissa retreats and Emily steps forward.

"She's gone?" is all she asks.

I nod my head and let the words crush me for what they really mean. Hadley isn't an Essence anymore, and neither is Edwin. Gone—forever. We aren't supposed to have an end to our forever.

The sun is fully set. The sky is dark and night is here. Birds are in the trees, stirring the branches while settling for the night. Animals claw and squirm in their own world, so completely separate from our own.

I hadn't known Emily and Melissa as well as Hadley, but I can see by the lost look in Emily's eyes that they must have been friends. Her body sways, wanting to chase after and save Hadley, but it's too late. Emily's hand goes to the stone that hangs from her neck, and she turns away, back to the heart of the lagoon. Melissa remains behind a few more moments, looking at the ground, unable to say anything until she notices her sister has walked off. She leaves also, following Emily.

I'm left alone without any further questions. The others don't bombard me as to why I couldn't stop Hadley or where she is now. All Hadley and I have done since other souls have come to Phantom Lagoon is warn them how dangerous it is to stay out after dark, yet we've broken our own rules. Hadley will speak as an example as to what can happen if you leave. Seeing the sun set will be feared unless you are within the trees of the lagoon, but maybe it's better that way. Heaven should be stumbled upon, not searched out.

I flit to the others within the lagoon. I don't make a sound, but eyes turn to me as I settle myself within the group. People with wary eyes cluster together like some monster comes to claim them all. They know who is missing within our family. Edwin and Hadley are gone—their absence echoes across the water.

"Luna?" someone says.

Giles steps forward to speak, but I shake my head and he stops. He has known Edwin since he was just a child. He knew Edwin better than I did; Giles had seen not just Edwin's bitter traits but also the good ones that made him act as the father he was and search for Hadley when she was missing. Giles saw Edwin, the loving man married to Lilly, who wished only to escape from this existence so he didn't have to suffer from the longing memories that never faded away.

It makes me envious. How dare he act as a coward and slink from a love he thought he couldn't have again? It's something we all suffer with in eternity. I want to forget Garren and how it is he who makes me push away any memories that came before Phantom Lagoon. I want to leave this place and see Heaven, but it will never be the Heaven I truly crave, because the one person I love most is here somewhere on Earth without me.

Arms wrap around me again. When I look up, I see they belong to Giles. I'm not sure if he's hugging me for his loss or my own, but I receive the comfort regardless.

"They're both gone," I whisper. The words are stronger than I feel. They don't waver or sink into each other, and it makes me think maybe I can do this, keep the people of Phantom Lagoon safe. Hadley had done it herself for so long while I was gone, now it is my turn to return the favor.

"I know. Edwin told me that he wanted to leave, whatever the consequences. I didn't know when, or if he would really do it, but I didn't think Hadley would follow."

"In the end he is her father, and she is his daughter. He came for her in the lagoon, and she followed him out." It seems so right for them to leave together. I drop my arms from Giles and he backs away.

Somber faces fill the lagoon. They look to me for guidance, and just like that, I've become a leader for them; the one who knows what to do and has an answer for why it is we disappear in the dark.

I step to the middle of the group and turn to face as many people as possible. "Edwin and Hadley are gone," I say, turning in a circle as I speak. As I do this I realize I don't know who most of these people are. I make a note to myself that soon I will hear all their stories and discover their spirits. "The sun is down. They can't come back." I raise my hand to the dark sky. Everyone watches my moves, but all are terrified to speak.

I stand, waiting for questions from the Essences collected here. *Why can't they come back? Where are they now?* But those queries never come. One by one people shift into their regular nightly routines. Small chatter starts within groups, but they converse only with whispers in respect for the souls who have been lost.

I leave them to settle for the night. As I pass, Conor, Jackson, and Theo look to me. They don't have questions, but I see in their stance they will offer help if I call upon them. I nod to them in some form of appreciation.

The cave of Phantom Lagoon is covered by green foliage, but I push away the leaves and vines, passing through. Curiosity leads me where I had been in a suspended sleep only a short time ago. Bodies of every Essence within the lagoon come into sight. Faces I've known, and faces I have yet to speak with. But I look for three bodies, all of whom I know very well.

Brielle is the first one I see, and she remains in the same position as when I first opened my eyes in the cave—lying on the floor with her legs curled in. Farther off is Hadley's body, her hands folded in, a ball gown floating around her as a cushion. Edwin is harder to find. His body is hidden behind a boulder, facing the wall. I imagine Edwin himself coming in this cave some time long ago and moving his human body so he would never have to see it again.

It surprises me to see their bodies here without their Essences. It almost doesn't seem right, but this cave will be an eternal record of who's been here, even if they've left. The only body missing is still my own.

I back from the cave again. When I uncover the foliage to leave, the crystal walls refuse to glimmer. The moon sings out in a sharp glow, but it doesn't reach the entrance.

People have already settled for the night. Some whisper their small conversations, but most lie down, looking to the sky in silence. I imagine those who had known Hadley and Edwin will mourn their lost souls, but they don't act as if this is a sad night. In a way Hadley and Edwin have done something we all crave—moving on. The only thing stopping the others from doing so is the unknown of what actually happens.

I circle around to the back of the lagoon, where the rock of the cave climbs high enough for me to stand over the lagoon. From high above I can see everyone, and it all feels like this is mine. All these people are here because of me, and I have to protect them.

Mystral started all this somehow. She needed me to create eternity for herself, but she also created it for others as well. Garren was the first Essence, not me. Yet he walks on this earth somewhere, and I don't know if he searches for me still or if I've been forgotten. Yet no matter what, I feel this small hope will always be in my heart that he will find me—and I'll stand with poise and grace in a gown that had once belonged to Sabine. Years, decades, or maybe even centuries from now, we will be together again, looking down at all those within Phantom Lagoon.

Mystral's words echo in my mind, so appropriate in this moment that I wonder if I'm the only one able to hear her words.

Take time and mend it. Stretch eternity like it may never break. Soothe infinity like it will always snap. Remember to cherish the night and seek the day. Postpone the moon and find forever, Aida de Luna.

The chant shakes me to the core. I had forgotten the words, but now the verses linger and vibrate within me like they are something so integral to my existence.

In a time so long ago, I had asked God to grant me mercy, to find charity, and to not let human flesh be burnt and scorched in the pestilence. And tonight the moon shines high in the night, relishing in that prayer I had said to the small boy who died, covered in buboes, trapped in his home. So many lives have slipped through my fingers—and now their souls are in my hands.

I am the curse that enabled the lagoon to take away human life.

I am the ghost that held an infant's corpse, only so it could find peace in a world so cruel.

I am the woman who fell in love but didn't know of the emotion until it was too late.

I am the Essence who has seen Heaven, only to be forbidden to speak of its allure.

I am life.

I am death.

I am mercy.

About the Author

Mandi Lynn started writing her first novel at thirteen, and at the young age of seventeen, *Essence*, hit the press. Since publishing her debut novel, Lynn has taught writing workshops, appeared on television, newspapers, and most importantly, graduated high school. While attending college, Lynn works part time at a salon as a stylist and continues to write future novels. Lynn can be found online creating YouTube videos about books, publishing, and all things reading.

Support the author! Review this book on Amazon and Goodreads!

Read her first novel now:
www.mandilynn.com/books/essence/

mandilynn.com

youtube.com/mandilynnVLOGS

twitter.com/Mandi_Lynn_

facebook.com/MandiLynnAuthor

Acknowledgments

I started writing this book before *Essence* was published. The draft of *I am Mercy*, which I had written at that time, has since been completely abandoned. The version you now hold in your hands is my heart and soul, much like *Essence* was.

Although 2014 was not my year, that's when I wrote the majority of this book. *I am Mercy* was my dumping ground, my way of exhaling all the emotions I couldn't speak.

To my mom and dad: Thank you for always supporting every decision I've made. For letting me transfer colleges, changing my mind left and right, but always keeping your faith in me, and pushing me to do the things I didn't think I could do.

To my mom: Thanks for reading one of the first drafts and telling me it had too many big words. I'll take that as a compliment.

To Aunt Karen: Thanks for being *I Am Mercy*'s first reader. Thank God you didn't hate it!

To Mémère: You've been gone for more than a year now, but you've found your way into this book. Chapter LXII is for you.

To Grampy: This book is dedicated to you because you are stronger than any person I've met. I don't know how you do it every day. I hope someday I can have a love as strong as yours for your family.**To Grammy:** I love you! Tell my mom how you paint your nails pretty!

To every single reader I have out there: You guys mean the world to me. A special thanks to Joseph Perry (again), Paige Couture, Karen LeClaire, Ryan Slattery, Anders Hokinson, Brista Drake, Kynan Pacheco, Kady Sciog, Mitchell Chapman, Antwon Saboor, and Amanda Fox who helped fund this book into print!

My readers are the reason I write, why I'm able to keep my mind sane. And, most of all, thank you for the emails. They push me to work harder every day. Someday I'll get my books on *The New York Times* Best Sellers list for you guys!

Made in the USA
Middletown, DE
18 November 2015